THE BEST AMERICAN MYSTERY STORIES 2010

THE BEST AMERICAN MYSTERY STORIES 2010

EDITOR LEE CHILD

CORVUS

First published in the United States of America in 2010
by Houghton Mifflin Harcourt.

This edition first published in Great Britain in 2010
by Corvus, an imprint of Atlantic Books Ltd.

A CIP catalogue record for this book is available from
the British Library.

ISBN: 978-1-84887-573-9

Printed in Great Britain.

Corvus
An imprint of Atlantic Books Ltd
Ormond House
26-27 Boswell Street
London WC1N 3JZ

www.corvus-books.co.uk

Contents

Foreword

EVERY YEAR, when I sit down to write the foreword to the new edition of *The Best American Mystery Stories,* two thoughts leap to mind. The first is: what can I write about that I haven't written about in the previous volumes? The second is: does anyone actually read it anyway, or do they (wisely) go straight to the fiction?

Well, just in case this book has found its way into the hands of a completist reader, here are a few things you should know.

- Mystery is a very broad genre that includes any story in which a crime (usually murder) or the threat of a crime (creating suspense) is central to the plot or theme. Detective stories are one subgenre, others being crime (often told from the point of view of the criminal), suspense (impending man-made calamity), espionage (crimes against the state, which potentially have more victims than a single murder), and such sub-subgenres as police procedurals, historicals, humor, puzzles, private eyes, noir, and so on.
- If you are expecting to read a bunch of what mostly passes for detective stories these days, you will be disappointed. Almost no one writes distinguished tales of ratiocination; observation of hidden clues and the deductions a brilliant detective makes of them is largely a lost art. Most contemporary detective stories rely on coincidence, luck, a confession, or flashes of insight by the detective (whether private eye, police officer, or an amateur who has taken time off from his or her primary occupation of cooking, gardening, knitting, writing, hairdressing, or shopping).
- Mystery fiction today is primarily devoted to the notion of "whydunit" rather than "howdunit" or "whodunit." Therefore, most tales are based on psychological scrutiny, whether by a detective, by the reader, or by the protagonist.

- The line between mystery fiction and literary fiction has become almost totally blurred. Such mystery writers as Elmore Leonard, Robert B. Parker, Dennis Lehane, George Pelecanos, James Ellroy, and others are certainly writing literary works. Such mainstream literary writers as Joyce Carol Oates, Michael Chabon, Paul Auster, Jonathan Lethem, Salman Rushdie, and others have written stories and books of mystery, crime, and suspense.
- This collection is devoted to the best-written mystery stories published in the 2009 calendar year. You can call them mysteries or crime stories or literary stories, and you will be right. The goal, as it is every year (and this is the fourteenth edition), is to collect the very best mysteries of the year, and I think we have succeeded—again.

The "we" referred to above includes my colleague Michele Slung, who examines thousands of stories every year to find the most worthy; Nat Sobel, the greatest agent in the world, whose impeccable taste has discovered dozens of first-rate tales that have been recommended for inclusion; the scores of editors of literary journals who keep me on their subscription lists and often point out work that merits extra attention; and of course, Lee Child, the guest editor. It is a cause of astonishment as well as gratitude that Child, an author who hits number one on bestseller lists in America, England, and who knows where else, was willing to take time out from a very full schedule to read the fifty stories I selected as the best of the year (or, at least, my favorites) and pick the top twenty, as well as write a superb, thoughtful introduction.

Also important, if less directly, to the ongoing success of this series are the previous guest editors, who have generously lavished so much time and attention on these annual volumes: the late Robert B. Parker, Sue Grafton, Evan Hunter (Ed McBain), Donald E. Westlake, Lawrence Block, James Ellroy, Michael Connelly, Nelson DeMille, Joyce Carol Oates, Scott Turow, Carl Hiaasen, George Pelecanos, and Jeffery Deaver.

While I engage in a nearly obsessive quest to locate and read every mystery/crime/suspense story published, I live in paranoid fear that I will miss a worthy story, so if you are an author, editor, or publisher, or care about one, please feel free to send a book, magazine, or tear sheet to me, c/o The Mysterious Bookshop, 58 Warren Street, New York, NY 10007. If it first appeared electronically, you must submit a hard copy. It is vital to include the author's contact information. No unpublished material will be considered for what should be obvious reasons. No material will be returned. If you distrust the postal service, enclose a self-addressed, stamped postcard.

To be eligible, a story must have been written by an American or Canadian and first published in an American or Canadian publication in the calendar year 2010. The earlier in the year I receive the story, the more fondly I regard it. For reasons known only to the dimwits (no offense) who wait until Christmas week to submit a story published the previous spring, this happens every year, causing much gnashing of teeth as I read a stack of stories while my wife and friends are trimming the Christmas tree or otherwise celebrating the holiday season. It had better be an extraordinarily good story if you do this because I will start reading it with barely contained rage. Since there is necessarily a very tight production schedule for this book, the absolute firm deadline for a story to reach me is December 31. If the story arrives twenty-four hours later, it will not be read. Really.

O. P.

Introduction

EVERYONE SEEMS TO KNOW what a short story is, but there is very little in the way of theoretical discussion of the form. A tentative definition is often approached from two directions simultaneously: first, Edgar Allan Poe is quoted as being suspicious of the novel, preferring instead that which can be consumed at a single sitting; and then Mark Twain is quoted as saying—of a letter, not a story—"I'm sorry this is so long; I had no time to make it shorter."

Some people attribute the second quotation to Pascal, but Twain is always a safe bet for quotes, and in either case the counterintuitive meaning is clear: it takes more time and greater effort to hone a narrative into a short form than to let it run a longer course. Combined with Poe's concept of the "single sitting," the short story is therefore seen as a delightfully well-crafted jewel, to be enjoyed by the connoisseur in the same way as a great meal or a glass of fine wine is enjoyed by a gourmet.

I'm not so sure.

To take issue with Poe first: his quote is full of self-interest. No one form has an inherent superiority over any other. All writers are scufflers at heart. We're all trying to earn our daily bread, and we'll do whatever sells. Poe's "single-sitting-as-a-virtue" trope was driven by what the market wanted. He was trying to keep the wolf from the door by writing for periodicals, of which there was a huge and increasing number during his lifetime. Believe me, if he could have sold thousand-page novels, he would have, and today he would be remembered for extolling their manifest superiority over shorter fiction. But the market wanted bite-size pieces, so bite-size pieces were what he wrote. Charles Dickens was in the same boat, but Dickens just broke up his (thousand-page) novels into chunks, and they were printed sequentially, to great acclaim, not least because the desire to know what happened next proved so powerful. Arthur Conan Doyle was somewhere between the two; the Sherlock Holmes canon is certainly mainly a series of short stories, but "Sherlock Holmes" is also a single, massive entity, loved and enjoyed for its totality rather than its episodic nature, as if the whole arc exists independently of its disjointed publication history, as one giant mega-novel.

And to take issue with the assumption behind the Twain quote: I absolutely guarantee that none of the stories in this anthology took longer to write than their authors' various novels. Not even remotely close. Yes, each sentence is crafted and polished; yes, each story was read and revised and then reread and revised again—but so is every sentence and chapter in a novel, and novels are much longer than short stories, and the effort expended is entirely proportional.

So, are the short stories in this collection *not* delightfully well-crafted jewels to be enjoyed by the connoisseur in the same way as a great meal or a glass of fine wine? Well, yes, they are, but not for the reasons given by conventional wisdom, but for a whole bunch of different reasons.

Short stories allow a little freedom. In their careers as novelists, the authors presented here are all, to some degree, locked into what they write, by economics and expectations. But in today's market, short stories have neither a real economic upside or downside; nor are they constrained to any real degree by reader expectation. So authors can write about different things, and more especially they can write in different ways.

Novels are assembled like necklaces, from a long sequence of ideas that combine like gemstones and knots; short stories can contain only one idea. Novels must take aim at the center mass of their amalgam of issues; short stories can strike glancing blows, even to the point of defining the idea only by implication. (As in Ernest Hemingway's famous six-word story: "For Sale. Baby Shoes. Never Worn.") To some degree the slightness of—or the partial knowledge of—the central issue or idea becomes a virtue. For instance, I was once in an expensive boutique on Madison Avenue in New

York City. It sold pens and notebooks and things like that. A woman asked to see some Filofaxes—small leather ring-binders designed for personal clerical use. She was shown two. She dialed her cell phone and said, "They have blue and green." She listened to the reply and said, "I am *not* being passive-aggressive!"

Now, there is no way that eavesdropping incident could inspire a novel. There's not enough there. But it could inspire a short story. Every writer has a mental file labeled "Great Ideas, Can't Use Them in My Novels," and short stories are where those ideas can find release.

Equally, every writer has mental files labeled "Great Voices, Can't . . ." and "Great Characters, Can't . . ." and "Great Scenarios, Can't . . ." and so on. Noir writers might want to try a sweeter setup at some point, and "PG" writers might hanker after a real "R" rating—or even an "XXX." The short story market is where those wings can be spread. The result is often a between-the-lines feeling of freshness, enthusiasm, experimentation, and enjoyment on the author's part. That's the feeling you'll find in this collection, and perhaps that feeling brings us to a better definition of exactly what a short story is—in today's culture, at least: short stories are a home run derby . . . the pressures of the long baseball season are put to one side, and everyone smiles and relaxes and swings for the fences.

LEE CHILD

GARY ALEXANDER

Charlie and the Pirates

FROM *Alfred Hitchcock's Mystery Magazine*

CALL HIM Juan Gama. That's what he goes by. He isn't Latino, but he's dark, thanks to Syrian blood on his mother's side. He can pass, at least with a nosy gringo tourist like this Charlie dude at the next table.

"Campeche has an amazing history," Charlie Peashooter is saying, guidebook open beside his sweet roll and orange juice. "The only city in the Americas other than Cartagena, Colombia, to be walled to thwart pirates. You surely know that, señor. My apologies if I am boring you."

Juan smiles blankly and nods, holding to the image that English to him is a foreign language. They are in La Parroquia, an open-air café on Calle 55. Morning eggs and coffee here is a homey routine Juan has fallen into. He knows that routines and patterns can be deadly, but six months in Campeche has slackened him.

Located on the Yucatán Gulf Coast, Campeche City is the size of Tacoma and Shreveport. It is tropical and picturesque, and nobody goes there. Juan Gama guesstimates a maximum of five hundred foreign visitors are in town at any one time, and that includes the Eurogringo variety. If they've determined that he fled south of the border, they would be scouring hot spots like Acapulco and Cancún, where one can debauch in style.

Juan Gama just turned twenty-four. Although he is nearly naked in shorts and T-shirt, he still manages to appear rumpled. His rimless glasses are smudged and his wavy black hair has a mind of its own. He is lanky and a bit awkward, and has accumulated fifteen pounds, much of it around the midsection. He hasn't been so relaxed in years.

"Pirate," he replies, pretending to struggle with the word.

"I should say so," Charlie says, consulting his guidebook. "Listen to this. English, Dutch, and French pirates regularly plundered Campeche after its founding in the 1500s. On February 9, 1663, they combined forces and killed every man, woman, and child. After the attack, Spanish colonial authorities decided to wall the city. The project was completed over the following half-century and eliminated the pirate menace. Any subsequent foray was driven off."

Not every woman was killed, not if you believe Teresa, Juan's lady, who can get cuckoo on the subject. Teresa just *knows* that a female ancestor of hers survived, a beauty, ravaged by a pirate captain. She's conflicted because of her pirate blood and what they did to her forebears.

Juan continues nodding, smiling.

Charlie initiated the conversation and introduced himself. He has a decade on Juan Gama. Slim and muscular and tanned, natty in slacks and pullover, his teeth are straight and white. The part in his sandy hair is as precise as a laser beam.

His appearance is agreeable and post-preppy, though his nose is too long and his features are too bunched to qualify him as Hollywood handsome. He smiles easily and his blue eyes never quite make contact. He is a baritone with perfect diction who wears heavy cologne.

Charlie has an aura of relentless congeniality. He looks to Juan like a game show host.

"Yes. Very hard times," Juan says, returning to his eggs.

"Indeed. The definition of piracy is more varied and complex these days. One dictionary defines it as unauthorized use of another's invention, production, or conception. They're referring primarily to copyright infringement. Those software companies are having fits, aren't they? Of course, the scope of piracy is even broader. For instance, the methodical manipulation of games of chance in three states. To the tune of two million dollars."

Juan Gama drops his fork and looks up.

Charlie Peashooter's smile is glorious. "Juan, you were thinking they would send a no-neck creature named Joe Knuckles?"

Juan Gama is genuinely speechless.

"Relax. That was the old way, in the old days. Please, finish your meal. Then we'll talk."

"I am a consultant," Charlie explains as they stroll the *malecon,* the boulevard that skirts the Gulf of Mexico. "Understand this, Juan. I was sent to negotiate, to resolve this difficulty. I am a reasonable person. My employers are reasonable people. That is my context."

They are walking beneath a fiery cloudless sky. The water is a vivid and murky green, like lime sherbet. "How'd you find me?"

"I'll continue addressing you as Juan if you don't mind."

"I don't."

"You trained and operated a brigade of card counters on a scale heretofore unseen. You went on a whirlwind tour and made your money before the casinos realized what had happened. Were they frat rats from your college, old chums?"

"No. Dormies, some still in school," Juan says.

"Compensation?"

"Fifty percent, less airfare and meals and hotel rooms."

"Hit and run, you were. A veritable blitzkrieg. You trained and rotated them so fast they were long gone before their photos circulated. Your system was devastatingly simple and effective. Blackjack dealers who thought they'd seen everything never knew what hit them. Hats off to you, sir."

"Uh, thanks. But, like, how'd you find me?"

"Resources. Everybody passed the hat and brainstormed. Your whereabouts was a challenge, sir."

"Card counting isn't a crime, you know. Having an idea what cards are left in the shoe shifts the advantage from the house to the player, that's all."

"It's a question of ethics."

Juan Gama laughs out loud.

"Oh, I admit it's hypocritical, but that's how it is. Nonetheless, my people want their money."

Juan is on the verge of losing his breakfast. He pauses, takes a deep breath.

Charlie places a hand on his shoulder and smiles genially. "Juan, please do try to relax. It's going to be all right. Bugsy and Moe and Icepick Willie haven't inundated that environment for decades."

Juan inwardly flinches. "You said negotiate?"

"That I did. The folks who run casinos nowadays have corporate bloodlines. They are cut from the entertainment conglomerates and tribal hierarchies. They understand that broken kneecaps don't enhance the bottom line. They understand compromise, they understand business decisions."

Juan nods grimly.

"A fifty-fifty split netted you in the neighborhood of one million smackeroos. You obviously live conservatively. Nevertheless, we wouldn't expect you to have every last penny squirreled away."

"You're right."

"We've written off your kiddy cohorts. I'm authorized to leave you ten percent free and clear. You give us ninety percent of the one million and keep the change. Down here, you're set for life. They look at the swindle as tuition for the education you gave them. Whadduya say, guy?"

"Uh. Yeah. Okay."

"When?"

Juan gazes out at the water. "Well, like I don't have it in a suitcase under my bed."

Charlie chuckles. "Ah. Offshore banks?"

"Grand Cayman," Juan improvises.

"You were a statistics major before leaving academia without your degree, Juan. A brilliant albeit indifferent student. I'm pleased to be part of bringing peace of mind and stability to your life."

"I appreciate that, Charlie."

"When do you think?"

"Tomorrow maybe."

"Let's say tomorrow, *definitely*. Thanks to the miracle of electronics, we can do the transaction at the speed of light. All we require is the will. La Parroquia for breakfast. I'm buying." Charlie gives him a slip of paper. "This is a wire transfer number. You say it's done. I make a confirmation call. You live happily ever after."

"Okay."

Charlie gestures to the water. "Today's the ninth of February. Quite a coincidence."

"Huh?"

"The anniversary of the massacre, the ultimate plundering." Charlie swings his arm inland, to the land gate, a man-made stone monolith. The attaching walls on this side are long gone. They are standing on land filled in the 1950s. "We're at sea level. Before the fortifications, they simply moored and marched right in. No natural defenses. Tragic, tragic, tragic."

Juan thinks of Teresa's pirates. There must be a moral to Charlie's story, but he doesn't ask what it is.

"Translated, Juan Gama is Spanish for John Doe," Charlie says. "Simplistic, yes, but you do have an engaging, impish quality."

Juan replies by staring at his feet.

Charlie says, "Alas, we live in a grown-up world, Juan."

Charlie sits on the edge of his bed. It is early evening, and he is watching the darkening horizon and the sea that is growing livelier by the minute. Charlie is five floors high, perhaps directly above where the pirates tied up. This hotel was the place to stay in Campeche during the go-go oil boom era, the late seventies and early eighties. Now it's frayed, not entirely clean, and almost empty.

That's just hunky-dory with Charlie. He doesn't particularly like people and he enjoys the privacy.

He assembles his Colt .25 automatic, disassembles it, and repeats the process until the finest film of oil coats every moving surface. He wipes the excess and admires the machined creation that fits in the palm of his hand.

Smuggling the weapon into the country was *no problema*. Charlie's clients flew him to Monterrey by private jet. From there he went charter to here.

He goes to the window and holds a round up to the fading light. In his home workshop, Charlie hollows his store-bought hollowpoints until the lead walls are nearly translucent.

Nobody can operate at my proximity, he thinks proudly. Nobody. And he's right. Charlie's affability permits him point-blank range. Everybody likes Charlie. Not even the most paranoid assignment knows what hits him.

Cold steel against the ear. An instantaneous recognition of betrayal. One low-velocity shot, no louder than a handclap, the auditory canal serving as nature's silencer. A gurgle, eyeballs rolling up like blinds, then nothingness. No muss, no fuss.

Medical examiners who have removed Charlie's slugs from brains of assignments he has turned into porridge comment that they resemble spiders. This is only one component in the legend of Charlie Peashooter, who uses a sissy gun and never misses.

Charlie slips the Colt into a pocket holster, mesmerized by what has become a spectacular display of lightning and howling wind and horizontal rain. Palm trees are bent like bows and there are whitecaps on the hotel's pool. He has never before been to the tropics and is amazed. The weather seems to be changing as fast as it does on the TV news where the talking haircuts speed up the satellite photos.

He worries about this Juan Gama assignment. His clients were so anxious that they dispatched him as soon as they isolated Juan and his breakfast ritual. Charlie hasn't the foggiest where Juan lives, though they did discover that he resides in the area with a woman named Teresa and her brother Perez.

Juan is a flighty young man who lacks graces. But he seems sensible. He should show tomorrow. After Juan Gama provides the magic number and the transaction is accomplished, Charlie will steer him someplace where he can complete his assignment. It isn't, after all, all about money. It's the principle of the thing.

Charlie shuts off the light. Early to bed, early to rise. That's his motto.

He stares at the flyspecked ceiling, again finding it peculiar that his clients often prioritize retribution above financial recovery. He puzzles over them as he does serial killers. He's never understood the breed. Why not kill for fun *and* profit?

He yawns, deciding that it takes all kinds.

Juan Gama stares at a ceiling that is not flyspecked. Teresa is an immaculate housekeeper.

"Your trouble, has it come for you?"

"Why do you say that?"

"How you were when you come home late from breakfast." Teresa hesitates. "How you are now, how you hold me after we make love tonight. You never hold me afterward."

Teresa is older than Juan. She is a kind, passionate woman with glossy black hair and trusting eyes. She has ample hips and comes up to his shoulders. She works as a travel agent at the hotels. Juan and she met on a day trip she led to the Maya ruin of Edzna. Juan was the odd man out in a group of French tourists.

Juan took her to dinner afterward. They ate broiled grouper and drank wine. They drank more wine and held hands. Teresa said he looked like he was lost. Not any longer, he said.

Teresa took Juan to her home in the old walled city. He has been there ever since, sharing the house with her worthless brother, Perez, who is his age. Teresa is lover, mother, and best friend to him, all that and more.

The walled city is in the throes of urban renewal. Lining narrow streets of flat, smooth blocks are row upon row of one- and two-story dwellings with ornate doors, wrought-iron balconies, and pastel stucco. Those that aren't already spiffed up are getting the treatment, buckets of paint dangling from precarious bamboo scaffolding. The town's being daubed in every jelly bean color except licorice.

Teresa's is tangerine. Her front room is a mini-museum. Descended from a longtime Campechano family —some great-great-greats of hers helped fight off the pirates, so she claims—she has old-timey portraits of them and bad dudes like Pegleg Pete and Blackbeard. In an armoire and mounted on a wall are a flintlock pistol, a cannonball, a blunderbuss, and a crossbow.

A gust from the storm has the wooden shutters clattering like drumsticks. Juan gets out of bed and secures them.

"I felt you were running from something, but you would never confide in me."

She is on her side, her back to him.

"I don't want to burden you," he says, not completely lying.

"You can, Juan."

"It'll be fine."

"Your name. Juan Gama. I know it is not real."

"Would you like my real—"

"No. I want to know you as I know you."

Juan Gama–John Doe, he thinks. He must have been out of his mind. Totally clueless. But he has gone through life treating life like a game.

He thinks she is asleep when she asks, "Have you seen Perez today?"

"No," he lies.

"I did not hear him come in. El Norte, this awful storm, I hope he is not caught in it."

Northers, the winter storms that occasionally blast through, the locals call them El Norte. "He'll be okay. He's a big boy."

"He is not a big boy, Juan. He is a child."

Juan pretends that he is dropping off.

"Sometimes, Juan, you remind me of Perez."

Juan does not drop off. He does not sleep a wink. He knows that as good a dude as Charlie seems to be, there are limits to his good nature.

If only I had money to give him, Juan laments.

Charlie Peashooter sips coffee at La Parroquia well past Juan Gama's breakfast time. He is disappointed in Juan, although not surprised. He cannot imagine greed clouding one's survival instincts, but that's human nature.

The storm has abated slightly. It is no longer curling eyelids inside out and raising tsunamis on mud puddles. It is not ideal flying weather. However, this is a blessing. Charlie overhears a taxi driver at the next table complaining to a waiter that nothing is landing at the airport because of high crosswinds and water on the runway.

The airport, Charlie thinks. On a hunch, he asks a waiter where Juan is and learns that Juan had told him that he was flying out of town this morning for a short trip.

Perez gazes out rain-streaked glass at the airstrip. A plane accelerates along the runway, its tires raising roostertails. It lifts off the ground just fine. His airliner from Mexico City could lift off just fine too to fly him to the capital on its return flight, but it isn't here. You can take off in this stuff, but you cannot land, so it has been diverted.

Perez doesn't understand flying, how you can go up but not down in foul weather. He orders another glass of whiskey from the bar. It would be just his luck if El Norte pours and blows for the three solid days. He feels at times like a big, black cloud hovers above him.

The gringo, his sister's boyfriend, who has never offered him a peso, had given him an airline ticket to cash in and meals and bar-hopping and a hotel room he had reserved in Mexico City. The gringo said he had business that was canceled, so why waste the trip?

The gringo has no business that Perez knows of and has not gone anywhere since he moved into Teresa's bed, but Perez did not argue with him.

Perez drinks and he smiles. He suspects that Teresa is behind this. She wants her brother out of the way for a few days so she can be alone with the gringo and extract a marriage proposal. While Juan isn't a terrible fellow for an Anglo, Teresa seems to like him more than he likes her.

Whether Juan stays or he goes, Perez has no strong opinion. He is rich like any gringo is rich, but no big money has materialized until this travel gift. The home belongs to Perez also and Teresa is a hard worker. Due to a combination of bad luck and bad bosses, Perez has had no success holding a job, but thanks to Teresa, there will always be beans and tortillas on the table.

"Are we in for forty days and forty nights of this? If you see a boat floating by loaded with animals, head for the hills."

Perez laughs at the corny joke by the gringo with the broken Spanish who is standing beside him.

"Of all the rotten luck," the gringo goes on. "My girlfriend is waiting at the Mexico City airport for me."

"Man, I know what you mean about bad luck," Perez says.

"Two weeks in Campeche on a consultancy assignment, she is as ready to see me as I am her. If you catch my drift."

Perez catches his drift. He is smiling broadly and winking. He is so suave and his voice is so perfect he should be a master of ceremonies on American television.

"You got my sympathy, man. I was going there on holiday. If you got money and I got money, you can find yourself a party anywhere."

The gringo sighs. "Too bad about our plane. My girl's sister is visiting us. She's your age and is hot as a firecracker."

Perez looks at him.

The gringo makes an hourglass gesture with his hands. Perez resumes observing airplanes spray water as they taxi. His last job was peddling wooden pirate ships on the street to tourists who did not want to buy them. Now that he finally has a wad of pesos in his wallet, the fates are depriving him of his fun.

The gringo snaps his fingers. "I have an idea. They say Mérida is clearing up. There must be outgoing flights. How far is it?"

Mérida, capital of Yucatán State, is an easy three-hour drive. Perez answers him and adds, "On account of the weather, it could take longer, but not much."

"I have a car, but I don't know the roads."

"I know the roads," Perez says.

"You'd be doing me a favor, taking the sister off my hands. You strike me as being capable of pulling that duty."

Another grin and wink. He is a nice, friendly man and they have a mutual problem.

"Why not?" Perez says. "What do I have to lose?"

Next day, Sunday, is as bright and hot as Juan Gama's mood is cool and gloomy. Teresa suggests that they take food and drink to the central plaza. There is a concert and big crowds. They can watch the people and listen to the music.

"You are troubled with the demons in your head and I worry about Perez. It will take our minds off these things," she says.

Juan shrugs. "He met a woman. That's all."

"He packed clothes before he went out yesterday and did not say a word to me."

"He's a grown man, Teresa."

"Only in years."

Juan lets it ride. Despite his offer to buy their food and drink from vendors, frugal Teresa packs bread, cheese, and sodas. For the eight blocks to the plaza, he carries their picnic sack in one hand and holds hers with his other. Since this is the end of him and her, this moment is incredibly bittersweet.

Juan is certain that Perez is in Mexico City, eating and drinking and living it up. When he stood Charlie up at La Parroquia, there were bound to be repercussions. Juan pictures Charlie beelining it to the airport to cajole Juan Gama's Mexico City itinerary from airline people.

If Charlie knew where he lived, he'd've come for him at Teresa's, not the café. Juan estimates that he has a one-day window to escape. Today.

On a bench in the plaza, he looks at the people and the band. He sees and hears nothing. His thoughts wander to roulette, the purest of the casino games.

The wheel itself, rich inlaid wood, spinning on precision bearings, is a work of beauty. At rest or in motion, it is mesmerizing. No participation whatsoever is required of the player. You lay your money on the felt and the dealer rakes it off.

Juan Gama, a statistics major with a mathematical brain; of all people, he should have known better. He could not stop himself any more than a heroin addict could keep a needle out of his arm. Like one of those degenerate gamblers, he lost the card-counting proceeds almost as fast as they came in.

He has enough money stashed for another year. Then what? He can worry about that then. Charlie is today's headache.

Easygoing Charlie, wouldn't he sympathize if Juan could convince him of his staggering roulette losses? What is that old saying? You're only a temporary custodian of the house's money. Wouldn't Charlie take back word to his bosses that they've had their money all along?

Yeah, right. And pigs can fly.

"Are you not feeling well?" Teresa asks.

"What?"

"You won't talk to me. You have been in a trance."

"Sorry."

She gets up. "Since you are not having any fun, I cannot have any either. Anyway, I am anxious to see if Perez is home."

Why not? Juan thinks, rising slowly. He puts his arm around her and, setting a slow pace, begins to tell her everything.

Charlie Peashooter is impressed. This little abode is as neat as a pin and the living room is an antique store with a military theme, including a rogue's gallery of buccaneer and colonial potentate portraiture. The feminine touch is apparent, with doilies and the scent of waxes. The decorator presumably is the sister of that unfortunate lad with the drinking problem.

In order to gain access to the airport terminal's interior, Charlie had purchased a ticket to Cancún. When he did not see Juan, it was logical that he utilized someone in this misdirection play. Another element in the logic: why would Juan blab to that waiter if he was skipping town? It had been easy enough to grease a ticket agent's palm to learn if a man named Perez had likewise purchased a ticket and to identify him.

Juan Gama's ill-gotten gains may not be in an offshore account,

Charlie theorizes. Perhaps, he thinks, Juan is old-fashioned, preferring to squirrel it in a mattress. His guess is close. In a shoebox in a
cubbyhole behind a closet, perhaps unbeknownst to the lady of the
house, is a shoebox containing fifteen thousand dollars in green-
backs and pesos.

Juan is teasing him with petty cash. They *will* have their chitchat
concerning that Grand Cayman numbered account.

Charlie peeks between curtains. The stinker, there he is, home
early from their picnic. His pleasantly plump lady friend is red-
eyed, squeezing her hankie for all it's worth. Charlie steps out of
the light.

"How could you do this to Perez?" a sniffling Teresa is saying not
for the first time. "To make a hunting decoy of him."

"Hey, like he's having a ball," Juan says. "Charlie's looking for
me, not Perez. Nothing will happen to him."

"Something already has. I can feel it. How could you lie to me
for these months?"

"I wasn't lying. I, uh, withheld. I was planning to tell you everything soon."

"Liar. When are you leaving me?"

"I have to go right away. I'll be back as soon as I can. I promise."

"Liar. What do I smell?"

They are inside. Juan is about to close the door, but he freezes.
He smells it too.

"A man's perfume. You do not wear any."

"I do," Charlie says, stepping out of a shadow. "Forgive me. The
door was unlocked."

"Liar," Teresa says, backing into Juan.

Juan steps protectively in front of her. "Charlie, I need an extra
day or two."

Charlie sighs and exhibits a compassionate frown. "Juan, Juan,
Juan. You should have been upfront. That hurts. I'd've worked
with you."

Juan hangs his head.

Teresa demands, "Where is my brother?"

"A fine young man. Dissipating himself in Mexico City, I'll bet-
cha. Oops, sorry, sis," Charlie replies with a wink.

"Liar. Liars. Both of you."

Charlie looks at Juan, his eyes widening playfully. "Well, I know where the term 'Mexican spitfire' originates, you lucky dog. Juan, now, this situation of ours?"

"One more day, Charlie. There's a mix-up on the account numbers—"

"You stop lying to him, maybe he will stop lying to me."

"Excuse me?" Charlie says to her.

Teresa looks at Charlie and his dead, cordial eyes. She has no expectation of prizes behind curtains.

"There is not any money except for what this man hides in my house he thinks I do not know about. Answer me where my brother is and you can take that money and go."

"No money?" Charlie says to him. "There *has* to be money."

"There is. Honestly, Charlie, there is."

Juan says "honestly" as car dealers in TV commercials do. Charlie realizes now that there is no money. An unsatisfactory development, yes, but the denouement will be the same.

He sidles to Juan, pats his arm, and says, "Money. If you say so. Splendid. Heck, we should go out to a telephone right now and resolve this. Let's get it out of our hair, okay?"

Juan's feet won't move.

Charlie gives him a winning smile and a nudge that is more than a nudge. "C'mon, big guy, one call does it all."

"No," Teresa says in a hoarse whisper.

But she is not speaking from where she was, behind Juan's slumped shoulders. She has shifted to the hallway shadows. He may have to do her also. Three assignments for the price of one. Life is so unfair.

He has already edged Juan outside. Hand firmly clamped to a wrist of his prey, Charlie reenters. He blinks, eyes adjusting to the darkness, and turns toward Teresa, igniting his smile. He glances at the wall with the pirate memorabilia. Something is missing.

Charlie reaches into his pocket when it dawns on him what it is. He reaches too late. The arrow pierces his throat as he draws his pistol.

"We drove your kind away once. We can do it again," Teresa says.

She is not talking to Charlie Peashooter, who is on the floor and cannot hear her. She is talking to Juan, who stumbles out the door and breaks into a run as she reloads the crossbow.

R. A. ALLEN

The Emerald Coast

FROM *The Literary Review*

THERE WAS NO BREEZE. The Gulf's blue-green surface was flat, and a haze — the waning vestige of a morning fog — hung above it. Listless waves slopped the tide line like a careless janitor. Waitron lit a cigarette and half-leaned half-sat on the wooden railing that enclosed the al fresco deck of Joe's Crab Trap. It was the midafternoon lull: bartenders prepping fruit garnishes for happy hour, busboys sweeping up sandy French fries, and the wait staff trudging through the personally unprofitable side work demanded by management in order to save money by not actually hiring someone to clean mirrors, dust woodwork, polish stainless steel, and whatnot.

Because of the haze, the glare was diffuse and everywhere and it burned into Waitron's retinae even in the shade of the deck's canopy. The haze muffled the beach noises: children squealing, the thump of a volleyball, snatches of music, the shrieks of gulls. He scanned the long white shore from east to west for as far as he could see. How many females could he discern between the vanishing points of his sight? Three hundred? More than five hundred? Certainly less than there were in August.

The need within him was rising, building like steam, his need for sex-plus. Sex-plus was a fulfillment that, he knew, average men never dream of; but it was his ultimate gratification. It came at a price, though, and the price was the need itself — the wanting — which was like hunger and thirst and a drug craving rolled into one. It was time to mark this territory and move on. He was first out in the shift rotation tonight and would be packed up and headed for Colorado in a few days, disappearing back into the floating world of the seasonal waiter. The time was right, like planets aligning in his favor. He would have to find the right one. He would try tonight.

"Robert?"

It would be Holcomb, the day-shift manager; the only one who addressed him by his real name. Hands on hips, Holcomb was standing just inside the doorway. He said, "You think you might dust the paddle fans anytime soon?"

Because he was tall, this was one of Waitron's side-work duties. He dead-eyed Holcomb for a beat or two. "When I finish this," he said, ashing his cigarette on the plank floor.

Holcomb went back inside.

There was nothing else Holcomb could say and they both knew it—the season was ending. Waitron turned his attentions back to the beach. How many between the ages of twelve and twenty-four? How many with the correct hair? The right body?

Now a hammering noise broke his reverie—a man replacing shingles atop the main building of the restaurant. Waitron watched him with detachment. The roofer was one of those construction worker types that, a few seasons ago, were everywhere in Destin. Scruffy hair and beard, shirtless and tanned impossibly dark, one of the numberless rabble drawn from the rural areas of the Southeast by the building boom now fizzling out along the Emerald Coast of the Florida Panhandle. He was just under medium-sized, monkey-built, a creature of sinew and vein. He wore a tool belt over cutoff jeans and a pair of filthy tennis shoes. To Waitron, he was a perfect specimen of his class: a cracker, a variety of Georgia/northern-Florida white trash whose life revolved around semi-skilled labor, cheap beer, and trailer park squabbles. It must be 120 degrees up there, Waitron mused—how does he stand it?

As if he could feel someone staring, the roofer stopped work and eased into a squatting position against the low slope of the roof, forearms resting on his knees, hammer dangling from one hand. He stared back at Waitron. The roofer had a crude tattoo—an eye —on his left triceps. A warning floated up from Waitron's memory. The roofer continued to stare at him with pale eyes set in a hawkish face. Waitron turned away.

Oakley paced the balcony, grinding on the mood he was in. "They call us trailer trash," he said. "And because the world has tarred us with this appellation, we are condemned to a brutish existence."

"I reckon what we're called is an accident of our births," Sparrow responded mildly. "I don't *feel* like trash." He'd been pounding nails since five A.M. in the broiling heat. Now freshly showered and in clean clothing, all he wanted was to relax with this beer while the sun set on the beautiful Gulf below. "You read some Hobbes when you were up in Fountain?"

"Yeah, I read *Leviathan*. I read that copy of *The Peloponnesian War* you sent. I read a lot. Ain't nothing changed: you do your forty-cent-an-hour job, you do your reps at the weight pile, you go to chow when they call you, and you sleep when it's lights out. There's still lotsa time left over to advance your education."

"You didn't go Mao-Marxist on me did you?" Sparrow joked.

"Nah. I'm just saying . . ."

Oakley had been out for three weeks. His doomed fascination with a jewelry store up in Dothan had bought him a stretch of two years and ten months.

Sparrow and Oakley had been best friends since grade school in a nameless, sun-struck tract of Section Eight housing on the outskirts of Mary Esther, Florida—itself a strip mall of a town that owed its existence to neighboring Eglin Air Force Base. They had shared the highs as well as the misery, looking out for each other in stir and out.

They were on the balcony of Oakley's second-floor crash in the old Spindrift Motel, a fifties-era relic, now condemned—pilings washed out by a June hurricane had destabilized the western wing. By this time next year, the pastel high-rise depicted on the billboard out front would take its place. Oakley was living there on the sly through the beneficence of Two-Eleven, the Spindrift's onetime handyman, now caretaker-cum-watchman pro tem and old jailing buddy to them both. It was no big deal to Two-Eleven, as he figured to be let go when the developer sent the dozers in—which might be any day now.

With two hundred feet of sand-covered extension cord, Oakley was stealing enough electricity from the absentee owners of the condo next door to power a refrigerator, a fifteen-gallon hot water heater, and a couple of lamps. There was no A/C, but it was late September, so the heat was tolerable for sleeping—just. Money for the necessities came in from day trips as a deckhand on the charter boats out of East Pass, baiting hooks for tourists, cleaning their catches, swabbing the decks and gunnels, lugging ice—the flunky work of a nautical factotum. But Oakley, not one to take direction in the first place and chafing at the dictatorial manner of the charter captains, was gaining a reputation as a malcontent on the marina. His other source of income, he'd told Sparrow, was "odd jobs."

They watched a young couple stroll out to the water's edge and settle onto a blanket. For Sparrow, the girl added a carload of black chips to the quality of the beachscape. She was a stunner, a cornsilk blonde not older than twenty. In defiance of a municipal ordinance laid down by the local guardians of social order, she was wearing a thong—coral in hue, a mere afterthought in terms of beachwear. Sparrow shivered. "You get laid since you got out?"

"Went and saw Amber a couple of times while that sheriff's deputy she moved in with was on duty, but she's turning into a candidate for *Girls Gone Wild.*"

Sparrow remembered the hot-and-haughty Amber. He emitted a dry laugh.

Oakley studied the thong girl for a moment and then looked away, as if the sight of her caused him pain. "I got money on my mind, bro. I lack funding. A man can't be who he really is without money. Which brings up my next point: I need to find Davy Redstone."

"Davy Redstone the fence?"

"Yeah. He owes me three dimes from that pawnshop B-and-E that I pulled before I went in. I heard he's hanging out at a bar north of the 331 Bridge, a slop chute called the Owl's Eye. I need you to go with me. I need you to watch my back."

"That was four years ago. Redstone's gonna balk on you."

"I will stress to him that a debt is a debt. He gives me any shit, I'll have to tune him up."

Sparrow nodded. He did not doubt that the prospects for *violencia* were distinct, if not imminent. Along with the alpha-dog precepts of your seasoned convict, Oakley had the muscle and the martial portfolio to back up a volatile nature. Problem was: Redstone traveled with an entourage. If it came to a dustup, they would be bucking the law of superior numbers.

"He'll have his homies cheek by jowl," Sparrow said.

"I got no choice."

"I'm there for you, bro."

Watch my back was the undeniable—the unquestionable—call

for support between them. And Sparrow's response was gold-standard true, true at the risk of incarceration, true past the point of injury, true *unto death*. It was his duty to a bond forged out of old hard times.

Duty. At one time, Sparrow would have greeted violent confrontation in service of this bond with gritty cheer. But he had turned thirty-three in March. Somewhere, Sparrow had read that thirty-three is an introspective watershed for even the thickest of men: they come to the sit-up-in-bed realization that times are flying. Like the tolling of a giant bell, it had been no different for him. He had been into some kind of criminality since the age of twelve—all of it larcenous, some of it violent, most of it with Oakley. But during his latest left-handed endeavor, Oakley had been behind bars. It was in collusion with an Atlanta-based counterfeiter—a former penitentiary colleague—that Sparrow spent two months passing bogus twenties in the Caribbean. The Feds were waiting for him at the gate at Miami International. On a half-dozen surveillance videos, he starred as the prosecution's witness against himself.

The government confiscated everything they could find; what they couldn't find, his lawyer wound up with. He'd bargained for thirty months and maxed it out at the Federal Correctional Institution in Marianna. It wasn't that he couldn't do the time; it was just that, in the joint, the judicial system is eating the front end off of your future.

Right after his release, he'd met, fallen in love, and moved in with Marlene, a clerical for a bail bondsman in Fort Walton. She had a four-year-old daughter who adored him for no reason whatsoever. So he had come to a conclusion: he didn't care if he had to be a roofer or a ditch digger or a dishwasher for the rest of his life, he wasn't going to do any more time. He had a duty to Marlene. And for little Jonquil, he was going to be the father she'd never known. Would Oakley understand his duty to them? Sparrow didn't think so. Right now, he wished he were at home with them, watching TV. But Marlene was up in Waycross visiting her mama, which was why he now found himself here with Oakley. He hoped they wouldn't find Redstone.

"When do you want to go?" Sparrow said.

"Now."

"My truck is on empty."

"We'll take my car."

"When did you get a car?"

"The other day. It's parked over in the Hampton lot. Keeping it around here might draw attention to my living arrangements. Grab the rest of them beers. Let's go."

Sparrow gave the beach a wistful last look. The wind was picking up.

The Hampton Inn was a two-block walk east on Scenic 98—the original beach-view part of Highway 98—and two blocks north. There was no view of the Gulf from this Hampton, and it attracted the folks that couldn't afford one—kids, mostly, or blue-collar families who scrimped to give their children a few days at the beach. From the rooftops, Sparrow would see them: mom, dad, and their youngsters, shuffling along in single file—serious as mourners—on the white gravel shoulders of the beach-access streets, wearing their sandals and bathing suits, loaded down with towels, coolers, floats, umbrellas, and other beach crap.

Oakley's ride was a late model Taurus. Sparrow got in and took its measure. "You boosted a rental," he said, checking the column.

"Yeah. But the plates are fresh."

"Goddamn."

Oakley was grinning like a dog eating cheese. "Don't worry, bro. I'll drive safe."

"Hi, folks, I'll be your waitron for your dining experience tonight," he said—his standard icebreaker that generally evoked a smile from patrons. "Would you like to start with a cocktail?"

The party was comprised of two fortyish couples and a teenaged girl—a daughter, he supposed. The adults wanted cocktails. While they decided, Waitron eyed the girl. Her hair was all wrong—too long, too light.

Leaving with their drink order, he noticed a lone girl at the bar. She was correct: petite, shoulder-length brunette hair, early twenties. Her face was okay—a poor man's Drew Barrymore. The glasses were an added attraction. By coming in here with that sluttish haircut, she was begging for sex-plus.

This was his last table. If the girl at the bar stayed until his checkout was over, it would be another sign.

She reminded him of number four, decomposing now for some two years in a hole fifty yards into a wooded area off of Highway 7 a few miles outside of Norwalk, Connecticut. Like the others, he had her GPS coordinates committed to memory: bargaining chips that would keep him off death row in case they caught him.

The sun went down. His table decided against dessert, but, to his annoyance, one of the women wanted coffee. He checked on the girl at the bar. She'd just ordered another margarita. His luck was holding.

After Waitron finished with his checkout, he marked time at the waiter's station, rolling silverware in paper napkins and watching the girl. Finally she finished her drink and paid, leaving, not by the door to the lot that bordered Scenic 98, but down the steps to the beach. Perfect. Waitron felt his nostrils flare; felt his lungs fill to the bursting point. He counted to ten and exited by the front door. He jogged through the parking lot to his car, where he grabbed the sack that contained the things he needed and then walked around the outside of the building to the beach. Her white shorts made her easy to follow as she walked eastward, barefoot in the surf-dampened sand.

Oakley had the pedal flat on the floor on their way back across Choctawhatchee Bay, speedometer bumping 110. The Taurus was bucking like a jackhammer because, having whacked a parked truck on their gravel-slurring escape from the Owl's Eye, the front end was out of alignment.

"Feels like we're coming apart," said Sparrow, gripping the arm-rest.

"We gotta get off this bridge," Oakley said. "If they called the five-o's, we could get bottled up."

Sparrow thought his prayers had been answered when they walked into the Owl's Eye to find that the fence was not there. They'd hung around for a while at the bar, casually pumping an evasive bartender about Redstone, and otherwise minding their own business.

Evening dissolved into night. The Owl's Eye was a dive and it possessed that seething atmosphere that all dives have, but things remained peaceful until a girl who was all teased-up hair and quick movements came up and wanted to know about Oakley's shamrock tattoo like it was some kind of message aimed at her from outer space.

Turns out: there was a narrow-minded boyfriend.

Oakley knocks boyfriend's eye out of its socket with a backhanded blow from a two-pound beer mug.

Boyfriend's friends materialize.

They fought a rearguard skirmish to the door, Sparrow swinging a barstool; Oakley brandishing the Spyderco folding knife that he kept clipped inside the waistband of his jeans.

The Taurus gained the causeway at the end of the 331 Bridge. A second later, they had to swerve to miss an SUV pulling out of a tourist trap called 3-Thirty-A.

Sparrow sucked his teeth. "Slow it down, willya."

Oakley dropped it down a notch or two. He said, "Ninety-eight is only a mile away. We get there, we'll be in good shape."

Sparrow wasn't so sure. Their remaining headlight was beaming off at a crazy angle, and they were trailing smoke like a crop-duster. "We're gonna have to ditch this vehicle PDQ," he said.

"Wonder where that fucking Redstone was," said Oakley.

When they got to Highway 98, they headed west into sparse traffic. Just east of Sandestin they passed a Florida Highway Patrol cruiser on the opposite side of the highway. The patrolie's head snapped in their direction as he went by. Sparrow turned around and saw the cruiser's roof lights come alive. "We got an audience," he said.

Oakley made a U-turn at the next opening in the median just as the cop was doing the mirror-image same 1,500 feet behind them. With his shirttail, Sparrow started wiping down the armrest and everything else he could remember touching.

"Damn," said Oakley. He slammed to a stop in the emergency lane. "Good-bye, Taurus."

They sprinted down a weedy embankment and vaulted a three-strand barbwire fence. Beyond the fence, they were quickly swallowed by the dense ground cover of a pine savanna. Branches whipping their faces, wiregrass snagging their feet, they crashed through. The highway, pulsing with blue light and echoing the squawk of a radio, faded behind. Saw palmetto spines stabbed through their jeans. Overhead, the slash pines cast bottlebrush silhouettes against a pumpkin moon.

Simultaneously, they tripped over a fallen log.

"What place is this?" Oakley puffed.

"Topsail Hill Park. It's a nature preserve," said Sparrow. "If we can get through it, we'll come out on deserted beach."

"How do you know?"

"I reroofed the park office and the pavilions in April. I read their brochures at lunchtime. The wind is blowing in off the Gulf. All's we gotta do is keep the breeze in our faces."

The sandy soil turned mucky, and suddenly they were chest high in cattails, and next, in water up to their waists. They backed out, lily pads clinging to them like greasy bandages.

"What now?" Oakley wanted to know.

"We stumbled into Morris Lake. If we work our way to the left, we'll run into a tidal marsh that drains it into the Gulf. We can follow it to the beach."

Twenty minutes later, they found Morris Lake's outfall; they felt their way along its edge, aided by lightning flashes from a storm percolating out over the Gulf.

"Yow! Shit!" Oakley yelped. "Something bit my leg."

"You see what was it?"

"Too dark. Them brochures mention snakes?"

"Yeah, got cottonmouth and rattlers, but a bunch of nonpoisonous ones too."

They could hear the surf now. A few minutes later, the scrub broke onto a twenty-five-foot sand dune crested by sea oats. The outfall creek, brimming with tannin-blackened water, cut through the dune and became an estuary flowing through the beach and into the Gulf. They clambered up the dune. Cloud-to-cloud lightning and intermittent moonlight delivered the blessed sight of the beach below them. A constant, storm-driven sea breeze drove the waves onto the shore with the intensity of a cymbal roll; salt spray stung their faces. Oakley tried to roll up the leg of his jeans to inspect his wound, but his calf was too swollen. "Pretty sure it was a snake," he said. "My leg's gettin' stiff on me."

Sparrow said, "We gotta walk two miles of this beach to Sandestin. We get there, we'll get you into the emergency room at Sacred Heart."

Mushing through the soft sand atop the dune, it quickly became apparent that their best time would be made on the more compact surface of the beach. They slid down the face of the dune. They could taste the storm's ozonic breath. An in-rushing cloudbank canceled the moonlight.

They walked along the base of the dunes, pushing west toward the lights of Sandestin's high-rise condos. The wind sheared their faces like a belt sander, and, more rapidly now, lightning fluxed cloud-to-cloud and into the water at the horizon.

"I thought you said this beach was deserted," Oakley said, pointing toward the water's edge.

The next lightning flash revealed two figures in copulation—a man was taking a woman from behind. They were facing the sea. The lightning bleached their skin a cadaverous white.

"Haw," said Oakley. "It's the doggy-style remake of Burt Lancaster and Deborah whatsherface on the beach in *From Here to Eternity.*"

It went dark.

Came another long flicker.

"Something ain't right about this frame," Sparrow said.

"True that. Let us file for discovery."

They strode closer, their approach masked by the roar of the elements. The man had something twisted around the woman's neck —a rope or belt—and her arms flopped like those of a rag doll with each thrust. In a voice loud enough to be heard above the combers, Oakley said, "Well, well, if it ain't Chester the Mo-lester. In the slam, we got a cure for you rape-o motherfuckers: it's called sticking my pecker up your comic-opera rectum."

He was skinny and basketball tall and he leapt away from the girl like he'd stepped on a third rail. The girl collapsed face forward onto the sand. Sparrow noted that her back was cut to shreds.

The guy got his pants up and lunged toward something metallic—a bowie knife—that was sticking out of the sand.

"He's got a banger!" Sparrow yelled as the man swept the foot-long blade in a wide arc toward Oakley's face.

Like an exercise-yard assassination, they split to either side of him. Sparrow heard Oakley's Spyderco snap into locked position. The man feinted at Oakley a second time. Oakley tripped backwards into the sand; the man moved in on him, bowie knife poised to plunge. Sparrow snagged the man's elbow, clutching it just long enough to keep him from stabbing Oakley. The man rounded on Sparrow. Sparrow threw a fistful of sand in his face.

The man made a noise in his throat and reeled backwards, clawing at his eyes. Oakley was on his feet again. "Eat this, Chester," he said as he jabbed his blade into the guy's midsection and then ducked beneath the reflexive chop of the big knife. Taking advantage of his opponent's blindness, Oakley cut the man repeatedly with his own blade, slashing and pinking, a quick gash across the forearm, one that missed the groin to strike the man's upper thigh. Sparrow thrust-kicked at the man's knees, trying to take him off of his feet, but either missed or landed glancing blows.

Oakley's hit count mounted, but three-inch wounds to the torso of a man whose bloodstream is blazing with adrenaline are hardly felt, much less immediately fatal.

At the water's edge, they spun in a death dance played out in total darkness punctuated by the blinding strobe of the lightning. Finally, Oakley managed to sink the full length of his pocketknife's blade into the man's lower rib cage; the man gasped. Sparrow tripped him, but as he fell, his blind thrashing with the heavy-bladed hunting knife caught Oakley across the belly as he was rushing in. While the man was trying to get back up, Sparrow kicked him in the temple and then again at the base of his ear. The man's grip on his knife went slack. Sparrow wrenched it free from his grasp and, with his left forearm pinning the man's throat, plunged the blade in and up through the man's solar plexus. Blood geysered into Sparrow's face. The man convulsed orgasmically for five seconds and lapsed into shock. Twenty seconds later he was dead.

Oakley was lying on his back in the sand, the front of his shirt soaked with blood. Sparrow bent over him and said, "Hey, bro. You okay?"

Oakley's eyeballs were rolled up. "Between the river and the steep came . . . serpents," he mumbled.

Sparrow shook him. "What? What's that mean?" He tried blowing into Oakley's mouth, but Oakley remained incoherent. Sparrow went over to the naked girl and rolled her over. She was limper than a boned capon. He splashed seawater on her; she made a noise. She was alive — for now.

Far down the beach, he saw headlights coming toward him. Sparrow rubbed a handful of sand on the handle of the bowie knife sticking out of the man's chest. To wash out his tracks, he sprinted along the edge of the surf; back to the natural ditch that Morris Lake's outfall made in the beach and waded up its dark waters until he was safely back among the pines.

Soon, the airspace above the shoreline lit up with beams and flashes of light—red, yellow, blue, and blue-white. Sparrow heard the helicopter and then saw the probe and sweep of its searchlight, the angry finger of society's god. He crawled beneath a gallberry bush. It was starting to rain.

Sparrow spent Friday night in the preserve. The rainfall varied from blinding sheets to drizzle. During the drizzle, he worked his way west through the brush until his terror of stepping upon an alligator or a snake in the darkness finally made him stay put in a thicket of swamp sweetbells.

Saturday blossomed hot, and the sun reached across ninety-three million miles to beat him like a child. He fell asleep from exhaustion in the middling shade of a scrub oak, but, an hour later, awoke in a panic of hot needle stings that were everywhere. Ants! He was covered in them. They were biting his face; they were in the crotch of his jeans; their mandibles clung to the dried blood of his many cuts and scratches. He hurdled through the shrubs to the blackwater depths of Morris Lake and—gators and snakes be damned!—plunged in. For the rest of the day, he holed up in a fetterbush in the lee of a dune. No one came in after him.

Well after dark on Saturday, he emerged from the bush—famished, dehydrated, mud-slaked, bug-bitten, and now ravaged by poison ivy—to make his way up ten miles of beach to Destin. If he came across late-night beach strollers or kids out crabbing, he would hide in the surf up to his chin and wait until they had passed.

Around three o'clock Sunday morning, Sparrow reached his truck.

The Sunday evening TV news said Oakley was in the ICU in a coma and that some waiter identified as Robert something-or-other was dead (good riddance) and that a girl—apparently a victim of a violent assault—was in critical-but-stable condition and was expected to recover but couldn't remember anything about what had happened. There was no mention of a fourth party, but Sparrow knew that the cops don't release the full story.

They'd come for him or they wouldn't. Oakley would live or he would die. Sparrow could accept that Life was bigger and more agile than he was.

Around nine o'clock, Sparrow heard a car door slam and then footsteps on the iron steps that led up from the driveway slab to the kitchen door of their mobile home. Marlene and little Jonquil were back from Waycross. Sparrow, slathered in Neosporin and hydro-cortisone cream, was sprawled on the couch in a pair of boxers.

Marlene dropped her suitcase when she saw him. "John," she cried, "what happened to you?"

"Nothing."

Hesitantly, she asked, "Are you okay?"

"Yeah."

Jonquil came in behind Marlene and clutched her mother's leg. "Is Daddy John hurt, Mama?"

"No, darling, he's okay. Go put your things in your room. Mama will fix you some supper when she gets unpacked," Marlene told her daughter, turning the child toward the rear of the trailer. "You want another beer, John?"

"Yeah."

"And you're sure about 'nothing' happening to you?"

"Yeah, I'm sure."

"Okay, then," she said as she headed for the kitchen.

Sparrow looked at the TV but it wasn't much in the front of his mind. Marlene wouldn't ask about it again. This was the way it was among their kind.

DOUG ALLYN

An Early Christmas

FROM *Ellery Queen's Mystery Magazine*

JARED SNAPPED AWAKE to the sound of laughter. On the bedside TV, Jay Leno was yukking it up with a ditzy blond celeb. Jared sat up slowly, dazed and groggy from too much brandy, too much sex. Fumbling around, he found the remote control and killed the tinny TV cackling, then looked around slowly, trying to get his bearings.

A bedroom. Not his own. Sunny Lockhart was sprawled beside him, nude, snoring softly with her mouth open, her platinum hair a tousled shambles. At fifty-one, Sunny had crow's-feet and smile lines, but her breasts were D-cup and she made love like a teeny-bopper. Better, in fact.

Gratitude sex. The best-kept secret in the legal profession. After settling cases involving serious money, clients were often elated, horny, and very, very grateful to the guy who made it happen.

Thanks to Jared's legal expertise, Sunny Lockhart was financially set for life, a free and independent woman of means. Unfortunately, she was also crowding fifty. Too old for Jared by a dozen years. And he had to be in the office to meet with a client at nine sharp.

Damn. Time to go.

Stifling a groan, Jared slid silently out of Sunny's rumpled bed and began gathering up his clothes.

Roaring down the shore road in his Mercedes SL500 through a gentle snowfall, Jared set his radio on scan, listening to the momentary snippets of songs flashing past. Mostly Christmas carols or country. Finally caught a tune he liked. "Back in Black," AC/DC. Cranking the volume, he slapped the wheel on the back beat, getting an energy surge from the music.

Couldn't stop grinning. Wondering if he could arrange a weekend getaway with Sunny. Getting hot and bothered again just thinking about it.

He paid no attention to the rust-bucket pickup truck rumbling down the side road to his left. Until he realized the truck wasn't slowing for the stop sign! The crazy bastard was speeding up, heading straight for him!

Stomping his brakes, Jared swerved over onto the shoulder, trying to avoid a crash. Knowing it was already too late!

Blowing through the intersection at eighty, the pickup came howling across the centerline, sheering off at the last second to slam broadside into Jared's roadster, smashing him off the road.

Airbags and the windshield exploded together, smothering Jared in a world of white as the Benz plowed through the massive snowdrift piled along the highway, then hurtled headlong down the steep embankment.

Wrestling through the airbag's embrace, Jared fought the wheel, struggling to control the roadster in its downhill skid. He managed to avoid one tree, then glanced off another. For a split second he thought he might actually make it—but his rear fender clipped a towering pine, snapping the car around, sending it out of control, tumbling end over end down the slope.

Bouncing off tree trunks like a pinball, the Benz was being hammered into scrap metal. The side windows shattered inward, spraying Jared with glass fragments. For a heart-freezing instant, he felt the car go totally airborne, then it slammed down nose-first into the bottom of the gorge with stunning force.

A lightning strike of white-hot agony flashed up Jared's spine, driving his breath out in a shriek. Freezing him in place. Afraid to breathe, or even blink, for fear of triggering the godawful pain again.

Christ. He couldn't feel his legs. Didn't know what was wrong with them, but knew it was serious. Total numbness meant his back might be broken or—

"Mister?" A voice broke through Jared's terrified daze. "Can you hear me down there?"

"Yes!" Jared gasped.

"Hey, I saw what happened. That crazy bastard never even slowed down. Are you okay?"

"I—can't move," Jared managed. "I think my back may be broken. Call nine-one-one."

"Already did. Hang on, I've got a first-aid kit in my car."

Unable to risk turning his head, Jared could only catch glimpses in his shattered rearview mirror, a dark figure working his way down the steep, snowy slope, carrying a red plastic case. Twice, the man stumbled in the roadster's torn tracks, but managed to regain his balance and press on.

As he drew closer, the mirror shards broke the image into distorted fragments, monstrous and alien . . . Then he vanished altogether.

"Are you there?" Jared gasped, gritting his teeth. Every word triggered a raw wave of pain.

"Almost. Stay still." The voice came from somewhere behind the wreck. Jared couldn't see him at all.

"You're Jared Bannan, the real estate lawyer, right?"

"Do I know you?"

No answer. Then Jared glimpsed the twisted figure in the mirror again. Climbing back up the track the way he'd come.

"Wh—where are you going? I need help!"

"I can't risk it." The figure continued on without turning. "Your gas tank ruptured. Can't you smell it? Your car could go off like a bomb any second."

"But—" Jared coughed. My God. The guy was right! The raw stench of gasoline was filling his nostrils, making it hard to breathe.

"Wait! Come back, you sonofabitch! Don't leave me! I have money! I'll pay you!"

At the mention of money, the climber stopped and turned around. But in the tree shadows, Jared still couldn't make out his face.

"That's more like it," Jared said. "I'll give you ten thousand dollars. Cash. Just get me out of this car and—"

"Ten grand? Is that all you're worth?"

"No! I mean, look, I'll give you whatever you want . . ." A flash of light revealed the climber's face for a split second. Definitely familiar. Someone Jared had met or . . . His mind suddenly locked up, freezing with soul-numbing horror.

The flash was a flame. The climber had lit a cigarette. "Oh, Jesus," Jared murmured softly, licking his lips. "What are you doing? Wait. Please."

"Jesus?" the climber mimicked, taking a long drag. "Wait? Please? Is that the best you can do? I thought shysters were supposed to be fast talkers."

Jared didn't answer. Couldn't. He watched in growing terror as the smoker tapped the ashes off, bringing the tip to a cherry glow. Then he flipped the cigarette high in the air, sending it arcing through the darkness, trailing sparks as it fell.

Jared's shriek triggered another bolt of agony from his shattered spine, but he was beyond caring. He couldn't stop screaming any more than he could stop the cigarette's fiery fall.

Leaving his unmarked patrol car at the side of the highway, Doyle Stark trotted the last hundred yards along the shoulder to the accident scene. A serious one, by north-country standards. A Valhalla County fire truck was parked crossways across one lane of the highway, blocking it. Two uniformed sheriff's deputies, Hurst and Van Duzen, were directing traffic around the truck on the far shoulder. Van flipped him a quick salute and Doyle shot him with a fingertip.

Yellow police-line tapes stretched from both bumpers of the fire truck to stakes planted in the roadside snowdrifts. The tapes outlined a savage gap in the snowy embankment, over the top and on down out of sight.

Detective Zina Redfern was squatting at the rear of the fire truck, warming her mittened hands in the heat of its exhaust pipe. She was dressed in her usual Johnny Cash black, black nylon *Police* parka over a turtleneck and jeans, a black watch cap pulled down around her ears. The woman took the term "plainclothes officer" literally. Even her combat boots were the real deal, LawPro Pursuits with steel toes. With a Fairbairn blade clipped to her right ankle.

"Sergeant Stark," she nodded, straightening up to her full, squared-off five-foot-five, one-forty. "Whoa, what happened to your eye?"

Six foot and compactly built, with sandy hair and gray eyes, Doyle was sporting a white bandage over his left brow.

"Reffing a Peewee pickup game," Doyle said. "Ten-year-olds watch way too much hockey on TV. What happened here?"

"A car crashed through the embankment, tumbled all the way to the bottom, then blew up and burned down to the frame. What's left of the driver is still inside. Beyond that, I'm not sayin' squat. I need you to see this with fresh eyes."

"Fair enough," Doyle nodded, picking up the edge in her tone. Zina had worked in Flint for four years before transferring north to the Valhalla force. She was an experienced investigator, and if something was bothering her about this . . .

He swiveled slowly, taking in the accident scene as a steady stream of traffic crawled past on the far shoulder. Wide-eyed gawkers, wondering what was up. Doyle knew the feeling.

Two sets of broad black skid marks met in the center of the lane, then followed an impossible angle to the torn snowbanks at the side of the road. "Who called this in?"

"A long-haul trucker spotted the wreckage as he crested the hill, around ten this morning. We caught a real break. The wreck's not visible from the roadside. If we'd gotten a little more snow during the night, the poor bastard might have stayed buried till spring. I marked off a separate trail away from the skid track," she said, leading him to a rough footpath up and over the berm. "There are footprints that . . . well, take a look for yourself."

Clambering to the top of the drift, Doyle stopped, scanning the scene below. A ragged trail of torn snow and shattered trees led down the slope to a charred obscenity crouched at the bottom of the gorge. A burned-out hulk that had once been an expensive piece of German automotive engineering.

The charred Mercedes-Benz was encircled by a blackened ring of torn earth and melted slush, its savagery already softening beneath a gentle gauze of lightly falling snow.

Joni Javitz, the Joint Investigative Unit's only tech, was hunched over the car, dutifully photographing the corpse. Even at this distance, Doyle could see the gaping mouth and bared teeth of the Silent Scream, a burn victim's final rictus. A few patches of skull were showing through the blackened flesh . . .

Damn. He hated burn scenes. The ugly finality and the vile

stench that clung to your clothing for days. In Detroit, cops called them Crispy Critters. But here in the north, no one in Doyle's unit joked about them. There's nothing funny about a death by fire. Ever.

Working his way warily down the slope, Doyle noted the uneven footprints in the snow of the roadster's trail. "Did the trucker climb down to the car?"

"The trucker didn't stop," Zina said. "He spotted the wreck and a little smoke. Wasn't sure what it was, but thought somebody should take a look."

"It was still smoking at ten o'clock? Any idea when this happened, Joni?"

"My best guess would be around midnight, boss, give or take an hour," Javitz said without turning. Tall and slender as a whip, she had to fold herself into a question mark to shoot the wreck's interior. "The car and the body are both cool to the touch now, but they're still ten degrees warmer than the ambient temperature. The State Police Crime Scene team is already en route from Gaylord. They should be here anytime."

"Okay . . ." Doyle said, swiveling slowly, taking in the scene. "We've got a hotshot in a Benz roadster who runs off the road at midnight, crashes and burns. Tough break for him. Or her?"

"Him, definitely," Joni said.

"Fine. Him, then. And why exactly am I here on my day off?"

Wordlessly, Joni stepped away from the car, revealing the charred corpse, and the deep crease in the driver's-side door.

"Wow," Doyle said softly, lowering himself to his haunches, studying the dent more closely. "Metal on metal. Red paint traces. No tree did this. Which explains the second set of skid marks on the highway. Somebody ran this poor bastard off the road . . ." He broke off, eyeing a small circle of dark red droplets, scattered like a spray of blood near the trunk.

"Plastic pellets?" Doyle said. "Any chance they're from the taillights?"

"Nope, the taillight lenses are Lexan," Joni said. "These pellets are definitely polypropylene, probably from a plastic gas container. A small one, a gallon or two. Like you'd use for a chainsaw or a lawn mower. The can was definitely on the ground outside the vehicle. I've already bagged up some residue to test for accelerants."

"I didn't see any skid marks from the other vehicle until the last second, just before it struck the Benz," Doyle mused. "From the depth of these dents, both cars must have been traveling at one hell of a clip. So car number two runs the stop sign at high speed, nails the Benz dead center, hard enough to drive it through the snowdrifts . . ."

"He's damned lucky he isn't down here too," Zina said.

"Maybe it wasn't luck," Doyle said, staring up the incline toward the highway. "If he hadn't hit the Benz, he definitely would have blown through the berm himself. And there's not much traffic out here at night. So, either he ran that stop sign, drunk, asleep, whatever, and the Benz had the million-to-one bad luck to get in his way or . . . ?"

"He wasn't out of control at all." Zina nodded, following Doyle's gaze up the hillside. "You think he drilled him deliberately?"

"Tell you what, Detective, why don't you hoof it back up the hill and check out that side road for tire tracks or exhaust stains in the snow. See if car number two was sitting up there, waiting for the Benz to show."

"Jesus," Joni said softly. "You mean somebody rammed this poor bastard on purpose? Then climbed down with a gas can and lit him up?"

"I don't like it either, but it works," Doyle agreed grimly. "Have you identified him yet?"

"The car's registered jointly to Jared and Lauren Bannan, Valhalla address."

"Jared Bannan?" Doyle echoed, surprised. "Damn. I know this guy. I've played racquetball against him."

"A friend?"

"No, just a guy. He's an attorney, a transplant from downstate, works mostly in real estate."

"A yuppie lawyer?" Zina said. "Should I cancel the Crime Scene team?"

The door to the classroom was ajar. Doyle raised his fist to knock, then hesitated, surprised at the utter silence from within. Curious, he peered around the doorjamb. A tall, trim woman with boyishly short dark hair was addressing the class. Soundlessly. Her lips were moving, the fingers of both hands flickering, mediating an animated discussion with a dozen rapt teenagers, who were answering with equally adept sign language, their lips miming speech, but with no sound at all.

It was like watching an Olympic fencing match, silvery signals flashing too quickly for the eye to follow.

The woman glanced up, frowning. "Can I help you?"

"Sorry to intrude, ma'am. If you're Dr. Bannan, we need a few minutes of your time."

"I'm in the middle of a class."

"This really can't wait, ma'am."

"My God," Lauren said softly, "are you absolutely sure it's Jared?"

"The identification isn't final, but he was carrying your husband's identification and driving his car."

"Jared wore a U of M class ring on his right hand," she offered. "Did the driver . . . ?"

Doyle nodded. They were in Dr. Bannan's office, a Spartan ten-by-ten box at Blair Center, the county magnet school for special needs students. Floor-to-ceiling bookshelves on three sides, Dr. Bannan's diplomas and teaching awards neatly displayed on the fourth wall. No photographs, Doyle noted.

"I didn't see a wedding ring," Zina said. "Did he normally wear one?"

"We're separated," Lauren said. "God. I can't believe this."

"Are you all right, Mrs. Bannan?" Doyle asked. "Can I get you a glass of water or something?"

"No, I'm . . . just a bit shaken. Do you have any idea what happened?"

"Your husband was apparently sideswiped on the shore road a few miles outside of town. Hit-and-run. His car went over a steep embankment, probably late last night. Midnight, maybe. He was pronounced dead at the scene. We're very sorry for your loss."

Lauren's mouth narrowed as she visibly brought her emotions under control. An elegant woman, Doyle thought. Slender as a willow with dark hair, a complexion as exquisite as a porcelain doll.

But not fragile. She took the news of her husband's death like a prizefighter rocked by a stiff punch. Drawing within herself to camouflage the damage.

After a moment, she took a deep breath, and carefully straightened her jacket.

"You said someone ran Jared off the road. What happened to the other driver?"

"We don't know yet, ma'am. Do you know why your husband might have been on that road last night?"

"No idea. Jared and I separated last year. Except for conferences with our attorney, I rarely see him. Why?"

Zina glanced the question at Doyle, who nodded.

"Judging from the skid marks, the collision may not have been accidental, Dr. Bannan," Zina said. "Do you know why anyone would want to harm your husband?"

"Whoa, back up a moment," Lauren said, raising her hand. "Are you saying someone deliberately rammed Jared's car?"

"We aren't certain yet, ma'am," Doyle said. "But the evidence does lean that way. At this point we're treating it as a possible homicide."

"For the record, would you mind telling us your whereabouts last night?" Zina asked.

Lauren glanced up at her sharply. "I was at home all evening. Alone. What are you implying?"

"Nothing, ma'am," Doyle put in. "It's strictly routine. We're not the enemy."

Lauren looked away a moment. "All right then. If you have questions, let's clear them up now."

"You said you separated last year?" Zina asked. "Have you filed for divorce?"

"We filed right after we separated. Last spring. March, I think."

"Do you have children?"

Lauren hesitated. "No. No children."

"Then help me out here, Mrs. Bannan. Without children involved, you can get a no-fault divorce in sixty days, and I'm speaking from experience. Was your husband contesting the divorce?"

"Only the property settlement. Jared earns considerably more than I do, so he felt he was entitled to a larger share. He kept coming up with new demands."

"Michigan's a community-property state," Doyle put in. "A wife's entitled to half, no matter who earns what."

"My husband is an attorney, Sergeant, though most of his work is in real estate. Fighting him in court wouldn't be cost-effective. We had our final meeting last Tuesday. He made an offer and I took it."

"But you weren't happy about it?" Zina said.

"Divorce seldom makes anyone happy."

"You're newcomers to the area, right?" Doyle asked. "When did you move north?"

"A little over two years ago."

"Why was that? The move, I mean?"

"Why?" Lauren blinked. But didn't answer.

That was a hit, Zina thought. Though she had no idea what it meant.

"I knew your husband in passing," Doyle offered, easing the silence. "I played racquetball against him a few times."

"And?" Lauren said, with an odd smile.

"And what? Why the smile?"

"Jared was the most competitive man I've ever known. Did he beat you, Sergeant?"

"As a matter of fact, he did. Twice."

"And did he cheat?"

"He didn't have to. He was quicker than I am. Why do you ask that?"

"Jared could be a very sore loser. I beat him at tennis once and he smashed his racquet to splinters in front of a hundred spectators. I filed for divorce a week later."

"Over a tennis match?" Zina asked, arching an eyebrow.

"It was such a childish display that I realized that Jared was never going to grow up. And I was tired of waiting. I wanted out."

"And now you are," Zina said. "Will the accident affect your financial settlement?"

"I have no idea. Money always mattered more to Jared than to me."

"Money doesn't matter?" Zina echoed.

"I was buying my freedom, Detective. How much is that worth? Can we wrap this up? I have a class in five minutes."

"You might want to make other arrangements, Doctor," Doyle suggested. "Give yourself a break."

"Working with handicapped kids is a two-way street, Sergeant. It keeps your problems in perspective. The last thing I need is to sit around brooding."

"You're not exactly brooding, ma'am," Zina noted. "If you don't mind my saying, you're taking this pretty calmly."

"I deal with problems every day, Detective. Kids who will never hear music or their mother's voices, kids with abusive parents. Last week I had to tell an eight-year-old her chemotherapy regimen had failed and she probably won't see Christmas. So this is very hard news, but . . ." Lauren gave a barely perceptible shrug.

"A thing like that would be a lot harder," Zina conceded, impressed in spite of herself.

"And yet the sun also rises," Lauren said firmly. "Every morning, ready or not. Are we done?"

"Just a few final questions," Doyle said quickly. "Your husband had a string of traffic citations, mostly for speeding. Was he a reckless driver?"

"Jared never hit anyone, he had great reflexes. But every trip was Le Mans for him. I hated that damned car."

"Was he ever involved in conflicts with other drivers?"

"Road rage, you mean? His driving often ticked people off, but he seldom stopped to argue. It was more fun to leave them in the dust."

"Which brings us full circle to question number one," Doyle said. "Can you think of *anybody* who might wish to harm your husband?"

Lauren hesitated a split second. *Another hit,* Zina thought, though not as strong as the first.

"No one," Lauren said carefully. "Jared was a charming guy, as long as you weren't playing tennis against him or facing him in court. If he was having trouble with clients, his office staff would know more than I do. He's with Lehman and Greene, downtown."

"How about you, ma'am?" Doyle asked. "The Benz is jointly owned, so it's at least possible your husband wasn't the intended victim. Have you had any problems? Threats, a stalker, anything like that?"

"No."

"What about your students?" Zina asked. "Your schedule includes mentally challenged students as well as hearing-impaired. Are any of them violent? Maybe overly affectionate? Seems like there's a lot of teacher-student hanky-panky in the papers."

Lauren met Zina's eyes a moment, tapping on the desk with a single fingernail.

"You two are really good," she said abruptly. "Usually the male plays the aggressive 'bad cop,' while the female plays the sympathetic sister. Reversing the roles is very effective."

"Thanks, I think," Zina said. "But you didn't answer the question."

"As I'm sure you're aware, Detective Redfern, some of my students have behavioral problems that keep them out of mainstream schools. But none of them would have any reason to harm Jared. Or me. Now if you don't mind, I'd like a minute alone before my next class. Please."

"Of course, ma'am," Doyle said, rising. "I apologize for the tone of our questions. We're sorry for your loss, Dr. Bannan." He handed her his card. "If you think of anything, please call, day or night."

Zina hesitated in the doorway.

Lauren raised an eyebrow. "Something else, Detective?"

"That kid you mentioned? What did she say when you told her the cancer had come back?"

"She . . . asked her father if they could celebrate an early Christmas. So she could give her toys to her friends."

"Good God," Zina said softly. "How do you handle it? Telling a child a thing like that?"

"Some days are like triage on the *Titanic*, Detective," Lauren admitted, releasing a deep breath. "You protect the children as best you can. And the battered women. And at five o'clock, you go home, pour a stiff brandy, and curl up with a good book."

"And tomorrow, the sun also rises," Zina finished. "Every single day. Ready or not."

In the hallway, Doyle glanced at Zina. "What?"

"I hate having to tell the wives. The tears, the wailing. Rips your freakin' heart out."

"The lady's used to dealing with bad news."

"She's also pretty good at dodge ball. She echoed half of our questions to buy time before she answered. Or didn't answer at all."

"She's got degrees in psych and special ed. She's probably better at this than we are. Anything else?"

"Yeah. Her clothes were expensive but not very stylish. She's a good-looking woman, but she dresses like a schoolmarm."

"She *is* a schoolmarm, sort of. What are we, the fashion police now?"

"Nope, we're the damn-straight real po-leece, Sarge. I'm just saying a few things about that lady don't add up. If a toasted husband can't crack your cool, what would it take?"

"You think she might be involved in her husband's death?"

"Let me get back to you on that. Who's next?"

"She said Bannan's office staff would know about any threats."

"Argh, more lawyers," Zina groaned. "I'd rather floss with freakin' barbed wire."

The offices of Lehman, Barksdale, and Greene, Attorneys at Law, occupied the top floor of the old Montgomery Ward building in downtown Valhalla. Old Town, it's called now. The historic heart of the village.

The new big-box stores, Wal-Mart, Home Depot, and the rest, are outside the city limits, sprawling along the Lake Michigan shore like a frontier boomtown, fueled by new money, new people. High-tech émigrés from Detroit or Seattle, flocking to the north country to get away from it all. And bringing most of it with them.

But Old Town remains much as it was before the Second World War: brick streets and sidewalks; quaint, globular street lamps. Nineteenth-century buildings artfully restored to their Victorian roots, cast-iron facades, shop windows sparkling with holiday displays, tinny carols swirling in the wintry air. Christmas in Valhalla.

Harbor Drive offers a marvelous view of the harbor and the Great Lake, white ice calves drifting in dark water out to the horizon and a hundred miles beyond.

Few of the locals give it a glance, but the two cops paused a moment, taking it in. They'd both worked the concrete canyons of southern Michigan, Detroit for Doyle, Flint for Zee, before returning home to the north. Beauty shouldn't be taken for granted.

Totally rehabbed during the recent real estate push, the offices of Lehman and Greene were top-drawer now, an ultra-modern hive of glass cubicles framed in oak with ecru carpeting. Scandinavian furniture in the reception area, original art on the walls. Doyle badged the receptionist, who buzzed Martin Lehman Jr. to the front desk. Midthirties, with fine blond hair worn long, thinning prematurely. Casually dressed. Shirtsleeves and slacks, loafers with no socks. No tie either. New Age corporate chic.

"How can I help you, Officer?"

"It's Sergeant, actually. I understand Jared Bannan works here?"

"He's one of the partners, yes. He missed a deposition this morning, though. Is there a problem?"

"Maybe we'd better talk in your office, Mr. Lehman. Wait here, Redfern. I'll call you if we need anything."

"Hurry up and wait," Zina sighed, leaning on the reception counter as Doyle and Lehman disappeared down the hallway. "Is there a coffee machine somewhere?"

"Over in the corner, I'll get—"

"Don't get up," Zina said. "You're on the job, I'm just hanging around. Can I get you a cup?"

"If you wouldn't mind," the receptionist said.

"My treat," Zina winked. "Working girls should look out for each other, don't you think?"

"Jared dead? Good God," Lehman said, sinking into the Enterprise chair behind his antique desk. "We played golf last Saturday, I can't—"

He caught Doyle's look.

"We flew down to Flint, there's an indoor course there," Lehman said absently. "It doesn't seem possible. Jared had so much energy . . . Had he been drinking?"

"Did he drink a lot?"

"Not really. He loved to party, though, and . . . look, I'm just trying to make sense of this."

"Join the club, Mr. Lehman. Your partner was apparently the victim of a hit-and-run that may have been deliberate. What kind of work did Mr. Bannan do here?"

"Real estate cases, mostly. He was a fixer. He brokered deals, arranged financing, resolved legal problems. One of the best in the state. We were lucky to land him."

"But since at least one party's unhappy in most business deals—"

"You know that I can't discuss Jared's cases with you, Sergeant. Attorney/client privilege applies."

"I'm not asking for specifics."

"Even so, our firm's reputation for discretion—"

"*Listen up, Mr. Lehman!* Somebody rammed your buddy's car off the road, into a ravine. Where he freakin' *burned* to death. Get the picture?"

"My God," Lehman murmured, massaging his eyes with his fingertips.

"I'm not asking you to violate privilege, but we could use a heads-up about any problem cases or clients that could have triggered this thing."

"That's not so easy. Jared specialized in difficult cases."

"Define difficult."

"Property cases where the parties are in conflict, foreclosures, or the disposal of assets during a divorce. Jared loved confrontations. He'd needle the opposition until they blew, then he'd file a restraining order or sue for damages, generally make their lives miserable until they settled."

"So he was what? Your hatchet man?"

"The best I ever saw," Lehman admitted. "The slogan on his office wall says REFUSE TO LOSE. He rarely did."

"That kind of attitude might make him a lot of enemies."

"It also made a lot of money. Real estate law is a tough game, and Jared's a guy you'd want on your team. Even if down deep, he scared you a little."

"Were you afraid of him?"

"I had no reason to be, we were colleagues. But in court or in negotiations, he was a ferocious opponent. No quarter asked or given."

"I get the picture." Doyle nodded. "Can you give me a quick rundown of any seriously unhappy customers?"

"Butch Lockhart would top the list," Lehman said, bridging his fingertips.

"The Cadillac dealer? Used to play linebacker for the Lions?"

"That's Butch. Jared represented Butch's ex-wife, Sunny, in a suit over their divorce settlement. He got their prenuptial agreement voided on a technicality and Sunny wound up with half of everything. Fourteen million for a six-year marriage."

"Wow. I'm guessing Butch is unhappy?"

"He threatened, and I quote, to 'tear Jared's head off and cram it up his ass' during a deposition. Looked angry enough to do it too. Naturally, Jared got the blowup on video. Butch's lawyers settled the same day. But there's more. Jared and Sunny Lockhart . . ."

"Have been celebrating?"

"Banging his clients was almost a ritual with Jared," Lehman sighed. "And Sunny lives in Brookside. Jared may have been coming from her place last night."

"Is Butch Lockhart aware of their relationship?"

"I would assume so. Jared and Sunny haven't been subtle about it."

"Noted," Doyle nodded. "Who else?"

"He recently brokered a deal for the Ferguson family. The three sons wanted to sell the family farm, the father didn't. Jared managed to get the old man declared incompetent. Mr. Ferguson threatened to kill him in open court, which clinched the case. Personally, I think the old man was dead serious."

"We'll look into it. Any others?"

Lehman hesitated, thinking. "Jared had a divorce case slated for final hearings next week. Emil and Rosie Reiser. They own the Lone Pine Boat Works on Point Lucien."

"What's the problem?"

"There's some . . . friction over the timing of the closing. Emil Reiser bought the boatyard ten years ago, built it up, married a local girl. They're splitting up and cashing out, but their daughter is very ill. Emil wanted to put everything on hold, but Jared has a buyer lined up who won't wait. The wife wants out immediately. Jared promised to make it happen."

"How?"

"I'm sorry, but that definitely falls under attorney/client privilege."

"Are you trying to tell me something, Counselor?"

"We both know the rules, Sergeant. I've already said more than I should."

"Fair enough. Lockhart, Ferguson, and Reiser are on the list. Who else?"

"Those are the top three. I'll scan through Jared's files, and flag any others that seem problematic."

"What about Bannan's wife? She said they're divorcing. Amicably?"

"No divorce is amicable, but they're both professional people. The discussions were *very* chilly, but civil. I'm handling—was handling—the paperwork for them."

"For both parties?" Doyle asked, surprised. "Isn't that unusual?"

"The only dispute was the terms of the settlement, and they hammered those out in meetings that I refereed. We wrapped it up last week."

"To everyone's satisfaction?"

"Jared was certainly satisfied. Lauren's harder to read. Jared and I have been friends since college. I could tell you the juicy details on every girlfriend he ever had, up to and including Sunny Lockhart. But I can't tell you a thing about his wife. He never talked about her. I do know that a few years ago, they had . . . a serious problem."

"What kind of problem?"

"That I truly don't know. But Jared had a *very* successful practice downstate, and we didn't recruit him, he called me up out of the blue. Said he wanted to make a fresh start."

"Trying to save his marriage?"

"Jared never took marriage all that seriously."

"How seriously did his wife take it? Should we be looking at her? Or a boyfriend?"

"Can't help you there, Sergeant. As I said, I simply don't know the lady well. I was surprised when I met her. She's a handsome woman, but not Jared's type at all. He liked them hot, blond, and bubbly and Lauren's the opposite. Cool, intelligent, and very private. I've seen more of her during the settlement conferences than I did the whole time they . . . sweet Jesus."

"What?"

"Their settlement isn't finalized." Lehman frowned. "We ironed out the details but nothing's been signed or witnessed."

"So? What's the problem?"

"It's void. All of it, even Jared's new will. As things stand, Lauren's still his wife and sole heir. She gets everything."

"How much are we talking about?"

"I really shouldn't—"

"Just a ballpark figure. Please."

"Very well. Property and investments would be . . . roughly two and a half mil. And Jared had a substantial life insurance policy. I'd put the total estate in the neighborhood of five million."

"Nice neighborhood," Doyle whistled.

"I'm afraid that's really all I can tell you for the moment," Lehman said, rising. "I'll fax you the information on any problem clients by the end of business today."

"I'd appreciate it, Counselor. About Bannan's death being a possible homicide? That stays between us."

"God. I don't even like to think about it, let alone tell anyone else."

"Thanks for your time, Mr. Lehman. I'm sorry about your partner."

"So am I, Sergeant," Lehman said, shaking his head glumly. "So am I."

Zina was waiting for Doyle on the sidewalk. "What'd you get?" she asked, falling into step as they headed for the SUV.

"A lot. Bannan was having an affair with Sunny Lockhart and half of his other clients, his life's been threatened at least twice, recently, and his widow stands to inherit five million. How'd you make out with the receptionist?"

"Same basic story. Bannan wasn't doing her, but he certainly could have. He was a killer negotiator who loved ticking off the opposition. He also got into a major shouting match with his partner last week."

"With Lehman? About what?"

"The receptionist wasn't sure; those flashy glass offices may look wide open but they're soundproof. The Reisers had just left, and Mrs. Bannan was waiting in reception. The argument could have been about either of them."

"Or something else altogether."

"Whatever it was, she said Bannan and Lehman were shouting loud enough to rattle the glass."

"Not loud enough, apparently. What else?"

"Bannan's clients loved him, in every sense of the word, especially the ladies. I'm feeling a little wistful that he never gave me a call."

"You hate lawyers."

"Only divorce lawyers. What's next?"

"Let's take the Lockharts separately, before they have time to cross-check their stories. I'll charm Sunny, you dazzle Butch."

"Can't I just beat it out of him?" Zina said. "The Lions sucked when Lockhart played for 'em."

*

"You're kidding?" Butch Lockhart grinned hugely, not bothering to conceal his delight. "That mouthy sumbitch is dead? For sure?"

"I'm afraid so," Zina said, eyeing him curiously. They were in Lockhart's office, a glass cubicle five steps up from the showroom floor that overlooked a gleaming row of Cadillacs that stretched the length of a football field. Lockhart loomed even larger than in his playing days, fifty pounds heavier now, a behemoth in a tailored silk suit, tinted glasses, tinted dark hair. A smile too perfect to be real.

"What kind of a car was he driving?" Lockhart asked.

"A Mercedes roadster."

"Better and better. A smart-ass yuppie buys it in his Kraut car. If he'd been driving a Caddy, he could've survived the accident."

"Actually, we don't think it *was* an accident, Mr. Lockhart. He was clipped by a hit-and-run driver. Would you mind telling me your whereabouts between ten and midnight last night?"

Lockhart stared at her, blinking, as the question penetrated his bullet skull. "Whoa, wait a minute, Shorty. Why ask me? What the hell, you think *I* killed him?"

"You did threaten to tear Mr. Bannan's head off in front of witnesses—"

"Maybe I would have, if I'd run into him in a bar after I'd had a few. But I didn't. And if I wanted him dead, I wouldn't need a car to do it. It's bad enough I had to take crap from that punk while he was alive, I'll be damned if I'll take any more now that he's toast. Especially from some backwoods taco bender. Get the hell out of my office."

"Actually, I'm not Latin, sir, I'm Native American," Zina said, rising. "Anishnabeg. And you're not required to answer questions without an attorney. No problem, I'll be happy to clear your name another way. How many red Cadillacs do you have in stock?"

"Red? What are you talking about?"

"The vehicle that struck Mr. Bannan's car left red paint scrapes on his door. I can just scrape paint samples from every red vehicle on your lots, then ship 'em to Lansing to see if any of them match. I'm sure your body shop can touch them up, good as new."

"Touch 'em up?" Butch echoed, standing up, towering over her. "Look, you little beaner—" He broke off, staring at the gleaming blade of the boot knife Zina slid out of her ankle sheath.

"I see two red Caddies out on your showroom floor," she continued calmly. "I'll just scrape some paint samples on my way out. Unless you'd like to be the sweet guy I know you really are and tell me where the hell you were last night, Mr. Lockhart. Sir."

"He was banging his new girlfriend," Zina sighed, dropping into the chair at her desk. "A high school cheerleader, no less." They were in the Mackie Law Enforcement Center, a brown brick blockhouse just outside Valhalla, named for a trooper killed by a psycho survivalist during a routine traffic stop.

Covering a five-county area, "the House" is shared by Valhalla PD, the Sheriff's Department, and the Joint Investigative Unit. Amicably, for the most part.

"How old is the girl?"

"Eighteen. Street legal, but just barely. She confirmed Lockhart's story. I politely suggested she might want to try dating guys her own age. She told me to stick my advice in the trunk of her brand-new Escalade. Paid-up lease, thirty-six months."

"She's eighteen and he's what? Forty?"

"Men are pond scum. I may have to switch to girls. What'd you get from Lockhart's ex?"

"Bannan was with her last night. They ate a late dinner, then thoroughly enjoyed each other's company. She fell asleep afterward. Her best guess is, he bailed out sometime after eleven. She has no alibi, but no motive either. He made her rich and she was in love with the guy."

"Or in heat," Zee said. "Scratch both Lockharts then, who does that leave?"

"Old Man Ferguson can't be too happy about being declared incompetent. And the Reisers, who have some kind of a beef over their scheduling. Plus pretty much everybody Jared Bannan ever met. The guy loved ticking people off."

"You're forgetting the widow. Five mil's a helluva motive, Doyle, and she definitely ducked some of our questions."

"Lehman said their relationship was pretty chilly. What did you make of her?"

"Same as you. She's smart, has great legs, and she's about to have five mil in the bank. Hey, maybe I will switch to girls. You want me to reinterview her while you run down Ferguson?"

"No, let's try the Reisers first. The boat works will close in an hour."

The Lone Pine boatyard was on the tip of Point Lucien, an isolated peninsula jutting into Grand Traverse Bay. A narrow, two-lane blacktop was the only access.

"Not much development out here," Zina noted. "Can't be many private shoreline sites left."

"Which should make the Reisers a bundle when they sell," Doyle said, wheeling the cruiser into the small parking lot. Switching off the engine, they sat a moment, listening to the lonely lapping of the waves and the cries of the gulls.

The yard wasn't much to look at. The only buildings were a cabin, a curing shed stacked with drying lumber, and the boat works itself, a long warehouse surrounded by a deck that extended out over the water, built of rough-hewn timbers culled from the surrounding forest.

A young girl was huddled in a lawn chair at the end of the dock, fishing with a cane pole, an ancient Labrador retriever at her feet. The dog raised its head, growling a warning as the two officers approached.

"Shush, Smokey," the girl said. "Daaa-ad! The police are here. Have you been bad again?" Her impish grin faded into a spate of coughing. She was muffled in a heavy parka, though the temperature on the point was a full ten degrees warmer than the inland hills. Lake effect. Her head was swathed in a turban against the cold, and to cover her baldness.

"Something I can do for you folks?" Emil Reiser asked, stepping out to meet them. He was a bear of a man, dressed for blue-collar work, red-and-black-checked flannel shirt, jeans, and cork boots. He needed a shave and his wild salt-and-pepper mane hung loosely to his shoulders. Two fingertips on his left hand were missing.

"Don't mind the dog, he's harmless, mostly. Is this business or pleasure?"

"It's business, Mr. Reiser."

"Yeah? Buying a boat, are you? 'Cause that's the only business I'm in."

"Actually, it's about your wife's attorney, Jared Bannan."

"Hell, what does that bastard—" Reiser broke off, glancing at his daughter, who was watching them intently. He flashed her a quick command in sign language and the girl turned away.

"She's hearing-impaired?" Doyle asked.

"Among other things." Reiser sighed. "We'd better talk inside. That kid can eavesdrop at fifty yards."

Reiser's workshop was like stepping back in time. The long room had four wooden hulls on trestles, in various states of completion. The air was redolent of sawdust, wood shavings, and shellac. Not a power tool in sight. But for the bare bulbs dangling from the ceiling beams, the works could have time-traveled from the last century. Or the one before that.

Zina wandered between the boats, running her hand over the hulls.

"Beautiful," she murmured. She paused in front of a rifle rack against the wall that held a dozen long guns, scoped Springfields and Remingtons, plus a pair of '94 Winchester lever-action carbines. "Expecting a war, Mr. Reiser?"

"They're hunting guns, miss."

"What do you hunt?"

"I don't, anymore. I build boats. And don't be wanderin' around back there. Workshops can be dangerous."

"Is that how you lost your fingertips?" Zina asked, rejoining them.

"My fingers?" Reiser glanced at them, as if he was surprised they were missing. "Yeah. Bandsaw, couple of years ago."

"Looks like it hurt," Doyle said.

"Compared to what?" Reiser snapped. "Your eye don't look so hot either, sport. Can we get on with this? I got work to do."

"I understand you had a beef with Jared Bannan?" Doyle said.

"My wife and I are breaking up. God knows, we've had enough trouble the past few years to wreck anybody. I got no beef with Rosie taking half of everything, though she's been doing more drinkin' than workin' lately. When this is over, I'll probably get drunk for a month myself."

"When what's over?"

"Our daughter is dying," Reiser said bluntly. "Cancer. You'd think being born deaf would be enough grief for any child, but . . ." He trailed off, swallowing hard.

"I'm sorry," Doyle said. "Truly."

"It can't be helped," Reiser said grimly. "All I asked from Bannan was a few extra months, so Jeanie could be at home until . . . her time. Rosie was okay with it, but Bannan said he had a big-bucks buyer lined up who wouldn't wait. Then Rosie's drunk-ass boy-friend put in his two cents. If Marty Lehman hadn't broken things up I swear I would've pounded 'em both to dog meat. But I never laid a hand on either of 'em. If Bannan claims I did, he's lying."

"Mr. Bannan isn't claiming anything," Doyle said mildly, watching Reiser's face. "He's dead. His car was run off the road last night."

"Jesus," Reiser said, combing his thick mane back out of his face with his shortened fingertips. "Look, I had no use for the guy, but I had no cause to harm him."

"Not even to get the extra time you wanted?" Zina asked.

"We already worked that out. My wife'll tell you."

"Where is she?"

"Stayin' at the Lakefront Inn, in town. On my dime. With her speed-freak boyfriend, Mal La Roche."

"We know Mal." Doyle nodded. "Would you mind telling us where you were last night?"

"Here with Jeanie, where else? You can ask her if you want, just don't upset her, okay? She's got enough to deal with."

"We'll take your word for it, Mr. Reiser. No need to bother the girl. Thanks for your time. And we're very sorry for your trouble."

Zina craned around to take a long look back as they pulled out of the boatyard. Reiser was at the water's edge, standing beside his daughter, his hand on her shoulder. Talking intently on a cell phone.

"We'll take your word for it?" she echoed, swiveling in her seat to face Doyle.

"As sick as that kid is, she probably goes to bed early, and she's hearing-impaired. How would she know whether Reiser went out? What did you make of him?"

"An edgy guy with a world of trouble. Given his state of mind, I wouldn't want to get crossways of him right now. You think his daughter's the kid Dr. Bannan mentioned? The one who wanted an early Christmas?"

"She's deaf, and the Blair Center is the only school for special needs students. Check with the school when we get back to the House. Meantime, we'll talk to Reiser's wife, confirm his story."

"Or not," Zina said.

"Rosie don't want to talk to you," Mal La Roche said, blocking the motel-room doorway, his massive arms folded. Shaggy and unshaven, Mal was a poster boy for the cedar savages, backwoodsmen who still live off the land, though nowadays they're more likely to be growing reefer or cooking crank than running trap lines. Mal has two brothers and a dozen cousins rougher than he is. Every cop north of Midland knows them by their first names.

"This isn't a roust, Mal, it's a murder case," Doyle explained. "We need to ask the lady a few questions, then we're gone."

"Or we can pat you down for speed," Zina added. "You look jumpy to me, Mal. Been tootin' your own product again?"

"I ain't—"

"It's all right, Mal, I'll talk to them." Rosie Reiser edged past Mal. Bottle-blond and blowsy, in a faded bathrobe, she looked exhausted, defeated. And half in the bag. "We'll talk out here, things are a mess inside. Is this about Mr. Bannan?"

"Your husband called you?" Doyle asked.

"He said you might be by," she nodded.

"Did he also tell you what to say?"

"I don't need him for that!" Rosie said resentfully. "I'm here, ain't I?"

"So you are," Zina said, glancing pointedly around at the rundown motel cabin, "though I can't imagine why. Your daughter—"

"Is where she needs to be! With her father, by the damn lake. His little princess. It's always about her! Has been since she was born. Never about me."

"Okay, what about you?" Zina said coolly. "Is this dump where you should be?"

"Just ask your questions and git!" Mal put in. "We don't need no lectures."

"What was the beef between your husband and Jared Bannan?" Doyle asked.

"It's over and done with."

"I didn't ask if it was settled. I asked what it was about?"

"It . . ." Rosie blinked rapidly, trying to focus through a whiskey haze. "I don't know. Something about . . . Emil wanted to wait until after Jeanie . . . you know."

"Dies?" Zina prompted coldly. "And Bannan had a problem with that?"

"He had some big-shot buyer lined up, but they wanted to break ground right away," Mal put in. "It's taken care of now, though. Jared and Emil worked it out."

"How?" Doyle asked.

"I don't know the details."

"Who was the buyer?"

"We don't *know!*" Rosie snapped. "I just know it's settled."

"Because your husband said so?"

"Screw this, I don't have to talk to you. You want to arrest me, go ahead."

"Why would we arrest you?" Doyle asked, puzzled.

"That's what you do, ain't it? So get to it or take a hike." She thrust out her wrists, waiting for the cuffs.

"We're sorry for your trouble, ma'am," Doyle sighed. "Have a nice day."

Zina started to follow him to the car, then turned back.

"Mrs. Reiser? It's none of my business, but losing a child must be incredibly difficult. You might want to wait a bit before you throw away your marriage for the likes of Mal La Roche."

"Hey," Mal began, "you can't—"

"Shut up, Mal, or I'll kick your ass into next week. Mrs. Reiser—"

"Butt out, Pocahontas," Rosie said, clutching La Roche's arm protectively. "At least Mal can show me a good time. Just because Emil's got no life don't mean *I* gotta live like a damn hermit."

"No, I guess not," Zee shrugged. "You're right, ma'am. You're exactly where you belong."

"It's the same kid," Zina said, hanging up her phone. "Jeanie Reiser is enrolled at Blair Center. Or was. A special needs student, hearing-impaired. She was taken out of school a few weeks ago, because of health issues."

They were in their office at the House.

"Which means Dr. Bannan knows Emil Reiser," Doyle mused. "Interesting."

"Interesting how?" Zina snorted. "Like *Strangers on a Train?* He kills her husband and . . . Who does she kill? Mal La Roche? Besides, neither one of 'em has an alibi."

"Maybe they aren't as tricky as the guys in the movie."

"Yep, that sounds like the doc all right. Dumb as a box of rocks."

"That's not what I—"

"Glad I caught you," Captain Kazmarek interrupted, poking his head in the door. Fifty and fit, "Cash" Kazmarek bossed the Joint Investigative Unit. An affable politician, he was also a rock-solid cop, twenty-five years on the Tri County Force. "I got a call from the Sheriff's Department at Gaylord. They have your truck. Red Ford pickup, passenger's-side front fender damaged, reported stolen yesterday. Found it an hour ago, abandoned in a Wal-Mart parking lot. What the hell happened to your eye?"

"Hockey game," Doyle said. "Did the security cameras catch anything?"

"Nope. The driver dumped it behind a delivery van to avoid the cameras. No prints either. None. Wiped clean, they said."

"A professional?" Zina asked.

"Could be," Kazmarek said, dropping into the chair beside Doyle's desk. "Or maybe some buzzed-up teenager with more luck than brains. Where are you on this thing?"

"We've got suspects, but it's a fairly long list," Doyle said. "Bannan majored in making enemies. Why?"

"Actually, a matter of overlapping jurisdictions has come up. I want you to drop a name to the bottom of your list."

"Let me guess," Zina said. "Dr. Lauren Bannan?"

"Lauren?" Kazmarek asked, surprised. "Is she a suspect?"

"The wife's always a suspect. Why, do you know her?"

"We've met. She's done some counseling for the department."

"No kidding? Who'd she shrink?" Zee asked.

"None of your business, Detective. And Lauren's not the name we need to move anyway. According to my sources, Emil Reiser has an ironclad alibi for that night."

"What alibi?" Doyle asked. "He claimed he was home alone with his sick kid. There's no way to verify that."

"Consider it verified," Cash said, rising briskly. "As far as we're concerned, Mr. Reiser was at the policeman's ball, waltzing with J. Edgar Hoover in a red dress."

"Hoover?" Zina echoed. "Are you saying the Feds want us to lay off Reiser?"

"I didn't mention the Feds, because a snotty FBI agent in Lansing asked me not to," Cash said mildly. "That crack about Hoover must have been a Freudian thing. Forget you heard it. Clear?"

"Crystal. Does this mean Reiser is totally off limits, Captain?"

"Not at all, this is a murder case, not a traffic stop. Just make sure you exhaust *all* other avenues of investigation before you look at Reiser again. And if you come up with solid evidence against him, I'll want to see it before you go public. Any questions?"

"You're the boss," Doyle said. "What about Mrs. Bannan?"

"I'd be surprised if Lauren's involved," Kazmarek said, pausing in the doorway. "But I'm obviously a lousy judge of character. I hired you two, didn't I?"

Zina and Doyle eyed each other a moment after Cash had gone.

"Federal," Doyle said at last.

"There's no way Reiser can be an informant," Zina said positively. "That boatyard's in the middle of nowhere and he's been out there for years."

"Which leaves WITSEC," Doyle agreed. "Witness protection."

"So Reiser gets a free pass just because he testified for the Feds once upon a time?"

"No way, in fact it makes him more interesting. But since he's officially at the bottom of our list now, let's see how fast we can work our way back down to him. Ferguson's the only suspect we haven't interviewed. We might want to look at Mal La Roche too, just on general principles—"

"That's the second time you've done that," Zina said.

"Done what?"

"Left the foxy doc off the list. She's got five million reasons to want her husband dead, Doyle, she's connected to Reiser, and she definitely ducked some of our questions. Or maybe you didn't notice? Because you're a guy and the doc definitely isn't."

"That's crap!" Doyle snapped. "I'm not . . ." He broke off, meeting Zee's level gaze. Realizing there might just be a kernel of truth in what she said. As usual.

"Okay." He nodded. "Straight up, do you seriously think she killed her husband? Or had it done?"

"I don't know. Neither do you. But she was definitely holding something back. Maybe it's connected to her husband's death, maybe not, but if we're crossing names off our list, I think I should question her again. Alone, this time. Girl talk. Unless you've got some objection? Sergeant?"

Doyle scanned her face for irony. He'd been partnered with Zina Redfern since she transferred north. Nearly four years now. And he still had no idea how her mind worked. Nor any other woman's mind, for that matter.

"Hell, go for it, Zee. Seeing a shrink might do you some good. Just be careful she doesn't have you committed."

"Screw that. I'm more worried about getting torched in my car."

Lauren Bannan delayed making the phone call as long as she could. She meant to make it after lunch, but wound up working at her desk well into the afternoon.

So she swore to make it the last call of the business day. Then forgot again. Sort of.

But when she stepped into the kitchen of the small lakefront cottage she'd leased after her separation, she knew she couldn't delay any longer. And like most tasks we dread, it wasn't as difficult as she'd feared.

Nearly eighty now, Jared Bannan's mother had been in a rest home in Miami for years. She was used to receiving bad news. In the home, it came on a daily basis.

"Don't make a big fuss over the funeral, Lauren," she quavered. "Jared never cared a fig for religion and I won't be coming. I'm sorry, but I'm simply not up to it. Hold whatever service you feel is appropriate, then send his ashes to me. He can be on the mantel, beside his father. I'll be seeing them both before long. How are you holding up, my dear?"

And Lauren started to cry. Tears streaming silently as she listened to words of comfort from an elderly lady she hardly knew. And would never see again.

"I'm all right, Mother Bannan," she lied. "I'll be fine."

Afterward, she washed her face, made herself a stiff cup of Irish coffee, then sat down at her kitchen table to scan the Yellow Pages listings for funeral homes.

The doorbell rang.

Padding barefoot to her front door, Lauren checked the peephole, half expecting Marty Lehman. He'd been hinting about offering her a shoulder to cry on —

But it wasn't.

"Detective Redfern," Lauren said, opening the door wide. "What can I do for Valhalla's finest?"

"Sorry to bother you at home, Dr. Bannan, but a few things have come up. Can you spare me a minute?"

"Actually, your timing's perfect, Detective. I have to choose a funeral home for Jared's service. Can you recommend one?"

"McGuinn's downtown handles the department funerals." Zina followed Lauren through the living room to the kitchen, glancing around the small apartment. It was practically barren. She'd seen abandoned homes that looked friendlier. "Love what you've done with the place."

"I'm still living out of boxes in the garage," Lauren admitted. "I took the place for the view. The back deck overlooks the lake. Sit down, please. I'm having Irish coffee. Would you like some?"

"Coffee's fine, but hold the Irish, please." Zina took a chair at the kitchen table. "This isn't a social call."

"Good," Lauren said, placing a steaming mug in front of Zina, sitting directly across from her. "I wouldn't know how to deal with a social call. Our friends were mostly Jared's business buddies. What do you need, Detective?"

"You sure you're up for this? You seem a bit . . . distracted."

"This hasn't been a day to relive in my golden years, but I'm not a china doll either. Cut to the chase, please."

"Fair enough. We've got an ugly murder on our hands, and you're screwing up our case."

"In what way?"

"By lying to us or withholding information."

"Holy crap," Lauren said, sipping her coffee. "That's pretty direct."

"You're not a china doll."

"No, I'm not," Lauren said, taking a deep breath. "I'm a special-ed teacher and counselor, licensed by the state and prohibited by federal law from divulging information obtained in my work. To anyone."

"Are you trying to tell me you know who killed your husband?"

"No. Absolutely not."

"But you know something?"

"Nothing that directly relates to Jared's death. And nothing I can discuss with you in any case."

"Reality check, Doc. A fair amount of evidence points directly at you. Shut us out and you could end up in a jackpot that can wreck your life, guilty or not."

"I'll help you in any way I can."

Leaning back in her chair, Zee sipped her coffee, reading Lauren's face openly. "All right. Let's hit the high spots. In our first interview, Doyle asked why you moved north. You ducked that question. Why was that?"

Lauren glanced away a moment, then met Zina's eyes straight on. "Jared and I needed a fresh start after the death of our son," she said flatly. "Jared Junior was born with a congenital heart defect. He lived five months. We hoped a new place might help. It didn't."

"I'm sorry."

"It was four years ago. I didn't become a counselor because I'm a good person who wanted to help others, Detective. I was only trying to save myself."

"How's it going?"

"A day at a time. Next question?"

"The big one. When Doyle asked who might have cause to hurt your husband, you hesitated."

"Did I?"

"You just did it again. Are you protecting someone?"

"I'm sorry," Lauren said, shaking her head slowly. "I can't."

"You *can't? I* can't believe you'd protect a killer over some damned technicality. Give me a name! Hell, give me his initials!"

"I just told you, I can't!"

"Jesus H. Christ!" Zina said, rising from her chair, leaning across the table. "In Flint I worked gangland, lady. The east side. I've known some hard-core bangers, but I've never met a colder case than you. The guy may have killed your husband!"

"You'd better go, Detective."

"Damn right I'd better, before I slap the crap out of you. But I'm warning you, Doc, if anybody else gets hurt because you held out on us? I'll burn you down, swear to God!"

*

Doyle was at his desk when Zina stormed in.

"She definitely knows something, but won't give it up," Zina said, dropping into her seat, still seething. "What did you get?"

"More than I wanted to," Doyle said absently.

"About who? Ferguson?"

"The old man's been in the county psych ward for a week, for evaluation. Twenty-four-seven observation. He's totally clear. So I ran Reiser through the Law Enforcement Information Net."

"Cash told us to lay off him."

"I didn't run his name, just his general description and those missing fingertips. Got a dozen possibles, but only one serious hit. A case I actually remembered, from twelve years ago in Ohio. I was a rookie on the Detroit force then. A Toledo hit man called the Jap rolled on the Volchek crime family, busted up a major drug ring. They wiped out his wife and kids as a payback."

"Nobody in our case is Japanese."

"Neither was the hit man. He got that nickname because he had some fingertips missing. Japanese Yakuza gangsters whack off their fingertips over matters of honor."

"Hell, Doyle, half my backwoods relatives are missing fingers or toes because they swing chainsaws for a living. That doesn't make 'em hit men."

"There's more. After the trial, the Jap disappeared. No mention of prison time, no updates on his whereabouts. Zip, zilch, nada."

"You think the Feds put him in the witness protection program?"

"Probably," Doyle agreed. "Let's say you've got a witness with a contract out on him. You can give him a new identity, even plastic surgery. But you can't grow his fingers back . . ."

"They stashed him in chainsaw country," Zina finished, "where nobody notices missing fingers. You think Reiser's this Jap?"

"I can't think of any other reason a backwoods boat builder would be waltzing with J. Edgar Hoover."

"And this hit man's daughter is in Mrs. Bannan's school, so they almost certainly know each other. Do you think she knows who he really is?"

"I know they've been talking a lot," Doyle said. "I pulled her telephone LUDs. She calls the parents of her students occasionally,

probably to discuss problems or progress. But over the past few
months she's been talking to Emil Reiser several times a week."

"His daughter's dying."

"And as her teacher, the doc would naturally be concerned."
Doyle nodded. "But they usually talk during business hours. She
calls the shop or he calls the school. Except for last Tuesday. She
called him at ten P.M. And two days later . . ."

"Somebody greased her husband," Zina whistled. "Wow. But can
we move on this? Cash told us to lay off Reiser unless we had rock-
solid evidence. All we've got is a possible connection between the
doc and a possible hit man. And I guarantee she won't give anything up. That's one tough broad."

"Cash ordered us to give Emil Reiser a pass. He didn't say anything about *Mrs.* Reiser."

"Rosie was already half in the bag this afternoon," Zina agreed.
"By now she's probably sloshed and looking for a shoulder to
cry on."

But Rosie Reiser wasn't at the Lakefront Inn. Her boyfriend told
them she'd been called to the hospital. An ambulance had brought
Princess Jeanie to the emergency room an hour earlier.

DOA.

They found Rosie Reiser in the ER waiting room, alone and dazed,
her hair a shambles, cheeks streaked with mascara like a mime's
tears. Her eyes were as vacant as an abandoned building.

"Mrs. Reiser," Zina said, kneeling beside Rosie's chair. "We're
very sorry for your loss. Can you tell us what happened?"

"Emil called. Said Jeanie was gone. She was fishin' off the end of
the dock, that kid loved bein' outdoors . . . But she dropped her
pole. And when Emil checked, she was . . ." Rosie took an unsteady
breath. "He called the ambulance, they brought her here. They let
me see her before they took her downstairs."

"Where's your husband now?" Doyle asked.

"He split. He knew when Jeanie died, the doc would give him
up. Figured you'd come for him."

"You mean Dr. Bannan knows who he is?"

"Hell, she was the one that warned him. That bitch almost got
me killed!"

"Warned him about what, Mrs. Reiser? What happened?"

"Our final hearing was coming up, Jared had a buyer lined up for the business, we could cash out and be gone. But Emil kept stalling, wanted to wait because of Jeanie. Him and Jared had a big blowout about it. After Emil stormed out, I told Jared about Emil being in witness protection, hiding out up here. Jared planned to out him in court, make Emil run for his damn life. That way I'd get everything, not just half."

"Clever plan," Zina said, her tone neutral.

"Marty Lehman didn't think so. He argued with Jared about it. Claimed Jared was an officer of the court, shouldn't give Emil up. Jared told him to screw himself. I thought we'd won. Then the doc tipped Emil what was up and he took Jared out. Told me if I opened my mouth, he'd do me and Mal the same way."

"How did Dr. Bannan find out about Emil?" Doyle asked. "Are they involved?"

"Involved?" Rosie echoed, puzzled.

"Are they lovers, Mrs. Reiser? Are they friends?"

"Hell, Emil's got no friends. We had to live like goddamn hermits out there." And she began to sob, great gasping yawps of self-pity.

"Mrs. Reiser, do you know where your husband might have gone?" Zina pressed.

"He went with Jeanie when they took her down. He didn't want her to be alone in that place."

"What place — whoa, you mean the morgue? Doyle, the morgue's in the basement. Reiser's still here!"

But he wasn't. They found the morgue attendant sitting on the floor, in a daze, his skull bloodied. He said Reiser clipped him with a gun butt. He was gone. And he'd taken his daughter's body.

Lights and sirens, flying through town pedal to the metal, Doyle driving, Zina hanging on to the dashboard crash bar.

Turning onto the Point Lucien road, he switched off the sirens without slowing. Not that it mattered. Reiser would be expecting them.

"Eavesdropping," Zina said suddenly.

"What?"

"When we were out here before, the girl was fishing. Emil signed for her to turn her back. He said she could eavesdrop at fifty yards. But she was deaf."

"He meant she could read lips."

"That's right. And where would a kid learn to do that?"

Doyle risked a quick sidelong glance, then refocused on the road. "In school," he nodded. "Dr. Bannan teaches hearing-impaired kids and she was in the anteroom when her husband and Lehman were arguing about outing Reiser."

"In an office with glass walls," Zee finished. "The secretary couldn't hear them, but the doc could have picked up the gist of their argument. And warned Reiser."

"And Reiser killed her husband to—Sweet Jesus!" Doyle broke off. "What the hell is all that?"

Ahead of them, the sky was glowing red, dancing shadows flick-ering through the trees as Doyle whipped the patrol car around, skidding broadside into the Lone Pine parking lot.

The boat works was engulfed in flame, a seething, crackling in-ferno fueled by the stacks of dried wood. Black smoke and sparks roiling upward into the winter night. Backlit by the blaze, Emil Reiser was calmly watching the fire consume years of his work. And his daughter. His whole life.

As Doyle and Zina stepped out of the car, Reiser turned to face them, his work clothes blackened with soot, his shaggy mane wild. Holding a hunting rifle cradled in his arms.

Doyle carefully drew his own weapon, keeping it at his side.

"Mr. Reiser, we'd appreciate it if you'd put that gun down, and step away from it."

"Not a chance, Stark. Just give me a few minutes. Jeanie wanted her ashes scattered out here, this is my last chance to do for her. Let the fire go a bit longer, then we'll get to it."

"To what?" Zina asked.

"You know who I am, don't you? And what I've done."

"You killed Jared Bannan?" Doyle asked.

"I did the world a favor with that one. I only wanted another month or so. Less, as it turned out. He was gonna wreck the little time Jeanie had left just to squeeze a few more dollars out of the deal. If anybody ever had it comin', that sonofabitch did."

"Was Bannan's wife a part of it?"

"Part of what?" Reiser asked, glancing absently at the fire, gaug-ing its progress.

"Did she know you were going to kill her husband?" Doyle pressed.

"She phoned me, warned me he was going to blow my cover. Tell her I said thanks."

"You can tell her yourself."

"No," Reiser said. "It's too late for that. Fire's about done. Let's get to the rest of it."

"Please don't do anything crazy, Mr. Reiser," Zina pleaded quietly. "Do you think your daughter would want this?"

"All Jeanie ever asked for was an early Christmas. She didn't even get that. Maybe it's an early Christmas where she is now. Hell, maybe it's Christmas every damn day. We'll see."

Zina and Doyle exchanged a lightning glance, reading the vacancy in Reiser's eyes. Knowing what it meant.

"Hold on, Mr. Reiser," Zee said, drawing her automatic. "Please, don't do this."

"Funny, that's what Bannan said. Don't. Please. Something like that. It didn't work for him either." Reiser jacked a shell into the chamber of his rifle. "It's on you two now, lady. You can send me over. Or come along for the ride."

And he raised the rifle.

Doyle fired first, spinning Reiser halfway around, then all three of them were desperately exchanging fire as the boatyard blazed madly in the background, flames and smoke coiling upward, smothering the stars of the winter night. A funeral pyre worthy of a princess.

"Do you think he was really trying to kill us?" Zina asked, fingering the rip in the shoulder of her black nylon *Police* jacket, the only damage from the fatal shootout.

"I don't think he cared. He sure as hell didn't leave us any choice." They were in the car, roaring back through town with lights and sirens. Leaving the smoldering boatyard to the firemen and the crime-scene team. And the coroner.

"What's your hurry?" Though she already knew.

"Like the man said, it's time to settle up. Any problem with that?"

"Nope. I told the doc if anyone else died, we'd be along."

"All right then."

It was past midnight when they skidded into Lauren Bannan's driveway. Doyle left the strobes flashing. Wanting the neighbors to know. He hammered on the door. No answer.

"I'm out here," Lauren called.

They circled the house to the rear deck. Lauren was standing by the rail, in black slacks and a turtleneck, looking out over the lake. Slivers of early ice floating ghostly in the dark waters, as far as the eye could see.

"Reiser's dead," Doyle said bluntly. "His daughter too."

Lauren nodded, absorbing it, showing nothing. "Did Jeanie go easily?"

"I . . . suppose so," he said, surprised by the question. "She died in her chair, on the dock."

"That's good. It can be far worse, with that type of cancer. What's the rest of it?"

"Emil Reiser killed your husband, Mrs. Bannan. He admitted it. Before we had to kill him."

"I'm sorry it came to that."

"It didn't have to! You could have stopped it! Warned us. The way you warned him. You knew what he'd do."

"No. I didn't know that. I thought—he'd bring pressure on Jared, that he'd contact the marshals or—"

"But you damn sure knew what happened after the fact! And you still didn't tell us."

"I couldn't."

"Because of some damned health regulation?"

"No. Not because of the law. I would have broken the law. Perhaps I should have. But my obligation wasn't to you, Sergeant, or even to my husband."

"Triage," Zina said quietly, getting it. "You told us the first day. It was too late to save your husband. Or Reiser. You were protecting the child."

"Jeanie's mother is a hopeless alcoholic, drowning in self-pity, with a violent boyfriend. If I'd warned you about her father, she would have spent her last days in foster care with strangers or even in court. She had so little time left and she was already dealing with so much. I simply couldn't do that to her."

"But you knew Reiser was a murderer!" Doyle raged.

"Actually, I didn't, not to a certainty. But it wouldn't have mattered. You saw them together. She worshiped him. And he treated her like . . ."

"A princess," Zina finished.

"What?" Doyle said, whirling on her. "You can't be buying into this crock?"

Zina didn't answer. Didn't have to.

"Are you here to arrest me?" Lauren asked.

Doyle eyed his partner, then Lauren, then back again.

"It's your call," Zina said.

"No," he said slowly. "Not tonight, anyway. But you're not clear of this, lady. You'll be answering a lot more questions before it's done."

"I'm terribly sorry about the way this played out, Sergeant. About what you were forced to do. I hope you can believe that."

"I don't know what I believe," Doyle said, releasing a ragged breath. "Let's go, Zee."

In the car, he sat behind the wheel without starting it, staring into the snowy darkness.

"I know what's bugging you," Zina said quietly.

"What's that?"

"It's one helluva coincidence. That warning Reiser, for the sake of his daughter, just happened to make the doc a very rich woman."

"You think she's capable of that?"

"I know she's awfully bright, Doyle. She has the degrees to prove it and she's one very cool customer. So is it at least possible? Damn straight. But given her choices? I don't know what I would have done."

"Nor do I," he admitted. "I just wish . . ."

"What?"

"I wish that kid had gotten her early Christmas, that's all."

"Hell, maybe she did," Zee said. "Maybe her father was right. Maybe where she is now, it's Christmas every day. Start the damn car, Doyle, before we freeze to death."

Doyle nodded, firing up the Ford, dropping it into gear. But as he pulled out, he realized Zina was still eyeing him. Smiling. "Now what?"

"My grandfather Gesh once told me he'd killed many a deer with one perfect shot," she said. "Right through the heart. But sometimes a buck will keep on running, a hundred yards or more. He doesn't realize he's been hit, you see. Right through the heart."

"I don't follow you," Doyle said.

"I know," Zina grinned, shaking her head. "I'm just sayin'."

MARY STEWART ATWELL

Maynard

FROM *Alaska Quarterly Review*

LEAVING MAYNARD HAD been a spur-of-the-moment decision. The keys were in the ignition, my suitcase was in the trunk, and he had gone in to make sure that the stove was off. What was I supposed to do, wait for him to come back so I could say for the thousandth time, "Please, Maynard, I don't want to go to Memphis"? This was my opportunity, and I took it. The hula dancer on the dashboard looked hipshot, and before I pulled out I pushed hard on her high hip to set her going.

I was counting on the fact that it would take him a while to realize I was really gone. He would worry that he might have misunderstood the situation. What would be more embarrassing than the cops pulling up at the same moment I got back from the grocery store, having run out to pick up some cheese doodles for the trip? Theresa would have to talk him into reporting the car stolen, and even then he would want to negotiate—to make the cops promise they wouldn't be mean to me. All told, it couldn't take less than a day and a half for them to get on the road.

The problem was that I only had one tank of gas. I had wanted to go to Florida, but when I looked at the map and looked at the needle dipping toward the three-quarters mark, I decided to go visit my cousin Stanley in North Carolina instead. I'd gotten a postcard from him the year before and I'd kept it because it was the only postcard anyone had ever sent me. On the front it had a picture of a beaver holding up a fish, and underneath it said "Catching the Big One in North Carolina." From what Stanley said on the card I thought it was the kind of town where you could just walk into the post office and ask for somebody and they'd draw you a little map on the back of a wanted poster, but when I did that the postman said, "You can't get there from here."

"That's the stupidest expression I've ever heard," I said. "You can get anywhere from anywhere."

"Not in a Cadillac you can't," the postman said. He had a little red mustache that glittered when he looked up to see who had rung the bell over the door. "He'll tell you," he said and disappeared into the back, leaving me with Milo. He smiled, and I was glad I had the little pistol that Maynard had given me for my eighteenth birthday tucked inside the lining of my purse.

I didn't know it yet, but Milo wasn't really scary. "How long are you planning to stay?" he asked as the Cadillac chugged up a slope that didn't seem to have any top to it.

"I don't know," I said. "I'll leave before winter, though. I hate winter. I always wanted to go to Florida, but my husband said it was too expensive."

"Your husband?"

"Well," I said, "he's not really my husband," and Milo laughed. I was surprised that he didn't seem to want to talk about the baby. All anybody wanted to talk about was the baby. For the last month Maynard and Theresa hadn't let me go anywhere, not even for a walk, as if I didn't know better than anyone when I was going to have it. Milo had stopped the car, and before I knew it he was helping me out, as gently as if I'd been an old lady. He was a lot bigger than Maynard. I had to tilt my head all the way back to look up at him. "Can you give me a hand with something?" I asked. "I need to store the car someplace for a while."

"I'm sorry, I just can't," Stanley said. He looked a lot worse than the last time I'd seen him. Almost all his teeth were gone, and he kept wiping his hands on the tablecloth. "I can't take care of a baby. I can give you a little money, though—not much, but a little. Enough to get to Florida, probably. Isn't that where you want to go?"

"Stanley," I said, "it's good to see you," and for a moment he stopped wiping his hands and looked at me. "This is a nice house," I said, and I meant it. It was cozy. Until you heard Stanley talking about Peter and Luke and John and realized they weren't just friends of his, you'd think he was a mostly normal person. "So tell me about Milo," I said.

"Oh no," Stanley said, shaking his head. "I don't know if I'd feel worse about setting you up with him or setting him up with you." But when Milo came over later that night, I could tell that Stanley was trying to leave us alone together. We stood out on the porch, where down in the valley we could see smoke rising like a kitchen fire.

I looked down into the tangled branches of what Milo called a laurel hell. The smoke rose from the middle, making a trail like a snuffed candle. He'd emptied the Cadillac's gas tank first so it wouldn't explode. "When will it stop burning?" I asked.

"By tomorrow, most likely." Milo put a sure, firm hand on the small of my back. I thought he looked worried, but with the beard it was hard to tell for sure. "No one sees the valley from this angle except me and Stanley," he said. "And the DEA."

I turned to face him, folding my hands under my belly and widening my eyes. I'd been practicing this pose for a long time, since before I met Maynard even. "Who are you?" I asked. "What are you doing here?"

"You tell me about yourself first," Milo said.

"There's nothing to tell," I said. But he didn't believe me, and when he came back the next day I knew I had to tell him at least part of the truth. Some men wouldn't have cared where you came from, but Milo wasn't one of them. "I lived with Maynard and his sister," I said. "They were nice to me, I guess, but you get tired of people being nice to you all the time. Anyway, it wasn't really about me at all; it was like they were being nice to the baby through me. And then Maynard decided that I went out too much and that I was going to have to stay at this special hospital in Memphis until the baby came, and I don't like hospitals, so I left."

"So it's not Maynard's baby?" Milo asked.

"Are you kidding?" I said. Because that was really funny to me. Then I remembered that Milo did not know Maynard. "I met him at the bus station," I said. "He hung around looking for girls like me. I know that sounds creepy, but it was just that he was too shy to meet people in the regular way. And I needed a place to stay, so it worked out for both of us."

"And there were other girls there at the same time?"

"Oh no," I said. "They'd left before I even got there. Your turn," and I poked him on the arm. He was lying on his back in Stanley's bed. Stanley was at his lab, and through the window we could smell the sweet smell of chemicals cooking. Milo turned and put a hand on my belly.

"Don't you worry about Maynard coming to look for you?" he asked.

"Oh, he'll find me," I said. "I was hoping to get to Florida just because it would cost them more to look for me down there, but it doesn't really matter. I'll get home one day and he'll be standing in the yard with Theresa. Theresa is his sister," I added, because I couldn't remember if I'd told him that. "She and Maynard look alike at first, but when you get to know them you realize that it's just the shape of the face. I think he'd be willing to let me go, but Theresa wouldn't let him. She'd say they'd spent too much money on me already."

Milo lay with his hand on my belly, as still as if he were listening for a train. He was very dark and sad, and I knew that something bad had happened to him. He had run away to the loneliest place he could imagine, to a godforsaken mountaintop where his only neighbor was a crazy man who talked to Saint Peter as if he were right there in the room, but trouble had been seeking him and had found him, even here. I was that trouble, and it was not the first time. "So you walk into the yard and Maynard and Theresa are standing there," he said. "What do you do then?"

"I was thinking they might like it down there with the car," I said.

Milo's hand stilled over my navel, and for a second I thought I might have the baby soon, against my will. Up until then I'd always thought we had an understanding. He lay quiet, and then he jumped up and got dressed in the kitchen.

I wasn't sure what I'd done. There is a time for saying things like that, just as there is a time for saying "I love you," and I'd been pretty sure I knew when it was. "I was just kidding," I called. In the doorway I saw Milo's shadow waver, and I coaxed him back into bed.

What I realized is that the Bible never gives you enough information. Putting the baby on the raft had been Stanley's idea—he'd had a vision, but he left me to figure out how to make a raft of bulrushes, whatever those were, and daub it with slime and pitch. I thought about going down to the library to use the computer and see if I could find a little diagram or something, but I've heard that they keep track of what you look for.

I won't lie: for a while I hoped that Milo would help me with the baby. I think if Maynard had seen me with a man like him, he would have turned around and gone right home. Or maybe Milo and I would have been in Florida by then, living not on the water, which would be too expensive, but close enough to it that you could hear the wind in the trees at night. That was what I thought at first, but I found out pretty quick that Milo didn't want anything to do with a baby. Sometimes at night I would go and stand at the cliff's edge and wonder what would happen to my body if I let myself fall — down into the laurel hell, coming to rest among the ripped empty packages of Sudafed and the wreckage of Maynard's Cadillac.

Stanley stayed sober for a whole day to help me, and he cut the cord and cleaned up after, but when the baby cried that night I had to roll myself out of bed and crawl across the floor to get to him. A few days later I washed up and went down the mountain to get a job, and the first thing I bought with my employee discount was a little yellow life raft. I was hiding in the bushes when the old man with the dog found it, and I stuffed my fist in my mouth to keep from screaming.

But things get better. One of the girls from work helped me dye my hair in the employee bathroom. They had me working in lingerie, and while I refolded the underwear that people had to rummage all through before they decided not to buy it, I'd catch a glimpse of myself in the mirror and smile like at a stranger. When the police came up to Stanley's, I felt enough like another person that I almost convinced myself when I told him that I had never been pregnant; I didn't know what that man from the post office was talking about. If I'd had a baby, I said, what hospital had I gone to? They'd checked every one within a three-hour drive, and nobody had a baby at home anymore.

I could feel Stanley watching me, and when they were gone he picked me up and swung me around in his arms. Later I found out that Milo had lied too, telling them he'd never met a pregnant lady at the post office and Stanley's cousin never had a belly that he'd seen.

It was summer, and even when we kept the windows open we sometimes had to change the sheets twice in one night. Stanley wandered around in the dark and we could hear him babbling and praying. Sometimes sleep wouldn't come at all, and we'd borrow Stanley's car and drive down to the neighborhood where the baby lived with his new family. The people who'd adopted him were just the ones you'd expect: the husband was a minister; the wife was fat and made cakes for bake sales. They'd named him Joshua. The newspapers had called him Moses, and I guess before he was adopted his legal name would have been Moses Doe. I told that to Milo and he said it sounded like a blues singer.

It felt nice to have Milo beside me. It was on one of those nights, driving around the part of town where the rhododendron were trimmed and did not look anything like hell, that I told him why I'd really left Maynard, I mean the main reason. I was looking for Theresa's cigarettes, and it was there in her underwear drawer —the list of all the girls who had lived with them before me. I knew that was what it was because my name was at the bottom, not my real name but the name they called me. They were all happy names: Jessica, Renée, Stephanie, and then mine there at the bottom, the only one without a line through it. "I don't mean they'd done anything bad to them," I said. "They probably just ran away like I did. But there had to be a reason why they didn't work out, don't you think? They'd all been there, and they'd all been pregnant, but there weren't any babies in the house. So then I started thinking, what did they know that I didn't? And then I started thinking that once my baby was born, Maynard and Theresa wouldn't have any more use for me. I tried to make him love me," I said. "It would have been safer, you know? But I don't think he did really."

Milo pulled me against him. He pressed against my hip, but even though it would have been okay probably—I mean no one would have seen us—I said, "No." We were parked across the street, and I could see the window that was the baby's window, which I knew because of the nightlight. On Milo's shoulder I would be tall enough to reach the sill. Why not, I thought. The baby was mine anyway. I would change his name back to Moses, and we would live in the house where you could hear the ocean in the trees. But there is a time for doing things if you're going to do them, and when it had passed we were still sitting there in the dark.

*

Where were the other girls—Stephanie, Carla, Amanda? I pictured them in big cities, in banks and libraries, walking through crowds of strangers. Their lips curled slightly and I saw that they were thinking of me too, pitying me for having run only to this mountaintop, where Maynard could still find me. I hated those girls. They must have had money, or someone to run away to who was better than Stanley. They shook their hair out like in shampoo commercials and smiled disdainfully. You could have done it if you wanted to, they said. You could have hitchhiked to Florida once the car broke down.

Milo wasn't with me the night the policeman was there. I drove to the baby's house alone, but I'd only made it twice around the block when I saw the cruiser. He stood by the driver-side door as if he were waiting for me, and since he'd already had time to read the license plate I figured that the best thing was to act as normal as possible. I parked across the street and rolled the window down. "Do you know how to get to Memphis?" I asked, which was stupid because Memphis was five hundred miles away.

Cops like to walk slow, I've noticed. Maybe it's because they're fat, or maybe it makes them feel important to think that someone has to wait for them. He leaned down by my window, bracing his hand on the ledge. "You come here a lot," he said.

"No, sir," I said. "I just got lost, that's all."

"You got lost last night," he said. "And the night before that."

He squatted beside the car, and I noticed the little red mustache strung across his upper lip. Before I could think, I asked him, "Do you have a brother who works at the post office?"

I knew what I'd said before he did. His hand went to his holster, and when he opened his mouth I could see the threads of spit that connected his lips. I opened the door and banged it into his chest. That must have knocked his pistol right out of his mind, because when I got the car turned around he was still kneeling in the middle of the road, one hand on his belly and the other raised as if signing for mercy. I thought of the dog worrying the life raft while I crouched in the wet bushes by the riverbank, and I hit him as hard as I could.

I didn't tell Milo what I'd done, but he must have read about the policeman's death and put two and two together because he stopped coming around. I stopped going to work. I slept a lot, and it seemed that whenever I woke up Stanley was standing by the open refrigerator fussing about how we were going to eat. Then I woke up and it was night, and I could hear him down in the laurel hell talking to John the Baptist. I went to the bathroom and on my way back I saw that he had found the little gun Maynard had given me and left it on the kitchen table. I wanted to tell him I would never need to kill myself. I could always go somewhere else; it was he and Milo who were stuck here. Then I tried to think when was the last time I had a conversation with Stanley that actually made sense, and I realized I couldn't remember.

When I woke again, I thought at first I was still dreaming. I had heard Maynard's voice in my head before, and this time he sounded just like he did in my nightmares, worried and fretful. But a Cadillac exactly like the Cadillac Milo had pushed off the cliff was parked in the driveway, and when I pinched myself to make sure I was awake they saw me. Theresa ran for the front door, but I got there first and shot the double-bolt. "What have you done with him?" she said. "Where is he, you selfish bitch?"

"Come on out, honey," Maynard said. "We're just excited to see you, that's all."

While I pulled on my bathrobe, I heard Theresa whisper, "Go around and see if there's a back door." But I opened it quick, surprising them. Maynard's face turned a strange color and he stepped back, feeling with his toes to make sure the ground was still there.

"That's the one you gave her," Theresa said. "It's not even loaded, I bet."

"Yes, it is," I said. I had bought the bullets at work and loaded them myself. "Walk," I said, and they backed up to the cliff edge. I knew I had to do whatever I was going to do, because Milo was coming down the path from his cabin and he was still too far away for me to guess what he was thinking. I looked in Maynard's eyes, which were as blue as Moses Doe's, though of course that's just a coincidence.

"Ashley," he said. "Please. Don't do this." But Ashley is not my name.

MATT BELL

Dredge

FROM *Hayden's Ferry Review*

THE DROWNED GIRL drips everywhere, soaking the cheap cloth
of the Ford's back seat. Punter stares at her from the front of the
car, first taking in her long blond hair, wrecked by the pond's am-
phibian sheen, then her lips, blue where the lipstick's been washed
away, flaky red where it hasn't. He looks into her glassy green eyes,
both pupils so dilated the irises are just slivered halos, the right eye
further polluted with burst blood vessels. She wears a lace-frilled
gold tank top, a pair of acid-washed jeans with grass stains on the
knees and ankles. A silver bracelet around her wrist throws off
sparkles in the window-filtered moonlight, the same sparkle he had
seen through the lake's dark mirror, which had made him drop his
fishing pole and wade out, then dive in after her. Her feet are bare
except for a silver ring on her left pinkie toe, suggesting the absence of sandals, flip-flops. Suggesting something lost in a struggle.
Suggesting many things to Punter, too many for him to process all
at once.

Punter turns and faces forward. He lights a cigarette, then flicks
it out the window after just two drags. Smoking with the drowned
girl in the car reminds him of when he worked at the plastics factory, how he would sometimes taste melted plastic in every puff of
smoke. How a cigarette there hurt his lungs, left him gasping, his
tongue coated with the taste of polyvinyl chloride, of adipates and
phthalates. How that taste would leave his throat sore, would make
his stomach ache all weekend.

The idea that some part of the dead girl might end up inside
him—her wet smell or sloughing skin or dumb luck—he doesn't
need a cigarette that bad.

Punter crawls halfway into the back seat and arranges the girl as comfortably as he can, while he still can. He's hunted enough deer and rabbits and squirrels to know she's going to stiffen up, and soon. He arranges her arms and legs to appear as if she's asleep and then brushes her hair out of her face before climbing back into his own seat.

Looking in the rearview mirror, Punter smiles at the drowned girl, waits for her to smile back. Feels his face flush when he remembers she's never going to.

He starts the engine. Drives her home.

Punter lives just fifteen minutes from the pond, but tonight it takes longer. He keeps the Ford five miles per hour under the speed limit, stops extra long at every stop sign. He thinks about calling the police, about how he should have already done so instead of dragging the girl onto the shore and into his car.

The cops, they'll call this disturbing the scene of a crime. Obstructing justice. Tampering with evidence. What the cops will say about what he's done, Punter already knows all about.

At the house, he leaves the girl in the car while he goes inside and takes a shit, his stool as black and bloody as it has been for months. It burns when he wipes. He needs to see a doctor, but doesn't have insurance, hasn't since getting fired.

Afterward, he sits at the kitchen table covered in unopened mail and smokes a cigarette. The phone is only a few feet away, hanging on the wall. The service was disconnected a month ago, but he's pretty sure he could still call 911, if he wanted to.

He doesn't want to.

In the garage, he lifts the lid of the chest freezer that sits against the far wall. He stares at the open space above the paper-wrapped bundles of venison, tries to guess if there's enough room, then stacks the meat on the floor, makes piles of burger and steak and sausage until he's sure. He goes out to the car and opens the back door. He lifts the girl, grunting as he gathers her into his arms like a child. He's not as strong as he used to be, and she's heavier than she looks, with all the water filling her lungs and stomach and intestinal tract. Even through her tank top he can see the way it bloats her belly like she's pregnant. He's careful with her as he lays her down in the freezer, careful as he brushes the hair out of her eyes again, as he holds her eyelids closed until he's sure they'll stay that way.

The freezer will give him time to decide, time to figure out what he wants. What he needs. What he and she are capable of together.

Punter wakes up in the middle of the night and puts his boots on in a panic, rushes out to the freezer. The girl's covered in a thin layer of frost, and immediately he realizes he shouldn't have put her away wet. He considers taking her out, thawing her, toweling her off, but doesn't do it. It's too risky. One thing Punter knows about himself is that he is not good at saying when.

He closes the freezer lid, goes back to the house, back to bed but not to sleep. Even wide awake, he can see the curve of her neck, the interrupted line of her collarbones intersecting the thin straps of her tank top. He reaches under his pajama bottoms, under the elastic of his underwear. He squeezes himself as hard as he can, until the pain takes the erection away.

On the news the next morning, there's a story about the drowned girl. Only the anchorman calls her missing instead and then says her name, says who she was. Punter winces. He knows just how hurtful that final word can be.

The girl is younger than Punter had guessed, a high school senior at the all-girls school across town. Her car was found yesterday, parked behind a nearby gas station, somewhere Punter occasionally fills up his car, buys cigarettes and candy bars.

The anchorman says the police are currently investigating but haven't released any leads to the public. The anchorman looks straight into the camera and says it's too early to presume the worst, that the girl could still show up at any time. Punter shuts off the television, stubbing out his cigarette. He takes a shower, shaves, combs his black hair straight back. Dresses himself in the same outfit he wears every day, a white T-shirt, blue jeans, black motorcycle boots.

On the way to his car, he stops by the garage and opens the freezer lid. Her body is obscured behind ice like frosted glass. He puts a finger to her lips, but all he feels is cold.

*

The gas station is on a wooded stretch of gravel road between Punter's house and the outskirts of town. Although Punter has been here before, he's never seen it so crowded. While he waits in line, he realizes these people are here for the same reason he is, to be near the site of the tragedy, to see the last place this girl was seen.

The checkout line crawls while the clerk runs his mouth, ruining his future testimony by telling his story over and over, transforming his eyewitness account into just another harmless story.

The clerk says, I was the only one working that night. Of course I remember her.

In juvie, the therapists had called this narrative therapy, constructing a preferred reality.

The clerk says, Long blond hair, tight-ass jeans, all that tan skin —I'm not saying she brought it on herself, but you can be sure she knew people would be looking.

The therapists had said, You were all just kids. You didn't know what you were doing.

When it's Punter's turn, the clerk says, I didn't see who took her, but I wish I had.

The clerk, he has black glasses and halitosis and fingernails chewed to keratin pulp, teeth stained with cigarettes or chewing tobacco or coffee. Or all of the above. He reminds Punter of himself, and he wonders if the clerk feels the same, if there is a mutual recognition between them. Punter reads the clerk's name tag: *OS-WALD*. The clerk stares at him and says, If I knew who took that girl, I'd kill him myself.

Punter shivers as he slides his bills across the counter, as he takes his carton of cigarettes and his candy bar. He doesn't stop shivering until he gets out of the air-conditioned store, until he gets back inside his sun-struck car.

The therapists had told Punter that what he'd done was a mistake, that there was nothing wrong with him. They made him repeat their words back to them, to absolve himself of the guilt they were so sure he was feeling. Punter said the words they wanted, but doing so changed nothing. He'd never felt the guilt they told him he should. Even now, he has only the remembered accusations of cops and judges to convince him that what he did was wrong.

*

Punter cooks two venison steaks in a frying pan with salt and butter. He sits down to eat, cuts big mouthfuls, then chews and chews,
the meat tough from overcooking. He eats past the point of satia-
tion, to discomfort, until his stomach presses against the tight skin
of his abdomen. He never knows how much food to cook. He always clears his plate.

When he's done eating, he smokes and thinks about the girl in
the freezer, how when walking her out of the pond, she had threatened to slip out of his arms and back into the water. He'd held on,
carrying her up and out into the starlight. He hadn't saved her—
couldn't have—but he had preserved her, kept her safe from the
wet decay, from the mouths of fish and worse.

He knows the freezer is better than the refrigerator, that the dry
cold of meat and ice is better than the slow rot of lettuce and left-
overs and ancient, crust-rimmed condiments. He knows that even
after death, there is a safety in the preservation of a body; there is a
second kind of life to be had.

Punter hasn't been to the bar near the factory since he got fired,
but tonight he feels the need for a drink. He needs to get away
from the house and the freezer. By eight, he's already been out to
the garage four times, and he knows he can't keep opening the
freezer lid, that if he doesn't stop staring at her, the constant thawing and refreezing will destroy her, skin first.

It's midshift at the factory, so the bar is empty except for the bartender and two guys sitting together at the rail, watching the ball
game on the television mounted above the liquor shelves. Punter
takes a stool at the opposite end, orders a beer, and lights a cigarette. He looks at the two men, trying to decide if they're men he
knows from the plant. He's bad with names, bad at recognizing
most people. One of the men catches him looking and gives him a
glare that Punter immediately looks away from. He knows that he
stares too long at people, that it makes them uncomfortable, but
he can't help himself. He moves his eyes to his hands to his glass to
the game, which he also can't make any sense of. Sports move too
fast, are full of rules and behaviors he finds incomprehensible.

During commercials, the station plugs its late night newscast, including the latest news about the missing girl. Punter stares at the
picture of her on the television screen, his tongue growing thick

and dry for the five seconds the image is displayed. One of the other men drains the last gulp of his beer and shakes his head. I hope they find the fucker that did that and cut his balls off, he says.

So you think she's dead then?

Of course she's dead. You don't go missing like that and not end up dead.

The men motion for another round as the baseball game returns from the break. Punter realizes he's been holding his breath, lets it go in a loud, hacking gasp. The bartender and two men turn to look, so he holds a hand up, trying to signal he doesn't need any help but puts it down when he realizes they're not offering. He pays his tab and gets up to leave.

He hasn't thought much about how the girl got into the pond or who put her there. He too assumed murder, but the who or why or when is not something he's considered until now.

In juvie, the counselors told him nothing he did or didn't do would have kept his mother alive, which Punter understood just fine. Of course he hadn't killed his mother. That wasn't why he was there. What he'd done afterward is why they had locked him away, put him behind bars until he was eighteen.

This time, he'll do better. He won't just sit around for months while the police slowly solve the case, while they decide that what he's done is just as bad. This time, Punter will find the murderer himself, and he will make him pay.

He remembers: missing her, not knowing where she was, not understanding, just wishing she'd come back. Not believing his father, who told him that she'd left them, that she was gone forever. Looking for her all day while his father worked, wandering the road, the fields, the rooms of their small house.

He remembers descending into the basement one step at a time, finding the light switch, waiting for the fluorescent tubes to warm up, stepping off the wood steps, his bare feet aching at the cold of the concrete floor.

He remembers nothing out of the ordinary, everything in its place.

He remembers the olive green refrigerator and the hum of the lights being the only two sounds in the world.

He remembers walking across the concrete and opening the refrigerator door.

More than anything else, he remembers opening his mouth to scream and not being able to. He remembers that scream trapped in his chest like a fist, never to emerge.

When the eleven o'clock news comes on, Punter waits for the story about the girl. He's ready with his small spiral-bound notebook and his golf pencil stolen from the Keno caddy at the bar. He writes down the sparse information. The reporter recounts what Punter already knows—her name, the school, the abandoned car. And then there's a clip of the local sheriff, who leans into the reporter's microphone and says, We're still investigating, but so far there's no proof for any of these theories. It's rare when someone just gets out of their car and disappears on their own, but it does happen. He pauses, listening to an inaudible question, then says, Whatever happened to her, it didn't happen in the car. There's no sign of a struggle, no sign of sexual assault or worse.

Punter crosses his legs, uncrosses them. He presses the pencil down onto the paper and writes all of this down.

The next clip shows the girl's father and mother standing behind a podium at a press conference. They are both dressed in black, stern and sad in dress clothes. The father speaks, saying, If anyone out there knows what happened—if you know where our daughter is—please come forward. We just want to know where she is.

Punter writes down the word *father*, the words *mother* and *daughter*. He looks at his useless telephone. He could tell these strangers what they wanted, but what good would it do them? His own father had known exactly where his mother was, and it hadn't done either of them any good.

According to the shows on television, the first part of an investigation is always observation, always the gathering of clues. Punter opens the closet where he keeps his hunting gear and takes his binoculars out of their case. He hangs them around his neck and closes the closet door, then reopens it and takes his hunting knife from the top shelf. He doesn't need it, not yet, but he knows television detectives always carry a handgun to protect themselves. He only owns a rifle and a shotgun, both too long for this kind of work. The knife will have to do.

In the car, he puts the knife in the glove box and the binoculars on the seat. He takes the notebook out of his back pocket and reads the list of locations he's written down: the school, her parents' house, the pond, and the gas station. He reads the time when the clerk said he saw her and then writes down another, the time he found her in the pond. The two times are separated by barely a day, so she couldn't have been in the pond for too long before he found her.

Whatever happened to her, it happened fast.

He thinks that whoever did this must be a local to know about the pond. Punter has never actually seen anyone else there, only the occasional tire tracks, the left-behind beer bottles and cigarette butts from teenage parties. He thinks about the girl, about how he knows she would never consent to him touching her if she were still alive, how she would never let him say the words he's said, the words he still wants to say. He wonders what he will do when he finds her killer. His investigation could be either an act of vengeance or thanksgiving, but it is still too early to know which.

Punter has been to the girl's school once before, when the unemployment office sent him there to interview for a janitorial position. He hadn't been offered the job, couldn't have passed the background check if he had. His juvenile record was sealed, but there was enough there to warn people, and schools never took any chances. He circles the parking lot twice then parks down the sidewalk from the front entrance, where he'll be able to watch people going in and out of the school. He resists the urge to use the binoculars, aware that he must control himself in public, that he must not act on every thought. This is why he hasn't talked in months, why he keeps to himself in his house, hunting and fishing, living off the too-small government disability checks the unemployment counselors helped him apply for.

The counselors, they hadn't wanted him to see what they'd written down for his disability, but he had. Seeing those words written in neat script didn't make him angry, just relieved to know. He wasn't bad anymore, just a person with a disorder, with a trauma. No one had ever believed him about this, especially not the thera-

pists in juvie, who had urged Punter to open up, who had gotten angry when he couldn't. They didn't believe him when he said
he'd already told them everything he had inside him. Punter knows
they were right to disbelieve him, that he did have feelings he
didn't want to let out. When Punter pictures the place where other
people keep their feelings, all he sees is his own trapped scream,
imagined now as a devouring ball of sound, hungry and hot in his
guts.

A bell rings from the building, and soon the doors open, spilling
girls out onto the sidewalk and into the parking lot. Punter watches
parents get out of other cars to go greet their children. One of
these girls might be a friend of the drowned girl, and if he can just
talk to her, then he might be able to find out who the drowned girl
was. He might be able to make a list of other people he needs to
question so that he can solve her murder.

The volume and the increasing number of distinct voices over-
whelms Punter. He stares, watching the girls go by in their uniforms. All of them are identically clothed, and so he focuses instead on their faces, on their hair, on the differences between
blondes and brunettes and redheads. He watches the girls smiling
and rolling their eyes and exchanging embarrassed looks as their
mothers step forward to receive them. He watches the breeze blow
all that hair around all those made-up faces. He presses himself
against the closed door of his Ford, holds himself still.

He closes his eyes and tries to picture the drowned girl here,
wearing her own uniform, but he can't. She is separate now, distinct from these girls and the life they once shared. Punter's glad.
These girls terrify him in a way the drowned girl does not.

A short burst of siren startles Punter, and he twists around in his
seat to see a police cruiser idling its engine behind him, its driver's-
side window rolled down. The cop inside is around Punter's age,
his hair starting to gray at the temples but the rest of him young
and healthy-looking. Hanging his left arm out the window and
drumming his fingers against the side of the cruiser, the cop yells
something, but Punter can't hear him through the closed windows,
not with all the other voices surrounding him.

Punter opens his mouth, then closes it without saying anything.
He shakes his head and locks his driver's-side door, suddenly afraid
that the cop means to drag him from the car, to put hands on him
as other cops did when he was a kid. He looks up from the lock to

see the cop walking toward his car. The cop raps on Punter's window and waits for him to roll it down. He stares at Punter, who tries to look away, inadvertently letting his eyes fall on another group of teenage girls.

The cop says, You need to move your car. This is a fire lane.

Punter tries to nod but finds himself shaking his head instead. He whispers that he'll leave, that he's leaving. The cop says, I can't hear you. What did you say?

Punter turns the key, sighing when the engine turns over. He says, I'm going right now. He says it as loud as he can, his vocal cords choked and rusty.

There are too many girls walking in front of him for Punter to pull forward, so he has to wait as the cop gets back in his own car. Eventually the cop puts the cruiser in reverse, letting him pass. Punter drives slowly out of the parking lot and onto the city streets, keeping the car slow, keeping it straight between the lines. Afraid that the cop might follow him, Punter sticks to the main roads and other well-populated areas, but he gets lost anyway. These aren't places he usually goes. A half-hour passes and then another. Punter's throat is raw from smoking. His eyes ache from staring into the rearview mirror, and his hands shake so hard he feels they might never stop.

At home, Punter finds the girl's parents in the phonebook, writes down their address. He knows now that he has to be more careful, that if he isn't then someone will come looking for him too. He lies down on the couch to wait for dark, falls asleep with the television tuned to daytime dramas and court shows. He dreams about finding the murderer, about hauling him into the police station in chains. He sees himself avenging the girl with a smoking pistol, emptying round after round into this faceless person, unknown but certainly out there, surely as marked by his crime as Punter was.

When he wakes up, the television is still on, broadcasting game shows full of questions Punter isn't prepared to answer. He gets up and goes into the bathroom, the pain in his guts doubling him over on the toilet. When he's finished, he takes a long, gulping drink from the faucet, then goes out into the living room to gather his notebook, his binoculars, his knife.

In the garage, he tries to pull up the girl's tank top, to get to the skin hidden underneath, but it's frozen to her. He can't tell if the sound it makes is the ripping of ice or skin. He tries touching her through her clothes, but she's too far gone, distant with cold. He shuts the freezer door and leaves her in the dark again but not before he explains what he's doing for her, not before he promises to find the person who hurt her, to hurt this person himself.

Her parents' house is out in the country, at the end of a long tree-lined driveway. Punter drives past, then leaves his car parked down the road and walks back with the binoculars around his neck. Moving through the shadows of the trees, he finds a spot a hundred yards from the house, then scans the lighted windows for movement until he finds the three figures sitting in the living room on the first floor. He recognizes her parents from the television, sees that the third person is a boy around the same age as the drowned girl. Punter watches him the closest, trying to decide if this is the girl's boyfriend. The boy is all movement, his hands gesturing with every word he speaks. He could be laughing or crying or screaming, and from this distance Punter wouldn't be able to tell the difference. He watches as the parents embrace the boy, then hurries back through the woods as soon as he sees headlights blink on in front of the house.

He makes it to his own car just as the boy's convertible pulls out onto the road. Punter starts the engine and follows the convertible through town, past the gas station and the downtown shopping, then into another neighborhood where the houses are smaller and more run-down. He's never been here before, but he knows the plastics plant is close, that many of his old coworkers live nearby. He watches the boy park in front of a small white house, watches through the binoculars as the boy climbs the steps to the porch and rings the doorbell. The boy does not go in, but Punter's view is still obscured by the open door. Whatever happens only takes a few minutes, and then the boy is back in his car. The boy sits on the side of the road for a long time, smoking. Punter smokes too. He imagines getting out of the car and going up to the boy, imagines questioning him about the night of the murder. He knows he should, knows being a detective means taking risks, but he can't do it. When the boy leaves, Punter just lets him go, then drives past the white house with his foot off the gas pedal, idling at a crawl.

He doesn't see anything he understands, but this is not exactly new.

Back at the pond, the only evidence he gathers is that he was there himself. His tire tracks are the only ones backing up to the pond, his footprints the only marks along the shore. Whoever else was there before him has received an alibi through Punter's own clumsiness. He knows how this will look, so he finds a long branch with its leaves intact and uses it to rake out the sand, erasing the worst of his tracks. When he's done, he stares out over the dark water, trying to remember what it felt like to hold her in his arms, to feel her body soft and pliable before surrendering her to the freezer.

He wonders if it was a mistake to bring her up from beneath the water. Maybe he should have done the opposite, stayed under the waves with her until his own lungs filled with the same watery weight, until he was trapped beside her. Their bodies would not have lasted. The fish and waves would have dismantled their shells, and then Punter could have shown her the good person he's always believed himself to be, trapped underneath all the sticky rot.

For dinner he cooks two more steaks. All the venison the girl displaced is going bad in his aged refrigerator, and already the steaks are browned and bruised. To be safe, he fries them hard as leather. He has to chew the venison until his jaws ache and his teeth feel loose, but he finishes every bite, not leaving behind even the slightest scrap of fat.

Watching the late night news, Punter can tell that without any new evidence, the story is losing steam. The girl gets only a minute of coverage, the reporter reiterating facts Punter has known for days now. He stares at her picture again, at how her smile once made her whole face seem alive.

He knows he doesn't have much time. He crawls toward the television on his hands and knees, placing his hand on her image just as it fades away. He turns around, sits with his back against the television screen. Behind him there is satellite footage of a tornado or a hurricane or a flood. Of destruction seen from afar.

Punter wakes up choking in the dark, his throat closed off with something, phlegm or pus or he doesn't know what. He grabs a handkerchief from his bed stand and spits over and over until he clears away the worst of it. He gets up to flip the light switch, but the light doesn't turn on. He tries it again and then once more. He realizes how quiet the house is, how without the steady clacking of his wall clock the only sound in his bedroom is his thudding heart. He leaves the bedroom, walks into the kitchen. The oven's digital clock stares at him like an empty black eye, while the refrigerator waits, silent and still.

He runs out of the house in just his underwear, his big bare feet slapping the cold driveway. Inside the garage, the freezer is silent too. He lifts the lid, releasing a blast of frozen air, then slams it shut again after realizing he's wasted several degrees of chill to confirm something he already knows. He knew this day was coming—the power company had given him ample written notice—but still he curses in frustration. He goes back inside and dresses hurriedly, then scavenges the house for loose change, crumpled dollar bills left in discarded jeans. At the grocery down the road, he buys what little ice he can afford, his cash reserves exhausted until his next disability check. It's not enough, but it's all he can do.

Back in the garage, he works fast, cracking the blocks of ice on the cement floor and dumping them over the girl's body. He manages to cover her completely, suppressing the pang of regret he feels once he's unable to see her face through the ice. For just a second, he considers crawling inside the freezer himself, sweeping away the ice between them. Letting his body heat hers, letting her thaw into his arms.

What he wonders is, Would it be better to have one day with her or a forever separated by ice?

He goes back into the house and sits down at the kitchen table. Lights a cigarette, then digs through the envelopes on the table until he finds the unopened bill from the power company. He opens it, reads the impossible number, shoves the bill back into the envelope. He tries to calculate how much time the ice will buy him, but can't figure it out. He could never do math or figures, can't begin to solve a problem like this.

The basement refrigerator had always smelled bad, like leaking coolant and stale air. It wasn't used much, had been kept because of his father's refusal to throw anything away rather than because of any sense of utility. By the time Punter found his mother there, she was already bloated around the belly and the cheeks, her skin already slick with something that glistened like petroleum jelly. He slammed the refrigerator door and ran back upstairs to hide in his bedroom, unsure what he should do. By the time his father came home, Punter was terrified he would know what Punter had seen, that his father would kill him too, that what started as a beating would end in murder.

But his father never said anything, never gave any sign that his wife was dead. He stuck to his story, telling Punter over and over how his mother had run away and left them behind, until Punter stopped asking about her.

He tried to forget, to believe his father's story, but he couldn't.

Punter tried to tell someone else, an adult, but he couldn't do that either, not when he knew what would happen to his father, not when he knew they would take her away if they knew where she was.

During the day, while his father worked, Punter went down to the basement and opened the refrigerator door. The first few times, he just looked at her, at the open eyes and mouth, at the way her body had been jammed into the too-small space, how her throat was slit like the throat of a deer his father had once shown him. The first time he touched her, he thought she was trying to speak to him, but it was just some gas leaking from her mouth, squeaking free from her too-full lungs. Still, Punter had pulled her out of the refrigerator, convinced for a moment she was somehow alive.

When he wrapped his arms around her, all that gas rolled out of her mouth and nose and ears, sounding like a wet fart but smelling so much worse.

He hadn't meant to vomit on her, but he couldn't help himself either.

Afterward, he took her upstairs and bathed her to remove the vomit. It was the first time he'd ever seen another person naked, and he tried not to look at his mother's veiny breasts, at the wet thatch of pubic hair floating in the bath water. Scrubbing her with a washcloth and a bar of soap, he averted his eyes the best he could. Rinsing the shampoo from her hair, he whispered that he was sorry.

It was hard to dress her, but eventually he managed, and then it was time to put her back in the refrigerator before his father came home. He tried to arrange her so that she would be more comfortable than she had been before.

Closing the door, he whispered good-bye. I love you. I'll see you tomorrow.

The old clothes, covered with blood and vomit, he took to the cornfield behind the house and buried them. After that, there was just the waiting, all through the evening while his father occupied the living room, all through the night while he was supposed to be sleeping.

Day after day, he took her out and wrestled her up the stairs. He sat her on the couch or at the kitchen table, and then he talked, his normal reticence somehow negated by her forever silence. He'd never talked to his mother this much while she was alive, but now he couldn't stop telling her everything he had ever felt, all his trapped words spilling out one after another.

Punter knows that even if they hadn't found her and taken her away, she wouldn't have lasted forever. After the first week, he had started finding little pieces of her left behind, wet and squishy on the wooden basement steps, the kitchen floor, in between the cracks of the couch.

Day after day, he bathed her to get rid of the smell, which grew more pungent as her face began to droop, as the skin on her arms wrinkled and sagged.

Day after day, he searched her body for patches of mold and then scrubbed them off.

Day after day, he held her hands in his, marveling at how, even weeks later, her fingernails continued to grow.

Punter sits on his front step, trying to make sense of the scribbles in his notebook. He doesn't have enough, isn't even close to solving the crime, but he knows he has to, if he wants to keep the police away. If they figure the crime out before he does, if they question the killer, then they'll eventually end up at the pond, where Punter's attempts at covering his tracks are unlikely to be good enough. Punter doesn't need to prove the killer guilty, at least not with a judge and a jury. All he has to do is find this person and then make sure he never tells anyone what he did with the body.

After that, the girl can be his forever, for as long as he has enough ice.

Punter drives, circling the scenes of the crime: the gas station, the school, her parents' house, the pond. He drives the circuit over and over, and even with the air conditioning cranked he can't stop sweating, his face drenched and fevered. He's halfway between his house and the gas station when his gas gauge hits empty. He pulls over and sits for a moment, trying to decide, trying to wrap his slow thoughts around his investigation. He opens his notebook, flips through its nearly empty pages. He has written down so few facts, so few suspects, and there is so little time left.

In his notebook, he crosses out father, mother, boyfriend. There is only one name left, one suspect he hasn't disqualified, one other person who has seen the girl. He smokes, considers, tries to prove himself right or wrong, gets nowhere.

He opens the door and stands beside the car. Home is in one direction, the gas station in the other. He reaches back inside the car for his things, leaving the notebook and binoculars behind but shoving the hunting knife into his waistband, untucking his T-shirt to cover the weapon. Punter knows it's just a guess, but he also knows that in the movies, when the detective has a hunch, it always turns out for the best.

It's not a long walk, but Punter gets tired fast. He sits down to rest, then can't get back up. He curls into a ball just off the weed-choked shoulder, sleeps fitfully as cars pass by, their tires throwing loose gravel over his body. When he wakes up, it's dark out. His body is covered with gray dust, and he can't remember where he is. He's never walked this road before, and in the dark it's as alien as a foreign land. He studies the meager footprints in the dust, tracking himself until he knows which way he needs to go.

There are two cars parked behind the gas station, where the drowned girl's car had been before it was towed away. One is a small compact, the other a newer sports car. The sports car's windows are rolled down, its stereo blaring music Punter doesn't know or understand, the words too fast for him to hear. He takes a couple steps into the trees beside the road, slows his approach to try and stay hidden. To control his breathing, he stops walking until his gasps for air grow quieter. Leaning against the station are two young men in T-shirts and blue jeans, nearly identical with purposely mussed hair and scraggly stubble. With them are two girls, a redhead and a brunette—still wearing their school uniforms and looking even younger than they are.

The brunette presses her hand against her man's chest, and the man's hand clenches her butt cheek. Punter can see how firmly he's holding her, how her skirt is bunched between his fingers, exposing several extra inches of thigh.

He thinks of his girl thawing at home, how he will have to soon decide how badly he wants to feel that, to feel her skin so close to his own.

He thinks of the boyfriend he saw through the binoculars and wonders if *boyfriend* is really the word he needs.

The redhead takes something from the unoccupied man and puts it on her tongue. The man laughs and motions to his friend, who releases his girl and picks up a twelve-pack of beer from the cement. All four of them get into the sports car and drive off together in the direction of the pond, the town beyond. Punter stands still as they pass, knowing they won't see him, that he is already—has always been—a ghost in their world. Punter coughs, not caring where the blood goes anymore. He checks his watch, the numbers glowing digital green in the shadows of the trees. He's not out of time yet, but he can't think of any way to buy more. He decides.

Once the decision is made, it's nothing to walk into the empty gas station, to push past the waist-high swinging door to get behind the counter. It's nothing to grab the gas station clerk—*OSWALD*, he reads again, before he shakes the name clear of his head—and press the knife through his uniform, into the small of his back. Nothing to ignore the way the clerk squeals as Punter pushes him out from behind the counter.

The clerk says, You don't have to do this. He says, Anything you want, just take it. I don't fucking care, man.

It's nothing to ignore him saying, Please don't hurt me.

Punter thinks, Not so brave now.

It's nothing to ignore the words, to keep pushing the clerk toward the back of the gas station, to the hallway behind the coolers. Punter pushes the clerk down to his knees, feels his own feet slipping on the cool tile. He keeps one hand on the knife while the other grips the clerk's shoulder, his fingers digging into the hollow spaces between muscle and bone.

The clerk says, Why are you doing this?

Punter releases the clerk's shoulder and smacks him across the face with the blunt edge of his hand. He chokes the words out. The girl. I'm here about the girl.

What girl?

Punter smacks him again, and the clerk swallows hard, blood or teeth. They're both bleeding now. Punter says, You know. You saw her. You told me.

Her? The clerk's lips split and begin to leak. He says, I never did anything to that girl. I swear.

Punter thinks of the clerk bragging, about how excited he was to be the center of attention. He growls, grabs a fistful of greasy hair, then yanks hard, exposing the clerk's stubbled throat, turning his face sideways until one eye faces Punter's. The clerk's glasses fall off, clattering to the tile.

The clerk says, Punter. He says, I know you. Your name is Punter. You come in here all the time.

The clerk's visible eye is wide, terrified with hope, and for one second Punter sees his mother's eyes, sees the girl's, sees his hand closing their eyelids for the last time.

The clerk says, I never hurt her, man. I was just the last person to see her alive.

Punter puts the knife to flesh. It's nothing. He doesn't have a choice now, and anyway, we're all the last person to see someone. He snaps his wrist inward, pushes through. That's nothing either. Or, if it is something, it's nothing worse than all the rest.

And then dragging the body into the tiny freezer. And then shoving the body between stacks of hot dogs and soft pretzels. And then trying not to step in the cooling puddles of blood. And then picking up the knife and putting it back in its sheath, tucking it into his waistband again. And then the walk home with a bag of ice in each hand. And then realizing the ice doesn't matter, that it will never be enough. And then the walk turning into a run, his heart pounding and his lungs heaving. And then the feeling he might die. And then the not caring what happens next.

And then.

By the time Punter gets back to the garage, the ice is already melting, the girl's face jutting from between the cubes. Her eyelids are covered with frost, cheeks slick with thawing pond water. He reaches in and lifts, her face and breasts and thighs giving in to his fingers but her back still frozen to the wrapped venison below. He pulls, trying to ignore the peeling sound her skin makes as it rips away from the paper.

Punter speaks, his voice barely audible. He doesn't have to speak loud for her to hear him. They're so close now. Something falls off, but he doesn't look, doesn't need to dissect the girl into parts, into flesh and bone, into brains and blood. He kisses her forehead, her skin scaly like a fish, like a mermaid. He says it again. You're safe now. They are just words but hopefully the right ones.

He sits down with the girl in his arms and his back to the freezer. He rocks her, feels himself getting wet as she continues to thaw all over him. He shivers, then puts his mouth against hers, breathes deeply from the icy blast still frozen in her lungs, lets the air cool the burning in his own throat, the horror of his guts. When he's ready, he picks her up, cradles her close, and carries her into the house. He takes her into the bedroom and lays her on the bed.

He lies beside her, and then, in a loud, clear voice, he speaks. He tries not to cough, tries to ignore the scratchy catch at the back of his throat. He knows what will happen next, but he also knows that by the time they break down his door, by the time they come in with guns drawn and voices raised, all this will be over. He talks until his voice disappears, until his trapped scream becomes a whisper. He talks until he gets all of it out of him and into her, where none of these people will ever be able to find it.

JAY BRANDON

A Jury of His Peers

FROM *Murder Past, Murder Present*

San Antonio (TX) Gazette, September 14, 1842:
The attorneys taken hostage by an arm of the Mexican Army three days
hence have not reappeared. The town is much perturbed, and there is some
talk of mounting a rescue effort.

THEY STRAGGLED BACK to San Antonio in ones and twos and
small groups as they were released from Perote Prison. Some traveled over land, some by boat across the Gulf of Mexico. But each
arrived bedraggled, thinner, and with watchful eyes. Some of the
men had families to greet their returns, most had friends, all had
practices. But it was hard to resume their lives. Nothing they could
lay their hands to seemed as worthwhile as just the fact of being
free.

For a while, it wasn't clear everyone was coming back. The Mexicans might well kill a few of their number as an example or because
they didn't have family to ransom them. While the released men
woke every morning overjoyed to find light coming through windows, a part of them remained in prison with their friends.

One of the last of the lawyers to return to San Antonio was William "Bill" Harcourt. He had spent more than a year in prison in
Mexico, and his hometown appeared very changed; both larger —
as he approached from the south on horseback, the buildings appeared a vast intrusion on the landscape — and smaller; when he
got to the heart of the city, the buildings were neither as many nor
as impressive as he remembered. He stayed at home for five days
and nights, he and his wife reliving their meeting, courtship, and
honeymoon, accelerated by past knowledge. For that long, not

even the nearest neighbors saw them, and it was as if Mrs. Harcourt had vanished along with her husband, rather than that he had returned.

But pleasant as it was to catch up on events and become reacquainted with his wife, staying in the house was too strong a reminder of confinement, so on the sixth day, Bill strolled downtown to his law office. It was a bright day in February and the walk cheered him. Being surrounded by people and buildings and commerce made him feel safe. But as soon as he stepped into the gloom of the offices, he thought, *Why do people choose to imprison themselves like this?*

Harcourt was not an imposing man. Of average size when he was taken hostage, he was now slender to the point of emaciation. Well under six feet tall, he still felt the whitewashed ceiling of the offices as a constant presence only inches above his head. His brown hair had grown thicker and longer and he hadn't yet cut it back, so he had the look of a frontiersman though he wore his best suit, one that had stayed safely in his closet all this time, with gray pants and a black frock coat with tails.

Harcourt broke into his first smile of the day when greeted by the clerk, Henry, a lad of barely twenty, who studied law in the offices while performing the clerk's duties: copying documents, running to the courthouse to peruse deeds, looking up statutes, emptying spittoons.

"Henry!" Harcourt cried, clapping the young man's shoulders. "Still clerking here?" It seemed a wonder to him that life had gone on as usual in his absence. Besides, what clerkly duties had he performed with all the lawyers in town vanished?

"Actually, I'm an attorney now, sir. I took my examinations six months ago."

"Good for you! Well, nature hates a vacuum. I guess the town needed to grow more lawyers while we were gone. Have you been busy?"

Henry looked embarrassed. Harcourt noticed the other people in the room.

At the time of the lawyers' abrupt departure from town on September 11, 1842, these offices had been shared by five lawyers. The entry room in which Harcourt and Henry now stood had served as a reception area, law library, and common room, with each lawyer having a small private office for receiving clients. Men were emerging from those offices now, two with smiles of greeting, one with a more interesting expression. A year and a half in captivity, learning the personalities and moods of the different guards, watching for signs of a beating or possible chance for ingratiation, had made Bill Harcourt a quick study of countenances, and he saw in these faces more than their owners intended. Even the smiles of his old partners had traces of apprehension. While they were glad to see him, they saw the possibility of imminent conflict. The stranger, who held a quill pen in his right hand, looked openly puzzled and anxious.

The next moment, there was a tumult of welcome, but Harcourt didn't forget his first impression. What conflict was hidden here?

Greeting him most effusively and openly was Samuel Maverick. Maverick was one of the leading lawyers in town, and though relatively new to Texas, one of the foremost citizens of San Antonio. He had been trying a case in court on September 11 when the invading Mexican forces captured the courthouse and every lawyer in town. Maverick had also been one of the first three prisoners released, but he had still spent six months in Perote Prison, so he and Harcourt were colleagues in more than the practice of law.

"You've been back almost a year," Harcourt said, "so I assume you've stolen all the legal business. Just like those cattle you refuse to brand, any client without another lawyer's name on him must belong to Maverick."

"I haven't had to steal them," Maverick said genially. "They've pressed themselves on me like fallen flowers when the tavern is empty."

"And express themselves just as satisfied with your services, I'm sure," Harcourt answered. The men laughed.

But raised voices from the last office gradually intruded on their reunion. Both men were even more sensitive to loud voices than Harcourt was to the flicker of an eyelid, because during their months of captivity, shouting had nearly always preceded a beating, or worse. These voices were only directed against each other, but they still drew the men's attention. Harcourt glanced inquiringly at Maverick, who rolled his eyes.

Harcourt recognized one of the voices, and a small smile shaped his thin lips. In Perote Prison, the lawyers had been chained to-

gether two by two. Being joined in that fashion creates either enduring friendship or such sensitivity that the other man's breathing becomes an irritant. One night, Maverick had gotten into a fist
fight with his chain mate. But Bill Harcourt and one of the men
now shouting in the adjoining office, John Lawrence, had become
fast friends—and confidants in more ways than one.

John had shared these offices with Harcourt for more than two
years, but they had only been acquaintances. Now, after a year
spent chained together, they were strange twins, their minds running along the same tracks. Somewhat. Bill knew the plans John
had shared and some secrets he hadn't meant to share, such as the
names he murmured in his sleep at night.

John had been a prematurely middle-aged thirty-year-old man
with a small pot belly, a shy wife of five years, a hearty laugh, but
thoughtful moods. Like the other captives, though, he was changed
now. Bill stepped into John's office and saw him pushing a younger
man away from the desk. The young man appeared a dandy in
tight white trousers, a gray vest with a gold watch chain across it,
and a blue coat with a flower in its lapel. Where had he gotten
a rosebud in February? It was a small mystery Harcourt's mind
brushed aside while taking in the man's even features, lively blue
eyes, and trace of a smile even as he was being pushed backward by
a man made lean and pale.

A woman in a small bonnet stood between them: Madelyn,
John's wife; thin and delicately featured, with light brown hair. One
of her hands reached toward her husband, importuning. The
other hand, Bill saw at a quick glance, was on the younger man's
arm, just before she removed it.

"Come, sir!" the young man said. "There's no thievery here. I
made an arrangement, first with your clerk, then with your wife—
whom some thought your widow. Without me, your practice would
have died completely."

John recovered himself. Perhaps he saw his old friend out of the
corner of his eye, or sensed the others clustering in the doorway.
"Thank you," he said, in the tone of a gentleman thanking a groom
for having kept his horse exercised. "But now, as you see, I've returned. You can find accommodations elsewhere or go back to
Austin."

"Oh, I like it here," the young man said. It was strange how his handsome face nonetheless seemed to find a sneer its most natural expression. "Truth to tell, people like me too. Some of your clients will not be so delighted with your return. You don't own them, you know."

"And they don't know you," John snapped. "When they do—"

The young man raised his voice, his eyes suddenly lit from within. "It's not only your clients who prefer me. I'm not trying to take over your life, Mr. Lawrence. But I think I can perform it better. I've sat in your chair, I've read your pleadings. I can do better. And not only there. You know, don't you? She must have told—"

Bill Harcourt was whipping across the room and over the desk without conscious thought. Harcourt's forearm was across the young man's throat and his fist in his stomach. When the man began choking, Harcourt recovered himself. He brushed off the younger man's jacket and spoke in his best courtroom voice. "Sorry for the strange introduction. I thought I saw a dangerous insect. Perhaps a scorpion. I am William Harcourt. You seem to have met my old friend, John Lawrence, whose office we're standing in. Hello, Madelyn. You look lovelier than ever."

To the young man's credit, he was not slow-witted or lacking grace. He removed his hand from his throat and nodded his head politely. By this time, he was aware of the crowded nature of the offices, and perhaps regretted the indiscretion he had been about to perform. It would not have done him much credit, not here. "My pleasure," he murmured. "You two must have a great deal to discuss after your adventure together."

Harcourt, who had mastered his anger completely, smiled. "Oh, John and I have had many months to discuss every topic."

The young man—Harcourt was beginning to think it a good idea to learn his name—gave him a frank look before regaining his smile. Then he turned it on John, who stood shuddering with fists clenched. He didn't have his friend Harcourt's composure. Like many mild men, he was not used to his own anger and couldn't master it quickly.

"You and I still have much to discuss," the young man said as he left the office, greeting the other lawyers affably on his way out. He didn't glance back at Madelyn, whose hand had removed itself from his arm in an instant when Bill had appeared.

"William," she said graciously, extending her hand to him.

So the three of them stood and chatted, as if nothing had just happened. Bill chatted amiably with Madelyn, but noticed that her other hand never extended to her husband's arm. John and Bill had been released from confinement at the same time, but obviously, John had needed less time to reacquaint himself with his wife and had been out in the world sooner.

Speaking of the last few days, Harcourt said to his former chain mate, "I felt like an amputee, with only my own two legs to account for. I had forgotten how to walk alone." John laughed, and laughter came from the doorway too. The three lawyers there knew exactly what he meant.

After a minute John took up his office, and his wife left alone.

Henry, the former clerk, had taken over William Harcourt's old office. Harcourt glanced into it, but showed no inclination to enter. "No, don't bother, Henry. You keep the desk. Let's wait to see whether I need it or another."

The other attorneys went off to the courthouse, but Harcourt demurred. In their absences, he owned the offices. He wandered into John's, or the office that had been John Lawrence's, wondering how it was changed. On the desk, he found a ledger book. John had always been very careful in his accounts. Harcourt leafed through it, noting columns of income and brief notations of services performed. Then the writing changed, though still recording similar transactions. Obviously, the young Austin lawyer had taken over John's account book, along with other parts of his life. Harcourt leafed through the book to the blank pages at the end, then sat musing.

As he had said, nature hates a vacuum and rushes to fill it. But nature has even stricter rules against two bodies occupying the same space.

The Texas Republic was short-lived (1836–1845), but no one living in it knew it would be. For all they knew, they had founded an enduring nation. Mexico, on the other hand, never acknowledged the sovereignty of the new country, still considering it a rebel province of its own. Its army continued to make raids into Texas, designed to humiliate more than to conquer. The Mexican President, Santa Ana, hated Texas, and no part of it more than San Antonio, the scene of his triumph at the Alamo, but which had shrugged off that tragedy to become the largest, most thriving city in Texas. The Alamo was in fact already a tourist destination, the shrine of Texas liberty. Two Mexican raids into San Antonio had wreaked havoc, and the second had accomplished its strange goal. Mexican soldiers had captured the courthouse and every lawyer in town, marching them deep into Mexico and captivity in the castle of Perote.

In Mexico, the imprisoned lawyers had often speculated on the nature of life in their absence. "I think people will be more civil to each other," one man had ventured. "They'll have to be, won't they, without courts to resolve their disputes?"

Samuel Maverick had shaken his shaggy head. "They'll kill each other," he'd intoned in his slow, gloomy voice, so suited to a courtroom. "The town will devolve back to the frontier. The law is what protects us from chaos, and none of us is very far removed from chaos."

In the darkness of the dungeon, Harcourt's voice had come slyly, like one of the vermin that crept through their sleeping straw. "I'm glad you didn't tell me until now that we were upholding civilization, like Atlas. I couldn't have borne up under the strain."

John Lawrence's laugh had been the first, followed by general hilarity, which they cut off quickly at the sound of an outer door. The Mexicans hated nothing so much as laughter from their captives.

Back in town now, on his second day home, Bill Harcourt wondered which of their speculations had been true. He dropped in on his friend the general store keeper, a onetime ranch hand who was smarter than his lot in life and had seen the need for mercantilism. His store prospered in dry goods, hardware, and feed. Prospered enough that he could sit on the porch and tell an old friend what life had been like in his absence.

"Oh, there was a mite more killing than usual, that's true, but hardly any that didn't need it. And we still had police, of course. There was no breakdown in law—no more than ordinary. A few folks had to sit in jail longer than they would have, I suppose, but no one had much sympathy for them. Two or three had their hangings delayed for want of a trial, but they seemed satisfied to wait."

"But the ordinary civil disputes," Bill questioned, "what did people do when they could no longer cry, 'I'll see you in court'?"

The shopkeeper shrugged. "They fought, of course. Sometimes right here on this street. Unless the dispute was between women, then they went at each other in slyer and more crippling ways. But mostly, men settled their differences the time-honored way."

"Trial by combat," Bill mused. He could see it taking place as if in front of him. "Older than law. And a good fist fight is much quicker and more satisfying than a trial, for both the participants and the spectators."

"Yup," the shopkeeper said complacently.

For the rest of the day and the next, Bill stayed away from his old friend John, and from the courthouse. In the last year and a half, his comradely desire to spend time with his colleagues had been more than satisfied. Instead, he walked around the town, refamiliarizing himself with the houses and buildings and trying to ignore the insubstantial quality they seemed to have now. He resumed acquaintances with his children and had long, quiet talks with his wife. In his absence, his wife had acquired more cattle and hired a man to plant more acres. She had done more than get by, enough so that he could wander about like a kept man for another week or more, and Bill didn't mind a bit. His wife's resourcefulness meant he didn't have to return immediately to the practice of law, and he felt no desire to do so. The old forms seemed strange to him, empty rituals. He picked up a deed in his old office and found its language ridiculous.

William Harcourt might never have tried a case again if not for the murder.

In the days of the Texas Republic, adventurers and settlers created a nation from their imaginations and faulty memories. Squatting in buildings that had housed the governments under Spain and then Mexico, they made institutions out of a traveler's fever dream of history. Their court system borrowed from England and stole from Spain, with bits of French thrown in for flavor. The beauty of this system was that a hometown lawyer could always claim he was working in one tradition or another, while the arcana of the law discouraged new competition.

But with all the hometown lawyers gone for so many months, inevitably a few others had moved in, down from Austin or over from

Nacogdoches. Common sense would say that these were not the brightest lights of their local bars. No one would leave a thriving practice to move into a town whose own lawyers might return any day. On the other hand, San Antonio was a booming town and needed legal transactions. A few out-of-town lawyers took the gamble, including the young dandy whom Bill had attacked in John's office. The young fellow turned out to have a name, Luke Enright. They would put it on a cheap tombstone if his body turned up.

Two days after his fight with John Lawrence, Enright's horse came in riderless, blood on its saddle. People knew the horse, and they knew Enright's last dispute.

The lawyers were all in the courthouse, an ostentatiously named one-story building on Main Street. Most lawyers spent most days in the courthouse, trying a case or observing a trial or researching land or water titles. Or gossiping, as they were doing at four o'clock of the afternoon when the chief of police came in. He might have been seeking a warrant, but finding the object of his search in the courtroom, he proposed to take him into custody that minute. "John Lawrence, you're under arrest for the murder of Luke Enright."

"Who?" asked one of the lawyers.

"The little bastard who took over my practice," John said. A good attorney would have shut his mouth before he could finish the thought aloud, but he had no attorney.

"He took over more than that," the chief said portentously. "While you were gone, he and your—well, he was a lodger in your house."

"My wife needed an income," John said, sounding sullen and unconvincing to everyone.

There were several rejoinders to that, referring to Mrs. Lawrence's needs, but no one spoke them aloud.

"And your wife is gone too," the chief announced as if it proved his point. "Did you kill them both at once?"

"No," another man said quickly. "I saw Mrs. Lawrence riding out myself, with luggage in her carriage."

"Which direction?"

"North. The Austin road."

"Horrified by what you'd done," the chief of police said to John, moving toward him.

John shook his head. "Just going to visit her sister for a while."

"You can explain to a jury," the chief said, reaching for John.

As he did so, the courtroom door opened, and everyone looked toward it. There was a certain apprehension in some of those gazes. One of the last times some of them had seen that door open, Mexican troops had come through it. But this late afternoon, the lowering sun only cast the shadow of one man. William Harcourt had returned to the courthouse.

He seemed to be well informed of what was happening. "What do you propose to do with the prisoner, Chief?" he asked briskly.

"Put him in jail, wait for—well, the circuit judge, I suppose."

"What about bail? He's entitled to indictment by a grand jury, as well. But we have neither magistrate to set bond nor district judge to call a grand jury."

The only district judge in the region had been captured along with the rest of the lawyers. One of the first three released, he had immediately returned to his home state of Mississippi, declaring it was unsafe to practice law in Texas. No one had yet been appointed or elected to take his place.

Judge was a position of distinction and honor, but it did not pay very well in the days of the Republic and offered no retirement pension. Lawyers took turns at the position, serving for a term or perhaps two out of a sense of duty, but always returning to more lucrative private practice. There were two men in the room who could claim the lifelong title of "Judge," but no current holder of the office.

"He'll just have to wait," the police chief declared. Everyone in the room murmured at that. The lawyers didn't like to think of their colleague sitting in jail with no legal recourse.

"I believe the Constitution entitles him to speedy trial if he demands it," another lawyer observed. Harcourt was glad he no longer had to do all the proposing. "That's right," another one said, "and a grand jury to determine whether there's cause to hold him."

"Well, we just don't have those things," the police chief said, beginning to sound sulky. He was usually comfortable in his authority, but being the only nonlawyer in a room full of attorneys made a man want to stand with his back to a wall.

"We can have," Harcourt said quietly.

The room went quiet. The nearly two dozen lawyers in the room looked around at each other. Most of them had served on a jury at one time or another, being readily available when a call for jurors went out. They were in a courtroom where hundreds of trials had been conducted. If any other group had thought of conducting an inquiry, they would have been a kangaroo court or a lynch mob, but this group could make it official.

"I don't want to sit in jail," John said. He hadn't moved from his chair.

"Would you rather be hanged tomorrow?" Sam Maverick said, stalking to the center of the room. "That's what we're talking about. There wouldn't be any appeal. This is real, John."

"Yes," the prisoner said. "I'd prefer that, if a jury of my peers thinks it just."

He sounded resigned and yet eager. Men looked at each other, wondering if they were ready to assume this responsibility. It was a moment before they realized that Bill Harcourt was speaking.

"Sam Maverick is one of the largest landholders in this county," he drawled as if telling a story. Bill stood by the jury box, leaning against its rail. "And we know he has large herds of cattle, some of them taken in fees. But he refuses to brand them. They roam free, so he can claim any unbranded cow is his."

"I've never—" Maverick began, but Bill waved him silent.

"Well, we are all mavericks now. Unbranded rogues, who answer to no one. That was the lesson of Perote. The lesson the Mexican general intended to teach us when he kidnapped us from this room. Our institutions are hollow, except as we give them form. There are only rules because we submit ourselves to the rule of law. Otherwise, this is a frontier. This building is a sham, unless we fill it with justice."

The men began to assemble themselves, some moving toward the jury box. Quickly, a lawyer named Early Jones was suggested and chosen as judge. Without much formality, the district clerk swore him in, with an oath to uphold the laws of the Republic of Texas.

"We need a prosecutor and the accused needs a defender," the new judge said.

Several lawyers moved toward John. Only Bill stepped toward the clerk. "I'll prosecute."

The silence was puzzled. Bill and John were known to be friends.

And they all knew Bill as a tenacious and thorough trial lawyer who had sent more than one man to prison while serving as a special prosecutor. Several lawyers, including John himself, looking up in surprise, wondered if Bill bore some secret grudge against the man with whom he'd been chained for more than a year.

"Unless there are any objections?" Bill asked, looking around.

No one said a thing. A few shook their heads.

"You need to take the oath," the clerk said.

Bill hesitated. "To do what?"

"Uphold the laws—" someone began, but another who had served one term as district attorney interrupted.

"The prosecutor is sworn to do justice."

"I'll take that oath," Bill said, and did so.

Samuel Maverick looked at the new prosecutor, then went to stand beside the accused. "I'll defend. If John will have me."

The defendant shook his hand, sealing the agreement.

A dozen men were sworn in as jurors. Others took seats inside the bar. They were all part of this. Without a consensus of opinion, there could be no resolution. Judge Jones assumed the bench and a more formal air. "Call your first witness."

Bill said, "Chief, come forward and give your evidence."

The chief of police walked slowly and suspiciously into their midst. No one cared about his suspicions. They knew this proceeding to be as legal as they could make it, whether they waited for a duly appointed judge or not. They would take their responsibilities seriously. No one seemed to feel this more strongly than Bill Harcourt, who looked sternly at the witness, ignoring the defendant's troubled stare.

"Well, there's the horse," the chief of police began slowly. "It's Enright's horse, all right. No one saw him ride out. The horse returned with blood on his saddle. Mr. Lawrence has no alibi for the whole morning. He's known not to be living with his wife since shortly after his return. Mrs. Lawrence is gone too, as if she knows—"

"Object to speculation," Maverick said quickly.

"There are Comanches still about, aren't there, Chief? Why would you not think young Mr. Enright merely the victim of an Indian attack?"

"No red man would let a horse go," the chief said positively. Men nodded at that. "Besides, there are also the quarrels. Besides the one some of you gentlemen saw, Mr. Lawrence and Enright exchanged words and almost came to blows two other times, one of them just yesterday afternoon. Now, Enright may have taken clients from several of you in your absence, but only Mr. Lawrence suffered so personal a loss."

They all turned to look at John, including the new judge. The accused tried to look composed.

"And this afternoon, John Lawrence returned to his office, cleared young Mr. Enright's things out, and resumed his practice as if he knew the matter was settled."

The accusation had been pretty speculative until then, but the chief's last words made good sense to everyone. "Your witness," Harcourt said.

Maverick had few questions, only establishing that the chief of police had no more evidence of Enright's demise or current whereabouts. "Do you think that's enough to condemn a man?" he asked, which was really aimed at his opponent.

"I haven't rested my case," Bill Harcourt said. "I suggest we adjourn this proceeding to John Lawrence's office."

The suggestion was unorthodox, but so was this entire proceeding. The law offices were just across the street. Within ten minutes, the offices were crowded. The jurors stood together against one wall of John's own office. "I'll call Henry Reynolds," Bill said, and the young clerk, now lawyer, came forward shyly.

Harcourt quickly established that the presumed deceased had used this office in John Lawrence's absence and had continued to do so even after his return. Disputes between the two men over possession of the office had grown more heated.

"And did you ever overhear any exchanges between *Mrs.* Lawrence and either of the two men? Come, Henry, you're sworn to give testimony."

A very mature look shot out of Henry's boyish face, turning his eyes much older for a moment. Only Bill caught the expression. "No, sir," Henry said staunchly. "They kept personal matters private."

"Not enough so," Bill remarked. He picked up a book from the desk, the same one he had handled two days earlier. "Do you recognize this?"

Henry nodded. "Mr. Lawrence's ledger book."

Bill held it up to an open page. "Like this office, not entirely his own anymore. Note the change in handwriting in the later pages. Please note also," he said to the jury, "that the income figures show a prospering practice. More so than when John kept it. I'll offer Republic's Exhibit One."

The book was admitted, and Maverick leafed through it, conferring quietly with his client.

Bill opened a drawer of the desk. His hand rummaged among the contents, and he drew out a pocket watch. "Do you recognize this?"

Several men did, from their expressions. "It looks like Mr. Enright's, sir. He told me once he'd inherited it from his grandfather. It was one of his most prized possessions."

Bill dropped it on the desk. "Yet here it sits. Does a man leave town and leave behind his most favored possession, as well as a thriving practice? The Republic rests. Gentlemen," he said to the jury, "even if this case remains open, I doubt there will be any more evidence one way or the other unless Enright's body turns up, and even that wouldn't tell us much. This matter can be settled tonight."

Samuel Maverick said, "The defense calls Martin Stenberg." After it was established that he was the man who had said earlier he'd seen Mrs. Lawrence riding out of town in her carriage, Maverick asked, "Which direction was she going, Martin?"

"I think I said. North, toward Austin."

"And she was traveling alone, with luggage?"

"Yes, sir."

"No more questions."

Bill just shrugged.

"The defense will call John Lawrence."

Defendants were not normally allowed to testify in their own defense, since it was presumed their testimony would be untrustworthy. Bill pointed this out.

"I'm calling him for a limited purpose, not to deny his guilt," Maverick said, and Bill let the legal point go.

"John," Maverick said sternly. "Where was your wife going?"

"We'd separated," John Lawrence said quietly. "You all seem to know that. She was going to stay with her sister."

"And where does her sister live?"

"Philadelphia."

"When she's gone to visit her sister in the past, how did she go?"

"To Galveston," the accused said quietly. "To take a ship."

Men, including jurors, nodded. The answer made sense. And Galveston was not north of them. It was south and east. "The defense rests," Maverick said abruptly.

Bill Harcourt made a brief summation. "Luke Enright may not have been well liked by the men in this room, but he deserves justice. He had increasingly violent quarrels with the defendant, then his horse turns up showing blood. Outside the courthouse, no more evidence than that would be needed. The young man had everything he wanted here. Why would he leave so abruptly? No, men, the chief of police is right. I ask for your guilty verdict."

Samuel Maverick had been looking over the two exhibits. When his turn came, he stood with both in his hands. Walking toward the jury box, he leafed through the ledger book. After the last page Harcourt had displayed, there were two dozen blank pages. But at the back, the new handwriting began again, with different names and figures. "Mr. Enright was apparently keeping track of more than his profits. These pages seem to be in a cipher. What did he want to hide? Which raises the question, what do we know about him? What did he leave behind, in Austin or elsewhere? When a man changes cities of residence, it's usually to escape something. I suggest, gentlemen, when a man writes different figures in a different place in the book, he's recording something other than what's recorded in the front. Could it be debts? Look at these numbers. They far outweigh the meager earnings in front. Could it be that the people to whom Enright owed these debts had caught up to him, or were about to do so? *There's* a reason for a man to light out in a hurry.

"And this was a lawyer. An angry young man who bore a grudge. There's no use to run if you're still pursued. Much better to make your creditors think you're dead. And if young Enright was going to fake his death, what better sweetness than to have his revenge at the same time? Initiate another quarrel with the man he hated, *then* flee."

Maverick surveyed the jurors, hardheaded lawyers who looked skeptical. *And flee without his horse?* they were clearly thinking.

"And leave with his lover. Yes. I hate to suggest scandal, but look at the facts. Mrs. Lawrence rode north. Not the direction she would normally take, but the direction from which young Enright came. They met, he cut himself and dripped blood on the saddle, and they rode away, Enright laughing to himself."

These jurors were lawyers, and not used to sitting silent in a courtroom. One said, "That's a fanciful picture, Maverick," and his neighbor added, "What about the watch he left behind? His most treasured possession. He wouldn't have run off without it."

The watch in question dangled from Maverick's hand. "This watch? The one he inherited from his grandfather? Look at the inside of the case, gentlemen. This watch has a manufacturer's date of 1838. It's very young for a treasured family heirloom."

He handed it across, and the jurors inspected it eagerly. Some looked at the defendant with new expressions, while others narrowed their eyes.

Bill Harcourt declined rebuttal argument. The verdict was swift. The jurors didn't even leave their box, only huddled together, then one stood to say, "Your Honor, we find the defendant not guilty."

The chief of police sputtered, but the new judge assured him that the verdict was as legal as a poll tax. The room surged around John with congratulations. It was important that nearly every lawyer in town had participated. They would spread the word. There might be speculation that the attorneys had protected one of their own, but not the kind of presumed guilt that would have dogged John Lawrence without this proceeding.

Besides, in the Republic of Texas there were rumors much more damaging to reputation than that one had killed a man. That suspicion added a touch of stature.

The men gradually cleared out of the offices. John declined offers of celebration until, with glances, the men understood that Bill Harcourt was lingering too. The men had a friendship to repair.

When the men were alone, John still sitting on his rickety wooden chair, Bill leaning back against the desk, Bill said simply, "Forgive me?"

John laughed. "I thought no one might volunteer to prosecute me, then there'd have been no trial and no exoneration. I owe you more—"

"Well, you know my passion for justice," Bill said archly.

"I do, actually."

Bill gave his friend a sidelong glance. "Stealing a man's liveli-hood, and his wife, and not being content with that, wanting to take his reputation as well, I call that worse than rustling. And"—his voice rose a little—"to do it while we were rotting in that hole. If you *had* killed him I'd call it just."

"When we were marched out of the courthouse on September 11 . . ." John began.

It was a date that would speak an entire narrative for the rest of their lives.

"—we were told we'd be released at the border. Then wondered whether we'd be murdered. Just coming back here seemed a dream of paradise. But I didn't have waiting for me what many of you had."

The childless marriage between John and his wife was, at least to the public eye, a cool one. And the names he had murmured in his sleep in Perote Prison had not been women's names. Bill wondered if young Henry knew the truth. If he did, he would keep it to himself. To Bill, a man's personal life and preferences were his own business, but here on the western frontier, a suggestion of unmanliness could ruin a man.

"After our year on the brink of death," he said, "other things seemed like small considerations."

John fingered the only exhibits from the hasty trial. "You introduced the only evidence in the trial," he said slowly. "This ledger. The first pages are in my writing, true, but then there are some pages torn out."

"Are there? Perhaps Enright wanted to put some space between your accounts and his."

John went on, in his quiet, lawyerly way. "The entries in the back are in the same handwriting, true, but no one has compared that writing to some of the pleadings Enright filed. The way you handled things, there wasn't time for that kind of investigation." Harcourt didn't answer. "And as for that watch, who knows whether that's the same one Enright carried or where it came from?"

"You're right. Perhaps Enright planted it there to implicate you, because he couldn't bear to leave behind the real one."

John gave him a look rather than an answer. "My point is that there wasn't time tonight to—to place this evidence here. It must have been done before I was accused. Even before I . . ."

Bill didn't want to hear a confession. "Maybe I was protecting myself," he said. "He trifled with more than one practice, and maybe with more than one wife. Or maybe I just took the opportunity while the rest of you went about your legal business to give the young man a stern lecture and run him out of here. Then made sure there'd be no accusations over his absence that could be sustained."

These would have been interesting speculations, between two other men. But these two knew the truth. John finally stood and walked close to his friend. "I know how fierce a litigator you are. It must have hurt you," he said, "to lose this trial."

"Lose?" Bill looked genuinely surprised. "You forget. The oath I took was to see justice done. I consider this trial one of my most significant victories." They went out together, into a new town.

William Harcourt—Bill—was induced to serve one term as judge, which he performed to universal respect, but declined reappointment. The end of his tenure coincided with the end of the Texas Republic. In the Mexican War that followed, he and his wife did well in cotton for uniforms. He was a colonel in the War Between the States, which touched Texas but lightly. He lived through turmoil and transformation and rebirth, and closed out his life toward the end of the century he had made his own, to great local renown, never having resumed the practice of law.

Nor did he and his old friend John Lawrence ever tell anyone each other's secrets.

PHYLLIS   COHEN

Designer Justice

FROM *The Prosecution Rests*

NEVER LONG ON PATIENCE, Harold Vekt was beginning to think
about giving up. His feet hurt and his beer-laden bladder was trying to get his attention.

His luck, he decided, stank. Forty minutes had passed since he'd
positioned himself behind the hedges leading to the elaborate
teak-and-glass entryway of the Waterside Club, on the edge of the
river that divided the city. Every departing couple had been ush-
ered into a taxi hailed by one of the plushly uniformed doormen,
or into a limo that glided up to the entrance at just the right moment.

Half of the women wore furs, although the night was mild. Many
of the men, and some of the women, carried leather briefcases.
All were well dressed and well groomed. Jewelry with possibilities
showed on all the women and many of the men.

Didn't any of them live within walking distance?

He was about to take a chance on assuaging his bladder in the
hedges when the door opened once again and a baritone voice
declared, "No thank you, Antonio. It's a fine evening. We'll walk
home." Vekt gritted his teeth and zipped up.

The couple appeared to be in their late forties, a few years
younger than Harold's mother. Though with their easy-street life,
he thought, they could look like that and be much older. The woman's hair was honey gold and sleekly coifed. She wore a beige fur
jacket over an amber silk dress, oval earrings of gold rimmed with
tiny diamonds, a thick gold bracelet, and a ring that was simple in
style but held a diamond of several carats. The man, in a three-

piece gray suit, wore a gold pocket watch and carried a tan leather briefcase of the old-fashioned envelope style, with a flap and two buckled straps.

The man and woman walked up First Avenue, busy and well lit, and turned east on Fifty-sixth Street. Vekt stayed three-quarters of a block behind them. They crossed Sutton Place; here no one else was about, and the bare but thickly branched trees dimmed the street lighting. Vekt grasped the weapon in the pocket of his gray hooded jacket and increased his pace until he was about twenty feet from them. "Excuse me, sir."

The couple halted and turned. "Yes?"

He moved closer. In his upturned left hand was a slip of paper. "I'm looking for ninety-two Sutton Terrace."

The man pointed toward the river. "Sutton Terrace is around that corner, but as far as I know, there's no ninety-two."

Vekt had closed the gap between them. He brandished the scrap of paper, and then his right hand was out with a slim-barreled black handgun and his left arm was tight around the woman's waist.

"Okay—the rules are: one, be quiet; two, open the briefcase and put your wallet in it. And if you happen to have a gun, remember that I can shoot her before you could even aim at me."

Staring, rigid, the man complied. Gargling noises came from the woman's throat. Vekt jabbed the gun into the back of her armpit and whispered fiercely. "Shut—up!"

He turned back to the man. "Now, your watch, with all its attachments." Into the briefcase went the Patek Philippe with its heavy gold chain and fob and Phi Beta Kappa key. "The wedding band too." It was of textured gold and about half an inch wide.

Vekt turned to the woman, keeping the gun in place. "Now your stuff—into the briefcase. First the purse."

"There's no—"

"Quiet. The purse." Her husband held out the briefcase; she dropped in the small cream leather bag with its mother-of-pearl clasp. "Your jewelry. All of it."

She started with the bracelet, using her teeth to undo the difficult catch. The earrings were next, then the solitaire, followed by a diamond wedding band that Vekt hadn't noticed.

He took the briefcase with his left hand. "Now, if you make any noise before I'm out of sight, I'll be back here before anyone else has time to show up. In which case you won't live to tell them anything." Shifting his gaze back and forth between them, he walked backward, aiming the gun.

He was ready to turn and run when a glint flashed in his left eye. It came from the base of the woman's throat.

Vekt dashed forward, grabbing at her neck for the thin gold chain with its small disc pendant.

"You stupid bitch — I said all of it!"

"NO!" she shrieked, flailing at him. "Not this! My baby! You can't take it! You can't have her!" She scratched his eyelids with one hand and pulled his greasy blond hair with the other.

He shoved the gun between her breasts and pulled the trigger. The husband was clawing at him; he shot without aiming and flew off down the street just as the first window opened in an adjacent building. He had not taken the chain.

Vekt flushed the toilet, huffing with relief, and jumped into the shower, making the water as hot as he could stand it. He soaped himself until he was coated with white, and then rinsed for ten minutes, gradually changing the mix until it ran ice cold.

Wrapped in a huge, thick, white towel, he strode with damp footsteps into the kitchen and pulled a bottle of Heineken from the refrigerator. But he put it back without opening it; his gut feeling told him that this was more than a beer occasion. He poured three ounces of Glenlivet over two chunky ice cubes in a thick tumbler and carried it into the living room, ready to assess the evening's proceeds.

Vekt began with high hopes and ended with exultation. Cash: $1,145 in the wallet, $312 in the purse. Credit cards: five, including two platinums. Jewelry: the best, and plain design, easy to dump. Except the watch: an intricate antique; he'd have to hold it for a while. Maybe even wear it; he could afford a three-piece suit. Except the earrings too, damn it. The name of a well-known brand of costume jewelry was stamped on the back. The bitch!

Vekt's friendly neighborhood fence was in a good mood. "These two" — the diamond rings — "let's say five thousand."

"Seven."

"Fifty-five hundred."

"They're at least twenty-five retail."

"Six."

"Done. How about the gold stuff?"

"The bracelet—mmmm—four hundred. This ring's a problem
—it has initials inside."

"So remove them."

"I will, but it ain't easy. And it leaves scars—reduces the resale
value. Seventy-five."

"Come on, Lou, it's a five-hundred-dollar ring."

"One hundred's the best I can do. Better than you'll get elsewhere."

Vekt conceded. He coaxed Lou out of fifty for each of the credit
cards and for the leather briefcase. He was now clean of almost all
the evidence. The purse and its trivial contents had been thrown
down a sewer; the gun and the blond wig went with it. Only the
antique watch remained, in the movable heel of a brown leather
boot, lined up in a closet with all his other footwear.

Vekt was startled by a hand touching his left forearm. His eyes and
mind had been wandering around the courtroom, from the gold
chains around the neck of a pudgy middle-aged juryman to the reporter who had all her parts in the right place under clothes that
showed them off.

He turned toward his attorney after a second nudge. "You must,
I repeat, must, pay attention," the man growled. "If a witness says
anything that you can challenge, write it down—push the paper to
where I can see it from the corner of my eye."

It was still a mystery to Vekt how he had lucked out with this lawyer. Wilson Herrera was nationally known for his high acquittal
rate and his six-figure fees. "Every attorney gets to do court appointments once in a while," was all he'd said in explanation.

The prosecutor's six-foot-two-inch frame, with its hint of a
paunch, moved agilely in its charcoal-gray vested suit as he faced
the witness over rimless granny glasses. Vekt took a perverse comfort from Luther Johnson's dark brown skin. Only two of the jurors
were black. Maybe the other ten wouldn't buy it from one of them.

"Detective Swayze. Tell us why you decided to arrest Harold Vekt
for the murder of Annabelle Jagoda."

"Her husband, Morris Jagoda, identified him in a lineup."

"And why did you include Mr. Vekt in the lineup to begin with?'

"Mr. Jagoda had identified his picture."

Vekt watched Hererra write, with a silver-plated Parker pen, *pic→l'up.*

"Is this the picture?"

The detective studied the stiff four-by-six paper. "Yes."

"What was the source of the picture?"

"Police files." Herrera underlined his cryptic notation.

"Describe the person as you see him in the picture."

"Long, narrow face, short, light brown hair, narrow eyes close together, sharp, straight nose, down-curved lips, small ears close to the head."

"Do you see the person in this courtroom?"

"Yes. The defendant." He pointed to Vekt with a jabbing motion. Johnson glared at Harold, then with deliberation shifted his gaze to the jury.

"Pass the witness."

Herrera rose. "Detective Swayze, did Mr. Jagoda provide a description of the person who had robbed him and shot his wife?"

"Yes."

The lawyer held out a page. "Does this statement include that description?"

Swayze scanned the printed sheet. "Yes."

"Please read the outlined phrase."

Swayze cleared his throat. "Shoulder-length blond hair."

It was Herrera's turn to look pointedly from the defendant to the jury. "Detective, you say Mr. Jagoda selected Mr. Vekt's picture and then identified him in a lineup. Was anyone else whose picture he was shown included in the lineup?"

"Uhh—no—the others were cops or civilian employees of the precinct."

"When Mr. Jagoda was viewing the lineup, what did you say to him?"

"I asked him to ID the perpetrator."

"To be more specific, did you say, 'Is the person who shot your wife among them?' or did you ask, 'Which of these people did it?'"

Swayze looked perplexed, then shrugged and shook his head. "I really don't remember." Herrera opened his mouth, then waggled his fingers in a dismissive gesture.

"Now, Detective, after Mr. Vekt was arrested, was a search of his apartment conducted?"

"Yes."

"Who conducted it?"

"I and my partner—Louis Walters—and two uniforms. Uniformed police officers."

"Describe the search—how thorough was it?"

"We looked in every closet, every drawer, every pocket, every cushion, every shoe, every food container. The toilet tank, the freezer."

"In other words, every possible place of concealment?"

"That's right."

"And what, if anything, did you find related to the robbery?"

"More than eight thousand dollars in cash."

"Just cash? No jewelry? No papers from Mr. Jagoda's briefcase, or the briefcase itself?"

"No. But Vekt could have easily—"

"Buts are not allowed, Detective. Was there anything at all that identified any part of the cash as having belonged to the Jagodas?"

"Why would a guy like Vekt have so much cash around unless—?"

"Please answer the question. Could you single out any of the cash as being proceeds of the robbery?"

"No."

"No further questions."

Johnson jumped up. "Redirect, Your Honor." The judge nodded.

"Considering the hair discrepancy, why did you accept Mr. Jagoda's identification of this picture and of Mr. Vekt in the lineup?"

"We had cautioned Mr. Jagoda to pay more attention to the permanent than to the changeable characteristics. He looked at this picture for a long time, turned the page, and then, suddenly, turned it back, saying—"

"Objection. Mr. Jagoda is the best source of what he himself said."

"Sustained. Mr. Johnson, you may pursue this when Mr. Jagoda is on the stand."

Vekt looked at the ceiling as Morris Jagoda entered the courtroom and walked stiffly toward the stand. Herrera jabbed his thigh. "The jury is watching you!" he hissed through clenched teeth.

Luther Johnson's body language managed to suggest deference and compassion as he began to question Jagoda. "I know, sir, that this is extremely painful for you. But it's necessary if justice is to be done. Please tell us what occurred on the night of March twenty-first last year."

Jagoda licked his lips. He rested his right hand on the ledge that held the microphone; his left arm hung at his side, bent slightly at an unchanging angle.

"We were on our way home from dinner, walking along Fifty-sixth Street. Someone called out to us, asked for directions. Then he pulled a gun and grabbed hold of Annabelle and demanded our valuables. We gave them to him—he instructed us to put everything in my briefcase—and he ran off. But he must have caught sight of the chain Annabelle was wearing with our daughter's pendant on it. He became enraged and ran back and grabbed for it. Annabelle became hysterical and tried to fight him off. He shot her, directly into the heart."

"Objection. Mr. Jagoda is not qualified to describe the course of the bullet."

Judge Patrick Quinn raised his bushy eyebrows. "Well—it hardly matters. The medical examiner has already testified to that fact." Herrera shrugged. The judge signaled Johnson to continue.

"Why did your wife, after surrendering all her other jewelry, resist his taking this item?"

Jagoda's eyes lost their focus. He seemed to have left the courtroom emotionally. The judge said, "Mr. Jagoda?"

"Yes—sorry.

"Felicity was our only child. We were nearly forty when she was born—our last chance. She was bright, lively, loving. Not the prettiest little girl in the world, but the most interesting, delightful, creative personality. For her third birthday we gave her a little round gold pendant, engraved with her initials intertwined with ours as though we were all holding hands.

"A few months later she became ill. She died of leukemia two months before her sixth birthday, after a great deal of suffering. She was brave too—did I say that? Annabelle put on the pendant and never took it off. She slept with it, she bathed with it. In the end, she defended it with her life, as though it were Felicity herself."

So that's what set the bitch off, Vekt thought. He scanned the jury out of the corner of his eye and squirmed.

Johnson waited a few seconds in the silent courtroom, then placed himself between the defense and prosecution tables. "Mr. Jagoda, did you get a good look at the person who shot your wife?"

"Yes. He is that man"—pointing—"in the light blue shirt and dark blue jacket."

"Please note that the witness has pointed out the defendant, Harold Vekt." Harold began to open his mouth but was glared down by Herrera.

"Would you tell us, Mr. Jagoda, if the defendant's appearance differs in any significant way from what it was at the time of the crime."

"His hair is different. It was blond, and much longer."

"Then how can you be certain it was he?"

"When I first saw his picture at the police station, there was something about it, but I passed it up because of the hair. But then I remembered that I'd been told to pay more attention to the permanent features than the changeable ones. And I suddenly recalled that as my wife pulled the robber's hair it had appeared to shift slightly, backward from the hairline.

"The eyes and mouth, the shape of the chin were exactly as I remembered them."

"One more question, sir. For how long a time would you estimate you had an opportunity to observe the defendant's face and become familiar with it?"

"I can't tell you in minutes or seconds. For as long as it took him to ask for an address, and for me to answer him; and for him to threaten us with his gun and demand our valuables, and for each of us to remove our valuables and put them in the briefcase, and for him to back away several feet and run forward again."

"I appreciate that you can't know the exact time lapse. But between two minutes and half an hour, which is closer?"

"Two minutes."

"How about between two minutes and fifteen minutes?"

"Fifteen. Definitely."

"Thank you, Mr. Jagoda. Pass the witness."

Herrera, four inches shorter and considerably bulkier than the prosecutor, rose from his chair but stayed behind the table.

"Mr. Jagoda, may I offer my sincere condolences for your losses."
Jagoda's expression did not change. "But you must appreciate that
describing the tragic nature of a crime does not provide evidence
that any specific person committed it."

"Objection."

"Sustained. Save it for the summation, Mr. Herrera."

"Sorry. Mr. Jagoda, you estimated the time you and the robber
were in each other's presence as between two and fifteen minutes,
closer to fifteen. During how much of that time were you actually
looking at his face?"

"I don't understand."

"Let's start with the time before he pulled the gun. When he
asked directions and you answered him. Were you looking at his
face throughout that time?"

"Well—I suppose so. What else would I have looked at?"

Vekt scribbled something. Herrera threw it a stony glance and
took an audible breath before continuing.

"Was he, for example, holding anything in his hand?"

Jagoda hesitated. "Ye-es. A bit of paper. I assumed the address he
wanted was on it."

"You assumed—so you didn't actually see it?"

"I tried to, but it was out of reach."

"You tried to. So then, for part of that time, were you not looking
at the paper rather than at the man's face?"

Jagoda was silent.

"Please answer."

"I would have to say yes."

"Now—let's get to the rest of the time, after the gun was displayed. How did you react when you first saw the gun?"

"I was horrified—paralyzed."

"Where were your eyes? What were you looking at?"

Jagoda sighed and closed his eyes. "The gun, mostly."

"And when you were putting your valuables into the briefcase,
what were you looking at?"

"The items I was handling, and the gun, and his face."

"When he turned his attention to your wife, what were you looking at?"

"Primarily the gun. It was jabbed into her side. I was terrified
that it would go off."

"So, would it not be accurate to say that for most of the duration of this event you were looking at the gun, not at the perpetrator's face?"

Jagoda's gaze left the attorney's face and swept out a semicircle across the floor, coming to rest on a far wall. Barely audible, he said, "Perhaps. I can't be sure."

Herrera nodded gently, as though he and the witness had arrived at an understanding. Then he moved a few steps closer to him. "Now, sir, is it correct to say that you identified the defendant first from pictures shown you by the police, and then from a lineup of six people?"

"Yes."

"What did Detective Swayze say to you as you prepared to view the lineup?"

"Objection. Your Honor, you've already ruled that the speaker is the best source—"

"In this instance," Herrera interrupted with a touch of indignation, "the speaker has already said he doesn't remember."

Judge Quinn looked from Herrera to Johnson to Jagoda, then pursed his lips and said, "Overruled. The witness may answer."

Jagoda nodded. "He instructed me to view each of the men carefully and select the assailant."

"'Select the assailant.' Were those his exact words?"

"I don't believe so, but—"

"Let me put it another way. Did he say, in effect, 'Is it one of them?' or did he say 'Which of them is it?'"

"The latter is closer."

"Let's clarify that. He asked not *if* one of them did it, he asked *which* of them did it. Is that correct?"

"Yes."

"Now, Mr. Jagoda, you said that shortly after your first sight of Mr. Vekt's picture you suddenly remembered that the robber's hair had seemed to shift as your wife pulled it. Why did you not say this in your first statement to the police, when you described the person as having shoulder-length blond hair?"

"I didn't remember it at the time. You must realize, I was in a state of shock."

"Yes," Herrera said softly, "tell us about that." Vekt looked up at him, puzzled.

Jagoda, focused inward, continued. "The police had found me sitting on the ground, in a complete daze, with Annabelle in my arms. I didn't realize that I had also been shot. They took me to the emergency room, where my arm was treated, then to the intensive-care unit to see her.

"As we entered I heard a doctor say to the detectives, 'She's still alive, barely. Frankly, with that wound, we don't know why.'

"I looked through a glass partition at a mass of technology: tubes, machines, all attached to this papier-mâché creature; yellowish-gray skin, concave cheeks—surely not my Annabelle."

Vekt stared at Herrera. Why was he permitting, even encouraging, this ploy for sympathy?

He drew a huge question mark on the yellow pad, but Herrera either failed or chose not to see it.

"The doctor was explaining to me," Jagoda was saying, "that all of her functions were being mechanically supported, but his words floated by me, carrying their meaning away. The electronic beeps speeded up, and there was a great deal of to-ing and fro-ing, but then the sound changed to an unmodulated signal, and everyone suddenly stopped moving. The doctor looked at his watch and"—Jagoda inhaled deeply—"pronounced Annabelle dead, at two-forty-six A.M.

"Very soon afterward, the police took my statement. So you can see why I might have left something out."

Herrera sighed, as though moved. "So what you mean to tell us, Mr. Jagoda, is that because of trauma you had forgotten about seeing the hairline shift, but that on a later occasion you suddenly recalled it?"

"Yes."

Two correction officers escorted Vekt to the defense table at 10:15 A.M.; everyone else, except the judge, was in place.

Herrera looked at him. Vekt straightened his tie. "How are you?" the lawyer asked.

"Slept lousy. That tear-jerking stuff—the jury ate it up. How come you let him go on like that?"

"Because it makes a very bad impression if you negate the victim's suffering." Vekt raised his eyebrows. "And," Herrera continued coldly, "we shall probably make use of it later in the trial."

Vekt opened his mouth, but just then Judge Quinn entered. "Remain seated, please. Mr. Johnson, have you any more witnesses?"

"One bit of redirect for Mr. Jagoda, Your Honor."

Morris Jagoda seemed to have lost weight since just the day before. Johnson asked him one question. "What was there about Mr. Vekt's picture that drew your attention to it despite the fact that the hair looked different?"

"The eyes and the shape of the mouth are rather unusual."

Vekt reflexively touched the betraying features. Herrera also had one more question for Jagoda: "What time was it when this person first approached you?"

"I can't say exactly. But we'd left the restaurant at about ten-oh-five and walked slowly, because Annabelle was wearing high heels. Probably ten-twenty or so."

"Ten-twenty. Thank you, Mr. Jagoda."

Vekt followed Jagoda's stiff descent from the witness chair and saw him take a seat at the end of the first row, next to a couple in their fifties who'd been there every day of the trial.

"What's he doing there?" he hissed. "I thought he wasn't allowed in."

"That was before he testified. Now it doesn't matter."

"It matters to me!"

Herrera's cheek muscles twitched. "His *wife* was murdered."

"Yeah."

The first witness for the defense was Harold's mother. "Mrs. Vekt, where, to your knowledge, was your son on the evening of March twenty-first?"

"He came to my place for dinner."

"Where do you live?"

"In Yonkers."

"Do you remember what time he left?"

"About ten minutes to ten."

"How do you know that?"

"We watched *Celebrity Poker* for a while, and he helped me unload the dishwasher. Then he had to rush off to make sure of catching the ten o'clock bus."

"And that bus arrives in the city about what time?"

"Maybe ten to eleven, if the traffic's light."

"Thank you, Mrs. Vekt. Pass the witness."

Johnson positioned himself about six feet from the witness stand. "Mrs. Vekt, how often does your son visit you?"

"Two or three times a month."

"How is it, then, that you remember this one instance so clearly?"

"It was the last time before he was arrested." Johnson blinked and turned his back to her momentarily.

"Mrs. Vekt, do you love your son?"

"You bet I do. He's a great kid." Harold smiled, hoping she wouldn't mention the gifts he'd given her.

"Wouldn't you, then, lie in order to keep your son out of prison?"

"I don't know."

"Please respond with yes or no."

"Objection," called Herrera, but Theresa Vekt spoke over him.

"I can't say yes or no. A person can't answer that sort of question unless they really need to decide about doing it. But I don't need to because I'm telling the truth."

"Right on, Mom," Harold mumbled, eliciting another squelching glance from Herrera.

"Sustained," the judge said, finally. He looked at Johnson. "Anything further?"

"No," the prosecutor grunted.

"Call your next witness, Mr. Herrera."

"Please call . . . ," Herrera said before he noticed that Harold was beckoning him. "Just a moment, please." He sat down, and Vekt leaned over to speak into his right ear.

"Put me on the stand. I'll knock 'em dead, the way Mom just did."

Herrera winced. He glanced around at the nearest spectators, then placed his mouth next to Harold's left ear and shielded it with his cupped right hand. "I thought we'd settled this. You have a legal right to testify, and if you are adamant I can't stop you. But in my *experienced* professional opinion, it would be extremely unwise —in fact, disastrous. So much so that I am unwilling to stake my reputation on it, and if you insist, I will apply to the judge to withdraw as your counsel. He might not consent, but the fact that I've asked will not do you any good."

The lawyer rose without waiting for a reply. Vekt stared at his back, no longer uncertain if Herrera knew he was guilty.

"Please call Dr. Madeline Smithers."
    "Objection! We see no legitimate purpose—"
    "You certainly understand the significance of—"
    "Let's not have cross-talk between the attorneys. Come."
    Johnson and Herrera leaned across the bench. Vekt strained to hear the whispers.
    Herrera: ". . . acknowledged expert . . ."
    Johnson: ". . . no relevance . . ."
    Herrera: ". . . solely on . . . severely stressed witness."
    Judge Quinn: "Gentlemen, lower your voices." The discussion continued inaudibly for about ninety seconds, and then the judge waved the attorneys away.
    "The witness may be called. But, Mr. Herrera—and you too, Mr. Johnson—she may be questioned only regarding her own expert knowledge, and not about the specifics of this case. Is that understood?"
    The attorneys, each looking dissatisfied, mumbled, "Yes."

Madeline Smithers differed from most witnesses in not swiveling her gaze furtively from defendant to prosecutor to jury as she entered the courtroom with brisk, sure steps. She took the oath firmly and swept the back of her taupe wool skirt free of wrinkles as she seated herself in an erect posture. She was slender, with smoothly groomed, graying dark hair and a long, oval face. Vekt's assessing eyes found only a plain gold wedding band and a hint of gold watch under the left sleeve of her suit jacket.
    Herrera was standing between the defense table and the jury box. "Please state for the record your full name, title if any, city of residence, and place of employment."
    "I am Madeline Curry Smithers, PhD. I reside in Chicago and am a full professor in the Psychology Department at West Chicago University."
    "Please describe the area of psychology in which you specialize."
    "For the past seventeen years my associates and I have been engaged in experimental investigation of perception and memory, in particular, the accuracy of eyewitness description and identification."

"In general terms, what have been your findings?"

"Unfortunately, inaccuracies and erroneous identifications have proven to be very common."

"Objection. What does 'very common' mean?"

"There will be more specific testimony."

"Overruled, provisionally."

Herrera turned back to the witness. "In your expert opinion, Dr. Smithers, what are the causes of eyewitness inaccuracies?"

"There are many influences on what we believe we remember. The wording of the questioning, for instance, can be crucial."

"Please give us an example."

"When a witness is asked to identify someone from among a group—either by photograph or in person—the police sometimes ask, 'Which of them is it?' rather than 'Is the person you saw among them?' Witnesses then tend to assume that one of the choices must be correct, and select the one closest to their recollection, however remote the resemblance.

"A witness may also sense, through subtle—usually unintentional—tonal and behavioral cues, which choice the questioner would prefer and respond accordingly."

"Doctor, can a traumatized person be suddenly 'jogged' into remembering what he previously did not?"

"Sometimes; however, trauma obstructs observation, and what is not initially perceived cannot be recalled. Our findings contradict the common assumption that everything we are in a position to observe is stored in our minds and available for retrieval. Perception tends to be very piecemeal; we construct whole memories by using these pieces as raw material and filling in the logical gaps. Such sudden 'remembering,' therefore, is often resolution of uncertainty rather than accurate recall."

"Regarding this transition from uncertainty to spurious certainty—"

"Objection to the word 'spurious.' Implies that such remembering is always inaccurate."

Quinn looked skeptically from Johnson to Herrera, then said, less than forcefully, "Sustained."

"In that case," Herrera intoned, "I ask you if indeed such memory recovery is always spurious."

"Not one hundred percent, but often enough so that one should be wary about relying on it."

"Objection! It's up to the jury to decide what testimony to rely on."

"Sustained. Strike everything after the word 'percent.'"

Herrera blinked and turned back to the witness. "Please tell us in what way, if any, accuracy of observation is affected if there's a gun involved in the traumatic incident."

"The tendency is for one's eyes to remain riveted on the gun, largely screening out everything else."

"Including faces?"

"Yes, I'm afraid so."

Herrera returned to the table and scanned a printed sheet. He rattled the page briefly, and Vekt's half-closed eyes snapped open.

"Dr. Smithers, have any of your studies involved the procedure known as a police lineup?"

"Yes. I've run two such studies, one with college students as subjects, the other using the general population. Identical studies, with closely matching results, have been carried out at several other universities.

"In each trial an incident was staged, and witnesses were later asked to identify the 'perpetrator' by choosing among six people in a lineup. In sixty-seven percent of the trials the wrong person was selected, whether or not the right one was among the six.

"Witnesses tend to select someone they've seen before in any context if that is the only familiar face. In one study, a man who had come into the room to empty wastebaskets just before a staged assault was lined up with five men who had not been present at all. Fifty-eight percent of the witnesses identified him as the one who had punched the 'victim' in the jaw."

Herrera allowed a silence of several seconds before asking, "Is this type of erroneous identification — that is, of persons who have been seen in other contexts — always of someone who has been seen in person?"

"Not at all. It may also result from a television or newspaper sighting, or from having been shown a photograph by the police."

"From having been shown a photograph by the police," Herrera echoed.

"Yes. Especially if no one else whose picture the witness was shown is included in the lineup." Herrera nodded.

"Please keep in mind," Smithers continued, "that such witnesses are not deliberately lying. They firmly believe that they are recalling what they actually saw."

Herrera impaled a juror in the back row with his eyes. "They firmly believe what is not in fact true. That is just what makes this especially dangerous and frightening."

"Objection!"

"Sustained. Please don't editorialize, Mr. Herrera."

"Sorry."

Vekt smirked.

"Has the jury reached a verdict?"

The foreman's long narrow body, in jeans and a green sweater, seemed to uncoil rather than just stand up. "Yes, Your Honor, we have."

Vekt's left leg began to tremble. The judge instructed him to rise; Herrera rose with him.

"Read your verdict, please."

The foreman, not smiling, said, "On every count, we find the defendant not guilty."

"WHEEE-OOOO!" Harold took great gulps of breath and seized his lawyer by the upper arms. "Great job, Herrera. Great job!" The attorney remained expressionless.

"The defendant is free to go," Judge Quinn announced. Harold snorted with pleasure as he saw the prosecutor and his assistant looking at each other disgustedly. Morris Jagoda sat with his head in his hands.

Vekt reached out to shake Herrera's hand, but the attorney was bending down to retrieve his briefcase from under the table. He removed a small manila envelope.

"I was instructed to give you this in the event you were acquitted. I have no idea what's in it, or from whom it originated. I don't want to know." Herrera swept his papers off the table into the briefcase, clicked shut its combination lock, and stalked out of the courtroom. Harold stared after him briefly, then shrugged and turned his attention to the envelope.

It was six-by-eight; nothing was printed or written on the outside. Its metal tab closing was reinforced with two strips of transparent tape.

"What's that?" Theresa Vekt had come up behind her son.

"I don't know—something from the lawyer."

"Not a bill?"

"Nah—the court's paying him. I'll look at it later." His implication that it was none of her business was accepted matter-of-factly. "How about celebrating at Dinky Jones's?"

The dimly lit wood-paneled tavern had survived through all the years of change in Harold's childhood neighborhood. They sat on stools at the far end of the bar and had a couple of beers each, talking little except for toasts to each other and Herrera and Smithers and the jury. Then Harold took his mother to the Yonkers bus, promising to come for dinner in a couple of days.

Back in his flat, he put the thick envelope on the coffee table and studied it, pressing it between his palms. Fetching a steak knife from the kitchen, he cautiously slit the seal and peered in, then eased out the contents: two tape-bound stacks of currency and a folded sheet of white paper. He flipped his thumb through the bills; they appeared to be all twenties. Then he unfolded the paper.

Mr. Vekt—

I have need of a person with your skills and stamina to do a job of work for me. Of several people considered, you appear to be the best qualified.

The job is a onetime errand, whose nature you will learn at the appropriate time. It is essential, and in your best interests, that you say nothing to *anyone* about this, starting right now.

If you wish to accept, please come to 774 West 32nd Street at 9:30 on Friday night. The building has several entrances; use the door at the far end, closest to the river. It will be unlocked from 9:25 to 9:35. You will be met and given further instructions. Please do not bring your own weapon.

Enclosed is an advance payment of one-tenth of your fee. The rest, if you earn it, will also come in small bills. Should you decide against taking the job, you may keep this money. The only thing that will be expected in return is silence.

The message was unsigned, but the stiff formality of its wording had a certain familiarity. Vekt wondered if Herrera himself had written it.

One hundred and twenty-five twenty-dollar bills. Times two. Five thousand dollars. One-tenth. He didn't care who. His career as a mugger, supplemented by occasional legitimate odd jobs when he was up against it, would scarcely produce that much in two years. It was creepy, but he could take care of himself. He knew it, and the guy, whoever he was, that wanted to hire him knew it too.

Light rain filmed Vekt's face as he walked west. Unexpectedly, the wait for the downtown bus had been only three or four minutes, and he reached his destination at 9:15. On the designated door the numbers 774 were formed out of bright blue plastic tape.

Vekt tugged on the unyielding vertical door handle, then knocked, futilely. The appointed time, apparently, was firm. Shivering from the dampness, he hugged himself and stamped his feet, glancing at his watch with increasing frequency.

Just as 9:25 popped in, Vekt heard a metallic scrape. He tried the handle again; this time only the door's great weight held it back. Slowly, he was able to pull it open.

Inside, there was total darkness. "Hey! You there?" Though he'd spoken softly, his voice reverberated. Suddenly there was blinding light, as multiple fluorescent bars fluttered on. He squeezed his eyes shut, then blinked several times before adjusting to the brightness.

He was facing a long, narrow corridor with whitewashed concrete walls. Blue tape arrows pointed down the center of the white floor. Vekt could not see where they ended.

"Anyone here?" He was louder this time, and so was the responding silence. Harold felt his scalp clench. His palm itched for a gun, but his only choices now were to accept the circumstances or forgo any possibility of earning a quick $45,000.

He proceeded warily about sixty feet along the blue trail, which made a left turn and an almost immediate right. A strip of blue disappeared under a battleship-gray door, which pushed open easily into a small bare rectangular room. The arrows continued at a diagonal. The head of the last one was angled toward a doorway in the corner.

"Son-of-a-bitch! What kind of stupid game is this?" Vekt aimed a punching shove at the narrow door, but it gave so easily that he lost his balance and stumbled through it into an unlit area. The lights in the room he'd just left cut off. With a loud clang, the door closed behind him.

"What the fuck is this?" He groped at the door, could not budge it, could find no knob or handle. "Turn the goddamn lights on!" He pounded on the door with both fists.

Suddenly the darkness was a bit less than total. He turned to see a small pool of light coming from a naked twenty-five-watt bulb hanging by its wire about six feet above the floor. Directly beneath it was a small square table, and on the table was a sheet of paper. He crossed the murky space and gingerly picked up the page, printed in the same typeface as the letter that had directed him here.

Dear Mr. Vekt,
  Welcome to the rest of your life.
  I own this property. It has been disused for several years. No one ever comes here. The walls, inside and out, are eighteen inches thick.
  Behind this table is a door leading to another room, the only other place you will ever be.
  In that room are a refrigerator, a sink (cold water only), and a toilet; also a rolled-up mattress with a blanket and two spare lightbulbs.
  In the refrigerator is a small supply of food. Use it sparingly; it will be replenished, but who knows when?
  The door to the room is on an automatic time lock set to open twice a day, at 8:00 A.M. and 8:00 P.M., and stay open for twenty minutes each time. (This will help you to know the approximate time of day after your watch battery runs out. That is, if you manage to keep track of day and night—there are no windows in your new environment.) During those intervals, do whatever you need to do and get out. The room has no outside air supply. If you need urgently to urinate at any other time use the storm drain in the center of this room.
  You have no hope of deliverance, even if you've broken the rules and told someone where you were going. All the blue tape will soon be gone, including the numerals on the

door. (There is no 774; the highest number on this street
is in the five hundreds.)

You will live, at most, as long as I do—or perhaps a few
days longer if there's food left when I die. My own life
expectancy is problematic—my heart was torn out by my
wife's death and when I've finished with you, I'll have
nothing left to do.

Now, of course, you know who I am. Have you figured out
yet that it was I who paid for your defense? Attorneys
such as Wilson Herrera do not ordinarily serve in "routine" cases, even by court appointment. Dr. Smithers
doesn't come cheap either. Neither knows the origin of
their fees.

Why have I done this? I prefer—for myself, at any
rate—personal vendetta to "criminal justice." I want to
control the exact specifications of your punishment, so
that I may savor it.

When you've digested the contents of this letter, put it
in the other room. It is the price of your next supply of
food.

There was no signature.

Harold Vekt commenced his accommodation to his fate by vom-
iting into the storm drain.

JOHN DUFRESNE

The Cross-Eyed Bear

FROM *Boston Noir*

FATHER TOM MULCAHY can't seem to get warm. He's wearing his bulky cardigan sweater over his flannel pajamas over his V-neck T-shirt. He's got fleece-lined cordovan slippers on over his woolen socks and an afghan folded over his lap. The radiator is clanging and hissing in the corner, and he's still shivering. He tugs his watch cap over his ears, wipes his runny nose with a tissue. He stares at the bed against the wall and longs for the sleep of the dead. The window rattles. The weather people expect eighteen to twenty inches from the storm. He sips his Irish whiskey, swallows the other half of the Ativan, opens Meister Eckhart, and reads how all of our suffering comes from love and affection. He slips the venomous letter into the book to mark his page. The red numerals on the alarm clock seem to float in their black box. He sees his galoshes tucked under the radiator, the shaft of the right one bent to the floor. He's so tired he wonders if the droopy galosh might be a sign from God. Then he smiles and takes another sip of whiskey.

He lifts a corner of the curtain, peeks out on the driveway below, and sees fresh footprints leading to the elementary school. Probably Mr. O'Toole, the parish custodian, up early to clear the walk, an exercise in futility, it seems to Father Tom. The snow swirls, and the huge flakes look like black moths in the spotlight over the rectory porch. How new the world seems like this, all the clutter and debris mantled in white. He looks at the school and remembers the childhood exhilaration of snow days. Up early, radio on, listening to 'BZ, waiting for Carl De Suze to read the cancellation notices: "*No school in Arlington, Belmont, and Beverly. No school, all schools, Bos-*

ton . . ." In the years before his brother died, Tom would wake Gerard with the wicked good news, and the pair of them would pester their mom for cocoa and then snuggle under blankets on the couch and watch TV while she trudged off to work at Filene's. They'd eat lunch watching Big Brother Bob Emery, and they'd toast President Eisenhower with their glasses of milk while Big Brother's phonograph played "Hail to the Chief." Maybe if Gerard had lived, if they'd taken him to the hospital before it was too late, maybe then their dad would not have lost heart and found the highway.

Father Tom woke up this morning—well, yesterday morning now—woke up at 5:45 to get ready to celebrate the 6:30 Mass. He opened his eyes and saw the intruder sitting in the rocking chair. Father Tom said, "Who are you?"

"I'm with the *Globe*."

"Mrs. Walsh let you in?"

"I let myself in."

"What's going on?"

The man from the *Globe* tapped his cigarette ash into the cuff of his slacks.

"No smoking in the room, Mr. . . . ?"

"Hanratty."

"I'm allergic."

"Does the name Lionel Ferry mean anything to you?"

Father Tom found himself accused of sexual abuse by a man who claimed to have been molested and raped while he was an altar boy here at St. Cormac's. Thirty-some years ago. A reticent boy whom Father Tom barely thinks about anymore, not really, now a troubled adult looking for publicity and an easy payday from the archdiocese, needing an excuse to explain his own shabby and contemptible life, no doubt. Out for a little revenge against the Church for some fancied transgression. Father Tom had no comment for this Mr. Hanratty. And he has no plans to read the morning papers. But he does know they'll come for him, the press, the police, the cardinal's emissaries. His life as he knew it is over. Already the monsignor has asked him not to say Mass this morning—no use giving the disaffected an easy target.

He never did a harmful thing to any child, but he will not be believed. He prays to Jesus, our crucified Lord, to St. Jude, and to the Blessed Virgin. Father Tom trusts that God would not give him a burden he could not bear. He puts out the reading lamp. He stuffs earplugs in his ears, shuts his eyes, and covers them with a sleep mask. He feels crushed with fatigue, but his humming brain won't shut down. He keeps hearing that Paul Simon song about a dying constellation in a corner of the sky. The boy in the bubble and all that. *"These are the days of . . ."* And then unfamiliar faces shape themselves out of the caliginous murk in front of his closed eyes and morph into other faces, and soon he is drifting in space and shimmering like numerals on a digital clock, and then he's asleep. In his dream he's a boy again, and he's sitting with Jesus on a desolate hill overlooking Jerusalem. It's very late, and the air, every square inch of it, is purple. Jesus weeps. Tom knows what Jesus knows, that soon Jesus will be betrayed. Jesus wipes His eyes with the sleeve of His robe and says, "You always cheer me up, Thomas," and He tickles Tom in the ribs. Tom laughs, tucks his elbows against his sides, and rolls away. "Do you like that, Thomas? Do you?" Tom likes it, but he tells Jesus to stop so he can breathe. "Stop, please, or I'll wet my pants!" But Jesus won't stop.

Father Tom wakes up when the book drops to the floor. He takes off the sleep mask, picks up the letter, unfolds it, and reads in the window light. *I'll slice off your junk and stuff it down your throat, you worthless piece of shit. I'll drench you with gasoline and strike the match that sends you to hell.*

While he's waiting for the monsignor to finish up in the bathroom, Father Tom considers the painting he's been staring at all his life. It hung in the front hall of the family's first-floor apartment on L Street when he was a boy, and he was sure it must have been called *Sadness* or *Gloom*. His parents had no idea what it was called. The painting was a gift from an Irish cousin on his mother's side was all they knew. One of the O'Sullivans from Kerry. Now it hangs on the wall above Father Tom's prie-dieu. As a boy he saw this ragged, barefoot woman sitting on a rock in the middle of an ocean with her eyes blindfolded and her head bandaged and chained to a wooden frame that he assumed to be an instrument of torture, but turned out to be a lyre, of all things, and the rock was really the world itself, and the title was actually and inexplicably *Hope*. He's been trying to understand the aspiration, the anticipation in this somber and forlorn study in hazy blues and pale greens all his life. Hope is blind? Does that even make sense? The lyre has only one string. So the music is broken. The dark sky is starless. All he's ever felt looking at the picture is melancholy and desolation. Hopelessness. Is that it? If you are without desire, you are free?

He hears the bathroom door open and Monsignor McDermott descend the creaky staircase. The bathroom reeks of Listerine and bay rum after-shave. He folds the monsignor's pearl-handled straight razor and puts it by the shaving brush and mug. He starts the shower and lets the room steam and warm while he shaves. He stares in the mirror and wonders what people see when they look at him. He cuts himself in the little crease beside his lip and applies a tear of toilet paper to the bubble of blood. He looks at his face and sees his father's blue eyes and his mother's weak chin. He removes the toilet paper and dabs the cut with a styptic pencil. Gerard was the handsome one.

Mrs. Walsh, bless her heart, has already brewed the coffee and filled his cup. "Will it be eggs and toast, Father?"

"Just coffee this morning, Mary." He stirs his coffee, lays the spoon in the saucer. "The monsignor left for Mass already, I see." For just a second there, Father Tom forgot that today is not like other days. "I never did what that man said, you know."

"That's between you and the Lord, Father. It's no business of mine." She walks to the sink and peers out the window. "Sixteen inches already, and no sign of a letup. There'll be snow on the ground till Easter."

"I can't even remember the boy very clearly."

"He was one of your favorites, Father. Altar boy, he was. Tim Griffin's nephew. You called him 'Train.' He had the vocation, you used to say."

"But didn't become a priest."

"Became a drunk and a burden to his dear mother, may her soul rest in peace." Mrs. Walsh sets the dishcloth to dry on the radiator and straightens the braided rug by the stove, a rug she made herself thirty-some years ago from her husband's and children's discarded clothing. There's Himself's blue oxford shirt right there and little Mona's corduroy jumper. When she sees the shirt, she

sees her dear Aidan in it and his gray suit and red tie on their honeymoon on Nantasket Beach. "There have been other accusations,
Father. Other men have come forward."

"I did nothing except be kind to those boys, give them the love
and attention they didn't get at home. I never—"

The doorbell chimes. Mrs. Walsh says, "That'll be Mr. Markey
from the cardinal's office. He'll be wanting a word with you." She
walks to the front door and adds over her shoulder, "He's a merci-
ful Lord, Father."

Mr. Markey unsnaps his earflaps and takes off his storm hat. He
holds it by the visor and slaps it against his leg, then hangs it on a
peg and toes off his shearling boots. He hands his gloves and scarf
to Mrs. Walsh and hangs his wool car coat on the hall tree, claps his
hands together, and rubs them. He takes Mrs. Walsh by the shoulders and plants a noisy kiss on her forehead. "And how's my favorite colleen today?"

Mrs. Walsh blushes. "Enough of the blarney, Mr. Markey."

Mr. Markey holds out his hand to Father Tom. "Francis X. Markey." They shake hands. Mr. Markey points to the parlor. "Care to
join me, Father?"

Father Tom sits on the edge of the sofa behind the coffee table,
his hands folded on his knees. Mr. Markey drops into the uphol-
stered armchair, leans his head back against the antimacassar, and
runs his fingers through his hair. "I gave the monsignor five bucks
and told him to get a forty-five-minute coffee at Dunkin' Donuts.
It's the only thing open between here and the expressway." He
leans forward. "You know why I'm here."

"I've been threatened, Mr. Markey." Father Tom slides the vicious letter across the coffee table.

Mr. Markey leans forward and reads it, steeples his fingers, and
brings his hands to his face. "It won't be the last, I would guess. I
should make one thing clear, Father. I don't care what you did or
didn't do. I don't particularly care what happens to you. I don't
care *about* you in any but the most Christianable way. I care about
Holy Mother the Church."

"I didn't do what I've been accused of."

"You're up to your neck in shit, my friend." Mr. Markey walks to
the French doors and closes them, then turns back to Father Tom.
"You attended O'Connell Seminary, am I right?"

"I did."

"Yes, you did. You guys had a regular fuck show going over there, didn't you?"

"I don't have to listen to this."

"Yes, you do. I'm the only guy who can keep you out of Concord." Mr. Markey takes a handful of Skittles from the bowl on the coffee table and eats a few. "You do not want to go to prison."

"I'm innocent. I won't go to prison."

Mr. Markey smiles and shakes his head. "They'll put you in protective custody, of course. What you need to understand, however, is that the guards are scarier than the inmates when it comes to pedophiles. They'll piss in your food, shit in your bunk, and they'll sodomize you with a control baton if you complain. They'll degrade you in every way they can. And then one day while you're playing cribbage with another kiddie diddler, the guards will turn away when some trusty goes after you with a lead pipe."

Father Tom puts his head in his hands. He takes a deep breath and sits back, stares at the ceiling. He hears Mrs. Walsh whispering—her prayers, no doubt—as she climbs the stairs. "Why has His Eminence sent you here, Mr. Markey?"

"I make problems go away." He shows Father Tom his handful of Skittles, rubs his palms together, holds out two fists and says, "Which hand has the candy?"

"The left."

Mr. Markey opens his empty left hand and then his empty right hand. He turns his palms to show he's not hiding anything. "Do you remember a priest named Dan Caputo?"

"Died last year. Had a parish in JP and did all that social justice work. 'Speak truth to power' and all that—he was an inspirational leader."

"But he had a secret, as so many of us do. The cops found his battered corpse in an alley in Chinatown, his pants down to his ankles, a cock ring on his dick, and what would prove to be semen on his lips. When they checked his ID and found out who he was, they called the cardinal, who called me."

"I didn't hear about any of this."

"Exactly. We got rid of the porn magazines and videos in his car. He died a hero." Mr. Markey sits in the armchair and looks at Father Tom. "The Catholic Workers named their new place after him. The Father Dan Caputo House of Hospitality." He laughs.

"Nothing is ever what it seems to be, Father." He reaches in his pocket. "Weather alert." He takes out his BlackBerry. "This event has all the makings of a Storm of the Century." He reads his text message. "Calling for three feet inside 128." He puts the Black-Berry away. "Now this is what we're going to do. First, I'm going to offer our Mr. Ferry a handsome settlement in exchange for a signed statement admitting that he has been lying about the moles-tations due to his profound depression and anxiety. He'll agree to check himself into a mental health clinic; you'll be reassigned to a desk job at the chancery for the time being, and in a while this ag-gravation will be forgotten."

"It's in the papers."

"You'll do a press conference at which you'll graciously and hum-bly accept Mr. Ferry's apology and forgive him."

"And if he doesn't agree to your conditions?"

"That would suggest that he is a man of principle. But a penni-less alcoholic, we both know, cannot afford principles."

"But if he surprises you, then we go to trial and I'm exoner-ated."

"Neither necessary nor desirable." Mr. Markey walks to the fire-place and leans against the mantle. "Let me ask your opinion, Fa-ther, about this epidemic of predatory priests. Not you, of course. The guilty ones like Geoghan and Shanley. That lot. And Father Gale over here at St. Monica's. The priesthood turns out to be a good place to hide in plain sight. Am I right?"

"I wouldn't call it—"

"Six hundred and fifteen million dollars the Church in the States paid out just last year. That makes two billion total. Fourteen thou-sand felonies by forty-five hundred pedophile priests. And it's only the tip of the iceberg, believe me." He squats and warms his hands over the fire. "I have a theory, for what it's worth." He moves his left hand into the flame and leaves it there. "A theory of arrested development."

"You'll burn yourself."

"You go to the seminary out of high school, and it's all paid for. You graduate and get your parish assignment—no chasing down leads, no job interviews." He pulls his hand out of the flame and examines it. "Along with the assignment comes food, clothing, and shelter, a salary, a woman to cook, clean up after you, and do your laundry. You get a professional allowance, health insurance, and a

pension. You snap on the Roman collar, and you have instant respect without having earned it."

"That's unfair."

"The Church stifles your emotional growth. You're a boy called
Father. Not just you personally, Father. All of you."

"Are you finished?"

"Then there's the disagreeable issue of celibacy. Troublesome,
am I right? Me, if I can't release a few times a week, Jesus, I'm impossible to live with. Sure, you can masturbate and remain celibate
and sane, but jacking off's a sin, so what to do?"

"Pray."

"You can pray away a boner?"

"One chooses to remain chaste, Mr. Markey. It's a sacrifice, not a
curse."

Mr. Markey puts his hands behind his head and shrugs his shoulders. "But why little boys? That's what I wonder, and then I think,
yes, of course, arrested development. If you're a boy yourself,
you're comfortable among other boys, and you also know an
abused boy would never say anything about sucking your cock for
fear the other kids would call him a fag. Shame keeps him quiet.
Am I getting warm, Father?"

"You think you know me, but you don't."

"Thomas Aloysius Mulcahy, born February 15, 1948, at Mass
General, second son to Brian, postal worker, and Kathleen, née
O'Sullivan, Mulcahy. Attended St. Cormac's Grammar School and
South Boston High; B student, perfect attendance in eleventh
grade. You had mumps, chicken pox, measles, and rubella. You
wore corrective glasses and corrective shoes. Your beloved brother
Gerard died of spinal meningitis in 1958, and your dad blamed
himself, drank more heavily, and abandoned the family six months
later. So there you were at ten, alone with a hysterical mother and
bereft of affection."

Father Tom closes his eyes and sees himself lying on the floor by
his mother's locked bedroom door, crying, not knowing if she was
also dead. He feels Mr. Markey's hand on his shoulder and opens
his eyes, wipes them.

"So you understood just how vulnerable boys who'd lost their
dads were. They needed the love and guidance of an older man,
and you reached out to them."

"You're making compassion sound obscene."

"You took them for ice cream, to Fenway, to the beach. Their mothers were so grateful. You were a savior. Lionel even thought you were using him to woo his mom. And, of course, with you being a priest, he was confused."

"You spoke with him?"

"Last night. He's still living in his mom's place on I Street." Mr. Markey stared out the window at the howling storm. "He said you took him to the movies."

"I took many boys to many movies."

"You bought popcorn, buttered popcorn. 'Butted,' he said. 'Hut butted pupcon,' and you held the box on your lap, and when he reached in for a handful, your fingers touched, and you let the touch linger. He said you licked the 'buttah' off his fingers—"

"He's lying."

"That could be. Or it could be false memories. That happens. But let me ask you this. Has any priest ever confessed abuse to you?"

"If any had, I wouldn't tell you."

"What would you do if Father X told you he boinked all the altos in the boys' choir?"

"I'd grant him absolution if he were contrite and determined not to sin again."

"That's it?"

"If thy brother trespass against thee, rebuke him; and if he repent, forgive him."

"Forgive, and ye shall be forgiven."

"I might also suggest counseling, therapy, prayer, and avoiding the near occasion to sin."

Mr. Markey picks up a copy of *The Pilot* off the coffee table and reads. *"Cardinal Law Appointed Archpriest at Vatican Basilica."* He shakes his head, rolls the paper, and slaps it against his leg. "Our ex-cardinal here once accused a six-year-old boy of negligence and culpability in his own repeated rapes. Under oath!" He drops the paper onto the coffee table. "I can't shake this paranoid fantasy I have of a fellowship of child-molesting priests all going to confession to one another, forgiving one another, and moving on as if nothing ever happened."

"One would need sincere contrition."

"They confess; they are contrite; they are forgiven." Mr. Markey checks his watch. "I'm going to need to speak with the monsignor alone. Maybe you should visit the church and pray for strength and guidance. By the time we see you again, everything should be taken care of." Mr. Markey puts his hand on the back of Father Tom's neck and squeezes. He pulls Father Tom's head toward his own until their foreheads touch. "Trust me."

Father Tom feels a hot current of pain buzz through his skull like his head's attached to a live electrical wire, but he's rigid, shaken, and speechless, and he can't pull away.

Father Tom lights a votive candle and prays for courage and understanding. He's always savored his time alone in a dark church where he feels hidden away. As a boy he'd arrive at five or six every Saturday morning, sit beneath the stained-glass window of the Last Supper, and pray the rosary. He wanted God to know that he was no Sunday Catholic; he was a boy God could count on, a soldier of Christ. Father Tom genuflects, walks to the pew beneath the Last Supper, and sits. The world seems far away. He remembers asking God to make him either dead or invisible. Dead he'd be with Jesus and Gerard; invisible he'd be alone.

He looks up at the window. Jesus has a mole under His right eye. The beloved John has his head on his arm and his arm on the table. His eyes are shut, and he's smiling like he's tasted the honeyed love of his Lord. The apostle Thomas stands behind the others, and all you see is his single wide eye peering above the heads at Jesus, the way Gerard's single eye peered above the hem of the blanket on the couch when he ran his foot along Tom's leg. "Quit it, Gerard, or I'll call Mom!"

When Gerard lay in his coma at the hospital, the nuns from St. Cormac's took up residence in his room and kept a twenty-four-hour vigil. They fussed and prayed over him. Sister Brigid saw the Angel Gabriel at the foot of Gerard's bed, weeping. Gerard was a saint, the nuns were certain. The ones He loves best, God takes first. When Gerard died in his mother's arms, the nuns hung framed photos of Gerard in every classroom alongside the president and the pope. Then the stories of Gerard's sanctity started, how he had healed a starling's broken wing with just a touch, how he could be both in church and in school simultaneously, how he could smell the presence of sin, how the statue of the Virgin Mary on the altar had wept at the moment of Gerard's passing.

What Father Tom will admit to if they ask—because it's pretty normal anyway—is that there are two selves in him. There's the self you see, the Father Tom he wants to be, the he who is pastoral, devout, compassionate, prudent . . . and what else? Vulnerable? Yes. And washed in the blood of the Lamb. And this is the bona fide Father Tom Mulcahy. And then there is the sinner, the carnal scoundrel who is impulsive, selfish, devious, and insatiable, a wolf inside who knows the secret of Father Tom's loneliness and hunger, and who would, if he could, twist Father Tom's selfless love and earnest affection into something loathsome and viperous. Father Tom will admit, this is to say, that he is indeed human and flawed, no better than they. And he'll explain to them his obsessive vigilance and tenacity in the battle with his pernicious other, and how he has always vanquished the interloping demon and has done so at a staggering price.

One day after sledding and making snow angels, he and Gerard built a snowman in the small backyard, and his brother took the carrot for the nose and stuck it down there and made it a weenie and told Tom to get down on his knees and eat it. He wouldn't, so Gerard pushed his face into the snow and sat on his head until Tom couldn't breathe, and he was terrified, and his mother wasn't here to save him.

He hears a noise, like someone dropped a hymnal, but when he looks around, he sees no one. He says, "Mr. O'Toole?" and hears his voice echo. He listens to the howling wind and to his beating heart. And then he hears his sobbing mother say, *Why Gerard, dear God?* They are in the hospital, and Tom is in a corner, peering past the nuns at his mother, prostrate on his dead brother's bed. *Why the beautiful one?* she says.

Father Tom prays for wisdom, guidance, and deliverance. He'll do God's will, and if God wants him to suffer unjustly, then so be it. But he's done with waiting. He'll speak with this Judas, this traducer, this Lionel Ferry, and give him a chance to confess his lies and to accept God's grace into his heart.

When Father Tom enters the sacristy, he's surprised by a man in a cumbersome green snow suit standing in a puddle of melting snow. "Mr. O'Toole?" Father Tom says. A black balaclava covers most of the man's face. His mustache is white with ice, and his glasses are opaque with fog. This man, who is apparently not Davy O'Toole, who is, Father Tom realizes, several inches shorter than the custodian, has a snowball in his left hand, which he lobs to Father Tom. When Father Tom catches the ball against his chest, the man swings what must be a club and strikes him on the side of his face, and he drops to the floor. His skull is shattered, he's certain, but it doesn't hurt. He hears the squeak of footsteps, hears the church door open, squeal, and slam shut. After several minutes, he opens the one eye that will, touches his face, and feels the drilling pain. His left ear is ringing.

Father Tom holds a handful of numbing snow over his swollen eye, presses the buzzer, and waits. He kicks aside some drifted snow and forces the storm door open. He knocks on the inside front door twice and then *shave-and-a-haircut.* A voice says, "Come in if you're beautiful." Father Tom drops the snow from his eye, shakes off as much snow as he can from his coat and slacks, steps inside the unlit parlor, and lets his eye adjust. "Hello!" He can see his breath. He can make out a sofa and a sleeping bag spread on the floor. He hears, "Be right with you. Gotta drain the lizard."

The parlor is spare, grim, disordered, and in need of a good airing out and thorough cleaning. The flock wallpaper is peeling and water-stained. Next to the sleeping bag is a white plastic lawn chair stacked with magazines. There's a small TV on the floor and a bookcase crammed with videotapes in black boxes. He hears, "Make yourself at home." He steps around pizza boxes—pepperoni and sausage, or are those mouse droppings?—and piles of funky clothing and sits in an old wooden kitchen chair with a slat missing from the backrest. He notices an unframed paint-by-number portrait of Pope John Paul II hung over the light switch by the closed door to what had been Lionel's bedroom. He sees those eyes that follow you around the room.

Lionel enters cradling a bottle of vodka. He's wearing a waist-length leather jacket with an extravagant fur collar, black patent leather shoes, and no shirt. His khaki chinos have been pissed in.

"Train?"

"Tommy Gun!"

"What's happened to you?"

"That's what we called you behind your back."

"You don't have to live like this."

"Your eye?"

"I fell."

Lionel flops onto the sofa. "I've been expecting you."

"You have?"

"For years." He drinks.

"We need to talk."

Lionel pats the sofa cushion. "Come sit with me."

"I'm fine here."

"I won't bite." He smiles. "I insist."

Father Tom moves to the sofa. "Did you write me a letter?"

"I never mailed it." Lionel touches Father Tom's arm. "I forgive you, Father. But I can't forget. That's the difference between me and God."

"I think you may have misunderstood my actions, Train."

"Of course you do. Otherwise, how could you live with yourself?"

"You don't want to do this to me."

"Do you remember my father's funeral? You drove me home from the cemetery."

"Kevin was a good man."

"He was an asshole." Lionel sniffles and sips the vodka. His eyes water, and he knows he could cry, but there'll be time for that later. "You bought me an ice-cream cone, pistachio with jimmies, and drove slowly. You said, 'I know for a young boy like you, Train, this is an awful loss.' By then you were patting my leg. You left your hand on my thigh . . ."

Father Tom unbuttons his coat and takes off his cap, pats down his thin, flyaway hair. He feels his forehead. He remembers those mornings in church when Jesus would come to him with His heart burning like a furnace, and the heat would blanket Tom, and he would sweat and lift his eyes to heaven, and Jesus would thrust a golden dart through his heart.

". . . and then your hand was in your pants, and your face was all squinched up, and all I could do was stare out the window and hope it would end, and the ice cream melted and ran down my arm until it was all gone."

"That did not happen, and I don't know why you want to think it did. I was offering you comfort and solace. I knew what it felt like to hunger for human touch. My father never held me, Train. Ever. My mother never did after Gerard died."

"Should I play my little violin?"

"I took your father's place."

"I'd wake up and you'd be in my bed."

"*On* your bed. Watching you sleep, like fathers have always watched their sons and imagined brilliant futures for them."

"That's fucked up."

"You were an affectionate boy. You brought out the tenderness in people. In me. And yes, I felt needed; I felt connected to another person for the first time since Gerard died."

"Did you wonder how *I* felt?"

"If it was a problem for you, you should have told me. I would have respected that. I had an understanding with myself. I thought I had your permission."

"If nothing sexual ever happened, why do I remember that it did?"

"Could you be making it up, Train?"

And then there's a knock, and Mr. Markey opens the door and steps into the room. He stamps his feet, tosses a fifth of brandy to Lionel and a newspaper to Father Tom. "You're famous, Father."

The man behind Mr. Markey takes off his glasses and his balaclava. He wipes his glasses with a hanky and puts them back on.

Mr. Markey says, "I believe you've already met my friend, Mr. Hanratty."

"Twice," Father Tom replies.

Mr. Markey says, "You'll excuse us, gents," and Lionel gets up and follows Mr. Hanratty down the hall to the kitchen.

"He's a reporter," Father Tom says.

Mr. Markey smiles. "Terrance doesn't write for the *Globe;* he delivers it."

Father Tom points to his face. "He did this to me."

"He can be a little feisty. I try to keep him on a short leash." Mr. Markey shrugs. "So tell me, Father, does our Lionel still make your heart beat faster?"

Father Tom stands and steps toward the door. "I'm not going to sit here and listen to this."

Mr. Markey grabs Father Tom's arm at the wrist and twists it until the palm is behind his back and the elbow is locked. "I've read somewhere that pain elevates our thoughts," Mr. Markey says, and he tugs at the arm until Father Tom feels like it'll snap at the wrist and shatter at the shoulder. "Of course, I'm not a theologian."

Father Tom is bent at the waist and in tears. "Please, you're hurting me."

"Keeps our mind off amusements."

"You're insane."

"Have you ever slept on a bed of crushed glass, Father?"

"Please, dear God!"

"Worn a crown of nettle?" Mr. Markey lifts the arm slowly. "These are not rhetorical questions, Father. Answer me."

"No, I haven't."

Mr. Markey releases Father Tom and shoves him back onto the sofa. "What excruciating bliss when the pain ends. You feel grateful to me right now, don't you?"

Father Tom can't move his arm.

"Thank me."

"Thank *you*?"

Mr. Markey leans over him. "Thank me!"

"Thank you."

"You're welcome." Mr. Markey tousles Father Tom's hair, pats his head. "Pain releases endorphins. You feel a little high. I believe you have practiced certain endorphin-releasing austerities yourself, have you not?"

"I'm not a masochist, if that's what you mean."

"The time you slammed your hand in the car door?"

"An accident."

"That's not what you told your therapist. Why on earth would you have wanted to punish yourself like that?" Mr. Markey walks to the window and admires the storm. "You don't get to see but one or two nor'easters like this in a lifetime."

Father Tom wonders if he could make it out the door before Mr. Markey catches him. And then what?

"I'm sure you struggled, Father, fought the good fight. You always wanted to do the right thing, but those little cock teasers wouldn't let you. Always with their sweet little asses and their angelic smiles." He leans forward and whispers: "You liked bending their heads back and kissing their exposed throats, didn't you? Absolutely divine, isn't it?"

"You filthy—"

"An ecstatic moment and yet so difficult to put into words." Mr.

Markey takes off his gloves and pulls up the sleeves of his car coat. "Nothing up my sleeve." And then he reaches behind Father Tom's ear and holds up a folded piece of loose-leaf paper. "What have we here?" He unfolds it. "My associate, Mr. Hanratty, discovered this in your dresser beneath your unmentionables while we were speaking earlier. It seems to be a list of boys' names. Should I read them?"

"Boys from the parish, boys I've worked with."

"But not *all* the boys you've worked with. What's special about these boys?"

"Everyone has his favorites."

Mr. Hanratty returns and hands a manila folder to Mr. Markey, who holds it up for Father Tom to see. "You can guess what this is, I'm sure."

"Class photos," Father Tom says.

"Of boys."

"Perfectly innocent," Father Tom says.

"They help you get off, I'll bet."

Father Tom feels the throbbing pain in his closed eye. "Look," he says, "it was a constant battle. I was always thinking about this . . . this abomination and trying not to think about it. I had no time for friendship or music or dreams or joy or charity or anything else that makes life worth living. If I had relaxed for a moment, I knew I might lose control. But I did not!"

"You are a victim of yourself. Is that what you're saying? *You're* the victim?"

Father Tom notices that the pope's painted eyes seem to shimmer in their sockets and spin like pinwheels and Mr. Markey's voice sounds tinny and far away, and then Lionel's a boy again, and he and Lionel are kneeling by the kid's bed saying their prayers, and then he tickles Lionel until Lionel begs him to stop, and Father Tom stops and says, *What a great relief when the pleasure ends.* And he drapes his arm around Lionel's shoulders and kisses his blond head, like a father saying good-night to his beloved son, and then, he can't help it, he tickles Lionel again until the boy yells, *Help!* And then Father Tom feels his head snap and realizes he's been slapped.

"Thanks, you needed that," Mr. Hanratty says.

"Why were you screaming for help, Father?" Mr. Markey puts the watch cap on Father Tom's head. "Let's go for a walk."

*

Mr. Markey closes the door behind them. He stands on the porch with Father Tom while Mr. Hanratty shovels a path through the waist-high drift to the middle of the windswept street where the snow is only shin- and ankle-deep.

"Where's Lionel?" Father Tom asks.

"Sleeping it off."

Father Tom pulls the cap down over his ears. The ringing in the left is worse. "What's the best I can hope for?"

"That we've been wrong all along, and there's no afterlife."

"That's absurd."

"That way you won't know you're dead. And in hell."

"You have no right to judge me."

"Who would want to live forever anyway? We'd be so bored we'd kill ourselves."

Mr. Markey leads Father Tom to the street. Mr. Hanratty spears his shovel into the snow. All Father Tom can see out of his squinted eyes are the slanting sheets of blowing flakes, the snowy hummocks of buried cars, and the indistinct facades of houses. He hears what might be the distant drone of heavy machinery or the blood coursing through his head. Mr. Markey and Mr. Hanratty stand to either side of him and lock their arms in his. Heads bowed into the wind, they begin their trudge down I Street.

"Where are you taking me?"

Mr. Markey says, "We thought you might need help."

"I *have* hope." Hope is the last emotion to leave us, Father Tom thinks. He sees the lyre player on her rock and speculates that you don't hope *for* something, do you? You just hope. To wait is to hope. Hope is a rebuke to the cold and starless sky. *I am,* it says. *I will be.* Father Tom sees movement to his right and makes out a bundled and hooded figure sweeping snow from a porch.

Mr. Markey leans his face to Father Tom's ear and says, "Not *hope! Help!*" The figure on the porch stops, regards the three lumbering gentlemen, turns, and goes into the house. And then Mr. Markey adds, "Sometimes a message must be sent," but what Father Tom hears is "Sometimes a messy, musky scent," and he wonders why this man is speaking in riddles. Mr. Markey tells Mr. Hanratty how we all have our burden to carry, and he points to Father Tom and says, "And this is the cross-eyed bear." Why would they call him that? Father Tom wonders.

When they reach Gleason's Market, Father Tom knows the rectory is around the block, and he's relieved to see that they're taking him back. They had him rattled earlier with that talk of no afterlife and all. But what else could they do, really? Soon he'll be sipping Mrs. Walsh's potato and barley soup after a hot bath, and then he'll go to his room and read and look out on this magnificent storm. Maybe he'll read right through his Graham Greene novels like he did the winter he was laid up with the broken leg. He sees a light on in the rectory kitchen, or at least he thinks he does. With all this bone-white snow in the air, it's not like you can actually look *at* anything. You look *through* the white. It's like peering at the world through linen. But then the light goes off, or was never on, and he thinks of the tricks your eyes can pull on you, like when you stare at the sky and the clouds seem to race up and away from you. No, the light is still on. He turns to Mr. Markey and says, "Everything's all right then?"

"Copacetic, Father." Mr. Markey looks at Father Tom's florid and swollen face, at his tiny blue eye, fixed in baggy lids like a turquoise bead on a leather pouch. A ragged little thin-lipped cyclops.

They walk past the rectory and follow a path that Mr. O'Toole has evidently plowed between the garage and the school. Father Tom looks up at the fourth-grade classroom and sees his nine-year-old self in the window by the pencil sharpener, nose pressed against the glass, looking down at him. When he peers out the window, Tom sees a battered old drunk being helped home by two friends, and he would like to know whose grandfather this is, but Sister calls him back to his seat for the spelling bee. Father Tom thinks now that he remembers that stormy morning when this ungainly procession passed below the window as he watched, but the old man could not have been him. A person can't be in two places at the same time. And then Monsignor McDermott is standing in the window. Father Tom would like to wave hello, but the men have his arms. The monsignor blows his nose and wipes it and then tucks his hanky up the sleeve of his cassock. Father Tom struggles to free the arm, and his escorts release him. He waves, but to an empty window. He considers screaming but doubts his voice would carry in the muffled stillness of the snow. And if it did? He lifts his arms, and the gentlemen lock theirs in his and walk.

"That's better," Mr. Markey says.

When they head up an alley and away from the rectory, Father Tom asks Mr. Markey, "Who do you think you are?"

"Nobody."
"You're somebody."
"Am I?"
"And I think I know you."

Father Tom is warm under this snowy blanket and would like to take off his jacket. He feels the icy snow whipping at his face and sees a pearl-handled straight razor lying on a bloom of crimson snow by his groin. He's on his back. His legs are buried beneath the drift. How long has he lain here? He gurgles, coughs, tastes blood in his mouth. He'd been dreaming of falling through a starless purple sky away from the vision of Christ when he realized he was tumbling toward the infernal abyss, and he screamed himself awake, thank God. His left arm is bent at the elbow and points to heaven. He tells the arm to move, but nothing happens. He might as well be telling someone else's arm to move. He remembers long ago lying helplessly in Lionel's bed with the dozing boy and trying to will him to turn, to rest his head on his, Father Tom's, chest and his slender arm on Father's waist. And later when Lionel whimpered and opened his teary eyes, Father Tom held him and said, "You've had a bad dream, Train, that's all. Don't cry, baby, don't cry. Don't cry."

But if he did not, in fact, scream himself awake moments ago, and if this is, indeed, hell, this frozen drift of blood and guilt, then Father Tom is happy to know that at least they don't take your memories away, which makes sense, because without a past you don't exist, and there can be no hell for you. He knows that his memories of love and affection will comfort and sustain him for eternity. And then he sees Mr. Markey and Mr. Hanratty standing over him. But when Mr. Hanratty pulls back his balaclava, Father Tom sees that it's Gerard, and he's with Jesus and not with Mr. Markey, and Jesus has His arm draped over Gerard's shoulders. Jesus waves at Father Tom and says, "So long, small fry!" They shake their heads and turn away.

"Stop, please!" Father Tom says, or thinks he says. And then he watches them somehow as they walk back in the direction of St. Cormac's, watches Jesus whisper into Gerard's ear, and the two of them turn again to glance back at him, but all they see is a black smudge in a white world that looks otherwise unsullied.

LYNDSAY FAYE

The Case of Colonel Warburton's Madness

FROM *Sherlock Holmes in America*

MY FRIEND MR. SHERLOCK HOLMES, while possessed of one of the most vigorous minds of our generation, and while capable of displaying tremendous feats of physical activity when the situation required it, could nevertheless remain in his armchair perfectly motionless longer than any human being I have ever encountered. This skill passed wholly unrecognized by its owner. I do not believe he held any intentions to impress me so, nor do I think the exercise was, for him, a strenuous one. Still I maintain the belief that when a man has held the same pose for a period exceeding three hours, and when that man is undoubtedly awake, that same man has accomplished an unnatural feat.

I turned away from my task of organizing a set of old journals that lead-grey afternoon to observe Holmes perched with one leg curled beneath him, firelight burnishing the edges of his dressing gown as he sat with his head in his hand, a long-abandoned book upon the carpet. The familiar sight had grown increasingly unnerving as the hours progressed. It was with a view to ascertain that my friend was still alive that I went so far against my habits as to interrupt his reverie.

"My dear chap, would you care to take a turn with me? I've an errand with the bootmaker down the road, and the weather has cleared somewhat."

I do not know if it was the still-ominous dark canopy that deterred him or his own pensive mood, but Holmes merely replied,

"I require better distraction just now than an errand which is not my own and the capricious designs of a March rainstorm."

"What precise variety of distraction would be more to your liking?" I inquired, a trifle nettled at his dismissal.

He waved a slender hand, at last lifting his dark head from the upholstery where it had reclined for so long. "Nothing you can provide me. It is the old story—for these two days I have received not a shred of worthwhile correspondence, nor has any poor soul abused our front doorbell with an eye to engage my services. The world is weary, I am weary, and I grow weary with being weary of it. Thus, Watson, as you see I am entirely useless myself at the moment, my state cannot be bettered through frivolous occupations."

"I suppose I would be pleased no one is so disturbed in mind as to seek your aid, if I did not know what your work meant to you," I said with greater sympathy.

"Well, well, there is no use lamenting over it."

"No, but I should certainly help if I could."

"What could you possibly do?" he sniffed. "I hope you are not about to tell me your pocket watch has been stolen, or your great-aunt disappeared without trace."

"I am safe on those counts, thank you. But perhaps I can yet offer you a problem to vex your brain for half an hour."

"A problem? Oh, I'm terribly sorry—I had forgotten. If you want to know where the other key to the desk has wandered off to, I was given cause recently to test the pliancy of such objects. I'll have a new one made—"

"I had not noticed the key," I interrupted him with a smile, "but I could, if you like, relate a series of events which once befell me when I was in practice in San Francisco, the curious details of which have perplexed me for years. My work on these old diaries reminded me of them yet again, and the circumstances were quite in your line."

"I suppose I should be grateful you are at least not staring daggers at my undocketed case files," he remarked.

"You see? There are myriad advantages. It would be preferable to venturing out, for it is already raining again. And should you refuse, I will be every bit as unoccupied as you, which I would also prefer to avoid." I did not mention that if he remained a statue an instant longer, the sheer eeriness of the room would force me out of doors.

"You are to tell me a tale of your frontier days, and I am to solve it?" he asked blandly, but the subtle angle of one eyebrow told me he was intrigued.

"Yes, if you can."

"What if you haven't the data?"

"Then we shall proceed directly to the brandy and cigars."

"It's a formidable challenge." To my great relief, he lifted himself in the air by his hands and crossed his legs underneath him, reaching when he had done so for the pipe lying cold on the side table. "I cannot say I've any confidence it can be done, but as an experiment, it has a certain flair."

"In that case, I shall tell you the story, and you may pose any questions that occur to you."

"From the beginning, mind, Watson," he admonished, settling himself into a comfortable air of resigned attention. "And with as many details as you can summon up."

"It is quite fresh in my mind again, for I'd set it down in the volumes I was just mulling over. As you know, my residence in America was relatively brief, but San Francisco lives in my memory quite as vividly as Sydney or Bombay—an impetuous, thriving little city nestled among the great hills, where the fogs are spun from ocean air and the sunlight refracts from Montgomery Street's countless glass windows. It is as if all the men and women of enterprise across the globe determined they should have a city of their own, for the Gold Rush built it and the Silver Lode built it again, and now that they have been linked by railroad with the eastern states, the populace believes nothing is impossible under the sun. You would love it there, Holmes. One sees quite as many nations and trades represented as in London, all jostling one another into a thousand bizarre coincidences, and you would not be surprised to find a Chinese apothecary wedged between a French milliner and an Italian wine merchant.

"My practice was based on Front Street in a small brick building, near a number of druggist establishments, and I readily received any patients who happened my way. Poor or well-off, genteel or ruffianly, it made no difference to a boy in the first flush of his career. I'd no long-established references, and for that reason no great clientele, but it was impossible to feel small in that city, for they so prized hard work and optimism that I felt sudden successes lay every moment round the next corner.

"One hazy afternoon, as I'd no appointments and I could see the sun lighting up the masts of the ships in the Bay, I decided I'd sat idle long enough, and set out for a bit of exercise. It is one of San Francisco's peculiar characteristics that no matter what direction one wanders, one must encounter a steep hill, for there are seven of them, and within half an hour of walking aimlessly away from the water, I found myself striding up Nob Hill, staring in awe at the array of houses.

"Houses, in fact, are rather a misnomer; they call it Nob Hill because it is populated by mining and railroad nabobs, and the residences are like something from the reign of Ludwig the Second or Marie Antoinette. Many are larger than our landed estates, but all built within ten years of the time I arrived. I ambled past a gothic near-castle and a neo-classicist mansion only to spy an Italianate villa across the street, each making an effort to best all others in stained glass, columns, and turrets. The neighborhood—"

"Was a wealthy one," Holmes sighed, hopping out of his chair to pour two glasses of claret.

"And you would doubtless have found that section of town appalling." I smiled at the thought of my Bohemian friend eyeing those pleasure domes with cool distaste as he handed me a wineglass. "There would have been others more to your liking, I think. Nevertheless, it was a marvel of architecture, and as I neared the crest of the hill, I stopped to take in the view of the Pacific.

"Standing there watching the sun glow orange over the waves, I heard a door fly open and turned to see an old man hobbling frantically down a manicured path leading to the street. The mansion he'd exited was built more discreetly than most, vaguely Grecian and painted white. He was very tall—quite as tall as you, my dear fellow—but with shoulders like an ox. He dressed in a decades-old military uniform, with a tattered blue coat over his grey trousers, and a broad red tie and cloth belt, his silvery hair standing out from his head as if he'd just stepped from the thick of battle.

"Although he cut an extraordinary figure, I would not have paid him much mind in that mad metropolis had not a young lady rushed after him in pursuit, crying out, 'Uncle! Stop, please! You mustn't go, I beg of you!'

"The man she'd addressed as her uncle gained the curb not ten feet from where I stood, and then all at once collapsed onto the pavement, his chest no longer heaving and the leg which had limped crumpled underneath him.

"I rushed to his side. He breathed, but shallowly. From my closer vantage point, I could see one of his limbs was false, and that it had come loose from its leather straps, causing his fall. The girl reached us not ten seconds later, gasping for breath even as she made a valiant effort to prevent her eyes from tearing.

"'Is he all right?' she asked me.

"'I think so,' I replied, 'but I prefer to be certain. I am a doctor, and I would be happy to examine him more carefully indoors.'

"'I cannot tell you how grateful we would be. Jefferson!' she called to a tall black servant hurrying down the path. 'Please help us get the Colonel inside.'

"Between the three of us, we quickly established my patient on the sofa in a cheerful, glass-walled morning room, and I was able to make a more thorough diagnosis. Apart from the carefully crafted wooden leg, which I reattached more securely, he seemed in perfect health, and if he were not such a large and apparently hale man I should have imagined that he had merely fainted.

"'Has he hurt himself, Doctor?' the young woman asked breathlessly.

"Despite her evident distress, I saw at once she was a beautiful woman, with a small-framed, feminine figure, and yet a large measure of that grace which goes with greater stature. Her hair was light auburn, swept away from her creamy complexion in loose waves and wound in an elegant knot, and her eyes shone golden brown through her remaining tears. She wore a pale blue dress trimmed with silver, and her ungloved hand clutched at the folds in her apprehension. She—my dear fellow, are you all right?"

"Perfectly," Holmes replied with another cough which, had I been in an uncharitable humor, would have resembled a chuckle. "Do go on."

"'This man will be quite all right once he has rested,' I told her. 'My name is John Watson.'

"'Forgive me—I am Molly Warburton, and the man you've been tending is my uncle, Colonel Patrick Warburton. Oh, what a fright I have had! I cannot thank you enough.'

"'Miss Warburton, I wonder if I might speak with you in another room, so as not to disturb your uncle while he recovers.'

"She led me across the hall into another tastefully appointed parlor and fell exhaustedly into a chair. I hesitated to disturb her further, and yet I felt compelled to make my anxieties known.

"'Miss Warburton, I do not think your uncle would have collapsed in such a dramatic manner had he not been under serious mental strain. Has anything occurred recently which might have upset him?'

"'Dr. Watson, you have stumbled upon a family embarrassment,' she said softly. 'My uncle's mental state has been precarious for some time now, and I fear recently he—he has taken a great turn for the worse.'

"'I am sorry to hear it.'

"'The story takes some little time in telling,' she sighed, 'but I will ring for tea, and you will know all about it. First of all, Dr. Watson, I live here with my brother, Charles, and my uncle, the Colonel. Apart from Uncle Patrick, Charles and I have no living relatives, and we are very grateful to him for his generosity, for Uncle made a great fortune in shipping during the early days of California statehood. My brother is making his start in the photography business, and I am unmarried, so living with the Colonel is for the moment a very comfortable situation.'

"'You must know that my uncle was a firebrand in his youth, and saw a great deal of war as a settler in Texas, before that region was counted among the United States. The pitched fighting between the Texians—that is, the Anglo settlers—and the Tejanos so moved him that he joined the Texas Army under Sam Houston, and was decorated several times for his valor on the field, notably at the Battle of San Jacinto. Later, when the War Between the States began, he was a commander for the Union, and lost his leg during the Siege of Petersburg. Forgive me if I bore you. From your voice, I do not think you are a natural-born American,' she added with a smile.

"'Your story greatly interests me. Is that his old Texas uniform he is wearing today?' I asked.

"'Yes, it is,' she replied as a flicker of pain distorted her pretty face. 'He has been costuming himself like that with greater and greater frequency. The affliction, for I do not know what to call it, began several weeks ago. Indeed, I believe the first symptom took place when he changed his will.'

"'How so? Was it a material alteration?'

"'Charlie and I had been the sole benefactors,' she replied, gripping a handkerchief tightly. 'His entire fortune will now be distributed amongst various war charities. Texas War for Independence charities, Civil War charities. He is obsessed with war,' she choked, and then hid her face in her hands.

"I was already moved by her story, Holmes, but the oddity of the Colonel's condition intrigued me still further.

"'What are his other symptoms?' I queried when she had recovered herself.

"'After he changed his will, he began seeing the most terrible visions in the dark. Dr. Watson, he claims in the most passionate language that he is haunted. He swears he saw a fearsome Tejano threatening a white woman with a pistol and a whip, and on another occasion he witnessed the same apparition slaughtering one of Houston's men with a bayonet. That is what so upset him, for only this morning he insisted he saw a murderous band of them brandishing swords and torches, with the identical Tejano at their head. My brother believes that we have a duty as his family to remain and care for him, but I confess Uncle frightens me at times. If we abandoned him, he would have no one, save his old manservant; Sam Jefferson served the Colonel for many years, as far back as Texas, I believe, and when my uncle built this house, Jefferson became the head butler.'

"She was interrupted in her narrative as the door opened and the man I knew at once to be her brother stepped in. He had the same light brown eyes as she, and fine features, which twisted into a question at the sight of me.

"'Hello, Molly. Who is this gentleman?'

"'Charlie, it was horrible,' she cried, running to him. 'Uncle Patrick ran out of the house and collapsed. This is Dr. John Watson. He has been so helpful and sympathetic that I was telling him all about Uncle's condition.'

"Charles Warburton shook my hand readily. 'Very sorry to have troubled you, Doctor, but as you can see, we are in something of a mess. If Uncle Patrick grows any worse, I hate to think what—'

"Just then a great roar echoed from the morning room, followed by a shattering crash. The three of us rushed into the hallway and found Colonel Warburton staring wildly about him, a vase broken into shards at his feet.

"'I left this house once,' he swore, 'and by the devil I will do it again. It's full of vengeful spirits, and I will see you all in hell for keeping me here!'

"The niece and nephew did their utmost to calm the Colonel, but he grew even more enraged at the sight of them. In fact, he was so violently agitated that only Sam Jefferson could coax him, with my help, toward his bedroom, and once we had reached it, the Colonel slammed the door shut in the faces of his kinfolk.

"By sheer good fortune, I convinced him to take a sedative, and when he fell back in a daze on his bed, I stood up and looked about me. His room was quite Spartan, with hardly anything on the white walls, in the simple style I supposed was a relic of his days in Texas. I have told you that the rest of the house also reflected his disdain for frippery. The bed rested under a pleasant open window, and as it was on the ground floor, one could look directly out at the gardens.

"I turned to rejoin my hosts when Sam Jefferson cleared his throat behind me.

"'You believe he'll be all right, sir?'

"He spoke with the slow, deep tones of a man born on the other side of the Mississippi. I had not noticed it before, but a thick knot of scarring ran across his dark temple, which led me to believe he had done quite as much fighting in his youth as his employer.

"'I hope so, but his family would do well to consult a specialist. He is on the brink of a nervous collapse. Was the Colonel so fanciful in his younger days?'

"'I don't rightly know about fanciful, sir. He's as superstitious a man as ever I knew, and more afeared of spirits than most. Always has been. But sir, I've a mind to tell you something else about these spells the Colonel been having.'

"'Yes?'

"'Only this, Doctor,' and his low voice sunk to a whisper. 'That first time as he had a vision, I set it down for a dream. Mister Patrick's always been more keen on the bogeymen than I have, sir, and I paid it no mind. But after the second bad spell—the one where he saw the Tejano stabbing the soldier—he went and showed me something that he didn't show the others.'

"'What was it?'

"He walked over to where the Colonel now slept and pointed at a gash in the old uniform's breast, where the garment had been carefully mended.

"'The day Mister Patrick told me about that dream was the same day I mended this here hole in his shirt. Thought himself crazy, he did, and I can't say as I blame him. Because this hole is in exactly the spot where he dreamed the Tejano stabbed the Texian the night before. What do you think of that, sir?'

"'I've no idea what to think of it,' I replied. 'It is most peculiar.'

"'Then there's this third vision,' he went on patiently. 'The one he had last night. Says he saw a band of 'em with torches, marching toward him like a pack of demons. I don't know about that. But I sure know that yesterday morning, when I went to light a fire in the library, half our kindling was missing. Clean gone, sir. Didn't make much of it at the time, but this puts it in another light.'"

Sherlock Holmes, who had changed postures a gratifying number of times during my account, rubbed his long hands together avidly before clapping them once.

"It's splendid, my dear fellow. Positively first-class. The room was very bare indeed, you say?"

"Yes. Even in the midst of wealth, he lived like a soldier."

"I don't suppose you can tell me what you saw outside the window?"

I hesitated, reflecting as best I could.

"There was nothing outside the window, for I made certain to look. Jefferson assured me that he examined the grounds near the house after he discovered the missing firewood, and found no sign of unusual traffic. When I asked after an odd hole, he mentioned a tall lilac had been torn out from under the window weeks previous because it blocked the light, but that cannot have had any bearing. As I said, the bed faced the wall, not the window."

Holmes tilted his head back with a light laugh. "Yes, you did say that, and I assure you I am coming to a greater appreciation of your skills as an investigator. What happened next?"

"I quit the house soon afterward. The younger Warburtons were anxious to know what had transpired in the sick room, and I comforted them that their uncle was asleep, and unlikely to suffer another such outburst that day. But I assured them all, including Jefferson, that I would return the following afternoon to check on my patient.

"As I departed, I could not help but notice another man walking up the side path leading to the back door. He was very bronzed, with a long handlebar moustache, unkempt black hair, and he dressed in simple trousers and a rough linen shirt of the kind the Mexican laborers wore. This swarthy fellow paid me no mind, but walked straight ahead, and I seized the opportunity to memorize his looks in case he should come to have any bearing on the matter. I did not know what to make of the Colonel's ghostly affliction or Jefferson's bizarre account of its physical manifestation, but I thought it an odd enough coincidence to note.

"The next day, I saw a patient or two in the afternoon and then locked my practice, hailing a hack to take me up Nob Hill. Jefferson greeted me at the door and led me into a study of sorts, shelves stacked with gold-lettered military volumes and historical works. Colonel Warburton stood there dressed quite normally, in a grey summer suit, and he seemed bewildered by his own behavior the day before.

"'It's a bona fide curse, I can't help but think, and I'm suffering to end it,' he said to me. 'There are times I know I'm not in my right senses, and other times when I can see those wretched visions before me as clear as your face is now.'

"'Is there anything else you can tell me which might help in my diagnosis?'

"'Not that won't make me out to be cracked in the head, Dr. Watson. After every one of these living nightmares, I've awakened with the same pain in my head, and I can't for the life of me decide whether I've imagined the whole thing, or I really am haunted by one of the men I killed during the war in Texas. Affairs were that muddled—I've no doubt I came out on one or more of the wrong Tejanos. So much bloodshed in those days, no man has the luxury of knowing he was always in the right.'

"'I am no expert in disorders of the mind,' I warned him, 'although I will do all I can for you. You ought to consult a specialist if your symptoms persist or worsen. May I have your permission, however, to ask a seemingly unrelated question?'

"'By all means.'

"'Have you in your employ, or do any of your servants or gardeners occasionally hire, Mexican workers?'

"He seemed quite puzzled by the question. 'I don't happen to have any Hispanos on my payroll. And when the staff need day labor, they almost always engage Chinese. They're quick and honest, and they come cheap. Why do you ask?'

"I convinced him that my question had been purely clinical, congratulated him on his recovery, and made my way to the foyer, mulling several new ideas over in my brain. Jefferson appeared to see me out, handing me my hat and stick.

"'Where are the other members of the household today?' I inquired.

"'Miss Molly is out paying calls, and Mister Charles is working in his darkroom.'

"'Jefferson, I saw a rather mysterious fellow yesterday as I was leaving. To your knowledge, are any men of Mexican or Chileno descent ever hired by the groundskeeper?'

"I would swear to you, Holmes, that a strange glow lit his eyes when I posed that question, but he merely shook his head. 'Anyone does any hiring, Dr. Watson, I know all about it. And no one of that type been asking after work here for six months and more.'

"'I was merely curious whether the sight of such a man had upset the Colonel,' I explained, 'but as you know, he is much better today. I am no closer to tracing the source of his affliction, but I hope that if anything new occurs, or if you are ever in doubt, you will contact me.'

"'These spells, they come and they go, Dr. Watson,' Jefferson replied, 'but if I discover anything, I'll surely let you know of it.'

"When I quit the house, I set myself a brisk pace, for I thought to walk down the hill as evening fell. But just as I began my descent, and the wind picked up from the west, I saw not twenty yards ahead of me the same sun-burnished laborer I'd spied the day before, attired in the same fashion, and clearly having emerged from some part of the Warburton residence moments previous. The very sight of him roused my blood; I had not yet met you, of course, and thus knew nothing whatever of detective work, but some instinct told me to follow him to determine whether the Colonel was the victim of a malignant design."

"You followed him?" Holmes interjected, with a startled expression. "Whatever for?"

"I felt I had no choice — the parallels between his presence and Colonel Warburton's nightmares had to be explained."

"Ever the man of action." My friend shook his head. "Where did he lead you?"

"When he reached Broadway, where the land flattened and the

mansions gave way to grocers, butcheries, and cigar shops, he stopped to mount a streetcar. By a lucky chance, I hailed a passing hack and ordered the driver to follow the streetcar until I called for him to stop.

"My quarry went nearly as far as the waterfront before he descended, and in a trice I paid my driver and set off in pursuit toward the base of Telegraph Hill. During the Gold Rush days, the ocean-facing slope had been a tent colony of Chilenos and Peruanos. That colony intermixed with the lowest hell of them all on its eastern flank: Sydney-Town, where the escaped Australian convicts and ticket-of-leave men ran the vilest public houses imaginable. It is a matter of historical record that the Fierce Grizzly employed a live bear chained outside its door."

"I have heard of that district," Holmes declared keenly. "The whole of it is known as the Barbary Coast, is it not? I confess I should have liked to see it in its prime, although there are any number of streets in London I can visit should I wish to take my life in my hands. You did not yourself encounter any wild beasts?"

"Not in the strictest sense; but inside of ten minutes, I found myself passing gin palaces that could have rivaled St. Giles for depravity. The gaslights appeared sickly and meager, and riotous men stumbled from one red-curtained den of thieves to the next, either losing their money willingly by gambling it away, or drinking from the wrong glass only to find themselves propped insensate in an alley the next morning without a cent to their name.

"At one point I thought I had lost sight of him, for a drayman's cart came between us, and at the same moment he ducked into one of the deadfalls. I soon ascertained where he had gone, however, and after a moment's hesitation entered the place myself.

"The light shone from cheap tallow candles and ancient kerosene lamps with dark purple shades. Losing no time, I approached the man and asked if I could speak with him.

"He stared at me silently, his dark eyes narrowed into slits. At last, he signaled the barman for a second drink, and handed me a small glass of clear liquor.

"I thanked him, but he remained dumb. 'Do you speak English?' I inquired finally.

"He grinned, and with an easy motion of his wrist flicked back his drink and set the empty glass on the bar. 'I speak it as well as you, *señor.* My name is Juan Portillo. What do you want?'

"'I want to know why you visited the Warburton residence yesterday, and again this afternoon.'

"His smile broadened even further. 'Ah, now I understand. You follow me?'

"'There have been suspicious events at that house, ones which I have reason to believe may concern you.'

"'I know nothing of suspicious events. They hire me to do a job, and to be quiet. So I am quiet.'

"'I must warn you that if you attempt to harm the Colonel in any way, you will answer for it to me.'

"He nodded at me coldly, still smiling. 'Finish your drink, *señor.* And then I will show you something.'

"I had seen the saloon keeper pour my liquor from the same bottle as his, and thus could not object to drinking it. The stuff was strong as gin, but warmer, and left a fiery burn in the throat. I had barely finished it when Portillo drew out of some hidden pocket a very long, mother-of-pearl-handled knife.

"'I never harm the Colonel. I never even see this Colonel. But I tell you something anyway. Men who follow me, they answer to this,' he said, lifting the knife.

"He snarled something in Spanish. Three men, who had been sitting at a round table several yards away, stood up and strode toward us. Two carried pistols in their belts, and one tapped a short, stout cudgel in his hand. I was evaluating whether to make do with the bowie knife I kept on my person, or cut my losses and attempt an escape, when one of the men stopped short.

"'*Es el Doctor!* Dr. Watson, yes?' he said eagerly.

"After a moment's astonishment, I recognized a patient I had treated not two weeks before even though he could not pay me, a man who had gashed his leg so badly in a fight on the wharf, his friends had carried him to the nearest physician. He was profoundly happy to see me, a torrent of Spanish flowing from his lips, and before two minutes had passed of him gesturing proudly at his wound and pointing at me, Portillo's dispute had been forgotten. I did not press my luck, but joined them for another glass of that wretched substance and bade them farewell, Portillo's unblinking black eyes upon me until I was out of the bar and making for Front Street with all speed.

"The next day, I determined to report Portillo's presence to the Colonel, for as little as I understood, I now believed him an even more sinister character. To my dismay, however, I found the house in a terrible uproar."

"I am not surprised," Holmes nodded. "What had happened?"

"Sam Jefferson stood accused of breaking into Charles Warburton's darkroom with the intent to steal his photographic apparatus. The servant who opened the door to me was hardly lucid for her tears, and I heard cruel vituperations even from outside the house. Apparently, or so the downstairs maid said in her state of near-hysterics, Charles had already sacked Jefferson, but the Colonel was livid his nephew had acted without his approval, theft or no theft, and at the very moment I knocked, they were locked in a violent quarrel. From where I stood, I could hear Colonel Warburton screaming that Jefferson be recalled, and Charles shouting back that he had already suffered enough indignities in that house to last him a lifetime. Come now, Holmes, admit to me that the tale is entirely unique," I could not help but add, for the flush of color in my friend's face told me precisely how deeply he was interested.

"It is not the ideal word," he demurred. "I have not yet heard all, but there were cases in Lisbon and Salzburg within the last fifty years which may possibly have some bearing. Please, finish your story. You left, of course, for what gentleman could remain in such circumstances, and you called the next day upon the Colonel."

"I did not, as a matter of fact, call upon the Colonel."

"No? Your natural curiosity did not get the better of you?"

"When I arrived the following morning, Colonel Warburton as well as Sam Jefferson had vanished into thin air."

I had expected this revelation to strike like a bolt from the firmament, but was destined for disappointment.

"Ha," Holmes said with the trace of a smile. "Had they indeed?"

"Molly and Charles Warburton were beside themselves with worry. The safe had been opened and many deeds and securities, not to mention paper currency, were missing. There was no sign of force, so they theorized that their uncle had been compelled or convinced to provide the combination.

"A search party set out at once, of course, and descriptions of Warburton and Jefferson circulated, but to no avail. The mad Colonel and his servant, either together or separately, voluntarily or against their wills, quit the city without leaving a single clue behind them. Upon my evidence, the police brought Portillo in for questioning, but he proved a conclusive alibi and could not be charged. And so Colonel Warburton's obsession with war, as well as the inscrutable designs of his manservant, remain to this day unexplained.

"What do you think of it?" I finished triumphantly, for Holmes by this time leaned forward in his chair, entirely engrossed.

"I think that Sam Jefferson — apart from you and your noble intentions, my dear fellow — was quite the hero of this tale."

"How can you mean?" I asked, puzzled. "Surely the darkroom incident casts him in an extremely suspicious light. All we know is that he disappeared, probably with the Colonel, and the rumor in San Francisco told that they were both stolen away by the Tejano ghost who possessed the house. That is rubbish, of course, but even now I cannot think where they went, or why."

"It is impossible to know where they vanished," Holmes replied, his grey eyes sparkling, "but I can certainly tell you why."

"Dear God, you have solved it?" I exclaimed in delight. "You cannot be in earnest — I've wracked my brain over it all these years to no avail. What the devil happened?"

"First of all, Watson, I fear I must relieve you of a misapprehension. I believe Molly and Charles Warburton were the authors of a nefarious and subtle plot which, if not for your intervention and Sam Jefferson's, might well have succeeded."

"How could you know that?"

"Because you have told me, my dear fellow, and a very workmanlike job you did in posting me up. Ask yourself when the Colonel's mental illness first began. What was his initial symptom?"

"He changed his will."

"It is, you will own, a very telling starting point. So telling, in fact, that we must pay it the most stringent attention." Holmes jumped to his feet and commenced pacing the carpet like a mathematician expounding over a theorem. "Now, there are very few steps — criminal or otherwise — one can take when one is disinherited. Forgery is a viable option, and the most common. Murder is out, unless your victim has yet to sign his intentions into effect. The Warburtons hit upon a scheme as cunning as it is rare: they undertook to prove a sane man mad."

"But, Holmes, that can scarcely be possible."

"I admit that fortune was undoubtedly in their favor. The Colonel already suffered from an irrational preoccupation with the supernatural. Additionally, his bedroom lacked any sort of ornament, and young Charles Warburton specialized in photographic technique."

"My dear chap, you know I've the utmost respect for your remarkable faculty, but I cannot fathom a word of what you just said," I confessed.

"I shall do better, then," he laughed. "Have we any reason to think Jefferson lied when he told you of the ghost's earthly manifestations?"

"He could have meant anything by it. He could have slit that hole and stolen that firewood himself."

"Granted. But it was after you told him of Portillo's presence that he broke into the photography studio."

"You see a connection between Portillo and Charles Warburton's photographs?"

"Decidedly so, as well as a connection between the photographs, the blank wall, and the torn-out lilac bush."

"Holmes, that doesn't even—"

I stopped myself as an idea dawned on me. Finally, after the passage of many years, I was beginning to understand.

"You are talking about a magic lantern," I said slowly. "By God, I have been so blind."

"You were remarkably astute, my boy, for you took note of every essential detail. As a matter of fact, I believe you can take it from here," he added with more than his usual grace.

"The Colonel disinherited his niece and nephew, possibly because he abhorred their mercenary natures, in favor of war charities," I stated hesitantly. "In a stroke of brilliance, they decided to make it seem war was his mania and he could not be allowed to so slight his kin. Charles hired Juan Portillo to appear in a series of photographs as a Tejano soldier, and promised that he would be paid handsomely if he kept the sessions dead secret. The nephew developed the images onto glass slides and projected them through a magic lantern device outside the window in the dead of night. His victim was so terrified by the apparition on his wall, he never thought to look for its source behind him. The first picture, threatening the white woman, likely featured Molly Warburton. But for the second plate . . . ."

"That of the knife plunging into the Texian's chest, they borrowed the Colonel's old garb and probably placed it on a dummy. The firewood disappeared when a number of men assembled, further off on the grounds, to portray rebels with torches. The lilac, as is obvious—"

"Stood in the way of the magic lantern apparatus," I cried. "What could be simpler?"

"And the headaches the Colonel experienced afterward?" my friend prodded me.

"Likely an aftereffect of an opiate or narcotic his family added to his meal in order to heighten the experience of the vision in his bedchamber."

"And Sam Jefferson?"

"A deeply underestimated opponent who saw the Warburtons for what they were and kept a constant watch. The only thing he stole was a look at the plates in Charles's studio as his final piece of evidence. When they sent him packing, he told the Colonel all he knew and they—"

"Were never heard from again," Holmes finished with a poetic flourish.

"In fact, it was the perfect revenge," I laughed. "Colonel Warburton had no interest in his own wealth, and he took more than enough to live from the safe. And after all, when he was finally declared dead, his estate was distributed just as he wished it."

"Yes, a number of lucky events occurred. I am grateful, as I confess I have been at other times, that you are an utterly decent fellow, my dear Doctor."

"I don't understand," I said in some confusion.

"I see the world in terms of cause and effect. If you had not been the sort of man willing to treat a rogue wounded in a knife fight who had no means of paying you, it is possible you would not have had the opportunity to tell me this story."

"It wasn't so simple as all that," I muttered, rather abashed, "but thank—"

"And an admirable story it was too. You know, Watson," Holmes continued, extinguishing his pipe, "from all I have heard of America, it must be an exceedingly fertile ground for men of mettle. The place lives almost mythically in the estimations of most Englishmen. I myself have scarcely met an American, ethically inclined or otherwise, who did not possess a certain audacity of mind."

"It's the pioneer in them, I suppose. Still, I cannot help but think that you are more than a match for anyone, American or other-wise," I assured him.

"I would not presume to contradict you, but that vast expanse boasts more than its share of crime as well as of imagination, and for that reason commands some respect. I am not a complete stranger to the American criminal," he said with a smile.

"I should be delighted to hear you expound on that subject," I exclaimed, glancing longingly at my notebook and pen.

"Another time, perhaps." My friend paused, his long fingers drumming along with the drops as he stared out our front window, eyes glittering brighter than the rain-soaked street below. "Perhaps one day we may both find occasion to test ourselves further on their soil." He glanced back at me abruptly. "I should have liked to have met this Sam Jefferson, for instance. He had a decided talent."

"Talent or no, he was there to witness the events; you solved them based on a secondhand account by a man who'd never so much as heard of the Science of Deduction at the time."

"There are precious few crimes in this world, merely a hundred million variations," he shrugged. "It was a fetching little problem, however, no matter it was not matchless. The use of the magic lan-tern, although I will never prove it, I believe to have been abso-lutely inspired. Now," he proclaimed, striding to his violin and picking it up, "if you would be so kind as to locate the brandy and cigars you mentioned earlier, I will show my appreciation by enter-taining you in turn. You've come round to my liking for Kreutzer, I think? Capital. I must thank you for bringing your very interesting case to my attention; I shall lose no time informing my brother I solved it without moving a muscle. And now, friend Watson, we shall continue our efforts to enliven a dreary afternoon."

GAR ANTHONY HAYWOOD

The First Rule Is

FROM *Black Noir*

"WHY YOU ALWAYS HATIN' ON THE MAN LIKE THAT?" Caprice asked, sounding like her feelings were hurt. "What'd he ever do to you?"

"He ain't done nothin' to me. But he ain't done nothin' for me, neither," C.C. said. "He ain't done nothin' for nobody, 'cept hisself."

Caprice thought about arguing with him, but she could see just from the way he was stretched out all over the couch, Seven-and-Seven held loosely in his left hand, feet dangling over the side, that her man was in one of his moods again. Say one word too many running contrary to his opinion now and your ass could wind up in the emergency room, trying to tell the doctors where it hurt through a mouth full of broken teeth.

She didn't understand C.C.'s problem with Miracle Miles and she never would. Wasn't Miracle on the television right now, four years after retiring from a decade-long, championship-studded career in professional basketball, bragging on the latest big shopping center he was helping to put up in the 'hood? Wasn't Miracle — smart, funny, and fine as a black man could ever be — what "giving back to the community" was all about?

Not in C.C.'s mind, he wasn't. C.C. could see Miracle for what he really was and had always been, just an overhyped baller with a shuck-and-jive grin white folks couldn't get enough of. From his earliest playing days in high school, they'd given him a fancy nickname and treated him like a superstar, paving the road with gold for him, first in college and then in the pros, just because he could dribble the rock between his legs and shoot a mini-mini-skyhook. But underneath all the bullshit he wasn't nothin' but a lucky punk, always in the right place at the right time to get paid. C.C. knew this for a fact because he'd seen the nigga long before all the hype set in, when Miracle was just a mediocre, sixteen-year-old point guard out of Princeton Heights High in Oakland named Stegman Miles.

He had game, yeah, but he wasn't all that. C.C. was the one who was all that. C.C. was running point for Jefferson back in those days, and there wasn't anything Stegman Miles could do that C.C. couldn't do better. C.C. could penetrate, dish, *and* shoot, from damn near anywhere on the court, and if he had to he could throw a little defense down on a fool too. Miles got more attention because he played what the reporters liked to call a more "disciplined" game, creating fewer turnovers while hitting the boards with greater intensity, but there was no doubt in C.C.'s mind he was the better player. He made All-City three years in a row and led Jefferson to the State Finals twice, and the second time around he got his chance to show folks who the real "miracle" man was. Jefferson and Princeton Heights went head-to-head and C.C. took Miles apart, outscoring him 32–18. Despite Miles's fourteen assists and nine rebounds, Jefferson won the game, and anybody who'd watched it would have had to see that Stegman Miles wasn't half the baller C.C. Cooper was.

Which C.C. would have gone on to prove, in both college and the pros, over and over again, had he not gotten himself shot, three weeks into his senior year at Jeff. He'd made a dumb mistake, let his boys talk him into trying to jack a Mexican ice cream vendor who, it turned out, liked to keep a nine on a shelf right beneath the service window of his truck, and that was the end of C.C.'s career. The bullet hit him just below his right kneecap and blew his leg up, left just enough muscle and bone behind for the doctors to sew back together.

Becoming a pro baller was the only ambition C.C. had ever known, and once it went away, so did any effort he might have made to stay out of trouble with the law. He'd always had an appreciation for the thug life and probably would have continued down that road no matter what; some things, even money couldn't change. But it seemed to C.C. that a nigga with a limp who barely qualified for a job busing dishes had no other choice but to be a gangster. You wanted to survive, to enjoy even the smallest taste of the good life, you had to take what the world didn't give you. So that's what C.C. did, finding only fleeting relief from his constant pain and outrage in boning, getting high, and scoring a few dollars here and there by committing petty crimes.

Meanwhile, Miracle Miles was becoming an American sports icon, collecting diamond-studded championship rings and million-dollar endorsement checks the way C.C. collected court appearances. He was flashy, he was upbeat, and he was a winner, just the kind of harmless black man white folks loved to idolize. As the years went by, C.C. watched him grow bigger and bigger, fame and bank account inflating in tandem like goddamn blimps threatening to black out the sky, and smoldered with resentment. It should have been him. Everything Miracle had should have belonged to C.C.

He had hoped it would all end when Miracle's playing days were over, that in retirement the nigga would blow all his bank and dwindle down to a fat, forgotten has-been, just as so many ex-athletes had before him. But to C.C.'s amazement, only the reverse occurred. Rather than kick back and party when he quit the game, Miracle simply moved on to a new one: big business. He took the money he made in ball and invested it in real estate, showing more smarts for retail development than he had for basketball, and hell if the punk didn't become phatter than ever. Now he was getting paid not to shoot the rock and smile on billboards, but to write books and give lectures, teach Fortune 500 CEOs how to do on Wall Street what he used to do on the court.

C.C.'s mother, the crazy bitch, had even bought him one of Miracle's books as a birthday present last month, thinking it would inspire him to get a job and straighten up. *The Miracle Rule Book* the shit was called; *How to Win in Business Without Having to Foul.* C.C. would have died laughing if he hadn't been so pissed. He threw the book across the living room after unwrapping it and didn't look at it again for four days. Then he picked it up, took it out to the back yard to trash it, and started reading it instead. He could read when he wanted to, he wasn't as illiterate as people thought, and now he wanted to. In spite of his hatred for the man, he was curious: was there really anything Miracles Miles could tell him about making coin he didn't already know?

In the end, the answer was no. It was the same old shit C.C.

had heard a million times before, *you gotta spend money to make money, study the market, timing is everything,* yadda-yadda-yadda. And of course, it was all delivered as one big basketball metaphor, Miracle offering the reader his own personal "rules of the game" as if putting mini-mall development deals together and makin' a no-look pass on the fast break were one and the same fucking thing. C.C. got as far as Chapter Three, then slammed the book shut and tossed it under his bed like a dirty sock, never to be thought of again.

Until moments like this one, anyway, when Miracle Miles was in the news again and there was no place on Earth a nigga could go to avoid hearin' about it. Here he was on ESPN—*ESPN!*—breaking ground at the site of his latest inner-city L.A. shopping center project, flashing teeth at the camera like a goddamn car salesman. Yeah, he was bringing name-brand retail stores to the community, but it wasn't the community he was thinkin' about. It was all the duckets he was gonna make in the process, same as always. Why was C.C. the only person in the world who could see through this fool?

"I'm gonna go over to Lottie's," Caprice said, getting up from her chair in the apartment's little dining room.

"Nah," C.C. said, still watching the television.

"What you mean, 'nah'?"

"I mean you ain't goin'. Soon as this is over, we gonna get busy."

Caprice sighed and sat back down, too experienced in the ways of her man to argue with him. "Why don't you turn it off now, then? You hate Miracle so bad, why you wanna keep watchin' it?"

"'Cause it's givin' me an idea."

"What—"

"Shut up and get your ass to the bedroom," C.C. said, reaching for the remote to kill the TV. Behind him, Caprice stood up and left the room, sulking in well-advised silence. She didn't need to know nothin' yet, but when he was ready, C.C. would tell the bitch what he was thinkin'.

She wouldn't like it, bein' a Miracle Miles fan and all, but she was gonna help him fuck the nigga up all the same.

The first thing Jerry Dunston did upon hearing that Butterby's was about to go into business with Miracle Miles was buy a basketball. It

was the first one he'd ever owned and would almost certainly be
the last. Jerry hated sports in general, and basketball in particular;
any game overpopulated by dope-smoking, tattoo-wearing, inartic-
ulate black guys who made more money in an hour than Jerry
made in a month was not his idea of entertainment.

Butterby's was one of the largest restaurant chains in the western
United States and Jerry was their rising star, a franchise salesman
only three years out of Stanford whose gift for gab seemed to be
adaptable to any need. Nobody could fake interest in something
he actually found thoroughly irrelevant or, worse, most suitable for
morons, better than he. Jerry would walk into a conference room,
chat like a giddy authority on whatever subject was most likely to be
near and dear to a client's heart, and then walk out again, usually
with the mesmerized client's money and misplaced affection firmly
in hand. If a viper could change colors like a chameleon, his manager Lou Merrill was fond of saying, that would be Jerry.

But feigning common interests with prospective clients and business partners was not Jerry Dunston's only patented sales tactic.
He also played some tricks of the trade that Lou would not have
found quite so amusing, as sensitive to outdated matters of ethics
as the old fool was. For one thing, Jerry liked to tweak spreadsheets
to exaggerate both Butterby's sales figures and the demographic
breakdown of its customer base, the latter to better meet a client's
likely priorities. If, for example, a client was looking for Butterby's
to appeal to a younger crowd, Jerry would fudge the numbers
to lend that appearance. Further, he had learned to commit the
fraud in such a way that, if caught, he could write the discrepancy
off as a software glitch, an innocent mistake that could easily be
corrected by pulling the offending report again. It was risky, but
almost always worthwhile, and he reserved its use in any case for
those clients he had judged to be either too green or too dense to
catch on.

In his earliest dealings with Miracle Miles's people, Jerry had
run this numbers game, confident that they wouldn't know the difference. Harvard-educated or no, they were underlings to a former
jock, a man to whom Butterby's was only giving the time of day because of the incredible name recognition he'd created by doing
spectacular things with a basketball over a twelve-year career. How
sophisticated could they really be? And as for Miles himself, he was

smart, sure; he had to be to have come this far in the dog-eat-dog commercial real estate game. But this idea some people had that he was a genius, a natural-born businessman with a mind on a par with those of all but a few Fortune 500 CEOs, was a crock. Miles was a likable college dropout with deep pockets and fortuitous instincts, nothing more and nothing less.

In any case, it was Miles's practice to let his people do all the heavy lifting, only inserting himself into negotiations when it was time to parry over the small details. Hence, following months of discussion, and weeks after a tentative agreement between Butterby's and Miraculous Enterprises, Inc., had been reached to bring Miracle Miles–branded Butterby's restaurants to various inner-city locations on the West Coast, Jerry was going to meet the man himself for the first time today. His fellows at Butterby's were beside themselves with excitement, but Jerry couldn't care less; were it his decision to make, he wouldn't be doing business with Miles at all. So what if Miles needed partnerships with franchises like Butterby's to get retail centers built in underserved urban areas? Butterby's was in business to make money, not revitalize the ghetto.

Still, a sale was a sale, and it was incumbent upon Jerry now to close this one with a bang. Asking Miles to autograph a basketball just before the meeting commenced was his idea of kissing the man's ass to maximum effect. He could have just bought a cheap rubber job at a local sporting goods store for fifteen bucks, but what he did instead was go online to drop $400 on an official game ball Miles had already signed. It wasn't enough for Jerry to appear to be a casual fan; he wanted Miles to think he was a fanatical one.

And hell if Miles didn't grin like a fool when Jerry popped the question in the Butterby's conference room, thrusting the ball and a Sharpie toward him. These jocks ate up public adulation the same way they snorted cocaine, Jerry thought; getting on their good side was as easy as teaching a smart dog to sit. Lou Merrill and Dan Kuramura, the other Butterby's execs in the room, looked on almost incredulously, having never seen Jerry exhibit the slightest interest in basketball before, but neither man said a word.

"I feel silly as hell doing this," Jerry said, gushing, "but I can't help it. If you could write something personally to me on this, Miracle, I'd really appreciate it."

Miles laughed, genuinely amused, and took the ball. "No problem. What's your name?"

"Jerry Dunston," Arvin Petrie said. A young, no-nonsense black man with the pinched, narrow face of a prosecuting attorney, Petrie was the Miraculous Enterprises exec with whom Jerry had been negotiating up to now.

Miles gave Petrie a look and raised an eyebrow. "This is our boy Jerry?"

Petrie nodded.

"Well, damn," Miles said, turning his famous megawatt smile upon Jerry again. "This will really be my pleasure."

Jerry didn't understand what he meant, but he didn't bother asking him to explain; if for some reason Petrie had been talking Jerry up earlier, that was all to the better. He watched Miles use the Sharpie to scrawl something unintelligible on the basketball, just above his signature, then took it back when it was offered.

"'Y-F-W-T-W-N'? What's that mean?" Jerry asked, curious.

But before Miles could answer, Petrie said, "I think we'd better get started," directing the comment at Lou Merrill, and Jerry's manager agreed with a nod.

They all took their seats at the conference table and got down to business. For nearly an hour, nothing seemed amiss, all the conversation following the predictable formalities of a major deal closing. But then the moment came to ink the contracts and things took an unexpected turn. Petrie intercepted the paperwork as Lou Merrill tried to pass it over to Miles, the expression on his face reaching even greater depths of solemnity, and said, "There's just one small amendment that'll need to be made here before Mr. Miles signs off."

Lou couldn't believe he was hearing right. He looked first to Miles for help, then to Jerry, but the former was unresponsive and the latter could only shrug.

"I don't understand."

Off a nod from Miles, Petrie produced a folder from his briefcase and slid it across the table toward the Butterby's VP.

"Back in my playing days," Miles said, "I learned to do something that I've carried over to my business practice. Before every road game in the playoffs, I'd dribble a ball all around the court, looking for dead spots in the floor. 'Cause if you hit one during a crucial part of the game, if could really mess you up, create a turnover you couldn't recover from." He turned to look directly at Jerry. "Gentlemen, I'm afraid you've got a dead spot on your floor."

Lou Merrill opened the folder Petrie had passed him and began scanning the pages within, his face growing more grim by the minute.

"What's going on?" Jerry asked, annoyed.

"I'm sure you must be wondering how my people got hold of deal memos that could only have come from Mr. Dunston's computer," Miles said to Lou, ignoring Jerry's question completely. "But all I'll say in response to that is that we have our resources, and what they were in this case should be irrelevant to you. The only thing you should really care about is what those memos prove about Mr. Dunston's apparent reluctance to treat all your clients and partners equally, and what Butterby's stands to lose if you allow him to continue working for you."

"I said, what the hell is going on?" Jerry asked again, leaping to his feet now. His shirt collar was soaked through with sweat.

Looking like a widower at his wife's funeral, Lou slid the folder of documents off to one side to let Dan Kuramura look them over and said to Jerry, "He's right. You've been juicing our numbers."

"What? That's crazy!"

Jerry reached across the table to snatch the documents out of Kuramura's grasp and started examining them himself. It was impossible, but he recognized them immediately, and all at once, the blood pounding through his head grew still.

"These are fakes," he said feebly. "There's no way—"

"We can't tell you who you can or cannot employ, of course," Petrie said, and Jerry looked over to see that both he and Miles were on their feet now, essentially calling the meeting to a close, "but we can take Mr. Miles's offer to partner with you off the table if Mr. Dunston is still drawing a Butterby's paycheck by the end of business day this Friday. It's entirely up to you."

And without another word, he and Miles started for the door.

On their way out, Miles peeled off to approach Jerry, who like a whipped dog involuntarily withdrew, not at all sure the man was above putting his fist through Jerry's face.

"You fucked with the wrong nigga," Miles whispered in his ear, winking. Then he flashed a particularly wicked version of his trademark smile and led Petrie out.

Hours later, sitting in a Butterby's executive office he could no longer call his own, Jerry was wondering how much of his $400 he could get back for the worthless basketball Miles had inscribed with the letters "YFWTWN" when the acronym suddenly made sense. Whether or not a "genius" lurked behind the House Negro effervescence of Miracle Miles, Jerry still couldn't say, but he knew for certain now that a killer most certainly did.

"I don't wanna do this," Caprice said again, for what had to be the ten-thousandth time, and C.C. had to give the girl props for courage, because the last time she'd said it, he'd almost taken her fool head off.

"I'm gonna tell you one last time: ain't nobody gonna hurt 'im," C.C. said.

"If somethin' goes wrong—"

"Ain't nothin' gonna go wrong. Long as you do exactly what I tol' you, ain't nothin' gonna go wrong."

Caprice didn't say anything more, but the pitiful look on her face said it was going to take an act of God to convince her. C.C. was planning to rob Miracle Miles at gunpoint tonight outside a Hollywood bookstore, using Caprice as bait, and even a high school dropout like Caprice knew how often things like that ended up with somebody getting killed.

Still, help C.C. she would because the alternative was to get beat so bad she'd probably wish she were dead herself. Her role in the plan as C.C. described it was fairly simple. Miracle never went anywhere alone, C.C. said; a bodyguard and a driver, at least, always accompanied Miracle to such events. The bodyguard would follow Miracle inside and stay with him during the signing, but the driver would likely stay out in the parking lot with the car. Caprice's job was to distract the driver just long enough for C.C. to slip inside the car only moments before Miracle was about to return to it. C.C. would quickly relieve the surprised fool of his cash on hand and jet, neither Miracle's driver nor his bodyguard wanting to try fucking with a man with a gun in the close confines of a limo. And Caprice? By the time the police or anybody else put her and C.C. together, he said, they'd both be long gone.

During the drive out to Hollywood, spilling all out of her best black dress like a whore with a rent bill due, Caprice practiced her controlled breathing and asked God to watch over them both.

C.C. was usually late for everything but this time they were early, arriving at the store over an hour before Miles was scheduled to start signing books. Still, a crowd was already forming inside and Caprice could feel her stomach lurching around like a bouncing waterbed.

"Why we gotta get here so early?"

"'Cause I wanna see who the nigga has with 'im and where his car's gonna be."

"But what're we supposed to do 'til he's ready to leave?"

"Same thing everybody else'll be doin'. Lookin' at books."

"We're goin' *inside?*"

C.C. glared at her. "I shouldn't have'ta explain my reasonin' to you, Caprice. And if I didn't need you lookin' good tonight, I'd slap you in your mouth just for askin' me to. We're goin' inside 'cause we gotta know when he's gettin' ready to come out, remember? This thing's gotta be timed just right or it won't work. All right? You understand now?"

She did, but she didn't like it. The whole thing was beginning to sound crazier and crazier to her.

Caprice entered the store a few minutes later, alone, as C.C. stayed outside to wait for Miles to show. She had almost a half-hour to kill, a packed house filling the space around her at an alarming rate, and she could only feign interest in books whose titles she could barely read for so long. She became increasingly certain that one of the staff, a middle-aged white man with the face and form of a scarecrow, was watching her intently, his right hand at the ready to grab the phone and call for security. She was about to flee, desperate for C.C.'s assurances that her fears were all in her head, when the celebrity they'd all been waiting for finally appeared.

Caprice heard a murmur from the crowd build to a dull roar and when she turned around, there he was, Miracle himself, walking through the door like a king entering his throne room. He was bigger than she could have ever imagined, towering over everyone as he slowly made his way to the table piled high with books that awaited him in the back, and his broad-shouldered, pale yellow suit fit his chiseled body with mouth-watering precision. He was smiling, of course, turning this way and that so that no one went untouched by his good cheer, and he even bumped fists with a few lucky people in the crowd.

Swooning, Caprice put a hand out to the wall beside her to keep herself from fainting.

Miracle finally reached his place at the table and sat down, and only then did Caprice notice that, just as C.C. had predicted, he wasn't alone. A brother as big and impenetrable as a cinder-block wall had come in with him, his face a humorless etching in stone. Standing now at Miracle's left shoulder as Miracle chatted up the store's manager, the big man stared straight ahead and crossed his hands in front of him, waiting for a reason to defend his employer to the death.

The sight of this giant brought Caprice back to reality with a thud and, remembering why she was here, she glanced over her shoulder to find C.C. standing at the tail end of the crowd, just inside the door. He smiled as if to say all was well and then gave his head an almost imperceptible shake, warning her off any further eye contact. Caprice turned back around, heart in her throat, and pretended to listen as the impish blond bookstore manager introduced Miracle Miles to his audience.

When she was done, the room erupted in applause and Miles began to talk about his book, selling it the way he sold everything else, with large doses of homespun charm and self-effacing humor. Any other time, Caprice would have been enthralled, but not tonight; tonight she was busy trying to keep her dinner from climbing back up into her throat. She liked this man. She admired this man. He was a hero to her, just as he was to thousands of other people, black and white. But in less than an hour's time, if she valued her life, she was going to help C.C. jack him for all the money on his person.

Or worse.

It was the "or worse" part that Caprice ultimately couldn't stop worrying over, because nothing ever came easy to Curtis "C.C." Charles and she couldn't imagine why this wack scheme of his should be any different. If it blew up in his face and Miles got killed somehow, Caprice knew she'd never be able to live with the guilt. She'd done a lot of fucked-up things in her life, to be sure, but she wasn't a bad person. Asking her to help him commit a crime that could wind up being the murder of a great man like Miracle Miles was more than C.C. had a right to do. No matter how much she loved him, and God knew she did love his pitiful ass, Caprice didn't owe C.C. as much as all this.

Emboldened by some power she didn't understand, she turned around and started to march out of the store.

Miles was still speaking but heads turned toward her all the same, so conspicuous was her desperation to depart. She didn't have to look at him to know that C.C. was staring daggers at her. Nonetheless, she kept her head down and kept moving, not stopping until the inevitable happened.

"Where the fuck you think you're goin'?" C.C. hissed at her under his breath, his right hand like a vise on her arm. Only the handful of people in their vicinity were paying them any attention so far, but if C.C. started to lose it, the star of this show would immediately cease to be Miracle Miles.

"I can't do it. Lemme go," Caprice said, pleading with him.

"You're gonna do it or I'm gonna kill you. Understand? You're dead."

For all his past crimes against her, he had never actually threatened her life before, and the precedent caused her to groan out loud, heartbroken. The pitiful sound again made her the central focus of the house, and this time the people eyeing her included Miles himself.

"You all right back there?"

C.C.'s hand fell away from Caprice's arm and he stepped back, leaving Caprice to answer the question for herself.

She turned and, somehow finding the will to smile, said, "Oh, yeah. I just need a little air, is all."

Before C.C. could stop her, she pushed past him to rush out the door.

He stood there for a brief moment, absorbing the singular gaze of what had to be over 150 people, Miracle Miles being the most openly analytical, and then shrugged, like this kind of innocent shit happened between he and his woman all the time.

"I better go check on her," he said, before slinking out the door like a tired old man.

C.C. thought sure Caprice was gone, but she was outside in the parking lot, shivering with fear and cold when he came around the corner to look for her.

Both of his hands were balled into fists, he didn't have enough self-control to prevent that, but he was strong enough to keep them at his sides as he closed on her.

"Please, C.C. Don't make me," she pleaded.

"You got one more chance." He gave her a brief glimpse of the revolver under the tail of his shirt, shoved down into the waistband of his pants. "I hear another word of argument out of your ass and I'll whack you right now, I ain't playin'."

"But he seen us together now! How—"

"So he seen us. So what? Don't nobody in that store know either one of us. Even if they know we're together now, it ain't gonna help 'em find us after we jet, is it? Huh?"

He'd already thought it all through, just in the short space of time between Caprice's exit from the store and this moment, and he had convinced himself it was true. It would have been better if no one had paid either one of them any mind, especially Miracle Miles, but C.C. could still jack Miles as planned without getting busted because he remained as anonymous as ever. The last time he and Miles had met was sixteen years ago. So what if Miles had seen his face?

"That's the nigga's car right there," C.C. said, nodding his head at a long white Lincoln limousine sitting in the middle of the bookstore's parking lot. "His driver's inside, listenin' to music, I think. You go on over there and start workin' his ass while I go back in the store and wait for Miles to finish.

"When I come back out here, I want that ride open and that driver off in a corner somewheres, I don't care how you get 'im there. You got that?"

Caprice hesitated, riding the last of her courage to its very end, and then silently nodded her head.

Bored damn near to tears, C.C. listened to Miracle Miles read from the book C.C.'s mother had given him for his birthday for fifteen minutes, once again standing at the front of the store close to the door, and almost gave it up. What a game Miles was running on these fools. He had a rule for this and a rule for that, do's and don'ts that were supposed to turn losers into winners every time, and it was all bullshit. Every word. Miracle Miles was a baller, nothing more and nothing less, and what he had to teach anybody about getting ahead in life wasn't worth the paper his "expert" advice was written on.

C.C. was so disgusted by Miles and the gullibility of his enraptured audience, he hadn't noticed that Miles's bodyguard was no longer standing at his elbow until somebody behind him said, "Come on outside with me, nigga," blowing the words into his right ear like a breathless lover.

The security man was pressed up against C.C.'s back, holding a nine down low where only C.C. could see it.

"And we don't want no drama, do we?"

C.C. thought about drawing his own piece, taking his chances in an all-out shoot-out, innocent bystanders be damned, but this was a short-lived temptation. Bad-ass gangsta that he was, C.C. discovered with some embarrassment that he wasn't quite ready to die.

The bodyguard guided him out, no one taking notice of them, and used the nine to steer him over to the white limo idling in the parking lot. C.C. looked around for some sign of Caprice, but she was nowhere in sight. Neither was she in the car when the bodyguard opened the back door for him and said, "Get in."

C.C. did as he was told and the man with the gun eased in after him, taking a seat across from C.C. before closing the door behind them. Over the bodyguard's right shoulder, on the other side of a smoked glass partition, C.C. could see Miles's driver sitting behind the limo's wheel. Alone.

"If you're lookin' for your girl, we sent her home," Miles's boy said, proving himself fully capable of smiling when the mood moved him. He held out an open palm, careful to keep the semi-automatic in his other hand trained on C.C.'s chest. "Let's have the piece. Careful."

C.C. gave him his revolver, too stunned and disoriented now to do anything else. What the hell was happening?

He got his answer a few minutes later when Miles joined them in the car, looking as happy and imperturbable as ever. He sat down next to his bodyguard, tapped on the glass behind his head, and the limo began to move.

"What the fuck's goin' on?" C.C. asked, unable to keep his growing sense of panic from creeping into his voice.

Miles just grinned at him. "Come on, C.C. Don't play dumb. You was gettin' ready to fuck me up, same as you did in the State Finals back in '93. Ain't that right?"

C.C.'s jaw dropped. Miles knew who he was. How in the hell was that possible?

Miles took C.C.'s revolver from his bodyguard and rolled it

around in his hands, looking it over with some amusement. "You were bad news then, and you look like bad news now. Wasn't hard to guess you hadn't come out here to get a book signed."

"Look here . . ." C.C. said, trying to generate something, anything, that sounded like a fully grown man's courage in the face of certain danger.

"I know what you think. Miracle Miles ain't nothin' but a pretty face. I punked 'im once, ought'a be easy to punk again, right?" He shook his head, and suddenly the expression on the man's face was very un-Miracle-like. "Uh-uh. I grew up on the street, same as you, brother. Only worse. Princeton Heights, Oakland, Cali, baddest fuckin' 'hood on the face of the earth. I could'a never got out'a there alive if I wasn't harder than any gangsta you'll ever know. You'd read my book, you would've understood that."

Fuck your book, C.C. thought to himself, but he didn't say it out loud because something had changed in Miles he didn't like. Something that made him genuinely afraid that the mistake he'd made tonight might cost him something more than another meaningless stretch in the pen.

"What you want me to do with him?" his bodyguard asked Miles.

"You? Nothin'," Miles said. And then he looked over at C.C. again, still flipping C.C.'s revolver around in both of his hands. "I got this one."

The following night, lying dead in a vacant field out in the wastelands of Sunland, months before his body was discovered and his murder written off as the inevitable result of a life misspent on crime, C.C. wasn't around to sit in on Miracle Miles's next book signing. And that was a shame. Because, if he had been, he might have heard something that would have explained how he had come to meet his cruel fate, and how the total sum of two pages in a book had probably made the difference between his meeting and avoiding it.

Finding it somehow fitting, Miles on this night regaled his adoring fans with a sampling from Chapter Three of *The Miracle Rule Book,* unwittingly choosing to start reading less than a hundred words from the spot where C.C., too overcome by jealousy and hatred for his old high school nemesis to go on, had chosen to stop.

"'Rule number four,'" Miracle read, "'is "Never forget a beat-down." The conventional wisdom says when you suffer a significant loss, you should put everything about it behind you and move on. But I don't agree. I think it's just as important to remember a crushing defeat as it is a huge victory, because you can use the pain of the former as motivation to succeed for the rest of your life. This is why I've always made it a point to remember everything about a major loss, including the names and faces of the people responsible for it. They may not know it, but I've had my revenge against them a thousand times over the years, even if it was only in my mind.'"

And to punctuate his point, Miles did what everyone here had hoped to see him do more than anything else in the world: laugh.

JON LAND

Killing Time

FROM *Thriller 2*

"WE'RE GLAD TO HAVE YOU ABOARD, Mr. Beechum," said
Roger Meeks, principal of Hampton Lake Middle School, rising
from behind his desk.

Fallon thought about how he'd killed the last man he shook
hands with and released the principal's flaccid grip quickly. That
man's name was Beechum and he'd had the misfortune to pick up
a sodden, weary Fallon hitchhiking on the side of a lonely inter-
state. Poor Beechum also had the misfortune of being in the process of relocating to a new state to take a new job and for having a
passing resemblance to Fallon. Passing in that they both had dark
hair and features, close enough to allow Fallon to effortlessly fool
principal Meeks with only minor modifications to his own appearance.

"Your résumé is quite impressive," Meeks continued, retaking
his seat and looking up from the pages before him. Their eyes met
and for just a moment Fallon thought the principal was studying
him, perhaps noticing the anomalies with the face of the now-dead
teacher clipped to the top sheet. But then he smiled. "I think
you're going to be very happy at Hampton Lake Middle School.
Let's show you the building."

The "tour," as Meeks called it, was important to Fallon. Though he
smiled through its course, careful to ask all the right questions, he
was actually cataloging various routes of escape and hiding. That
his former employers were after him was not in doubt at all, any
more than the fact they would eventually be successful. Because

Fallon had failed them. Worse, Fallon had misbehaved by executing those sent to make him pay for his failure.

His former employers would have been wise to let him go and be done with it. But they couldn't take the chance Fallon would come after them. Here he became a victim of his own well-deserved reputation. His background in Special Forces had taught him to not just accept killing, but embrace it as a skill to be mastered like any other: with practice. The means—knife, gun, bare hand, explosives—mattered not at all, only the result. And with Fallon the result was always the same.

Except once. And now because of that he was on the run. Killing time in the guise of a middle-school English teacher. Or Language Arts, as they called it these days.

Meeks continued the tour of Hampton Lake Middle School in perfunctory fashion, Fallon nodding and smiling at all the appropriate times. The building was T-shaped with two long hallways separated by an enclosed courtyard adjoining a perpendicular two-story wing at the building's front end located farthest from the road. A gym and presentation room were located in the back end, the cafeteria in the front. Fallon noted a drop ceiling heavy enough to support a man's weight, accessing a crawl space that ran the length of the building on both sides. The location of the sub-basement, containing the electrical and heating elements, was more difficult to pin down at this point.

Normally, Fallon would look for places to stash weapons as well. Here he didn't consider that to be a factor. If he was found, escape would be the thing, not confrontation.

"Now," Meeks said, the cursory tour over, "let's show you your classroom."

Eighth-grade honors English, Language Arts, was just finishing an abridged, heavily censored version of a book called *Catch-22*. Fallon rented the movie that night and didn't really get most of it, except the title concept of a wartime pilot in search of a loophole to be deemed too crazy to fly. Fallon thought parts were supposed to be funny, but didn't laugh and was glad when it was time for the class to move on to *Frankenstein*. Fallon hadn't read that book either, but he'd seen the movie, the old one with Boris Karloff, and figured that was close enough.

His classroom overlooked the front of the building, including an oval-shaped drive that enclosed a parking lot used by teachers as well as visitors. Fallon couldn't see the main entrance but had a clear view of any vehicle approaching it, which was the next best thing.

"So who do we think is the villain in the story?" Fallon asked his class.

His remark was greeted by shrugs and quick glances cast amidst his young charges. Having no real concept of how to teach exactly, he'd constructed his classes around discussion. Fortunately, he'd come at a time of the semester devoted to literature and didn't expect to still be around for the next unit. More than a month in any one setting would be tempting fate indeed.

"The villain?" Fallon prompted, leaning back so he was halfway sitting on the lip of his desk.

"Frankenstein," a boy named Trent said from the rear. Trent had floppy hair and the first signs of acne.

Fallon liked him because he recognized a worn patch in the rear pocket of his jeans as the outline of a switchblade. Fallon looked into Trent's eyes and saw emotionless, stone-cold resignation. A boy after his own heart.

"Not the monster," Trent continued, without further prompt. "The doctor."

"Why?" Fallon asked him.

"'Cause he fucked with nature."

The moment froze, everyone staring at Fallon in shock. Trent resumed again, saving him the bother of coming up with an appropriate response.

"So the monster kills all these people, terrorizes the village, scares the crap out of people. But it's not his fault, not really."

"So he's not responsible for his own actions?" Fallon challenged.

"Poor bastard doesn't even know what he's doing. Blame Frankenstein for bringing him to life."

"Like parents," a frizzy-haired girl named Chelsea chimed in between crackling chomps on a wad of gum, sending a brief laugh rippling through the classroom.

"Maybe that's Shelley's point," someone else said.

"So the monster's not evil," Fallon raised.

"No," came the multiple response.

"But he's not good either."

"No."

"So what is he?"

"The same as everybody else," Trent said, booted feet propped up on the desk before him.

Five weeks earlier Fallon had received his next job through the usual means. A text message sent to his cell phone dispatched him to a public e-mail website. He logged in at the nearest FedEx-Kinko's and entered the coded details into his PDA. Fallon never knew the reason for his targets' selection. He only needed to know who and where; sometimes how and when. His log-on automatically triggered the deposit of half his fee into a previously designated offshore bank account.

Setting up a kill could take considerable time, up to several weeks, a period during which Fallon became intimately acquainted with the habits of his targets without immersing himself into the minutiae of their lives. The last job was different because it specified the target's entire family be included. Someone out to set an example, obviously, make a point.

Discussion here was not an option. Even if Fallon had wanted, he couldn't have asked for confirmation and clarification. And if the fact that the target's family consisted of a wife and three young children bothered Fallon, there was no way to contact his employer to change his mind. The URL from which his assignment had been sent was a dummy site automatically deactivated as soon as Fallon logged off. Declining a job was never an option, once the mechanical triggering apparatus made Fallon an even richer man. Catch-23.

Wiring the target's house with explosives was easy enough, doing it in a way that would make it look like a tragic accident only slightly harder. The only drawback: he'd have to trigger the blast manually himself. Not an attractive prospect considering he much preferred being somewhere else far away when the explosion ripped lumber and concrete, flesh and blood, apart.

Fallon was not a man prone to question or marred by pangs of conscience. And the early stages of the job progressed without being terribly struck by either. A man like Fallon could not view human beings with any higher regard than, say, crash-test dummies or department-store mannequins. They were his means to an end, though with ample funds for a secure retirement in place he was hard-pressed to say exactly what those ends were. Except he couldn't retire; he enjoyed his work too much. Catch-24.

And his latest assignment should have gone down like all the others, all in place and on schedule. Fallon following his instructions to the letter to make sure all family members were inside before triggering the blast.

Detonators were a thing of the past mostly, cell phones the thing these days. Simple matter of wiring the trigger chip with a number and then dialing it at the appropriate time. There'd be a brief delay, several seconds or more, but that wasn't a problem in this case.

Fallon took his throwaway cell phone from his pocket and dialed. Let it ring once and then settled back to wait from his car parked safely down the street, counting the seconds out in his head.

One . . . two . . . three . . .

By *five,* Fallon began to feel edgy, and at *ten* he redialed, let it ring twice this time. Counted the seconds again.

Same result. Nothing.

Setbacks were nothing new to Fallon; failure something else again. There was no time to consider what had gone wrong. Better to focus on damage control, what to do from here. Fallon had weapons, a bounty of them. But murdering an entire family in the suburbs with guns and knives without a clear plan of access and approach would be a desperate move not befitting a professional of his level. Worse, he'd be acting rashly with the eventual outcome dictated by fortune instead of forethought. Better to come back, rethink the next step tomorrow.

Except tomorrow turned out worse.

The next book on the honors English list was called *Johnny Got His Gun.* Fallon couldn't find a movie version, but the book was short and supposedly about war, so he decided to read it.

The book *was* short. And Fallon understood nary a word, much less what the book was supposed to be about. Antiwar, that much was clear, if nothing else. So he decided to focus the class's discussion on war itself, something he knew plenty about.

But Mr. Beechum, of course, didn't, which meant Fallon couldn't appear to either. He listened to the surprisingly intelligent, unsettling comments made by his students. Unsettling because it made him realize how much he missed that part of his life for its simplicity and clarity. The ability to kill for a cause with impunity. Of course, the cause meant little to Fallon; it was the impunity he embraced with a fervor and passion unknown in any previous segment of his life.

An unpleasant end to his military career was as expected as it was inevitable. Fortunately, there were plenty of private firms willing to pay far more while letting him practice his same skills. That, too, ended badly, in an embarrassing scandal for the company and yet another inglorious dismissal for Fallon. But there was no shortage of work for a man with Fallon's skills, and he'd been stateside barely a week when a similarly ex-member of the same private firm came calling with an offer to join a network of professionals whose work was appreciated instead of vilified. Fallon didn't bother himself with delusions of morality, of right and wrong. He did what he did, and he liked it. Simple as that.

The class agreed with the book's antiwar stance. Fallon wished he'd been able to tell them the true side of things. About the various pleasures a man could derive from watching a face explode to a bullet or the guttural gasps a victim makes when a knife digs deep, shredding flesh and muscle. He wished he could explain that violence was something to neither be shunned nor embraced. It simply was.

Just like him.

To make his point, Fallon decided to stray from the lesson plan and introduce the only story he actually remembered reading as a boy. Read so much the pages actually disintegrated, the words disappearing until there were no sentences left and Fallon reluctantly discarded the handout. He hadn't thought of that story in a very long time until now, glad to find a copy ripe for photocopying in the school library.

"'The Most Dangerous Game,'" the librarian said, reading over Fallon's shoulder as collated copies spit out from the machine's feeder. "A true classic. But a bit violent, don't you think?"

When Fallon returned the following morning, the target family was gone, whisked away in the dawn hours by shadowy men in black

SUVs, if the neighbors were to be believed. FBI or federal marshals, no doubt, extricating Fallon's targets into witness protection.

Fallon had never failed before, but there were percentages involved in everything and here the odds had finally caught up with him. He found himself obsessing over every move he had made to retrace where he'd gone wrong. The wiring perhaps. Maybe a bad chip. A reception or transmission problem even.

That was why Fallon was awake in his motel room when they came. Four of them, all well armed and well skilled enough to know not to drive their car too close to his room in the motor court. But they'd left their headlights on a second too long, enough to alert Fallon that someone was coming.

He gauged the distance suggested by the strength of the headlights and counted the seconds again.

One . . . two . . . three . . .

The door blew inward at *six*, Fallon unleashing a fusillade that was every bit the equal of his four would-be killers. So much passed through his mind as the bullets chewed up the walls around him and the smell of blood mixed with sulfur and cordite. The roar from the three guns he managed to reach drowned out the screams mostly, and Fallon was screeching away from the scene before another light snapped on in any of the nearby rooms.

The reality of the moment struck him, and fast. The fact that his employers wouldn't stop with these four men, especially since Fallon had so effortlessly executed them, was no less a reality than the fact that his time as a contractor was effectively over. There was no redemption or second chances. He had gone from the very best at what he did to irrelevant in the seconds it had taken him to gun down four men.

Catch-25.

Fallon had effectively prepared for this moment, while never really considering it a possibility. Money would not be a problem; he had plenty of it stashed away. The issue was getting to it safely, making the necessary arrangements with according precautions, and such things took time. He'd have to disappear without the use of any of his various identities, all of which could be compromised now. His employers and conduits knew too much about him, his habits and patterns. Disappearing meant relying on none of them, becoming someone else entirely while laying the groundwork for his permanent departure from parts known.

There were plenty of Third World countries into which he could vanish, only to resurface as a man with a different identity boasting the kind of skills that were always in need. Fallon couldn't imagine himself wallowing away the time on a beach, no matter how beautiful or plentiful the women. His life had been defined by killing for too long to either risk or want change.

For now going off the grid meant avoiding all forms of security cameras and public transportation, including buses, trains, and airplanes. Rental cars were out as well, and stealing too many cars could leave the kind of pattern he needed to avoid.

That left hitchhiking. Mr. Beechum's was the fifth car in a week to chance picking him up. Fallon didn't kill the others and hadn't expected to kill Beechum until the ditzy man kept speaking enthusiastically of the new job to which he was headed. That's when the plan unfolded for Fallon, and the best he was able to do for Beechum in return was kill him in quick, painless fashion.

"I love kids" was the last thing the teacher said. "Making a difference in their lives and all."

In that moment Fallon couldn't have known the kind of difference he'd end up making.

Fallon saw the two vans creep toward the school's entrance when he was in the third day of discussing "The Most Dangerous Game." They were noteworthy first for the fact they drove onto the grounds down the wrong side of the U-shaped drive fronting the building and second because the vans wore the markings of a professional cleaning service. Such markings always allowed for unquestioned access to buildings, public and otherwise, but why would a middle school with a full janitorial staff need a professional cleaning service?

Fallon's heart began to beat faster as the vans drifted out of his line of sight. Two vans meant a dozen men or more, certainly overkill on the part of his former employers. And if they had ascertained his presence here at Hampton Lake, they'd be much better off laying an ambush instead of storming the building in full awareness of his conceivable escape.

That reality should have made him feel better.

But it didn't.

Instincts had saved his life often enough for Fallon to learn to trust them, and right now they were scratching at his spine like scalpels peeling back the flesh.

"Rainsford's my kind of guy," Trent was saying from his customary perch in the back of the room, biker boots propped up on the desk before him.

"Go on," Fallon managed to say, not really paying attention. His eyes strayed out the window again, but the vans did not reappear. He moved closer to the glass, hoping to better his angle.

"Dude, he kicks General Zaroff's ass. And it was Zaroff's own fucking fault."

"Why?" Fallon asked, intrigued in spite of the nagging feeling that wouldn't go away.

"Because he'd been playing the game too long. Hunting men, who knows how many of them."

"So why stop?"

"Because he should've known he'd meet his match. Sooner or later. It's like, you know, inevitable."

Fallon moved away from the window, suddenly intrigued. "So why'd he keep doing it? Come on, people, put yourself in Zaroff's shoes."

"'Cause it's all he had," said a girl in the front row. "All he knew."

"What else?"

"He was good at it," someone else answered. "When you're that good, you don't think anybody'll ever beat you."

"Was Rainsford better at the game than the general?" Fallon asked his class.

"No," said Trent. "Zaroff lost 'cause he got lazy. When you get lazy, you get beat every time. But Rainsford, he was a hero."

"Why?"

"He saved lives. Of Zaroff's future victims. Not all heroes mean to be heroes, if you get my drift."

"May I have your attention please?"

The voice of Principal Meeks boomed over the school's PA system.

"All students and teachers, please report to the gymnasium immediately. That's all students and teachers, please report to the—"

The principal's voice cut off in midsentence, as if he'd accidentally hit the wrong switch. Fallon watched his students begin to rise from their desks, replaying Meeks's words in his head—not for content so much as cadence. Something all wrong about the tone and import. Fallon knew the sound of a man under duress because he'd put countless men in just that position.

When you get lazy, you get beat every time . . .

"No," Fallon said before the student closest to the door could open it. "Back to your seats."

"But—"

"Back to your seats."

The edge in Fallon's voice had his students returning to their desks without further question. The hallway beyond filled with students spilling out of nearby classrooms, the heavy trampling of feet signaling the approach of those emerging from the two-story wing at the building's head.

"Mr. Beechum?"

Fallon swung toward the windows again. They only opened inward at the very top, enough to provide ventilation but not escape.

"Mr. Beechum?"

Fallon didn't answer. Mr. Beechum was gone.

"Trent," Fallon said, the persona shed, cold eyes boring down on the boy who'd been his favorite, "give me your switchblade."

"My wh—"

"Now, Trent."

The voice not raised, just measured and certain.

"It's a butterfly knife."

Trent fished the butterfly knife out of his backpack, brought it up to Fallon, and extended it toward him in a trembling hand. Fallon wished he could smile at him reassuringly, the way Mr. Beechum would.

Except Mr. Beechum had left the building.

"Okay," Fallon said, "everyone line up starting on this wall and wrapping around to the back of the room. Shoulder to shoulder. Very close. Out of sight from the door."

"Why?" a girl asked, moving to obey.

Fallon didn't answer. Beyond his classroom, the thick flow of students and their teacher escorts continued down the corridor, oblivious to whatever might be transpiring. Fallon hoped he was wrong, but knew he wasn't. He had spent his life as Zaroff, the odds stacked heavily in his favor. But now suddenly he found himself as Rainsford, the underdog.

When you're that good, you don't think anybody'll ever beat you.

Well, whoever had come in those vans was in for a big surprise, weren't they?

The moments passed in silence broken only by the loud breathing of his students. Or maybe it wasn't loud. Maybe Fallon just heard it that way.

The hallway emptied, a few stragglers passing the windowed door and then no one. A pause, then fresh footsteps crackling atop tile alone followed by the creaking echo of doors being thrust open, each growing louder.

Fallon snapped the butterfly knife's blade into position.

A boy whimpered. Two girls began to sob, then a third.

Fallon pressed a single finger against his lips, signaling them to be quiet, ducked back so he was out of sight from the doorway.

The heavy footsteps drew closer. The knob rattled, door easing inward.

A student gasped.

A man lurched past Fallon, never seeing him, clearing his route of escape. Fallon's eyes shifted between the door and the high-end submachine gun the man was now steadying: on Trent who'd started defiantly forward, boots clacking against the tile.

Fallon saw the man's finger curling round the trigger in the last moment before he pounced. Arm wrapped around the man's neck to silence him as he drew Trent's butterfly knife on a sharp upward angle required to slice through bone and gristle, digging into the lungs and shredding them.

The man gurgled and rasped, fighting against Fallon as bloody froth poured from his mouth. Fallon snapped his neck for good measure, studying his face as he dragged him across the room before the horrified stares of his students.

The man was Arab; Fallon could tell that from sight as well as smell. Smells were important to him. You spend enough time all over the world, in the various cesspits of humanity, and you begin to know men by their smells as much as anything. An Arab, all right, and in that moment Fallon realized everything he had been dispatched to Iraq to prevent had finally come to pass. The foreign stink come home.

Fallon was free to escape now. Two vans meant a dozen men at least, the other eleven likely scattered throughout the building. He could flee the building without so much as killing another, or, perhaps, just one. Maybe use one of their vans as his escape vehicle and leave them to whatever debacle they intended to perpetrate on the school and the world. It wasn't his world anyway, not anymore.

Or was it?

He glanced at Trent and his other students, bunched tighter together now, hugging each other as they stared at him in terror the way they would a monster, like the one Frankenstein had created. Or maybe General Zaroff, mad for the hunt.

Johnny got his gun, all right.

Flee and these students, *his* students, would inevitably end up in the gym with the others. Perhaps to be made an example of for disobeying. Terrorists like these were not very original, and that awareness sparked a memory in Fallon's head of Chechnyan terrorists taking a school over in that particular godforsaken nation hostage. The students brought to the gymnasium, just like here. And then the gym was blown up while the whole world watched.

No, not very original, but effective all the same.

Fallon tried to imagine how he'd do it, how many men in the gym versus how many patrolling and securing the building. He settled on four in the gym, eight for the building.

Seven now.

Fallon stooped down and began working the dead man's jacket free.

"I need you all to stay here," Fallon told his students. "Don't make a sound and wait for me to come back for you." Then, to Trent, "You're in charge."

They looked at him as the stranger he had become even before he'd donned the terrorist's jacket and bandana, squeezed his feet into the dead man's work boots, and slung his submachine gun from his shoulder. Enough to pass for the dead man from a reasonable distance, which was the best he could hope for. The 9/11 hijackers had never all met each other, but this kind of operation was different, requiring practice and synchronization. They would know the building as well as he did; every crawl space, every nook and cranny. The difference, of course, was he knew the terrorists were here while they had no idea he was.

Wait for me to come back for you . . .

Why had he said that? Fallon wondered, once he was in the hall-way, careful to leave the door open as all the others on the hallway were. It would be so easy for him to flee the building now before the inevitable appearance of the authorities on the scene. That was no longer an option for him, the challenge, the game, before him much too great to consider walking away from.

But was he Zaroff or was he Rainsford?

The building was eerily quiet, save for the din coming from the gymnasium area, where nearly seven hundred students were being crammed in even now. Fallon tried to remember all the details of the Chechnyan school seizing. Those terrorists had waited for the authorities to arrive, waited for them to mount their ill-fated raid, before triggering the explosives and killing hundreds. It would be the same way here, the strategy aimed at drawing the most attention possible. Round-the-clock coverage on the networks for days before the entire country paid witness to a mass murder in prime time.

Fallon made sure to conceal the considerable bulk of his shoulders within the terrorist's shapeless, now bloodstained, jacket. He tied the dead man's bandana low over his forehead, hoping it would conceal the differences in their faces and hair from the distance he required. He made sure the walkie-talkie, simple Radio Shack variety, was secured to his belt and started back up the corridor the way the dead terrorist would if he were retracing his steps.

At the head of the hallway, the office directly on his left and the science wing just down the hall to his right, Fallon glimpsed another of the terrorists rushing away from the main entrance with extra chains clanking. By now, all such doors would have been secured and wired with explosives, to deter both escape from within and attack from the outside. Fallon had a clear shot at the man but opted not to take it until he was sure no others were in the vicinity. Instead he made his footsteps just loud enough to be heard. Then swung about, gun leading, back to the stairwell up which number two had rushed.

"Hey," the man called to him in Arabic, *"shoo hada?"*

Fallon's response to the man asking him "What is this?" was to swing and fire. A single headshot that dropped the terrorist where he stood. He crumpled to the steps and slid halfway back down the stairs. Not Fallon's intention, but by this point instinct had taken over.

Two down.

Fallon heard footsteps converging on the stairwell from opposite directions on the second floor. He crouched over the body, submachine gun angled at the main entry doors as if to suggest that's where the deadly fire had originated. He could see the plastic explosives layered into place over the glass. Not the way he would've done it exactly, but still effective.

The footsteps grew louder, voices in Arabic shouted his way. Fallon swung when the two men were close enough to take in a single sweep. Two shots, both to the head again to be sure.

Four down.

This time his shots coincided with the rattling echo of machine-gun fire coming from the other end of the building. Screams and cries answered the barrage, greeted by a second longer one that drove the students and teachers to silence. Four to six of the remaining terrorists would be down there. Doors chained from the inside, denying him both access and the element of surprise. Without either, never mind both, the game would be over.

Fallon's Radio Shack walkie-talkie crackled. He snapped it from his belt, listened.

"Shoofi mafi? What's the matter?"

"Mafi Mushkil," Fallon replied, hoping he had chosen the right word in Arabic. "No problem."

"Dilwaati. Hurry."

Fallon clasped the walkie-talkie back on his belt and headed down the stairs, banking left toward the school's science wing as the blare of sirens descended on the Hampton Lake Middle School.

The students of his eighth-grade honors Language Arts class were arranged two-by-two, fourteen deep, with Fallon bringing up the rear. After rousing them from the classroom against the tearful protestations of many, he placed Trent at the head of the group to lead the way toward the gym.

He'd encountered another terrorist in the science wing who approached him in the half-light, noticing the ruse too late and making the mistake of trying to right his submachine gun. Fallon was close enough to use Trent's butterfly knife this time, a single swipe across the man's throat for silence and surety.

He spent just over a minute gathering up two vials of clear liquid in one of the science labs and ran into another of the terrorists, literally, at the head of the corridor. Their eyes had met; the terrorist's gaping, Fallon's steeling as his hands came up, thumbs pressing into the man's eyes to mash brain tissue and send him spasming toward death.

Six down.

Then back fast to his classroom to enact the final phase of his plan, the students suitably scared and confused. He marched them down the hall toward the gymnasium, pretending to prod with the submachine gun while concealing a capped glass vial in either hand.

A hundred feet away, a pair of terrorists guarding that booby-trapped entry to the building spotted him coming and twisted his way, keeping tight to the wall while shouting instructions Fallon ignored. They approached on either side of his marching phalanx and as soon as they were close enough to realize something was very wrong, Fallon popped the caps off his vials and tossed the acid compound at their faces. Not directly on line, but enough splashing home to send their hands upward to comfort their ravaged eyes.

Fallon took each down with a single, quick burst, then pushed his shocked charges on faster. Through the glass doors and half-wall he glimpsed a nonstop onslaught of police vehicles and media vans, continuing with his charges toward the chained entrance to the gym.

He moved to the front of the apparent stragglers he had rounded up, pounding on the door and then swinging away with gun leading.

"Open up! Hurry!" he screamed in Arabic, desperation forced into his voice. "They're in the building!"

The chains rattled, locks and explosives being thrust aside. The double-door entrance jerked open by a sweaty man who bled garlic through his pores.

Fallon started shooting, willing to sacrifice a few innocents to get the last of the job done. He felled the three terrorists converging on the door, before turning his attention on the one who had yanked it open because his hands were too full to go fast for a weapon. That man had barely hit the floor when Fallon whirled sideways, scanning the room for motion.

He fired at whatever moved, like a cheap arcade game now, hoping no bystanders got caught in the fire but knowing he couldn't let that concern stop him. He fired his last spray upward into the sprinkler apparatus, activating a spray of water, which almost instantly doused the cavernous room and drenched its occupants.

His submachine gun clicked empty. Fallon was twisting to retrieve the sidearm of a dead terrorist when a bearded rail of a man came at him, showcasing a detonator as he blithered away in Arabic.

"Maashallah! Maashallah!"

Fallon palmed Trent's butterfly knife, locked the blade into place.

"Maashallah! Maashallah!" The man's wild hair a soaked tangle that swept over his face, seeming to merge it with his beard.

"Maashallah!"

Fallon snapped his hand outward, sending the knife whizzing through the air. It took the final terrorist in the eye, buried to the hilt in his brain. He fell to the floor. The detonator rattled across the floor.

Fourteen down, Fallon thought, realizing his initial estimate had been off as he looked up and let the cascading water wash over his face. *And not a single bystander with them.*

Fallon emerged from the boys' locker room wearing the uniform and visor of a SWAT officer who'd gone in there to secure the site. Confusion was his ally now, confusion and chaos as the police stormed the building to find bodies everywhere and had to sort through the tales of the mysterious teacher who had killed them. They'd never believe it at first and before they did, Fallon would be gone.

In the foyer beyond the gym, he passed his eighth-grade honors Language Arts class being questioned by an expanding bevy of officers. Fallon kept his head turned low and to the side, cocking his gaze back just once to meet Trent's when he was almost to the door.

"So if he wasn't Beechum, any of you have an idea who he was?" an official in plain clothes was asking his students.

"Rainsford," Trent said, as his eyes locked and held with Fallon's through the SWAT visor. "His name was Rainsford."

DENNIS LEHANE

Animal Rescue

FROM *Boston Noir*

BOB FOUND THE DOG in the trash.

It was just after Thanksgiving, the neighborhood gone quiet, hungover. After bartending at Cousin Marv's, Bob sometimes walked the streets. He was big and lumpy and hair had been growing in unlikely places all over his body since his teens. In his twenties, he'd fought against the hair, carrying small clippers in his coat pocket and shaving twice a day. He'd also fought the weight, but during all those years of fighting, no girl who wasn't being paid for it ever showed any interest in him. After a time, he gave up the fight. He lived alone in the house he grew up in, and when it seemed likely to swallow him with its smells and memories and dark couches, the attempts he'd made to escape it—through church socials, lodge picnics, and one horrific mixer thrown by a dating service—had only opened the wound further, left him patching it back up for weeks, cursing himself for hoping.

So he took these walks of his and, if he was lucky, sometimes he forgot people lived any other way. That night, he paused on the sidewalk, feeling the ink sky above him and the cold in his fingers, and he closed his eyes against the evening.

He was used to it. He was used to it. It was okay.

You could make a friend of it, as long as you didn't fight it.

With his eyes closed, he heard it—a worn-out keening accompanied by distant scratching and a sharper, metallic rattling. He opened his eyes. Fifteen feet down the sidewalk, a large metal barrel with a heavy lid shook slightly under the yellow glare of the streetlight, its bottom scraping the sidewalk. He stood over it and heard that keening again, the sound of a creature that was one breath away from deciding it was too hard to take the next, and he pulled off the lid.

He had to remove some things to get to it—a toaster and five thick Yellow Pages, the oldest dating back to 2000. The dog—either a very small one or else a puppy—was down at the bottom, and it scrunched its head into its midsection when the light hit it. It exhaled a soft chug of a whimper and tightened its body even more, its eyes closed to slits. A scrawny thing. Bob could see its ribs. He could see a big crust of dried blood by its ear. No collar. It was brown with a white snout and paws that seemed far too big for its body.

It let out a sharper whimper when Bob reached down, sank his fingers into the nape of its neck, and lifted it out of its own excrement. Bob didn't know dogs too well, but there was no mistaking this one for anything but a boxer. And definitely a puppy, the wide brown eyes opening and looking into his as he held it up before him.

Somewhere, he was sure, two people made love. A man and a woman. Entwined. Behind one of those shades, oranged with light, that looked down on the street. Bob could feel them in there, naked and blessed. And he stood out here in the cold with a near-dead dog staring back at him. The icy sidewalk glinted like new marble, and the wind was dark and gray as slush.

"What do you got there?"

Bob turned, looked up and down the sidewalk.

"I'm up here. And you're in my trash."

She stood on the front porch of the three-decker nearest him. She'd turned the porch light on and stood there shivering, her feet bare. She reached into the pocket of her hoodie and came back with a pack of cigarettes. She watched him as she got one going.

"I found a dog." Bob held it up.

"A *what?*"

"A dog. A puppy. A boxer, I think."

She coughed out some smoke. "Who puts a dog in a barrel?"

"Right?" he said. "It's bleeding." He took a step toward her stairs and she backed up.

"Who do you know that I would know?" A city girl, not about to just drop her guard around a stranger.

"I don't know," Bob said. "How about Francie Hedges?"

She shook her head. "You know the Sullivans?"

That wouldn't narrow it down. Not around here. You shook a tree, a Sullivan fell out. Followed by a six-pack most times. "I know a bunch."

This was going nowhere, the puppy looking at him, shaking worse than the girl.

"Hey," she said, "you live in this parish?"

"Next one over. St. Theresa's."

"Go to church?"

"Most Sundays."

"So you know Father Pete?"

"Pete Regan," he said, "sure."

She produced a cell phone. "What's your name?"

"Bob," he said. "Bob Saginowski."

Bob waited as she stepped back from the light, phone to one ear, finger pressed into the other. He stared at the puppy. The puppy stared back, like, How did I get *here?* Bob touched its nose with his index finger. The puppy blinked its huge eyes. For a moment, Bob couldn't recall his sins.

"Nadia," the girl said and stepped back into the light. "Bring him up here, Bob. Pete says hi."

They washed it in Nadia's sink, dried it off, and brought it to her kitchen table.

Nadia was small. A bumpy red rope of a scar ran across the base of her throat like the smile of a drunk circus clown. She had a tiny moon of a face, savaged by pockmarks, and small, heart-pendant eyes. Shoulders that didn't cut so much as dissolve at the arms. Elbows like flattened beer cans. A yellow bob of hair curled on either side of her face. "It's not a boxer." Her eyes glanced off Bob's face before dropping the puppy back onto her kitchen table. "It's an American Staffordshire terrier."

Bob knew he was supposed to understand something in her tone, but he didn't know what that thing was so he remained silent.

She glanced back up at him after the quiet lasted too long. "A pit bull."

"That's a pit bull?"

She nodded and swabbed the puppy's head wound again. Some-one had pummeled it, she told Bob. Probably knocked it uncon-scious, assumed it was dead, and dumped it.

"Why?" Bob said.

She looked at him, her round eyes getting rounder, wider. "Just because." She shrugged, went back to examining the dog. "I worked at Animal Rescue once. You know the place on Shawmut? As a vet tech. Before I decided it wasn't my thing. They're so hard, this breed . . ."

"What?"

"To adopt out," she said. "It's very hard to find them a home."

"I don't know about dogs. I never had a dog. I live alone. I was just walking by the barrel." Bob found himself beset by a desper-ate need to explain himself, explain his life. "I'm just not . . ." He could hear the wind outside, black and rattling. Rain or bits of hail spit against the windows.

Nadia lifted the puppy's back left paw—the other three paws were brown, but this one was white with peach spots. Then she dropped the paw as if it were contagious. She went back to the head wound, took a closer look at the right ear, a piece missing from the tip that Bob hadn't noticed until now.

"Well," she said, "he'll live. You're gonna need a crate and food and all sorts of stuff."

"No," Bob said. "You don't understand."

She cocked her head, gave him a look that said she understood perfectly.

"I can't. I just found him. I was gonna give him back."

"To whoever beat him, left him for dead?"

"No, no, like, the authorities."

"That would be Animal Rescue," she said. "After they give the owner seven days to reclaim him, they'll—"

"The guy who beat him? He gets a second chance?"

She gave him a half-frown and a nod. "*If* he doesn't take it," she lifted the puppy's ear, peered in, "chances are this little fella'll be put up for adoption. But it's hard. To find them a home. Pit bulls. More often than not?" She looked at Bob. "More often than not, they're put down."

Bob felt a wave of sadness roll out from her that immediately shamed him. He didn't know how, but he'd caused pain. He'd put some out into the world. He'd let this girl down. "I . . ." he started. "It's just . . ."

She glanced up at him. "I'm sorry?"

Bob looked at the puppy. Its eyes were droopy from a long day in the barrel and whoever gave it that wound. It had stopped shivering, though.

"You can take it," Bob said. "You used to work there, like you said. You—"

She shook her head. "My father lives with me. He gets home Sunday night from Foxwoods. He finds a dog in his house? An animal he's allergic to?" She jerked her thumb. "Puppy goes back in the barrel."

"Can you give me till Sunday morning?" Bob wasn't sure how it was the words left his mouth, since he couldn't remember formulating them or even thinking them.

The girl eyed him carefully. "You're not just saying it? 'Cause, I shit you not, he ain't picked up by Sunday noon, he's back out that door."

"Sunday, then." Bob said the words with a conviction he actually felt. "Sunday, definitely."

"Yeah?" She smiled, and it was a spectacular smile, and Bob saw that the face behind the pockmarks was as spectacular as the smile. Wanting only to be seen. She touched the puppy's nose with her index finger.

"Yeah." Bob felt crazed. He felt light as a communion wafer. "Yeah."

At Cousin Marv's, where he tended bar twelve to ten, Wednesday through Sunday, he told Marv all about it. Most people called Marv *Cousin* Marv out of habit, something that went back to grade school though no one could remember how, but Marv actually was Bob's cousin. On his mother's side.

Cousin Marv had run a crew in the late '80s and early '90s. It had been primarily comprised of guys with interests in the loaning and subsequent debt-repayal side of things, though Marv never turned his nose down at any paying proposition because he believed, to the core of his soul, that those who failed to diversify were always the first to collapse when the wind turned. Like the dinosaurs, he'd say to Bob, when the cavemen came along and invented arrows.

Picture the cavemen, he'd say, firing away, and the tyrannosauruses all gucked up in the oil puddles. A tragedy so easily averted.

Marv's crew hadn't been the toughest crew or the smartest or the most successful operating in the neighborhood — not even close — but for a while they got by. Other crews kept nipping at their heels, though, and except for one glaring exception, they'd never been ones to favor violence. Pretty soon, they had to make the decision to yield to crews a lot meaner than they were or duke it out. They took Door Number One.

Marv's income derived from running his bar as a drop. In the new world order — a loose collective of Chechen, Italian, and Irish hard guys — no one wanted to get caught with enough merch or enough money for a case to go Federal. So they kept it out of their offices and out of their homes and they kept it on the move. About every two-three weeks, drops were made at Cousin Marv's, among other establishments. You sat on the drop for a night, two at the most, before some beer-truck driver showed up with the weekend's password and hauled everything back out on a dolly like it was a stack of empty kegs, took it away in a refrigerated semi. The rest of Marv's income derived from being a fence, one of the best in the city, but being a fence in their world (or a drop bar operator for that matter) was like being a mailroom clerk in the straight world — if you were still doing it after thirty, it was all you'd ever do. For Bob, it was a relief — he liked being a bartender and he'd hated that one time they'd had to come heavy. Marv, though, Marv still waited for the golden train to arrive on the golden tracks, take him away from all this. Most times, he pretended to be happy. But Bob knew that the things that haunted Marv were the same things that haunted Bob — the shitty things you did to get ahead. Those things laughed at you if your ambitions failed to amount to much; a successful man could hide his past; an unsuccessful man sat in his.

That morning, Marv was looking a hair on the mournful side, lighting one Camel while the previous one still smoldered, so Bob tried to cheer him up by telling him about his adventure with the dog. Marv didn't seem too interested, and Bob found himself saying "You had to be there" so much, he eventually shut up about it.

Marv said, "Rumor is we're getting the Super Bowl drop."

"No shit?"

If true (an enormous *if*), this was huge. They worked on commission—one half of one percent of the drop. A Super Bowl drop? It would be like one half of one percent of Exxon.

Nadia's scar flashed in Bob's brain, the redness of it, the thick, ropey texture. "They send extra guys to protect it, you think?"

Marv rolled his eyes. "Why, 'cause people are just lining up to steal from coked-up Chechnyans."

"Chechens," Bob said.

"But they're from Chechnya."

Bob shrugged. "I think it's like how you don't call people from Ireland *Irelandians*."

Marv scowled. "Whatever. It means all this hard work we've been doing? It's paid off. Like how Toyota did it, making friends and influencing people."

Bob kept quiet. If they ended up being the drop for the Super Bowl, it was because someone figured out no Feds deemed them important enough to be watched. But in Marv's fantasies, the crew (long since dispersed to straight jobs, jail, or, worse, Connecticut) could regain its glory days, even though those days had lasted about as long as a Swatch. It never occurred to Marv that one day they'd come take everything he had—the fence, the money and merch he kept in the safe in back, hell, the bar probably—just because they were sick of him hanging around, looking at them with needy expectation. It had gotten so every time he talked about the "people he knew," the dreams he had, Bob had to resist the urge to reach for the 9mm they kept beneath the bar and blow his own brains out. Not really—but close sometimes. Man, Marv could wear you out.

A guy stuck his head in the bar, late twenties but with white hair, a white goatee, a silver stud in his ear. He dressed like most kids these days—like shit: pre-ripped jeans, slovenly T-shirt under a faded hoodie under a wrinkled wool topcoat. He didn't cross the threshold, just craned his head in, the cold day pouring in off the sidewalk behind him.

"Help you?" Bob asked.

The guy shook his head, kept staring at the gloomy bar like it was a crystal ball.

"Mind shutting the door?" Marv didn't look up. "Cold out there."

"You serve Zima?" The guy's eyes flew around the bar, up and down, left to right.

Marv looked up now. "Who the fuck would we serve it to—Moesha?"

The guy raised an apologetic hand. "My bad." He left, and the warmth returned with the closing of the door.

Marv said, "You know that kid?"

Bob shook his head. "Mighta seen him around but I can't place him."

"He's a fucking nutbag. Lives in the next parish, probably why you don't know him. You're old school that way, Bob—somebody didn't go to parochial school with you, it's like they don't exist."

Bob couldn't argue. When he'd been a kid, your parish was your country. Everything you needed and needed to know was contained within it. Now that the archdiocese had shuttered half the parishes to pay for the crimes of the kid-diddler priests, Bob couldn't escape the fact that those days of parish dominion, long dwindling, were gone. He was a certain type of guy, of a certain half-generation, an almost generation, and while there were still plenty of them left, they were older, grayer, they had smokers' coughs, they went in for checkups and never checked back out.

"That kid?" Marv gave Bob a bump of his eyebrows. "They say he killed Richie Whelan back in the day."

"*They* say?"

"They do."

"Well, then . . ."

They sat in silence for a bit. Snow-dust blew past the window in the high-pitched breeze. The street signs and window panes rattled, and Bob thought how winter lost any meaning the day you last rode a sled. Any meaning but gray. He looked into the unlit sections of the barroom. The shadows became hospital beds, stooped old widowers shopping for sympathy cards, empty wheelchairs. The wind howled a little sharper.

"This puppy, right?" Bob said. "He's got paws the size of his head. Three are brown but one's white with these little peach-colored spots over the white. And—"

"This thing cook?" Marv said. "Clean the house? I mean, it's a fucking dog."

"Yeah, but it was—" Bob dropped his hands. He didn't know how to explain. "You know that feeling you get sometimes on a really great day? Like, like, the Pats dominate and you took the 'over,' or they cook your steak just right up the Blarney, or, or you

just feel *good?* Like . . ." Bob found himself waving his hands again
". . . good?"

Marv gave him a nod and a tight smile. Went back to his racing
sheet.

On Sunday morning, Nadia brought the puppy to his car as he
idled in front of her house. She handed it through the window and
gave them both a little wave.

He looked at the puppy sitting on his seat and fear washed over
him. What does it eat? When does it eat? Housebreaking. How do
you do that? How long does it take? He'd had days to consider
these questions—why were they only occurring to him now?

He hit the brakes and reversed the car a few feet. Nadia, one
foot on her bottom step, turned back. He rolled down the passenger window, craned his body across the seat until he was peering
up at her.

"I don't know what to do," he said. "I don't know anything."

At a supermarket for pets, Nadia picked out several chew toys, told
Bob he'd need them if he wanted to keep his couch. Shoes, she
told him, keep your shoes hidden from now on, up on a high shelf.
They bought vitamins—for a dog!—and a bag of puppy food she
recommended, telling him the most important thing was to stick
with that brand from now on. Change a dog's diet, she warned,
you'll get piles of diarrhea on your floor.

They got a crate to put him in when Bob was at work. They got
a water bottle for the crate and a book on dog training written by
monks who were on the cover looking hardy and not real monkish,
big smiles. As the cashier rang it all up, Bob felt a quake rumble
through his body, a momentary disruption as he reached for his
wallet. His throat flushed with heat. His head felt fizzy. And only
as the quake went away and his throat cooled and his head cleared
and he handed over his credit card to the cashier did he realize,
in the sudden disappearance of the feeling, what the feeling had
been: for a moment—maybe even a succession of moments, and
none sharp enough to point to as the cause—he'd been happy.

"So, thank you," she said when he pulled up in front of her house.
"What? No. Thank *you*. Please. Really. It . . . Thank you."

She said, "This little guy, he's a good guy. He's going to make you proud, Bob."

He looked down at the puppy, sleeping on her lap now, snoring slightly. "Do they do that? Sleep all the time?"

"Pretty much. Then they run around like loonies for about twenty minutes. Then they sleep some more. And poop. Bob, man, you got to remember that—they poop and pee like crazy. Don't get mad. They don't know any better. Read the monk book. It takes time, but they figure out soon enough not to do it in the house."

"What's soon enough?"

"Two months?" She cocked her head. "Maybe three. Be patient, Bob."

"Be patient," he repeated.

"And you too," she said to the puppy as she lifted it off her lap. He came awake, sniffing, snorting. He didn't want her to go. "You *both* take care." She let herself out and gave Bob a wave as she walked up her steps, then went inside.

The puppy was on its haunches, staring up at the window like Nadia might reappear there. It looked back over his shoulder at Bob. Bob could feel its abandonment. He could feel his own. He was certain they'd make a mess of it, him and this throwaway dog. He was sure the world was too strong.

"What's your name?" he asked the puppy. "What are we going to call you?"

The puppy turned his head away, like, Bring the girl back.

First thing it did was take a shit in the dining room.

Bob didn't even realize what it was doing at first. It started sniffing, nose scraping the rug, and then it looked up at Bob with an air of embarrassment. And Bob said, "What?" and the dog dumped all over the corner of the rug.

Bob scrambled forward, as if he could stop it, push it back in, and the puppy bolted, left droplets on the hardwood as it scurried into the kitchen.

Bob said, "No, no. It's okay." Although it wasn't. Most everything in the house had been his mother's, largely unchanged since she'd purchased it in the '50s. That was shit. Excrement. In his mother's house. On her rug, her floor.

In the seconds it took him to reach the kitchen, the puppy'd left a piss puddle on the linoleum. Bob almost slipped in it. The puppy was sitting against the fridge, looking at him, tensing for a blow, trying not to shake.

And it stopped Bob. It stopped him even as he knew the longer he left the shit on the rug, the harder it would be to get out.

Bob got down on all fours. He felt the sudden return of what he'd felt when he first picked it out of the trash, something he'd assumed had left with Nadia. Connection. He suspected they might have been brought together by something other than chance.

He said, "Hey." Barely above a whisper. "Hey, it's all right." So, so slowly, he extended his hand, and the puppy pressed itself harder against the fridge. But Bob kept the hand coming, and gently lay his palm on the side of the animal's face. He made soothing sounds. He smiled at it. "It's okay," he repeated, over and over.

He named it Cassius because he'd mistaken it for a boxer and he liked the sound of the word. It made him think of Roman legions, proud jaws, honor.

Nadia called him Cash. She came around after work sometimes and she and Bob took it on walks. He knew something was a little off about Nadia—the dog being found so close to her house and her lack of surprise or interest in that fact was not lost on Bob—but was there anyone, anywhere on this planet, who wasn't a little off? More than a little most times. Nadia came by to help with the dog and Bob, who hadn't known much friendship in his life, took what he could get.

They taught Cassius to sit and lie down and paw and roll over. Bob read the entire monk book and followed its instructions. The puppy had his rabies shot and was cleared of any cartilage damage to his ear. Just a bruise, the vet said, just a deep bruise. He grew fast.

Weeks passed without Cassius having an accident, but Bob still couldn't be sure whether that was luck or not, and then on Super Bowl Sunday, Cassius used one paw on the back door. Bob let him out and then tore through the house to call Nadia. He was so proud he felt like yodeling, and he almost mistook the doorbell for something else. A kettle, he thought, still reaching for the phone.

The guy on the doorstep was thin. Not weak-thin. Hard-thin. As if whatever burned inside of him burned too hot for fat to survive. He had blue eyes so pale they were almost gray. His silver hair was cropped tight to his skull, as was the goatee that clung to his lips and chin. It took Bob a second to recognize him—the kid who'd stuck his head in the bar five-six weeks back, asked if they served Zima.

The kid smiled and extended his hand. "Mr. Saginowski?"

Bob shook the hand. "Yes?"

"Bob Saginowski?" The man shook Bob's large hand with his small one, and there was a lot of power in the grip.

"Yeah?"

"Eric Deeds, Bob." The kid let go of his hand. "I believe you have my dog."

In the kitchen, Eric Deeds said, "Hey, there he is." He said, "That's my guy." He said, "He got big." He said, "The size of him."

Cassius slinked over to him, even climbed up on his lap when Eric, unbidden, took a seat at Bob's kitchen table and patted his inner thigh twice. Bob couldn't even say how it was Eric Deeds talked his way into the house; he was just one of those people had a way about him, like cops and Teamsters—he wanted in, he was coming in.

"Bob," Eric Deeds said, "I'm going to need him back." He had Cassius in his lap and was rubbing his belly. Bob felt a prick of envy as Cassius kicked his left leg, even though a constant shiver—almost a palsy—ran through his fur. Eric Deeds scratched under Cassius's chin. The dog kept his ears and tail pressed flat to his body. He looked ashamed, his eyes staring down into their sockets.

"Um . . ." Bob reached out and lifted Cassius off Eric's lap, plopped him down on his own, scratched behind his ears. "Cash is mine."

The act was between them now—Bob lifting the puppy off Eric's lap without any warning, Eric looking at him for just a second, like, The fuck was that all about? His forehead narrowed and it gave his eyes a surprised cast, as if they'd never expected to find themselves on his face. In that moment, he looked cruel, the kind of guy, if he was feeling sorry for himself, took a shit on the whole world.

"Cash?" he said.

Bob nodded as Cassius's ears unfurled from his head and he licked Bob's wrist. "Short for Cassius. That's his name. What did you call him?"

"Called him Dog mostly. Sometimes Hound."

Eric Deeds glanced around the kitchen, up at the old circular fluorescent in the ceiling, something going back to Bob's mother, hell, Bob's father just before the first stroke, around the time the old man had become obsessed with paneling — paneled the kitchen, the living room, the dining room, would've paneled the toilet if he could've figured out how.

Bob said, "You beat him."

Eric reached into his shirt pocket. He pulled out a cigarette and popped it in his mouth. He lit it, shook out the match, tossed it on Bob's kitchen table.

"You can't smoke in here."

Eric considered Bob with a level gaze and kept smoking. "I beat him?"

"Yeah."

"Uh, so what?" Eric flicked some ash on the floor. "I'm taking the dog, Bob."

Bob stood to his full height. He held tight to Cassius, who squirmed a bit in his arms and nipped at the flat of his hand. If it came to it, Bob decided, he'd drop all six feet three inches and two hundred ninety pounds of himself on Eric Deeds, who couldn't weigh more than a buck-seventy. Not now, not just standing there, but if Eric reached for Cassius, well then . . .

Eric Deeds blew a stream of smoke at the ceiling. "I saw you that night. I was feeling bad, you know, about my temper? So I went back to see if the hound was really dead or not and I watched you pluck him out of the trash."

"I really think you should go." Bob pulled his cell from his pocket and flipped it open. "I'm calling 911."

Eric nodded. "I've been in prison, Bob, mental hospitals. I've been a lotta places. I'll go again, don't mean a thing to me, though I doubt they'd prosecute even *me* for fucking up a *dog*. I mean, sooner or later, you gotta go to work or get some sleep."

"What is *wrong* with you?"

Eric held out his hands. "Pretty much everything. And you took my dog."

"You tried to kill it."

Eric said, "Nah." Shook his head like he believed it.

"You can't have the dog."

"I need the dog."

"No."

"I love that dog."

"No."

"Ten thousand."

"What?"

Eric nodded. "I need ten grand. By tonight. That's the price."

Bob gave it a nervous chuckle. "Who has ten thousand dollars?"

"You could find it."

"How could I poss—"

"Say, that safe in Cousin Marv's office. You're a drop bar, Bob. You don't think half the neighborhood knows? So that might be a place to start."

Bob shook his head. "Can't be done. Any money we get during the day? Goes through a slot at the bar. Ends up in the office safe, yeah, but that's on a time—"

"—lock, I know." Eric turned on the couch, one arm stretched along the back of it. "Goes off at two A.M. in case they decide they need a last-minute payout for something who the fuck knows, but big. And you have ninety seconds to open and close it or it triggers two silent alarms, neither of which goes off in a police station or a security company. Fancy that." Eric took a hit off his cigarette. "I'm not greedy, Bob. I just need stake money for something. I don't want everything in the safe, just ten grand. You give me ten grand, I'll disappear."

"This is ludicrous."

"So, it's ludicrous."

"You don't just walk into someone's life and—"

"That *is* life: someone like me coming along when you're not looking."

Bob put Cassius on the floor but made sure he didn't wander over to the other side of the table. He needn't have worried—Cassius didn't move an inch, sat there like a cement post, eyes on Bob.

Eric Deeds said, "You're racing through all your options, but they're options for normal people in normal circumstances. I need my ten grand tonight. If you don't get it for me, I'll take your dog. *I* licensed him. You didn't, because you couldn't. Then I'll forget to feed him for a while. One day, when he gets all yappy about it, I'll beat his head in with a rock or something. Look in my eyes and tell me which part I'm lying about, Bob."

*

After he left, Bob went to his basement. He avoided it whenever he could, though the floor was white, as white as he'd been able to make it, whiter than it had ever been through most of its existence. He unlocked a cupboard over the old wash sink his father had often used after one of his adventures in paneling, and removed a yellow and brown Chock full o'Nuts can from the shelf. He pulled fifteen thousand from it. He put ten in his pocket and five back in the can. He looked around again at the white floor, at the black oil tank against the wall, at the bare bulbs.

Upstairs he gave Cassius a bunch of treats. He rubbed his ears and his belly. He assured the animal that he was worth ten thousand dollars.

Bob, three deep at the bar for a solid hour between eleven and midnight, looked through a sudden gap in the crowd and saw Eric sitting at the wobbly table under the Narragansett mirror. The Super Bowl was an hour over, but the crowd, drunk as shit, hung around. Eric had one arm stretched across the table and Bob followed it, saw that it connected to something. An arm. Nadia's arm. Nadia's face stared back at Eric, unreadable. Was she terrified? Or something else?

Bob, filling a glass with ice, felt like he was shoveling the cubes into his own chest, pouring them into his stomach and against the base of his spine. What did he know about Nadia, after all? He knew that he'd found a near-dead dog in the trash outside her house. He knew that Eric Deeds only came into his life after Bob had met her. He knew that her middle name, thus far, could be Lies of Omission.

When he was twenty-eight, Bob had come into his mother's bedroom to wake her for Sunday Mass. He'd given her a shake and she hadn't batted at his hand as she normally did. So he rolled her toward him and her face was scrunched tight, her eyes too, and her skin was curbstone-gray. Sometime in the night, after *Matlock* and the ten o'clock news, she'd gone to bed and woke to God's fist clenched around her heart. Probably hadn't been enough air left in her lungs to cry out. Alone in the dark, clutching the sheets, that fist clenching, her face clenching, her eyes scrunching, the terrible knowledge dawning that, even for you, it all ends. And right now.

Standing over her that morning, imagining the last tick of her heart, the last lonely wish her brain had been able to form, Bob felt a loss unlike any he'd ever known or expected to know again.

Until tonight. Until now. Until he learned what that look on Nadia's face meant.

By 1:50, the crowd was gone, just Eric and Nadia and an old, stringent, functioning alcoholic named Millie who'd amble off to the assisted living place up on Pearl Street at 1:55 on the dot.

Eric, who had been coming to the bar for shots of Powers for the last hour, pushed back from the table and pulled Nadia across the floor with him. He sat her on a stool and Bob got a good look in her face finally, saw something he still couldn't fully identify—but it definitely wasn't excitement or smugness or the bitter smile of a victor. Maybe something worse than all of that—despair.

Eric gave him an all-teeth smile and spoke through it, softly. "When's the old biddie pack it in?"

"A couple minutes."

"Where's Marv?"

"I didn't call him in."

"Why not?"

"Someone's gonna take the blame for this, I figured it might as well be me."

"How noble of—"

"How do you know her?"

Eric looked over at Nadia hunched on the stool beside him. He leaned into the bar. "We grew up on the same block."

"He give you that scar?"

Nadia stared at him.

"Did he?"

"She gave herself the scar," Eric Deeds said.

"You did?" Bob asked her.

Nadia looked at the bar top. "I was pretty high."

"Bob," Eric said, "if you fuck with me—even in the slightest—it doesn't matter how long it takes me, I'll come back for her. And if you got any plans, like Eric-doesn't-walk-back-out-of-here plans? Not that you're that type of guy, but Marv might be? You got any ideas in that vein, Bob, my partner on the Richie Whalen hit, he'll take care of you both."

Eric sat back as mean old Millie left the same tip she'd been leav-

ing since Sputnik—a quarter—and slid off her stool. She gave
Bob a rasp that was ten percent vocal chords and ninety percent
Virginia Slims Ultra Light 100s. "Yeah, I'm off."

"You take care, Millie."

She waved it away with a "Yeah, yeah, yeah," and pushed open
the door.

Bob locked it behind her and came back behind the bar. He
wiped down the bar top. When he reached Eric's elbows, he said,
"Excuse me."

"Go around."

Bob wiped the rag in a half-circle around Eric's elbows.

"Who's your partner?" Bob said.

"Wouldn't be much of a threat if you knew who he was, would
he, Bob?"

"But he helped you kill Richie Whalen?"

Eric said, "That's the rumor, Bob."

"More than a rumor." Bob wiped in front of Nadia, saw red marks
on her wrists where Eric had yanked them. He wondered if there
were other marks he couldn't see.

"Well then it's more than a rumor, Bob. So there you go."

"There you go what?"

"There you *go*," Eric scowled. "What time is it, Bob?"

Bob placed ten thousand dollars on the bar. "You don't have to
call me by my name all the time."

"I will see what I can do about that, Bob." Eric thumbed the bills.
"What's this?"

"It's the ten grand you wanted for Cash."

Eric pursed his lips. "All the same, let's look in the safe."

"You sure?" Bob said. "I'm happy to buy him from you for ten
grand."

"How much for Nadia, though?"

"Oh."

"Yeah. Oh."

Bob thought about that new wrinkle for a bit and poured himself a closing-time shot of vodka. He raised it to Eric Deeds and
then drank it down. "You know, Marv used to have a problem with
blow about ten years ago?"

"I did not know that, Bob."

Bob shrugged, poured them all a shot of vodka. "Yeah, Marv
liked the coke too much but it didn't like him back."

Eric drank Nadia's shot. "Getting close to two here, Bob."

"He was more of a loan shark then. I mean, he did some fence, but mostly he was a shark. There was this kid? Into Marv for a shit-load of money. Real hopeless case when it came to the dogs and basketball. Kinda kid could never pay back all he owed."

Eric drank his own shot. "One fifty-seven, Bob."

"The thing, though? This kid, he actually hit on a slot at Mohe-gan. Hit for twenty-two grand. Which is just a little more than he owed Marv."

"And he didn't pay Marv back, so you and Marv got all hard on him and I'm supposed to learn—"

"No, no. He *paid* Marv. Paid him every cent. What the kid didn't know, though, was that Marv had been skimming. Because of the coke habit? And this kid's money was like manna from heaven as long as no one knew it was from this kid. See what I'm saying?"

"Bob, it's fucking one minute to two." Sweat on Eric's lip.

"Do you see what I'm saying?" Bob asked. "Do you understand the story?"

Eric looked to the door to make sure it was locked. "Fine, yeah. This kid, he had to be ripped off."

"He had to be killed."

Out of the side of his eye, a quick glance. "Okay, killed."

Bob could feel Nadia's eyes lock on him suddenly, her head cock a bit. "That way, he couldn't ever say he paid off Marv and no one else could either. Marv uses the money to cover all the holes, he cleans up his act, it's like it never happened. So that's what we did."

"You did . . ." Eric barely in the conversation, but some warning in his head starting to sound, his head turning from the clock to-ward Bob.

"Killed him in my basement," Bob said. "Know what his name was?"

"I wouldn't know, Bob."

"Sure you would. Richie Whelan."

Bob reached under the bar and pulled out the 9mm. He didn't notice the safety was on, so when he pulled the trigger nothing happened. Eric jerked his head and pushed back from the bar rail, but Bob thumbed off the safety and shot Eric just below the throat. The gunshot sounded like aluminum siding being torn off a house. Nadia screamed. Not a long scream, but sharp with shock. Eric made a racket falling back off his stool, and by the time Bob came around the bar, Eric was already going, if not quite gone. The overhead fan cast thin slices of shadow over his face. His cheeks puffed in and out like he was trying to catch his breath and kiss somebody at the same time.

"I'm sorry, but you kids," Bob said. "You know? You go out of the house dressed like you're still in your living room. You say terrible things about women. You hurt harmless dogs. I'm tired of you, man."

Eric stared up at him. Winced like he had heartburn. He looked pissed off. Frustrated. The expression froze on his face like it was sewn there, and then he wasn't in his body anymore. Just gone. Just, shit, dead.

Bob dragged him into the cooler.

When he came back, pushing the mop and bucket ahead of him, Nadia still sat on her stool. Her mouth was a bit wider than usual and she couldn't take her eyes off the floor where the blood was, but otherwise she seemed perfectly normal.

"He would have just kept coming," Bob said. "Once someone takes something from you and you let them? They don't feel gratitude, they just feel like you owe them more." He soaked the mop in the bucket, wrung it out a bit, and slopped it over the main blood spot. "Makes no sense, right? But that's how they feel. Entitled. And you can never change their minds after that."

She said, "He . . . You just fucking shot him. You just . . . I mean, you know?"

Bob swirled the mop over the spot. "He beat my dog."

The Chechens took care of the body after a discussion with the Italians and the Micks. Bob was told his money was no good at several restaurants for the next couple of months, and they gave him four tickets to a Celtics game. Not floor seats, but pretty good ones.

Bob never mentioned Nadia. Just said Eric showed up at the end of the evening, waved a gun around, said to take him to the office safe. Bob let him do his ranting, do his waving, found an opportunity, and shot him. And that was it. End of Eric, end of story.

Nadia came to him a few days later. Bob opened the door and she stood there on his stoop with a bright winter day turning everything sharp and clear behind her. She held up a bag of dog treats.

"Peanut butter," she said, her smile bright, her eyes just a little wet. "With a hint of molasses."

Bob opened the door wide and stepped back to let her in.

"I've gotta believe," Nadia said, "there's a purpose. And even if it's that you kill me as soon as I close my eyes—"

"Me? What? No," Bob said. "Oh, no."

"—then that's okay. Because I just can't go through any more of this alone. Not another day."

"Me too." He closed his eyes. "Me too."

They didn't speak for a long time. He opened his eyes, peered at the ceiling of his bedroom. "Why?"

"Hmm?"

"This. You. Why are you with me?"

She ran a hand over his chest and it gave him a shiver. In his whole life, he never would have expected to feel a touch like that on his bare skin.

"Because I like you. Because you're nice to Cassius."

"And because you're scared of me?"

"I dunno. Maybe. But more the other reason."

He couldn't tell if she was lying. Who could tell when anyone was? Really. Every day, you ran into people and half of them, if not more, could be lying to you. Why?

Why not?

You couldn't tell who was true and who was not. If you could, lie detectors would never have been invented. Someone stared in your face and said, *I'm telling the truth.* They said, *I promise.* They said, *I love you.*

And you were going to say what to that? Prove it?

"He needs a walk."

"Huh?"

"Cassius. He hasn't been out all day."

"I'll get the leash."

In the park, the February sky hung above them like a canvas tarp. The weather had been almost mild for a few days. The ice had broken on the river but small chunks of it clung to the dark banks.

He didn't know what he believed. Cassius walked ahead of them, pulling on the leash a bit, so proud, so pleased, unrecognizable from the quivering hunk of fur Bob had pulled from a barrel just two and a half months ago.

Two and a half months! Wow. Things sure could change in a hurry. You rolled over one morning, and it was a whole new world. It turned itself toward the sun, stretched and yawned. It turned it-self toward the night. A few more hours, turned itself toward the sun again. A new world, every day.

When they reached the center of the park, he unhooked the leash from Cassius's collar and reached into his coat for a tennis ball. Cassius reared his head. He snorted loud. He pawed the earth. Bob threw the ball and the dog took off after it. Bob envisioned the ball taking a bad bounce into the road. The screech of tires, the thump of metal against dog. Or what would happen if Cassius, sud-denly free, just kept running.

But what could you do?

You couldn't control things.

LYNDA LEIDIGER

Tell Me

FROM *Gettysburg Review*

Friday

FOR HER OWN GOOD, Zandra's family had been ordered to tell her things, not to ask questions.

Nevertheless, Tom always greeted her with, "Hey, Zee. How're you doing?"

Today she replied as usual, "Not . . . so . . . bad," in her clear but halting whisper. The sameness of her answer confirmed that there was nothing in it she pondered, nothing that could frighten or befuddle her. It was a pleasantry, not a true question.

"You look wonderful. Better every day," he said. Then he squeezed her good hand, the left one, and tried to think of suitable things to tell her.

No one knew how much, if anything, she could see. That was one of the forbidden questions. The CAT scans were inconclusive as to how much the optic nerve had been damaged, but Tom had seen her scrutinizing Christmas and get-well cards inches from her face; several times she'd mentioned "shadows." He didn't understand why the doctors hedged. Surely it didn't take years of medical school or a barrage of sophisticated tests to determine whether a person could see. Furthermore, how could it be something about which a patient and her doctors could disagree? "The memory of sight," they were theorizing these days. It would be simple to ask her, "What color is my sweater?" but he was afraid. The doctors knew what was best. Her HIV test had come back negative, and that was the most important thing.

"I've been growing a beard," he told her.

"I . . . know," she said.

"You do?" he said, too eagerly, and she smiled.

"Scratchy," she whispered.

He rubbed his chin. "Oh. Right." He always kissed her hello and good-bye.

"Why . . . ?" She took a deep breath.

"Just for a change, I guess. And to sleep a few minutes later in the morning."

Zee sighed, or groaned.

Betsy, his latest girlfriend, thought the sprouting beard made him look like Steven Spielberg. He wasn't sure that was a good thing. For the past four months, he'd been a grudging student in her cinematic College of One, dutifully squinting at the subtitles in her Kurosawa DVDs, struggling to see the genius in Wertmüller. If she really wanted to compliment him, she'd say the beard made him look like Welles or Eisenstein. Someone she truly respected.

He and Zandra had both had a few relationships in the four years since the divorce, but he never felt comfortable talking to her about them. He worried that not only would she not be jealous, but that she would see in his failed romances vindication of her own decision to leave him. At the start, women always told him how thoughtful and good he was, how solid. After a time, they began criticizing him for repressing his feelings, for not taking risks. Eventually they accused him of being cold, self-absorbed, and inflexible. Tom let them yell at him, and then he let them go.

If Betsy had hit the anger stage, she was hiding it; some feminine protocol undoubtedly governed how to behave toward a man whose ex-wife has nearly died. With an almost missionary zeal, she continued to cook elaborate foreign dishes to accompany the foreign movies. Last week, before a Satyajit Ray film, she'd made an Indian dinner, roasting and grinding the spices herself. He concentrated so hard on eating slowly and appreciatively and making the appropriate comments that he couldn't say whether he'd even enjoyed the food.

Zandra was an enthusiastic but ungifted cook whose motto was "Always add something to a recipe to make it your own." She was prone to dumping soy sauce or cinnamon into her spaghetti, or throwing a handful of sunflower seeds into her brownies. In some ways, it was the most foreign food Tom had ever eaten, but he always found something good to say about it, even the time when she pressed miniature meat loaves into muffin tins and an hour later unmolded hot, crumbly hockey pucks.

After they separated, every month or so she had him over for dinner. In return, he might unstick a window or drill a hole for a coat hook or fix something that required Super Glue, about which she was inexplicably phobic. These were YTB jobs. "You're The Boy," she'd elucidated years ago when a mousetrap in their college apartment needed emptying. He found pleasure in being The Boy, and opportunities abounded in her new house. Although, as a real estate agent, she had first crack at the choicest properties, for some reason she had been smitten by a ramshackle cabin just outside of town. She loved the ugly old flowered kitchen linoleum and positively prized the dented zinc countertops. It pained him to see how different a home she'd chosen from the bright, clean split-level where they'd raised Caitlin, whereas he'd moved into a condo that was a downsized version of it, complete with a redwood deck protected by indoor-outdoor carpeting and a rain gauge that he could easily read through the sliding glass door. When she'd explained why she wanted a divorce, she described their marriage as a slow starvation. He made her repeat it twice, irrationally thinking she might have meant to say *salvation.*

He had tried to make her happy. He never forgot their anniversary (red roses) or her birthday (a gift certificate at a day spa). He always put the toilet seat back down. Little things could be important. When she expressed a like or dislike, he paid attention. There was the time she complained that he never surprised her. A few days later, he secretly filled her car with gas and had it washed. She never noticed.

"I'm getting new carpeting," he told her now. "Wall-to-wall. The floor won't feel so drafty, and it'll keep the wood like new." He thought she gave him a look. "It's sort of grayish brown with flecks. The clerk said it won't show the dirt." Betsy called it "pre-soiled."

Zee was staring at him. "Why . . . ?" she exhaled. She seemed exhausted.

"Because I'm such a slob. A regular ape-man." He thumped his chest like a cartoon gorilla. "Remember that song?"

She didn't respond.

In college, she used to sing to herself, "Come on and love me, be my ape-man girl." The lyrics went on about being happy in an ape-man world: living in a tree, eating with your hands, that sort of thing. One of these days he should surprise her with a CD. Some music store clerk into the oldies—it was an oldie already by the time they were in college—might recognize it from the few lyrics he could remember. Zee probably had the original record stashed somewhere in her cabin, but he wasn't about to go looking for it.

He hadn't been back there. No one had. When she needed clothing, someone went shopping. She seemed to have given up asking about the new clothes, as she had about her head injury and what everyone was instructed to call "the accident." Before long, arrangements would need to be made to box up her things. The place would have to be cleaned and put back on the market, although Tom was certain that no one who knew its history would want to live there. Zee could never move back there, even if she recovered. It was no longer safe. That was one more thing that had been taken from her. Tom had begun investigating the cost of renting a hospital bed and hiring a nurse to come in during the day. It wouldn't be hard to convert his study. He could buy a bigger TV, hang a bird feeder or two in the window for the flashes of color, put a little CD player on the nightstand so she could listen to audio books. Zee had always loved mysteries. He hadn't said anything to her yet, of course. Or to Betsy.

As he paced, Zee's eyes tracked him—following the sound of him, the doctors would say. She was waiting for him to tell her something else.

"It's snowing," he told her. "It's terribly cold. You're lucky to be someplace warm. The weatherman said it's already one of the ten coldest winters on record."

She was still waiting.

"Hey, Mom. Looking good," Caitlin sang out as she breezed into the hospital room. Around her mother, she'd developed this new tendency to breeze, bustle, chatter, flutter, babble, and generally behave like some crazed perpetual-motion machine.

"Thank . . . you," her mother whispered.

She did look good these days, relatively. With that horrible shunt removed from her skull, her hair was growing back. It was coming in gray, either because of the trauma or because she'd secretly been dyeing all these years. At least she was wearing fun purple sweats, instead of a hospital gown, now that she was off the tubes. Caitlin used to worry that if she herself went blind, people would dress her in clashing stripes and plaids, maybe even T-shirts with moronic slogans, and laugh at her behind her back. Now she worried that if someone tried to kill her, she might not die.

She shrugged off her parka and snatched up yesterday's mail from the bedside table, in the process sending the telephone crashing to the floor. "Sorry. Enter the ox," she said, stooping to slap the jangly thing back together. Who in their right mind would call someone in her mother's condition anyway? Telemarketers, most likely. Invasive cretins. She prayed for one—just one!—to call while she was there. She stood and rifled through the cards. "Oooh, Aunt Eileen's in Africa again."

"Ethi . . . opia," her mother said.

"Right!" Caitlin cheered, as if her mother were a clever contestant on some TV game show. She had forgotten how to talk like a normal person. Now she was bright and brisk, frantically awkward. Strutting and fretting. Life's but a walking elbow. In her own way, she felt as inappropriate as her aunt, who was jetting blithely around the world—even if it was her job—and dashing off chirpy little notes on embossed hotel stationery. As if anyone cared what the weather was like in Addis Ababa! Aunt Eileen, who was five years younger, had been born old, Mom claimed. "Don't feel bad about being an only child," she'd advised Caitlin more than once. "Someday, when you're least expecting it, you'll find your true sister, like I did with Peg." Their meeting in a Laundromat as college freshmen was a family legend. "I thought this chain-smoking blonde was stealing my clothes out of the dryer. But she happened to have a Bullwinkle sweatshirt exactly like mine. Wottsamatta U!" It still made her laugh.

Caitlin imagined that her father had fallen in love with Aunt Eileen all those years ago, which would have been much more sensible of him. Her mother would have been her aunt! *No, I wouldn't have been born,* she reminded herself. *I wouldn't be* me, *anyway.*

"Dad . . ." her mother began.

"He was here? Good," Caitlin said. He came every afternoon at 4:30, after her mother's last therapy session. Visitors were allowed in only one at a time, so, without discussing it, the regulars had settled into time slots, putting in predictable, orderly twenty-minute shifts, occasionally conferring with one another if they happened to meet in between. "I think Dad's going through a midlife crisis. His beard?" She restacked her mother's get-well cards, rapping them sharply on the tabletop like a blackjack dealer straightening his deck. Her mother seemed to wince. "I thought only bald guys felt they had to grow beards when they hit fifty. Although he hardly ever takes off that baseball cap, so who can tell what his scalp is up to."

"Scratchy," her mother whispered.

"Definitely," Caitlin agreed.

She wondered if her mother regretted the divorce. How important could all those "bored-and-suffocating" complaints—the confidences Caitlin had loathed hearing—seem to her now? Both of her parents would be happier together, even like this. Mr. In-Sickness-and-In-Health would have dutifully taken care of Mom for the rest of his life and been grateful, because for once he would have known exactly what to do. Unlike his present role. As a devoted ex-husband, he was doing his best, but with the apologetic sheepishness of an actor who wasn't yet off-book. Caitlin had been considering majoring in theater before Everything Happened, as the family referred to it. Now she might as well become a professional bowler, get paid for knocking things down and making a racket, though it was probably harder than it looked. That would be something to tell her mother: "I'm thinking of dropping out of college. I can't see the point in anything."

When the doctors said, "Tell her things," they didn't mean: "Tell her the boy who broke in and pressed a pillow to the back of her head, then a .22 against the pillow, was younger than her daughter. Tell her that after he zipped up his jeans and left her for dead, he went out for a Big Mac. Tell her that when the police caught him a couple of hours later, he explained that he had been bored."

"Tell me if this hurts." Caitlin leaned over the metal guardrail and rubbed her mother's new claw, gently bending the curved fingers outward. "Oh, I almost forgot." She rooted in her backpack for a little plastic bottle. "Grandma thought you might like this. It's got coconut oil and aloe?" She squirted out a dollop of lotion and warmed it in her palms. "She swears by it. You know she still creams her hands and wears cotton gloves to bed every night? She's incredible."

Grandma, unlike Dad, was rising to the occasion. If she had any hesitation about how an ex-mother-in-law should conduct herself, you couldn't tell. She greeted disaster with a sort of satisfaction, as if now that the worst had happened, she could finally stop worrying about it.

With the dorms closed, Caitlin was thankful to be spending the semester break with her, tucked up in the sewing room hide-a-bed and awakening to the odor of cigarette smoke and coffee. It smelled better than fresh-baked Christmas cookies. There was no question of going back to the cabin, and no need. (Thank god her mother wasn't the type for a cat or houseplants.) She would have sprung for a motel before staying with her father. His latest virtually lived there, a middle-aged, semi-anorexic pseudo-waif who never stopped talking. Or cooking. At the sad little Christmas Eve dinner the five of them had gathered for at Grandma's, old Heavens-to-Betsy, as Grandma secretly called her, unveiled a plate of brownies that she bragged were from Katharine Hepburn's family recipe. Caitlin and her father exchanged glances. He had to be remembering the time her mother had made what was supposedly George Washington's eggnog but was closer to latex enamel, the kind that covered in one coat. Kate's famous brownies, big surprise, were chocolate caulk. In a way, Caitlin felt sorry for earnest, bony Heavens-to-Betsy in the way she felt sorry for all optimists, all myopic dogs barking up a lifetime of wrong trees, but it was too much trouble to try to set her straight. She wished, utterly without hope, that her father would ask her mother to get back together again, and that her mother would say yes.

"Poor Mommy," she crooned to her mother, the way she had once comforted her baby dolls. "Poor, poor Mommy." She massaged her mother's hands until the beachy scent of the lotion rose from the bed.

Her mother's nose wrinkled.

"Nice, isn't it?" Caitlin sniffed her own hands. "You know, I hear this is the original recipe for Marie Antoinette's very own piña coladas?"

Her mother made the peculiar noisy grin that was her new way of laughing.

It was a made-to-order Christmas miracle for the media. Shot in the head the day before Thanksgiving, popping out of her coma bright and early Christmas Day, smiling and squeezing hands by

New Year's Eve. It was so damned miraculous that Marian couldn't explain why she was having such a hard time feeling lucky. Lucky was how everyone was supposed to feel, what the reporters wanted to hear, so they could write:

> "We're shocked and terribly disappointed that the boy won't be tried as an adult, of course," declared the victim's former mother-in-law, seventy-two-year-old Marian Sladek, "but this is the season of forgiveness. As we remember the Son who was born to die for our sins, so must we also remember that even the misguided child whose thoughtless act shattered so many lives is somebody's son."

It was a hell of a lot more heartwarming than what she had actually said when Channel 6 showed up on her doorstep this morning, which was, "Lucky? Do we feel lucky because some worthless punk turned a bright, wonderful, hard-working woman into an invalid for the rest of her life, robbed a daughter of her mother, and for punishment he'll be lying on his can watching TV for a few years, courtesy of my taxes?" The young reporter holding the microphone cringed, and for a moment Marian pitied her: a paid jackal in a poorly cut plaid coat that would add twenty pounds on camera. "There was someone like Alexandra on *Oprah* the other day," Marian told her, "and when she said she forgave the drug-crazed hoodlum who tried to murder her for three dollars and a bus pass, the audience applauded. And cried, of course." Channel 6 bobbed her head and smiled hopefully. "But I'm telling you," Marian went on, "that we have entirely too much forgiveness nowadays. Forgiveness for cruelty, stupidity, intolerance. Forgiveness for selfishness and cowardice. We have lost our capacity for outrage. That is not what Jesus meant by turning the other cheek."

The reporter sputtered an apology and left with her cameraman. Channel 6 would never air the segment. *Oprah* was on a different network.

It was from studying Buddhism that Marian, an unwavering lifelong Christian, had accepted rage as her savior. In a stress-management seminar that Marian's company had sponsored several years before her retirement, the instructor had led the participants in a Buddhist meditation: "Breathing in, I know I have anger in me; breathing out, I know I am the anger." It had taken only three exhalations to reduce Marian to helpless sobs, cross-legged on her green plastic mat, in front of everyone. She understood that her anger had been protecting her all along from a vast, unsuspected cavern of sadness—she refused to call it despair—and decided then and there to love it, to hang on to it for dear life.

When the elevator doors opened, she walked down the long white hall, lugging her usual tote bag full of surprises for Alexandra. As she had once focused on stimulating her son, and later her granddaughter, when they were small, she now searched out things that would engage those of Alexandra's senses that weren't in question, items that might remind her of who she used to be. Give us this day our daily bundle. In this case: mail and a comic strip to be read aloud, a manicure kit so she could polish Alexandra's nails, a pine needle–filled sachet to tuck under the pillow, and a new pair of soft, nubby socks.

In the hall, a candy striper wobbled on a stepladder as she took down the shiny red and green ornaments that hung from the ceiling. In a few weeks there'd be hearts, then shamrocks, Easter eggs . . . Marian saw herself plodding through all those days, clutching her tote bag with one hand, her stalwart friend, Rage, with the other. She gnawed the inside of her cheek.

Alexandra was propped up in bed, facing the window. Who knew what she saw?

"Hi, darling." Marian kissed her. "It's colder out there than a Republican's heart."

With an effort, Alexandra whispered, "Com . . . mie."

Marian burst out laughing. "Bless your heart." She was thrilled whenever Alexandra made any sort of joke, or responded to one. Humor, after all, was one of the higher brain functions. "Even in the cold, everything's gorgeous with all that new snow. Like an exquisite pen-and-ink drawing," she went on as she took off her coat. "I love the bare trees. The way you see tiny little twigs you can't even imagine in the summer when the leaves are so full?" She sniffed. "Do I smell coconut?" she said.

"Cait . . . lin."

"Oh, good, she did your hands. Because I've brought a little treat." She took out the manicure kit and helped Alexandra feel the files, the cuticle stick, the buffer. "This shade might be too orangey for you, but I adore the name. Coral Shores. It makes you think of the ocean and warm sunshine, doesn't it? A gorgeous white sand beach, and at the edge of it, palm trees with those immense green fringy tops, like a hat Carol Channing would wear."

Alexandra said nothing—concentrating, perhaps, on the word-picture Marian worked so hard to paint. Or wondering who on earth Carol Channing was. Marian envisioned the blindness as a membrane between Alexandra's eyes and brain, a membrane that will and imagination could break. She prattled on while she did Alexandra's hands; occasionally she was rewarded with a smile or a sound that was close to a laugh. Marian knew she'd pay for it tonight, bending over the guardrail like this until her back stiffened. She didn't care. If Channel 6 had asked her why she cared so much about the woman who had broken her son's heart, how would she have answered?

> "We're the poor child's only family," said the elder Mrs. Sladek of her forty-nine-year-old daughter-in-law. "Her parents are dead and her only sibling is flying all over the world on business, or I have no doubt she'd be here right now. Although," she added delicately, "they've never been terribly close. As for my son—broken-hearted? So you would think. I honestly can't say for sure. He's not cold, exactly, just tepid. Always has been. I'm sure Dr. Phil and his ilk would blame his upbringing: a father who left, a mother who overcompensated by giving him everything and leaving him nothing to want. But some people simply aren't born passionate. When I met Alexandra, on the other hand, I recognized her instantly as a kindred spirit." In conclusion she said quietly, "I have always, always loved my daughter-in-law very much."

She had to release Alexandra's hand to get a tissue. To her mortification, her absurd imaginary press conference had left tears in her eyes.

"You won't believe what I had at the feeder today," she said, searching Alexandra's face for a sign of interest but going on anyway. "A tufted titmouse! A pair of them. Titmice. Tom still can't hear that word—much less say it!—with a straight face. Why are men such adolescents? Of course, those despicable starlings scared them away. The big, speckled pigs practically bathe in the feeder and knock the seeds everywhere. The man at the bird store says the starlings are just like poor relations who show up and eat you out of house and home. You can't starve your family just to get rid of them, so what choice do you have?"

Alexandra appeared to be sleeping. Clever, exciting Marian had stimulated her right into a doze, with two nails still to be done. She dabbed them with the little brush, then held Alexandra's hands and blew lightly on the wet polish. "Here's the ocean breeze blowing across the coral shores," she whispered. When she thought the nails were dry, she changed Alexandra's socks. Her daughter-in-law's feet were cool and waxy-looking. Recently, the right one had started to droop and stiffen in an odd position. Marian tugged the thick new sock over it, then gently worked to straighten the foot, as the therapist no doubt had just done half an hour earlier. Alexandra grunted, and Marian let go. She dropped the old socks into her bag, to be washed at home. The hospital had a service, but you couldn't trust them not to lose things, and she didn't like the idea of someone who didn't know Alexandra handling her clothing. Marian straightened slowly. Her spine made a sound like cookies being crushed with a rolling pin for a crumb crust. The sachet would keep for another time, she decided; the pine was one smell too many.

As she struggled back into her coat, it nagged at her that she hadn't read Alexandra her mail, which she should have done first thing instead of launching into one of her bird-nerd monologues, as Caitlin called them. One envelope looked like a card from the office. The other agents were decent people, but once it became obvious that Alexandra's career there was over—you can't show houses you can't see—they didn't know how to behave toward her. The one with the Minneapolis postmark had to be from Peggy, Alexandra's college friend. Peggy had a good heart, which Marian admitted was the sort of thing you said about irresponsible, lost women whose hair was a different color every time you saw them, but who never did anything that was downright immoral.

Alexandra opened her eyes. She bumped her hands clumsily together, trying to raise them to her face.

"Here, sweetheart." Marian bent again and clasped Alexandra's hands, lifting them to eye level. Alexandra rolled her head from side to side, as if studying first her healthy, moving hand, then the weak one that curled in on itself like a hatchling. All they had in common were ten perfect ovals, gleaming coral.

Saturday

Peg almost didn't come when she suspected that she was getting a cold. She deliberated about checking with the doctors, but it wasn't as if the problem was Zee's immune system. A million things worse than a cold were no doubt being pumped through the hospital's ventilation ducts every second. These days, you could go in for a hysterectomy and die of Legionnaires' disease—provided some incompetent anesthesiologist didn't do you in first. Besides, the Zee she knew and loved wouldn't fight her way out of a coma to die of the sniffles. Peg was haunted by her vision of Zee not fighting, of forcing herself to be still and submit until it was finally over. Only it wasn't over, not quite. Afterward, lying there bruised and half-naked in her torn clothes, but *alive,* she must have thought she was finally safe. What had she felt when that asshole kicked her over onto her stomach, when the hard piece of metal nuzzled at her skull through the pillow he pressed to the back of her head? Did she plead, promise anything? Was she angry, scornful, utterly cool? Or numb, the way you get when time stops?

Peg found herself taking deep breaths in the elevator. Hospitals had always terrified her; sick people made her want to run. Zee wasn't really sick, she was recuperating. And she was still herself—Marian had stressed that—only tired and weak and aphasic. "A bit slow to find the words," Marian elaborated, as if Peg herself were a bit slow. When the elevator slid open on all those in-your-face cheery handmade Christmas decorations, Peg thought first of an elementary school, then a nursing home. Suddenly she was afraid to take deep breaths.

It didn't matter that it was just the rehab ward, no diapered screamers strapped into wheelchairs here. Her automatic mouth breathing kicked in to shut out the acid tang of urine, antiseptics, and boiled food. She couldn't separate the smell from the memory of smell. Which was even more ridiculous considering that she'd been sneezing for a day and a half and felt like a cork was stuffed up each nostril.

She was angry with herself for being such a baby, for not coming sooner, for letting acres of acoustic tile and white linoleum induce a low-grade panic attack, for making lists of what might be acceptable things to say, safe topics. To Peg, "Discretion is the better part of valor" had always meant: "It's tough to keep your mouth shut." She knew Zee was going to be different. She also knew it was vitally important to act as if everything was the same. She'd never been good at acting. Whatever the opposite of a poker face was, she had it. A domino face? One wrong move, and everything collapses. Marian had prepared her for the fact that Zee might be blind, but

Peg knew that whatever was on her face would be in her voice too. She and Zee had never been able to bullshit each other. Face it, they were probably seriously flattering themselves if they thought they'd ever bullshit anyone. They'd always been a matched pair of heart-on-sleeve buffoons. It was that "always" she had to get beyond. Forget the past and the person Zee had been. Be ready to appreciate the current Zee. Be here now. Another philosophy that wasn't exactly second nature to Peg.

She walked slowly, reading the room numbers. A few feet from Zee's door, she stopped to compose herself and run through her mental list of cheerful comments. She felt like a fraud and an idiot. But it didn't take a clairvoyant to read the invisible writing over the door of every hospital: Abandon mope, all ye who enter here. For god's sake, with all that Zee was going through, Peg could certainly find the guts to be upbeat, couldn't she?

You look fantastic!

(For a person who's supposed to be dead!)

I hear you're improving like crazy!

(The doctors are withdrawing your nomination for Most Likely to Be a Turnip Forever!)

I'm sure you'll be out of here and back to normal in no time!

(Do you think the bullet in your brain will set off airport metal detectors?)

Things could be worse!

(Think of that diabetic man in Florida whose surgeon amputated the wrong leg!)

The drive down from Minneapolis was gorgeous!

My motel room is a hoot!

If a coward dies a thousand deaths, isn't that practically as good as having nine lives?

All of this, of course, was about herself and not about Zee at all. Peg gave herself a brief shake, like a wet dog—an onlooker might have mistaken it for a shudder—and went in to see her friend.

Zee's bed faced away from the door, toward a big, frost-etched window with a sun catcher hanging in the middle. Some kind of yellow bird. Marian and her animals!

It was the hand Peg saw first, resting on the metal guardrail and looking normal enough except for the freshly painted nails in an unsettling shade of salmon. Then she realized Zee wasn't alone.

A scruffy-looking older man rose from his chair in the corner. "Peg?"

"My god. Tom?" She reached out to shake hands as he lurched forward to embrace her. Awkwardly, she patted his rib cage for a moment before they disentangled themselves. She knew from his face that he was smelling every Marlboro Light she'd smoked in the car.

"I can come back," he said. "I didn't know you were coming."

"I wrote. A few days ago. I should have called." But if she didn't call, no one could tell her not to come.

"No problem. I'll get some coffee and see you in twenty minutes." He gathered his coat and gloves from the chair. Something in her expression must have prompted him to explain, "Doctor's orders. To keep her from getting too tired." Less brusquely, he said, "Evidently Mother didn't fill you in on the routine."

"We haven't talked much," Peg said.

"Is that . . . Peg?" A whisper from the bed.

"Nobody knew she was coming, Zee," Tom said. "Her letter . . . went astray or something. I'll come back in a while and we can finish our visit, okay?" He turned to Peg. "She doesn't talk much, but she understands everything. And she hears perfectly. You don't have to shout."

"Shouting never crossed my mind," Peg said, and he reddened. "I'm generally quite well behaved in hospitals." Caitlin had been only a toddler when Zee unexpectedly said one day, "I married my father. It seemed like a good idea at the time."

"Peg?" Zee whispered again.

"Sorry. I'll get out of your way," Tom said. "I'm gone."

Peg, plucking off her gloves, watched him hustle out of the room.

"Well, that was certainly weird," she said to Zee, who only smiled and smiled.

Zee's surgical buzz cut, her new gray stubble, gave her a reduced, severe appearance, like a retired general. Yet it took mere seconds to stop seeing the lack of her former hair: shoulder length, whiskey-colored, sixties straight. Peg had never been religious, but something about Zee's . . . *immutability* . . . awed her, even frightened her a little.

She hunched over the guardrail for a clumsy hug and kiss. Zee's left arm hugged her back.

Peg dug a tissue from her pocket and blew her nose twice. "Damn cold," she said. "I didn't take anything because I was afraid I'd fall asleep while operating heavy machinery."

"Me . . . too," Zee said. She pressed a button that raised her torso several inches. "Your . . . trip?"

"Oh, you know," Peg said, shucking her coat. "I spent the whole drive rehearsing what to say. Important stuff, you know? Nothing about the weather or hospital food or, god forbid, current events. I had an appendectomy a few years back, and everyone who visited just wanted to talk about Libya. Or was it Liberia? It was awful." Zee was smiling. "So I had this idea that we'd talk, really talk, like we used to. But now that I'm here, all I can think is that being together is enough." She hid her face, her shameful domino face, in her hands. "Oh god, I'm sorry. I'm going all cosmic on you."

"They . . . all . . . talk," Zee said. "No one . . . tells . . . me . . . things."

"Really," Peg said. "Really? Well, forget Libya. And Liberia. I'm out of the loop. I can't help you there." She heard herself with the horror of someone who was spending her last minutes on the *Titanic* organizing her sock drawer. "Jesus. I hate being so damned nervous."

"You're . . . part of my . . ." Zee trailed off, distressed.

"Yes?" Peg said. "What? Your . . . life?"

Zee shook her head. "My . . ." She tapped her chest.

"Your heart?" Peg said. "Zee, you know I always sucked at charades."

Zee squeezed her eyes shut.

Peg groaned. "I'm sorry I'm so—"

"My . . . self," Zee whispered, radiant with relief that the word had surfaced.

"Oh, Zee." Peg's throat closed.

Zee slowly reached up and fumbled for Peg's hair. "What color . . . ?"

Peg laughed. "My new hair person calls it 'champagne caramel.' An hour of being wrapped in tin foil, for this?" She held up an end. "Split all to hell. You probably can't see it, but—" She stopped. She was conscious of Zee working a piece of hair between her fingers as if she could learn something from the texture. "You can't see me?"

Zee took some time formulating her answer. "I can . . . picture you."

"But you don't look blind," Peg said, as if it was something she could talk Zee out of.

"I look . . . ?"

"Well, normal. Like you're actually focusing on me."

"Not . . . scary?" Zee whispered. "No . . . bullshit."

"Hey. Tammy Faye Bakker was scary. Did anyone tell you she died? She would have liked these fingernails. I take it you didn't pick the color?" Peg paused and took her friend's hand. "Zee, tell me. Can you see anything at all? I mean, when your eyes are open or closed, is there a difference?"

Abruptly, Zee's hand clenched. Her perfect new nails stabbed Peg's skin.

"What is it?" Peg said. "Are you all right?"

Zee's head rolled from side to side in a kind of frenzy. She no longer seemed to focus on anything.

"Sha . . . dows . . ." There was fear in her voice, and anguish. "Shapes."

"That's something, at least. Maybe the rest will come back. What do the doctors say?"

Zee labored to raise her head. She strained her mouth open as wide as possible. "NOTHING!" she whispered. Her head flopped back onto the pillow, and she started to cry.

"Shh. Shh." Peg stroked Zee's cheek. With her other hand, she lifted Zee's palm to rest against her own wet face so they could feel each other's tears. "Blood sisters."

Snow blew past the window. It was like being inside a glass paperweight that a giant, unseen hand kept shaking and shaking. Peg wanted to scream at it to stop. Instead, she said softly, "Tell me about the shadows and I'll tell you everything I know. Anything. I promise."

Monday

Tom believed it was all for the best, and the doctors concurred. So had Marian and, reluctantly, Caitlin.

Peg meant well, certainly. And, to be fair, she hadn't been warned. Honesty was an overrated virtue; it wasn't the sort of thing you brandished right and left without considering the consequences. Peg couldn't have known how wild Zee would be, how distraught. Tom was thankful he'd returned to her room promptly. He'd considered giving the old friends a little extra time together, after Peg had driven for hours through all that snow. As it turned out, twenty minutes had been more than enough.

After the sedative wore off, Zee remained calm. She simply refused therapy. And food. It grieved Tom to see her intubated again. The doctors speculated that forcing her to confront the incident had caused shock and depression. With time, and the proper medication, it would pass. Surely she would even resume speaking to him. If anyone deserved her coldness and anger, it was Peg, not he. It was Peg, as Zee said, who took away the shadows.

No one prevented Peg from going to Zee's room — her former room — the next day. She was simply informed that Mrs. Sladek had been moved to a ward where the only visitors permitted were family members. Unfortunately, the room number could not be given out; the phone had been temporarily disconnected to give the patient some rest. Predictably, Peg had left Tom a voice mail ranting about kidnapping and false imprisonment. She threatened to go to the police. He called her back at the motel today just to be sure she had checked out and was on her way home. He prayed that she wouldn't involve the reporters.

The only one who hadn't agreed with his regrettable but necessary action was Betsy. In her opinion, Zandra should have been exposed to little bits of the truth all along, to lessen the shock. Tom had betrayed her trust. He kept everything to himself because he was a control freak. Knowledge is power. Peg was a heroine; why, Betsy wouldn't be surprised if she slipped past the nurses by pretending to be Zandra's long-lost sister, just in from Africa.

When Tom proposed that she had seen too many movies, Betsy called him a pious oaf and said that his beard made him look Amish, nothing against the Amish.

"Remember *Sunset Boulevard*? That's who you remind me of, you and Zandra. You're playing Max to her Norma Desmond." She shook her head. More quietly, she said, "Everyone in that movie was so alone."

She looked in his eyes for so long that he thought she might kiss him good-bye. Instead, she simply turned and walked out, grabbing her *Rashomon* DVD but leaving him the sushi, although she knew perfectly well how he felt about seaweed. She and Zee, he thought wistfully, would have liked each other.

Zee's new room looked out on a parking lot. Ironically, now that she could see—at any rate, that was how he interpreted her re-mark about the shadows—she didn't have much of a view. Nor did she seem to care. She had turned her face to the wall, literally and figuratively. Somehow it was easier to talk to her, now that he knew she wouldn't answer. It was a good time to finally tell her what was on his mind. If her usual nurse was on duty, he could ask if she knew anyone who might be interested in the sort of situation he was envisioning. She had never been overly friendly to him, but she was tender with Zee.

He groped in his pocket for the CD and the reassuring hard edges of its smooth plastic case. He expected Caitlin to be amused when he related how he went into a music store and repeated "be my ape-man girl" until the tattooed and perforated clerk coaxed the title out of the computer and pointed him to the section where he'd find the Kinks. Instead, Caitlin rolled her eyes and snorted. "Why didn't you just Google?" She couldn't believe that he'd bought some embarrassing clock-radio-CD player instead of an iPod. But he and Zee could listen together to the CD player, and it was small enough to leave room on the nightstand at home for one of those wireless indoor-outdoor thermometers. Zee would be able to see at a glance when it was extremely hot or cold and feel grate-ful that she never had to go out for anything.

You could set your clock by 814's ex. Right on schedule, he was marching down the hall, today with what Nurse Paltz hoped was only a radio but feared might be one of those karaoke contrap-tions. It had gotten worse ever since Oliver Sacks went on *60 Min-utes* with that elderly woman, a stroke victim who couldn't talk. He got her to sing "Daisy"—only every seventh word or so, and not half so well as Hal the computer in that old outer-space movie when the astronaut was disabling him, but it started a wave of hope-ful people trundling in with everything from guitars to electronic keyboards and worse, desperate to break through to their loved ones. Most went away heartbroken. It would be better all around if the hospital set some rules.

In general, Paltz neither approved nor disapproved of what went on in these cases: the heaps of childish gifts, the gabble of one-sided conversations. She admired that energy, that optimism. People were entitled to whatever gave them comfort, including the illusion of giving comfort to someone else. Or the illusion that you could cure someone with love. As if only the alone and friendless died! Day after day, the visitors came with their gadgets and good intentions. They reminded her of children snatching at the string of a balloon that kept on drifting farther and farther away.

Of course, 814 was different. She had come out of one coma already. The family had had their miracle. This time around, although the muteness was clearly self-imposed, everyone went on behaving as if she were still a helpless victim instead of an angry woman who was asserting virtually the only power she had left. Paltz had seen it before. Sometimes it was the patient's recovery, not the initial trauma, that tore a family apart. Especially when the person who was returned to them was not the person they had lost. Face it: people had different definitions for recovery.

If the ex had asked Paltz's advice, she would have counseled him to skip the music and simply talk. Say he was sorry. Try to explain why he had behaved like an idiot and banished the friend, or even confess that he couldn't explain. But no, there was the music. It was too faint to identify. No one was singing along. Yet.

How many times a week did that poor old woman grope her way through "Daisy" for the sake of her family or a roomful of med students? Still, perhaps it gave her life focus; perhaps it brought her more visitors. Paltz no longer cried easily, but the other day that space movie had been on TV again, all chopped up with commercials for minivans and acid-reflux remedies, and when Hal started to lose his mind and sing slower and slower, she broke down and sobbed like a fool. Her grandchildren laughed at her. She didn't blame them.

She had just given 810 his meds when the crash came from 814. The music stopped. It took her a moment. Then she got the picture. In the silence that followed, she waited for the ex to come dashing down the hall, apologetic and panicky. Let him beg for a sedative: she intended to stand her ground. She would tell him that anger was often part of the healing process; it was usually an encouraging sign when they started to fight back. Of course, it was entirely possible that he wouldn't consider it good news. It might not fit with his plans. Paltz chided herself for being uncharitable. The ex generally had a smug look, but, to be fair, it was often hard to tell what was on a bearded man's mind.

When no one came looking for her, she collected a broom and dustpan and started down the hall, uncertain whether she was motivated by duty or raw, unprofessional curiosity. Where on earth had that woman found the strength? Paltz was careful to compose her expression; there was a mess to be cleaned up, and it wouldn't do to appear pleased.

PHILLIP MARGOLIN

The House on Pine Terrace

FROM *Thriller 2*

THERE WAS an intercom attached to the ice-white wall and I used it to call up to the house on Pine Terrace. The voice that answered was the voice on the phone. He sounded just as pleasant now as he had then. Not uptight like I expected a john to be. While we were talking, I heard an electronic hum and the iron gate swung inward. We broke off and I drove my Ford along a winding drive past stands of palm trees. The house was at the end of the drive.

My father left my mother when I was too young to remember him. From a remark here and a remark there, I've figured out that it was no big loss. I do remember that we were always dirt poor. Mama was part of a crew that cleaned houses. You don't get rich doing that, but you do get to see how the other half lives. A few times, when she couldn't get anyone to watch me, she risked getting fired by bringing me with her. The only place she brought me that I remember clearly was the house on Pine Terrace.

When I was little, Mama called me "Princess." She said someday I would marry a prince and live in a castle and be rich. I've never been married, I'm working on rich, and this is the castle I'd live in if I had my way. I dreamed about this house. Fantasized about it when I was alone and feeling lazy. Wished for it when I was younger and really believed I could do anything.

The house was so white the rays of the sun reflected off it. It was long, low, modern, and perched on a cliff with a view of the Pacific that was so breathtaking you'd never get tired of it. There was a Rolls-Royce Silver Cloud parked near the front door. Farther down the drive was a sports car so expensive that someone in my tax bracket couldn't even identify it. I looked at my Ford, thought about the small, singles apartment I lived in, and suddenly felt like a visitor from another planet.

What I saw when the front door opened confused me. Daniel Emery III was one of the handsomest men I'd ever seen. He was six-one or -two, broad-shouldered, and tanned a warm, brown color that made you think of tropical beaches. He wore a yellow cashmere V-neck sweater and tight white jeans. There were no gold chains, diamond pinky rings, or the other swinger jewelry turnoffs. He was, in other words, the male equivalent of his dream house and I wondered what in the world a guy like this with a place like this wanted with a call girl.

"You're Tanya?" he asked, using the phony name I'd given when he phoned in response to the ad in *Swinger's Weekly*.

"And you must be Dan," I answered, pitching my voice low and sexy.

He nodded as he gave me the once-over. I was sure he would like what he saw. His smile confirmed my belief.

"You certainly fit your description in the ad."

"You're surprised?"

"A little. I figured there'd be a bit of puffing."

I smiled to show him that I appreciated the compliment.

"Can I get you a drink?" he asked.

"No, thanks," I said, starting to hate what I was going to do. "And we should get the business part out of the way so it won't interfere with your pleasure."

"Sure, the money," Dan said. "One thousand in cash, you said. I've got it here."

He handed me an envelope and I thumbed through the ten crisp hundred-dollar bills inside it.

"One more thing," I said. "What do you expect for this?"

He looked puzzled. "Sex."

"What kind of sex? Do you want straight sex or head? Anything kinky?"

"I thought you said you'd do anything I wanted and would stay the night for a thou."

He was starting to look worried.

"That's right. And you understand there's no rough stuff."

"That's not my style. Now, have we got the business out of the way?"

"Unfortunately, no," I said, flashing my badge. I could hear the trunk of the Ford open as my partner, Jack Gripper, got out. "I'm a policewoman, Mr. Emery, and you're under arrest for prostitution."

What a waste, I remember thinking. I meet the guy of my dreams, who lives in the house of my dreams, and instead of balling him, I bust him. Life can sure be cruel. Then, he phoned.

"Officer Esteban?" he asked, sounding just as pleasant as he'd been during the ride to the station house.

"Yes."

"This is Dan Emery. You arrested me for prostitution three weeks ago."

"Oh, yes. I remember."

"I didn't bother getting a lawyer. You had me dead to rights. I just faced the music and pled guilty about twenty minutes ago."

"Good for you. I hope the judge wasn't too tough."

"The fine wasn't much, but the process was pretty humiliating."

"Hopefully, it won't happen again."

"That's for sure. So, the reason I called. Actually, I wanted to call you before, but I thought I should wait until my case was over. Otherwise, I was afraid it would sound like a bribe."

"What would?"

"My dinner invitation."

Five years as a cop had taught me how to stay cool in the tensest situations but I was completely flummoxed.

"I don't know . . ." I started.

"Look, you're probably thinking I'm some kind of weirdo, what with answering that kinky ad and all. But, really, I'm not like that. I did it as a lark. Honest. I haven't been with a prostitute since college and I've never had a call girl. I don't even subscribe to that paper. I picked it up at my barber while I was waiting for a haircut. It just seemed like fun. Really, I'm very embarrassed about the whole thing. And I have been punished. You have no idea what it's like for a guy to admit he had to pay for sex in a courtroom packed with giggling people."

I laughed.

"Good," he said, "I've got you laughing. Now, if I can just get you to go out with me I'll be batting a thousand. What do you say?"

*

I said yes of course, and dinner was everything I'd hoped it would be even if the restaurant was elegant enough to make me feel a little uncomfortable and I didn't recognize half the dishes on the menu. Dan turned out to be a perfect gentleman with a sense of humor and none of that macho bullshit that I'm used to from the cops I've dated. The only thing that bothered me that first night—and I say bothered only because I needed a word here, not because I really gave it any thought then—was his reluctance to talk about himself. He was an artist at steering the conversation back to me whenever I'd try to find out a little about him. But I was so used to guys who only wanted to talk about themselves that it was actually a bit of a relief.

I didn't sleep with Dan after our first date or our second. I didn't want him thinking I was an easy lay. The third time we dated he invited me to his house instead of going to a restaurant and he cooked a dinner to die for. We ate on the flagstone patio. The air felt like silk, the view was spectacular, and not having sex with him seemed downright silly.

The next two months were like a fairy tale. We couldn't keep our hands off each other and I missed him every minute we were apart. Sergeant Groves couldn't figure out why I was being so nice to him. He knew how upset I'd been when he took me out of narcotics and put me into the call-girl sting operation. I'd yelled sex discrimination and he asked me who else he could use as a call girl. The whole thing was supposed to be temporary, anyway.

During those two intense months I learned a little bit more about Dan, and everything I learned made me like him more. Dan was an orphan, whose parents had died in a car crash on vacation in the south of France during his sophomore year at USC. He'd been living in an apartment on his own and continued to stay there until he graduated, even though he'd inherited the house on Pine Terrace. Dan told me that he'd been very close to his parents and the house contained too many memories. It had taken a while before he could stay there without being overcome with sadness.

The family lawyer had provided Dan with advice and an allowance until he turned twenty-one and was allowed to control his inheritance. Even though he was rich enough so he didn't have to work, he was employed as a stockbroker at a small, exclusive brokerage house run by an old college friend. At one point, he confided that he was doing well enough at work to keep up his lifestyle without having to tap into his inheritance.

I didn't go out of my way to tell anyone about Dan but it's hard to keep secrets from your partner.

"The john?" Jack Gripper said, unable to keep the surprise out of his voice.

"Yeah," I answered sheepishly.

"It's the house, isn't it?"

We'd passed the house once on the way to interview a witness and I'd told Jack how I'd been in it as a kid and how it was my dream house. After arresting Dan, he'd asked me if the house was the one I'd told him about and I'd said it was.

"Geez, Jack, why don't you just come right out and call me a gold digger?"

"Hey, I'm not casting any stones."

Gripper really is nonjudgmental. I guess that comes from being a cop for so many years and seeing as much of life as he has. After our brief discussion about Dan and me, he never brought up the subject again, and I didn't either.

We were in bed when Dan first told me he loved me. I hadn't pushed it. Just being with Dan was enough. I've always kept my expectations low. Like I said, I'd grown up poor and I'd fought for everything I had. My apartment was the nicest place I'd ever lived in. Most of the guys I'd dated hadn't lived much better. I was starting to build a nest egg, but I could have done what I was doing for the rest of my life and never put away enough to live like Dan.

I don't want you to think his money was everything, but money is always important if you grow up without it. I want to think I was in love, but I'm not sure I know what love is. I never saw it in my mother's relationship with the occasional man she brought home. Working the streets, I've seen enough women with split lips and enough men with stab wounds to know that love isn't what it's cracked up to be. I've never seen shooting stars or heard bells ring with anyone I dated. Not even with Dan. But, he did feel comfortable and he was sure good in the sack and I guess I felt as close to him as I've ever felt to anyone.

When he said, "There's something we have to talk about," my first thought was he was going to call it off.

"So talk," I said, trying to make it sound like a joke.

The full moon hanging over the ocean made seeing in the dark easy enough. Dan rolled over on his side. He looked troubled.

"We've been together, what? Two months?"

"Sixty-one days, twenty hours, three minutes, and one arrest," I answered, still trying to keep things light. "But who's counting."

Dan smiled, but it was only for a second. Then he looked sad.

"My little flatfoot." He sighed.

"What's wrong?"

"I love you, but I don't know if I can trust you."

That got my attention and I sat up.

"What do you mean, you can't trust me," I snapped, hurt and a little angry.

"How much of a cop are you, Monica? And how much do I mean to you?"

I thought about that. More the second part of the question than the first. He'd just told me he loved me. What was he leading up to? I thought about living here, driving the Rolls, wearing clothes like the clothes I saw on movie stars.

"I love you too, Dan. And I'm not so much of a cop that you can't trust me with anything."

"That's what I hoped you'd say. Look, I'll level with you. Dating a cop was as much a kick at first as dialing a call girl. I'm not sure there wasn't even a little bit of a revenge motive in it. You know, getting you in bed after you'd arrested and embarrassed me."

I started to say something, but he held up his hand.

"No. Let me get this out. It's not easy for me. That's how it started, but that's not the way it is now. When I said I love you I meant it, but I'm not sure you'll want to stay with me when you hear what I have to say.

"You like this house and the cars and my lifestyle, don't you?"

"That's not why I've been seeing you," I answered defensively.

"I didn't say it was. Aren't you curious about how I can afford to keep them up?"

"You told me that you're doing well at work, and about your inheritance. Besides, it's none of my business."

"You really don't have any idea of how much it costs to live like I do, do you?"

"Where is this going?" I asked, suddenly growing a little concerned.

"If you learned something bad about me, that I was doing . . . that I was dishonest. What would happen?"

"To us?" I answered, confused.

"As a cop. Would you turn me in?"

I looked at him and I thought about us. Like I said, I wasn't sure I loved him, but I liked him enough to know my answer.

"I don't turn in my friends."

"Then I'll say what I have to say and you can decide what you want to do. I haven't been completely honest with you about my financial situation." Dan looked embarrassed, a look I had never seen before. Not even when I'd busted him. "I always thought my parents were loaded, and I assumed I'd inherit what they had, so I never really applied myself in school. I'm pretty bright—I've got a good IQ—but college was one big party and I graduated without many practical skills.

"Soon after my parents died I had a rude awakening. This house, a vacation home, a trust fund, and some stocks were all I got. It wasn't peanuts but I learned that they weren't as well-off as I'd thought.

"It never occurred to me that I'd have to pay property taxes, the upkeep on a house like this, and all the other expenses parents worry about but don't discuss with their children. The lawyer who probated the estate taught me the financial facts of life. I held out for a while, but eventually I had to sell the vacation home. Then I used up my trust fund and sold off a lot of my stocks to keep up this lifestyle. Like I said, I have no marketable skills."

"What about the brokerage?" I asked.

"Oh, that's real, and I am doing okay, but what I earn just about covers the property taxes and expenses for a place like this."

"Why don't you sell it?"

Dan looked me in the eye. "Would you? If you had a house like this wouldn't you do whatever you had to do to keep it?"

I didn't say anything. What could I say? I knew I'd kill to keep this house if it were ever mine. Dan smiled sadly. He reached up and touched my cheek. The heat of his hand felt so good that I missed it when he took it away.

"I knew you'd understand. That's why I love you. We're so different, but we're the same in the ways that count."

"If you don't make enough to afford . . . everything, and you didn't inherit enough to keep it . . . ?" I asked.

Dan broke eye contact. "There's no way to sugarcoat this, Monica. I've been dealing."

"Narcotics?" I said, stunned. He nodded.

"Cocaine, mostly. No heroin. I wouldn't do that. Some marijuana. I'm careful. I sell to select customers, friends mostly, some of my clients. It's actually the only thing I've ever done well on my own."

I got out of bed and walked to the window. I didn't know what to say.

"Why are you telling me this?" I asked. "Do you have any idea of the spot you've put me in?"

"I do appreciate the moral dilemma I've created for you, but it's not going to be a problem anymore. I love you and I knew I couldn't keep seeing you if I didn't come clean about this. I respect what you do, being a cop. I don't ever want to compromise you."

I turned back toward the bed. "Well, you have. I should bust you after what you've confessed to me."

"You don't have to, Monica. I told you so there wouldn't be any secrets between us, and the reason I'm telling you now is that it's all going to stop. I had to make a choice between you and dealing, and it wasn't even close. But I didn't know how you'd feel about that. If you'd still want to stay with me."

"Why should I object if you stop selling dope?"

"You don't understand. If I stop dealing, *this,*" he said, waving his hand around the room, "is all going to end; the house and the cars and the restaurants and . . . everything."

"What do you mean?"

"What I said. Without the cocaine, I can't afford the lifestyle and there won't be any more cocaine."

"Because of me?"

"That's the biggest part of it, but there's also a practical reason. If I was religious I'd see the hand of God at work." Dan smiled. "I knew I loved you soon after we met and I knew I'd have to stop dealing if I wanted to keep you, but I didn't know how I was going to get out of the life. The people I worked for are very dangerous. I was afraid of what they'd do if I told them I wasn't going to deal for them anymore and they found out I was dating a cop, and they would have found out. These guys are very connected. I . . . Well, I worried—really worried—that they might hurt you, or threaten to hurt you if I told them I was going to quit."

"Jesus, Dan," I said, really worried because I knew what he said was true. There are dealers that wouldn't think twice about killing a cop.

"It's okay, Monica. You don't have to worry." He laughed. "Talk about your acts of God." He smiled. "The week before we met, my connection was busted. Then, right after you arrested me, the DEA arrested the head of the cartel he worked for."

"Who was he?"

"Alberto Perez." I'd heard about the bust. Perez was big. "They got him in Miami with millions of dollars worth of coke and they got most of his organization too. It's *finito*."

"Your connection didn't sell you out?"

"I worried about that a lot. When we started dating I was waiting for the other shoe to drop. But it didn't, and I think I know why. I'm small potatoes. The Feds aren't going to waste time on someone who deals at my level. You know that. Besides, I'd sold all my product. I was supposed to get some more from the shipment they confiscated. So, I'm clean. There'd be no hard evidence I was a dealer, even if they wanted me. It's been two months now. More since my connection was arrested. So, I'm guessing I'm safe."

I turned back to the ocean but I didn't see it. I was thinking too hard about how much I trusted Dan and what I was willing to do to keep him.

"So, what will you do?" I asked to stall for time.

"I'll have to sell most of what I have. I can get a bundle for the house. The cars will have to go. I sat down with my accountant. I'll be in good shape if I watch my money. But the life you've seen me lead, that's over."

The house! I couldn't bear it. To be this close to living the life I'd dreamed of living for so many years, and then to have it snatched away. Dan was talking but I wasn't listening. I was upset, but there's this thing about me. I can wall off my emotions when I need to make a serious decision. It comes in handy as a cop and it was coming in handy now. I had a good idea of how I could save the house, but I wanted to think before I said anything to Dan. There was too much at stake. So I got back in bed and I wrapped my arms around him and kissed him.

"I love you, Dan," I said. "I want to be with you. You'll be okay. We'll be okay. We'll be working stiffs. That's not so bad. I've been one all my life. You'll see. We'll be fine."

Dan rested his head on my shoulder. "You don't know what this means to me. I was so worried you'd leave me when you found out how big a phony I am."

"You're not a phony. You just got hooked on this lifestyle the way your customers got hooked on coke. And it's not like you'll have to go cold turkey. We're going to do fine once you sell this stuff.

"And it is only stuff," I said, but I didn't mean that.

I was still working the call-girl sting and busting johns kept me away from Dan for a week. I didn't like the work. To tell the truth, it made me feel sleazy. Most of the poor bastards we arrested had never been in trouble with the law before. They looked so pathetic when I flashed my badge. I guess it was the futility of it all that got me. We were never going to stamp out prostitution. It was the world's oldest profession for a reason.

I felt the same way about drugs. People were always going to want something to make them feel better, even if it was only for a little while, and they were going to buy coke or a hooker even if it was illegal. I thought they should legalize drugs and prostitution and let us concentrate on murderers, con men, and armed robbers, but no one in the state legislature cared what I thought, so I spent most of the week after Dan told me about his problem dressed like a high-priced tart.

I spent the other part checking up on Dan. I cared for him, but I'm not naive. He'd lied to me about dealing and I wanted to know if he'd lied about anything else. I used the usual Internet sources to find out what was on the Web. He was quite the socialite and the history he'd given me checked out. Then I ran a check on the house, his cars, and everything else he had ever owned. Everything he'd told me checked out there too. Finally, I used my computer to tap into federal and state law enforcement files that are only available to cops. All I found was a DUI from his sophomore year in college that was resolved when Dan went into a diversion program. All in all, I was satisfied that Dan was being straight with me, so I set up a meeting with some people I know.

I told Dan my idea after dinner at an inexpensive Mexican restaurant in my neighborhood. Dan joked that I was trying to break him into our new life, but I really liked the place and I liked being able to wear jeans to dinner and not having to worry about not knowing what the dishes on the menu were.

I kept the conversation at dinner about police work, telling Dan war stories about some of the weird things cops encounter on the job, and I waited until we were back at the house on Pine Terrace before I told him what I'd been doing.

"How's everything going?" I asked.

"How's what going?"

"You know, selling the house, the Rolls?"

He looked sad. "I've talked with a few realtors to get an idea of what it will bring. The Rolls and the Lamborghini will go next week."

"Maybe not," I said.

"What do you mean?"

I felt as if I was standing on a ledge about to jump. I had no idea how Dan would react to what I was going to propose or whether we'd still be together after I had my say.

"There may be a way to save the house and everything else."

"I'm not following you."

"I might be able to put you in touch with someone."

"I'm still not following you."

"You're not the only one with secrets," I said nervously. "I've been doing a few things I shouldn't too."

Dan stared at me open-mouthed. "You don't mean . . . ?"

"I'm not gonna be a cop all my life. I've seen how cops live and what cops make. I want to be someone, Dan. I was working narcotics until we started this call-girl sting. About a year ago I was involved in a big bust. Peter Pride."

"You were in on that?"

I nodded.

"Pride walked."

"Yes, he did. Want to know why?"

Dan didn't say anything.

"Key evidence disappeared and I started a Swiss bank account. Nothing huge, but something for my old age."

"Didn't some cop get busted for that? I thought I read . . ."

I nodded. "That was the one part I didn't like. Bobby Marino. I had nothing to do with that. Pride hated him and he set him up. It doesn't matter now and there's nothing I can do about it. But, I can fix you up with Pride. What do you say?"

Dan's tongue flicked out and he wet his lips.

"I don't know. These guys I was dealing with . . . They were bad but Pride's a killer."

"They're all killers, Dan, but Pride's a killer who pays well. I've been tipping him off for a year now. He likes me. You need this," I said, waving my hand at the view, "and I need you. What do you say?"

"Let me think. Pride is a whole new ball game."

Dan called me a week later and we met for lunch. While we waited for the waitress to bring our order he held my hand.

"I've been thinking about Pride and I'll do it."

"Oh, Dan," I said, because it's all I could think to say. He smiled and tightened his grip and I squeezed back. I was that happy.

"One thing, though," he said.

"What's that?"

"From now on, you're out."

I started to protest, but he cut me off.

"I mean it. I didn't like getting arrested, even for a misdemeanor like prostitution. I don't even want to think what would happen if they arrested a cop for what you're doing."

"I'm a big girl, Dan."

"I've never doubted that, but I'm sticking to my guns. From now on, I'm the one taking the risks or the house goes on the market, as planned."

Sergei Kariakin was Russian Mafia, which meant he didn't just kill babies for fun, he ate them too. The only place he was called Sergei or Kariakin was on his rap sheet where his name was followed by "aka Peter Pride." Sergei loved America, which he called "the land of criminal opportunity," and he had adopted an alias he thought sounded like the name of a movie or rock star. The fact that he was as ugly as his crimes and couldn't carry a tune didn't faze him and no one dared point out these problems.

Normally, there were several firewalls between Peter and the narcotics and sex slaves that were his bread and butter, but he'd made a mistake two years ago and had faced certain conviction until the key evidence in his case disappeared from the police evidence locker. I had a gambling problem back then and someone had told Peter's lawyer about it. One evening, a very polite gentleman who never gave me his name made me a proposition. Within a week, my gambling debt had been retired and Peter's problem had been solved. I stopped gambling cold turkey, but I stayed on Peter's payroll, dropping timely tips about raids and snitches when I could get away with it.

My meeting with Pride took place in the dead of night in a deserted industrial park. Neither of us could afford to be seen socializing with the other. At first, Peter was reluctant to bring Dan into his organization. Even if he hadn't been picked up after Alberto Perez was arrested, Pride worried that Dan was on the DEA's radar screen. I told him I'd poked around and, as far as I could tell, the DEA didn't know Dan existed. I pitched Dan's upper-class clientele and the opportunity it presented to Pride to broaden his market.

A week later, Dan and I met Peter in an abandoned warehouse at three in the morning. The meeting ended with Peter agreeing to front Dan a kilo of cocaine. If everything went well, there was a promise of more to follow. I was so pumped up on the way back to Pine Terrace that I didn't feel the effects of being up for more than twenty-four hours. As soon as we were inside the house I started ripping off Dan's clothing. I don't even remember how we got from the entryway to the bedroom.

The next afternoon, I was so beat I had trouble keeping my eyes open. I staggered into police headquarters and found a note asking me to see Sergeant Groves. Groves was a handsome black man with a trim mustache and a serious demeanor. It was rare for him to lighten up and he looked even more tense than usual when I walked into his office and found him sitting with Jack Gripper and a man and a woman I didn't recognize.

"Shut the door, Monica," Groves ordered. I did and he motioned me into the only available seat.

"You're in deep shit," he said.

There was a DVD player on Groves's desk. He hit the play button and I heard myself telling Dan how I'd helped Peter Pride beat his case. My heart seized up. The conversation had taken place in the bedroom of the house on Pine Terrace. I wanted to ask how they'd recorded it, but I was too frightened to speak.

"That confession will send you away," Groves said.

My throat was as dry as the Sahara. I knew I shouldn't say anything without a lawyer, but I still asked, "What do you want?"

"Pride," answered the woman.

I was in shock, but part of my brain was running through my alternatives.

"You can't use that tape. You'd have to have bugged the house."

"We can use it if we planted the bug with the permission of the owner," she said, and I felt myself die a little.

Dan had been arrested the day after his connection was busted. Jack Gripper had been in on the arrest and he remembered what I'd told him about the house. Bobby Marino had gone down for stealing the evidence in Pride's case, but I became a suspect when a snitch in Pride's organization told the police that he'd heard a woman took the evidence. One of the tips I'd given Pride had been a setup. Sergeant Groves had given the location and time of the raid only to me. When there was no one at the house that was raided and they knew I was guilty, Gripper and I were switched to the call-girl sting and Dan was told to give me a call. Nature took its course after that.

When I found out that Dan had betrayed me I went from shock to anger to bitterness. I saw him once more after my arrest when we were preparing for the setup that eventually put Peter Pride away. He told me he was sorry and really did love me, but he'd had no choice. I don't believe he loved me, but, even if he did, I knew he'd forget about me when the next woman came along; someone who wasn't serving the sentence that would keep me in prison for at least seven years.

There is no view from the cell I share with Sheila Crosby, a forty-two-year-old embezzler, but I can still see the view from Dan's bedroom when I close my eyes.

Sometimes I imagine that I walk out of prison and Dan is waiting for me in the Rolls. We ride to the house on Pine Terrace and I take a shower to wash away the jailhouse stench. After the shower, we make love. When Dan is asleep, I walk out onto the patio and watch the approach of a storm that's been brewing in the Pacific. It's a magnificent storm, and when it passes I am as untroubled and serene as the Pacific after that storm. And I am married to my prince and I am rich and I live in a castle on Pine Terrace.

CHRIS MUESSIG

Bias

FROM *Ellery Queen's Mystery Magazine*

JACK-O'-LANTERNS LIT the crisp evening with their complicit
leers, but Frank Creegan sensed a worse mischief coming round.
Something else slouched below the dark horizon, pushing the
dead ahead of it like a wave.

Coming up on the intersection of 29A and Drowned Meadow
Avenue, he heard yet another call on his scanner. Red and blue
lights flashed up ahead at the Usoco station. He cut over to the
right, trying to remember who would be on duty at the pumps at
8:00 P.M.

He parked on the shoulder. Aside from a familiar white sedan
parked at the side of the station, the police cruiser was the only vehicle in the lot. Check that — a huge bicycle leaned by the air pump
that jutted from the brick wall between the closed bays.

Creegan crossed the macadam with a heavy heart. An odd-
looking man in an oversized bicycle helmet turned to look at him
from the office door. Creegan recognized him as a resident of
the adult home near the train station, an odd young soul given to
slow-motion tours of the town on his twenty-eight-inch dinosaur
of a bike. Creegan remembered the red eyes of its oversized re-
flectors and the swath of the battery-driven headlamp patrolling
the dusk — one of God's special sentries.

Officer Ray Evers stood just inside the office talking into his portable radio. The uniformed patrolman gave Frank a surprised but
not unwelcoming look.

"You doing a double tour, Lieutenant?"

"No. I was just down the block and heard the squawk. This is my neighborhood. This is where I usually buy my gas. Who's on their way?"

Evers shrugged. "Everybody. Won't be room to breathe in here."

Creegan took out his notebook. The helmeted figure beside them shifted from one sneaker to the other with his hands up in front of his chest like a T. rex. This near to the pale chin and cheeks, Creegan saw salt-and-pepper stubble belying the childish mannerisms.

"Is this man a witness, Evers?"

"I don't think he saw the shooting, but he did find the body and call 911. I was just around the corner. This didn't happen very long ago."

"On that phone?" Creegan pointed his chin at the pay phone by the inner door connecting office to work area.

"No, he used the booth on the corner out there. He was waiting in it when I pulled in."

"What's his name?"

"Jeremy Jordan—J.J., they call him."

"Who's they?"

"Well, shopkeepers, neighborhood people. You know. He's harmless and keeps to himself, but he tools around."

"Did he see anybody?"

"I really just got here, Lieutenant. And he's a little . . . addled."

The benighted one did not seem to know he was being talked about.

"You see what you can get out of him while I take a look. Excuse me, J.J., I need to get by."

Creegan was ready for it now. He looked down at the floor as he placed his steps. A thin cordite haze scratched at his throat and nose. As Evers went outside to give Creegan more room, he said, "I asked the dispatcher to get hold of the station owners."

Creegan nodded and looked over the counter.

The stitching on the dead man's blue coveralls spelled out *Sal,* but it was Turgot, all right. He was on his back with his head propped in the corner of the cramped space. Creegan looked down on him with his hands by his sides; then he sidestepped carefully to the right so he could see around the edge of the counter and get a look at the body full-length.

He squatted down to get an angle on two apparent entry wounds.

The lower one was even with the sternum on the left side. It had produced a sopping patch darker than the dark shirt. The other wound was a hand's length above the first, near the collarbone, less bloody. No blood seeping from underneath the body.

Turgot's face stared past him, not quite emptied of the good nature that had greeted every entrant to the store: "Hello, buddy!" The ghost of amiable welcome overlapped in Frank's imagination with the ringing percussion of confined shots. He raised his right hand and sketched the sign of the cross over the body.

"I think he was more into Allah," said Evers from the doorway.

Frank looked up at him; Evers retreated and began questioning J.J.

Frank's eyes kept busy, and he stayed in his crouch. A small green pencil, the stubby kind without eraser, was resting on the dead man's left thigh, up near the groin. Frank stood and his left knee clicked. He kept panning the room.

A blotter-sized calendar covered most of the countertop. The day squares contained appointments, calls, deli orders, and so on, in several different kinds of handwriting. The expired days were marked off with diagonals.

Someone had scrawled a small swastika on the top edge on the customer's side. The penciled image stood out from what had been three fingers of blankness. Doodling cluttered the other three margins, penned and penciled perhaps by employees as they idled on the business phone—but no other swastikas.

He read the upside-down entries for that day, and then he returned to the bent cross. No more than a half-inch square, the cursive rounding indicated something hastily done. He took his eyes away and did another three-sixty.

Evers's sergeant pulled up. The patrolman moved toward the car, pulling J.J. gently after him.

No casings in sight. Maybe a revolver, or the guy knew enough to pick them up. Or they'd rolled under the motor-oil rack or the soda cooler where Crime Scene would hopefully find them.

He looked again at the body. The blind gaze was locked on the cubbies behind the counter. Frank's professional self refused to be drawn into the mystery of that deceptive intensity, but he could not help thinking about the history here.

Turgot had worked at the station for several years, often doing both shifts seven days a week. Frank had never pried, but he guessed much of the man's pay went to an extended family in Turkey. Human industry, blood ties, and then murder setting it all awry—for what? Beer and cigarettes? How much treasure could the emptied cash drawer have possibly held in between the night drops? It would take some doing to balance out this equation.

Sergeant Mike Monafferi appeared in the doorway.

"Lieutenant?"

"I know the deceased, Mike," Creegan said, which was not strictly true, but he wanted to rationalize his intrusion. "I live less than two miles from here."

"Whattaya think? Robbery-murder?"

"Probably." But he came back to the swastika. "If you don't mind, I'm going to hang around until the investigators get here."

"There's only one coming from Homicide. Spread pretty thin tonight. Two floaters washed up from the Sound in different spots, and there's that big bloody smash-up on Memorial Parkway."

Creegan nodded; he'd heard the radio exchanges, hammer strokes from a dark forge.

Swastikas: the range brand of madness, which had begun reappearing on the facades of synagogues, Jewish tombstones, and the garage doors of African Americans settling into what had been exclusively white neighborhoods. The crooked marks had been incubating in the playrooms of crackpots. Hadn't Manson carved one into his forehead? A special unit had even been proposed to investigate the rising number of hate-related crimes.

A third patrol car rolled up, followed shortly by the precinct detectives in an unmarked car. The sergeant went out to them.

The Crime Scene vans were all over the county, so Evers and a female officer were set to taping off the half-acre lot and bordering sidewalks to keep the gathering tramplers back. A detective began talking to J.J. The other, Ivey Coleman, a guy with a good work ethic, started toward Creegan but was called back by his partner.

Creegan stayed in the cramped office, continuing to move his eyes methodically across every surface at every level. One of the fluorescents winked and *tsked* overhead, not helping matters. It was the only sound in the room, although a small portable TV flickered on a side shelf. It was turned down so low that the local news played like a tiny mime show—a quiet, peripheral companion.

Maybe Turgot had reduced the volume politely when the killer came in to him. No doubt exterior shots of the station would soon be feeding into the tiny screen, creating a fitful hall of mirrors.

On the counter, flush with the wall below the windowsill, was a small cardboard box filled to the brim with the same type of green pencil that lay upon the body. Frank leaned over and saw that the pencils were presharpened and had been stamped with gold lettering: *North Hills Country Club.*

The pencils were obsolete; Peconic County had recently taken over the struggling private course and renamed it High Meadow Golf Club. Crews were already at work on the refurbishment. Apparently, just the one pencil was missing from the box, although several others were displaced into a tiny logjam.

Past impressions: Turgot rubbing his palms together, then a hand darting out to rearrange some item on the counter, always aligning and making the most of things that fell into his possession—the courtesy pens, promotional calendars, notepads with little logos or tiny letterheads on them, all straightened into a personalized symmetry on the counter, the walls, or the surrounding shelves. Outside, a tall, thirtyish guy with dark hair was crossing the macadam. His overcoat was much more stylish than Frank's. It was the new guy in Lieutenant Stout's crew, Joe Vecchio.

The son-in-law of a state assemblyman and a law-school graduate, Vecchio was getting a shot at the most prestigious unit in the county. It wasn't the first time Frank had seen one of these preordained climbs up the ladder of influence. Yet, Homicide assignments had never been indiscriminate plums; curried or not, investigators had to demonstrate a proven combination of persistence and intelligence to be considered for that crack squad.

Vecchio stopped by Monafferi's car. Creegan watched him through the plate glass and was watched in turn as the homicide investigator listened to the others. Vecchio sent Coleman's partner, K. P. Satcher, over to help the uniforms canvass the onlookers and then headed toward the office with Ivey close behind. He stopped in the doorway with no detectable emotion on his square, handsome face. "Lieutenant Creegan, headquarters wants you to call the chief of detectives. He's at home." No self-introduction; no readable tone.

"I'm not officially here, Detective Vecchio."

The other nodded tightly but said nothing. What was going on here?

"All right. In the meantime, I'd like to make a suggestion about the scene." He made sure he also caught Ivey's eye and ear.

"Don't worry," Vecchio said. "I already got the word to defer to you on everything."

"Excuse me?"

"The chief wants you to call right away. You can have them patch you through on my radio. This way you can get it straight from the . . . source's mouth."

Vecchio had parked right behind Frank. Chief Dewey picked up after one ring. The long and the short of it was that Frank's old friend wanted him to baby-sit Vecchio until he could break loose an experienced secondary from the rest of hell night.

Creegan made believe he had a choice.

"Okay," he said, "but if I start this, I want to be in on the finish."

"Suit yourself, Frank. Just make sure this Vecchio kid don't screw the pooch."

Creegan hung up the handset. Then he deliberately checked the interior of Vecchio's car.

Homicide investigators were assigned specific vehicles whose interiors were usually good indicators of their drivers' habits. This one did not look or smell like a fast-food eatery. Nor was it littered with odds and ends of paperwork.

A polyethylene file box sat square in the middle of the rear seat, and a fat binder in county colors occupied the passenger seat. The official plastic dividers were outnumbered by paper flaps that stuck out like a rawhide fringe. He flipped it open to the title page and read by reflected light: "Forensics and the Modern Investigator—A Seminar in Advanced Scene Analysis."

Crime Scene pulled up as he emerged from the car. Creegan asked one of the techs to push the tape line out beyond the corner booth the cyclist had used for his 911 call.

"I don't think anyone's used the phone since we got here," Frank said. "I want to keep it that way, and we need to get the tramplers back farther, but not so far they don't feel talkative. I'll have Monafferi block off Drowned Meadow Avenue."

The tech had worked scenes with Creegan before and just nodded. Like everybody else, though, he was trying to figure out what the hell an off-duty shift commander was doing at a felony murder scene.

A responder from the volunteer firehouse sped past on 29A, heading west; an EMT vehicle and a pumper were not far behind, flashing by with operatic wails and big, blasting honks, gravitating to their own scene of misrule.

Vecchio was out of sight as Creegan strode back to the office; but from Ivey's hovering posture, Frank could tell the murder investigator was down taking a look behind the counter.

Vecchio rose up to his full height just as Frank reached the open door.

"What do you think?" Creegan asked. "What's your first impression?"

The other's brow drew down slightly. He said, "Not everybody trusts first impressions." Did he think he was being tested?

"I know, but it's a way to start brainstorming."

"Well, it looks like a robbery gone bad. What was that suggestion you were going to make before you went out for your call?"

Creegan positioned himself in front of the counter.

"Here's the way part of this feels," he said. "Either the shooter or somebody with him reached over real quick and fumbled out a pencil from that box there. He scribbled this little swastika right-handed on the blotter, real fast and sloppy, standing on this side, and then he flung the pencil towards the body, which was already on the floor. See it there on his leg? Maybe not the shooter, but an accomplice who watched his friend pull the trigger and grab the cash and decided on impulse that he had to do *his* bit."

Vecchio listened intently. "Okay," he said. "We can probably eliminate our bike rider from doing any impulsive drawing. He acted out his every move for Evers. He came in to ask the victim to hook on the air hose so he could pump up a soft tire and as soon as he saw the body he backed out, hands up in front of him like this, and ran for the phone booth."

They looked out into the lot, which was fairly well lighted. Monafferi was still working on J.J., but he seemed exasperated. J.J.'s body stooped in an absent, almost meditative posture. Where's he looking? Frank wondered. Somewhere off to the right where a wooded lot abutted the macadam.

"That drawing," Vecchio resumed. "That could have been done anytime after they pulled off last month's sheet. And why couldn't your friend here have had the pencil in his hand when he got shot?"

"We're theorizing. He was a lefty, though, and he only used pens. He would hand a pen to anyone who was signing a charge slip— can't use pencil for that—and when he wrote a note he always pulled a pen out of his top pocket—usually an insurance company or tree-trimmer's promotional thing. See there?"

He pointed at the clicker end of a yellow-and-white ballpoint protruding from the pocket in between the bullet wounds. A kind of guilt about this easy summoning of Turgot's mannerisms chafed the edges of his thought process. He pushed through it.

Vecchio grasped Creegan's familiarity with the victim, but he seemed to have trouble with Frank's intuitive leaps. What could he say, though, to someone who had methodically cleared nearly every homicide he had handled before moving up to command? Frank sympathized.

"If it had been in his hand," he said, "I think it would have ended up on the floor, maybe off to his left where his southpaw is stretched out. I know that's in no way conclusive, but I'm sure he wasn't using a pencil."

He looked over at the box. "That's a fresh supply of pencils. Let's find out how and when they got here. I think it'll help our odds if we get the techs to work hard on the pencil and the box. They'll be all over the blotter and the counter, but I'm hoping the pencils will give us a pristine chronology."

"But this probably started as a robbery, right?"

"Well, the killer or killers probably took the money. Turgot's pockets don't look tampered with, but they may have been emp-tied out too. We'll see if his wallet's gone when we move him. But whether that was the prime motive, I don't know. That little Nazi logo there makes me think twice."

"Someone in the shop probably would have erased it or scratched it out if it was made earlier," Vecchio conceded.

"Good point."

Vecchio's eyes went out to those questioning the score or so of neighbors who'd walked over from nearby homes.

"I told them to start knocking on doors after they get through with the crowd. Are you going to stay with us while we collect evidence?"

"Yeah, sure; I'll be back in a minute. You stay with it. Ivey here is good with scene work."

As he hit the outer air, Frank let out a breath and saw it vaporize in the deepening chill. He relieved Monafferi of J.J. and stood side by side with the latter, trying to get in synch with his field of vision. The faraway gaze was aimed toward underbrush with a dark backdrop of adult maples and some pines. Creegan looked harder and saw a void about a jeep's width near the back corner of the parking area. Fire trail?

"Hey, J.J. Did you see something happen over there?"

Creegan pointed with a grand gesture at the woods. J.J. leaned right and a little in front of his questioner, as if he were trying to see around a corner and farther along the trail.

"Did you see someone go in there, J.J.?"

J.J. straightened and the fingertips of the T. rex hands began rubbing together.

"J.J., did you?"

"Yeah. Two guys."

"When was that? Tonight when you found Turgot?"

"Who's Turgot?" J.J. asked, and his helmet slipped down a little on his furrowed brow.

"The man inside. The one who was shot."

"His name is Tony. He said to call him Tony."

"Did you see the two men go into the woods just before you found Tony?"

"Yeah. They was runnin'."

Creegan looked at Monafferi. Together they assessed the lighting in the lot, the full moon riding clear of the scattered clouds behind them.

"Did they go in through that trail, J.J.?"

"Yeah. They ran in there. Can't ride through there anymore. Too many sticks and bushes."

Even as they spoke, a middle-aged couple wielding a flashlight strolled out of the overgrown trail and teetered on the cement curbing, watching the show.

"There're houses back there with a dirt road access off of Twenty-nine," Creegan said aloud, remembering.

"Yeah," J.J. said. "Little houses but no sidewalks and no streets."

Monafferi whistled at a tech, and then headed for the clueless couple.

"Did you get a good look at the two guys, J.J.? Were they coming out of the office when you rode in?"

The fingers stopped rubbing and curled in toward J.J.'s palms as he scanned his memory.

"No. Just two guys runnin' into the woods. I didn't see them in the office. No." His index fingers unfurled. "No."

"Did you see their faces? No? Did they have masks or hats on?"

"One guy had a baseball hat on backwards. The other guy had his hood up."

"Like a sweatshirt hood? Yeah? Dark shirts, light? What kind of pants?"

Nondescript clothing, maybe jeans, grayish tops.

"What color was their skin?"

J.J.'s shoulders started to rise like they were being reeled up into the sky; his eyes squinted almost shut. "White," he said. "They ran white."

"What do you mean?"

"They ran white, not black."

"Okay, J.J. Can you stay with us for a while? I want you to talk to Detective Coleman about what you saw. We'll give you a ride home in one of the police cars if you can stay." Frank signaled Ivey.

J.J. nodded, but had a second thought. "What about my tire? Tony can't set up the hose 'cause he's dead."

"We'll see. Let me get the detective over here."

They stood waiting for Ivey, oddly matched, the damp chill working into fingers and feet.

Walt Overholser, the ME, appeared and did a strange duck walk under the yellow tape, heading for the office with big, outturned feet slapping the pavement. Frank looked at the high-shouldered, aging figure. What a target that man must have made as a corpsman on Guadalcanal.

"That's the Scarecrow," J.J. said. He looked radiant, like a celebrity hound who's just spotted an idol.

But Creegan did not share his joy. Overholser had had his usual morbid effect upon him, breathing upon his worry for his son Michael, ashore in Lebanon with the Fleet Marines. Frank had his own surreal, quarter-century-old memories of hitting the beach in Beirut under the watchful eyes of women in bikinis and men astride horses and dusky kids dancing excitedly on the sand as he and his fellow Marines rode by in their amphibians on the way to the airport. Every generation seemed to have its Barbary shore, didn't it?

Acting out of this sudden melancholy, he put an arm around J.J.'s shoulders. But the body inside the baggy clothing tensed with a strength beyond muscularity. Creegan dropped his arm. "Detective Coleman's coming now," he said. "I want you to tell him about everything you did and saw from the time you biked in—especially about the two men who went into the woods. Okay? Then we'll get you home."

"I don't live at home."

"Back to the place you're staying, then."

A couple was conferring across the tape with the female officer: the Hodges, both short, slender, faces looking like they'd been slapped repeatedly. They were dressed for a formal affair that must have seemed very frivolous now. The officer turned. He nodded and she lifted the tape for them.

They were nice people, in their early forties, and had owned this place fifteen years without mishap, other than a larcenous night-manager. Al Hodge started talking from a dozen paces. "My God, Frank, your guy said Turgot was shot dead. They wouldn't say that unless they knew for sure, right? It's not someone else in there, is it?"

"I'm afraid it is him, Al."

Annie Hodge leaned into her husband with a contorted face that was painful to watch. She struggled to open her throat.

"He . . . *we* were robbed?" she asked. "Did he get shot . . . because he wouldn't give up . . . the stupid money?"

Creegan shrugged sadly. "Folks, did he have any enemies that you're aware of?"

"Turgot?" they said together.

"How about family disputes? Money problems? Expensive habits?"

"The only thing he ever got for himself was that white Chevy there, which he considered an investment. Right, Annie?"

"No run-ins with customers?"

"He was my meeter and greeter, for God's sake. You always got the treatment, didn't you? And he *never* forgot a face."

"Just asking; there's always crazies. But no one who might have had a problem with his being a foreigner, say?"

"He never said anything about that. And I've never had a crank call or letter about it either."

"Okay, but let me know if anything pops out of the memory bank. We'll need a list of your other employees too."

"He got along fine with the mechanics and his relief."

"Yes. But maybe they saw him having problems with someone that you didn't hear about. Let's find out about today's customers — the past week's. Maybe further back. Where'd he live?"

"He has people over in Drowned Meadow Depot. He had a room as small as a kid's there. God, those folks are gonna wail when they hear this. Talk about a bunch that pulls together."

"Can I have the address?"

He took it and put the Hodges with Satcher to work up lists of staff and customers and to sort out receipts.

Fresh tape now reached into the gaping darkness of the woods. Beams of light touched here and there under limbs and behind underbrush. A tech was breaking out the big lights, although only daylight would allow a proper ground search.

Monafferi came up. "A car was parked in a turnaround off that lane running from 29A to the bungalows. The couple that tromped in noticed it earlier. Beat-up old compact. Gray or light blue. No plate info. Didn't see anybody parking it or leaving in it. There's four families back in there; the ones that were at home didn't see anything. One guy thought he heard some firecrackers go off at about the right time."

The wind rushed through the pine tops with a highway sound. "Keep at it, Sarge," Creegan said and headed back to the office. He could see Vecchio pointing out something to a tech. Frank considered the detective's knitted brow and his narrowed eyes. The eyes lifted up from Turgot and rested on Frank without relaxing at all.

Frank's rear bedroom had a picture window. He looked out with post-shower lassitude at the long, narrow yard. The grass was still green, but shot with silver, and had begun humping and clumping for the winter. A great oak towered over the thinned woods at the far end of the property. His gaze rose up the dark, rough bark, but he could not see the crown from this angle.

He had a troublesome pride in the ancient tree; he had never seen a larger one on the Island. It had withstood many hurricanes over the decades, although Agnes had snapped off a huge limb that had once pointed to the horizon like the arm of an archangel.

He and Mike had borrowed a monster extension ladder, some heavy ropes, and long saws so that they could separate the splintered bough from the upright trunk. The sawn lengths still stretched out in the shade at the back of the lot, moldering but substantial, like fallen columns. Mike had been very aware of being a real help to him, clearly doing a man's work. The proud young face still shone out from a timeless grotto in Frank's memory. He had seen the same expression on his son's face when they had gone down to Parris Island to see him graduate from boot camp.

Elsewhere in the house was the murmuring chorus of his wife and daughter and younger son. Laundry was thrashing; female lines from *The Merchant of Venice* were being rehearsed. Curtis would be readying his arm. Frank thought about a quick nap before driving out to see the boy pitch in the fall-ball championship.

The phone rang. It was Vecchio. As Frank listened, he imagined his kid on the mound, looking toward an empty seat in the bleachers.

Fred Stout stood in the dark hall outside the interrogation room drinking boiled coffee from a Styrofoam cup. He was a blocky, large-pored man, with a brain that had as low a center of gravity as his body. He graced Frank with a direct look as he took another sip of sludge.

"Frank. Wonder Boy told the shrimp we had a synagogue break-in and that we think some old friends of his are involved. We got him a couple years back for helping two kids mess up Brith Sholom cemetery. The others were juveniles, but he was eighteen and took the heat. He's bitter about that, so now that he thinks he can pay them back, he's not being shy. I guess you got some bad news for him, right?"

Stout got a silent profile rather than an answer as Frank set up by the two-way glass. "Come on, Frank, before I can shake somebody loose, you'll have this cleared."

"Lieutenant Creegan?"

They both turned toward Ivey, coming up with his notebook fanned open. "Satch caught up with the victim's family. The brother-in-law says he brought dinner over for the victim last night about six-thirty, about an hour and a half before the shooting, and he was as cheerful as always. No one else was there and he didn't talk about any hassles.

"Oh, and I know you were real curious about those pencils, right? Well, the brother-in-law works for the county crew upgrading the golf course where the pencils came from. He says it was him that brought them. He handed over that box to the victim at dinnertime last night. The box was still taped shut when he gave it to him."

Creegan thanked him. They continued watching the Q and A, and Frank put his hand up when it seemed Stout was going to make another overture. He wanted to read the suspect and observe Vecchio's technique without any distractions before going in.

Dwight Apgard was almost without shape inside his baggy clothes. His hooded sweatshirt was a dingy gray devoid of logo or script. Under the table, the legs of his bleach-streaked jeans looked like they were draped over sticks. The dots and smudges of his pinched little features barely disturbed the roundness of a small, close-cropped skull. He looked as if he would crack like an egg.

Vecchio was listening intently while Dwight rewrote history, explaining how not he but someone else had masterminded the vandalism he'd been busted for. Evidently Apgard Senior had had to remortgage to make good on the property restoration, a consequence that had clearly taken Dwight's life to a deeper circle of hell.

"You think he's the twerpetrator?" Stout asked.

"No. He's a passenger, I believe. We use him to get to the real guy. Here we go."

Vecchio greeted Frank politely, feigning a trace of surprise at his appearance. Apgard tore his eyes away from his attentive listener, wondering perhaps if the wind had just veered.

"Dwight, this is Lieutenant Creegan. He's working the case too. He might have some news for us."

Creegan sat down diagonally across from Dwight.

"You look like a priest with those glasses on and that turtleneck," Dwight said.

Frank gave him a sad, crinkling look and then said, "Dwight, forget about this vandalism stuff. There was a shooting last night, and I know you were there when it happened."

Vecchio widened his eyes and looked from one to the other. Dwight's face began to mottle.

Vecchio said, "No way! Is that true, Dwight? Damn, I guess I have to read you your rights." He did so with a hurt smile.

Stunned, but still clinging to their barely vacated rapport, Dwight waived his rights to an attorney.

"I don't know nothin' about a shooting," he said after the formalities. "Where did it happen?" He sat back with folded arms, mimicking Vecchio's widened eyes.

Frank turned to his left and said, "Detective, his print turned up at the gas station where that attendant was killed last night."

"Really." Vecchio looked even less cordially at Dwight.

"Oh," the young man said. "You're talkin' about the Usoco deal. I heard about that on the news. Hey, I been in there a few times to buy gas. Maybe *that's* why you found my prints. But I haven't been in there for a while."

Frank was shaking his head. "That pencil you used to leave your mark. That's what the fingerprint was on. The box of pencils it came from got dropped off last night, just before the man was shot, so I know you were there. We also have a witness who saw *two* people leaving the scene. I guess it's just a matter of letting him get a look at you in a lineup. But, here's the thing. I think your *pal* did the shooting, not you. Who were you with, Dwight? That's who we really want."

Dwight's arms tightened into a self-hug; he twisted sideways. "I wasn't there last night."

Vecchio took the folder Creegan had brought in and looked inside. "Huh! Sorry, Dwight, there's no doubt about the match. You were in there *after* those pencils were dropped off."

Creegan took in the torqued posture, the scrawny arms wrapping the rib cage. "Dwight, if you're the only one we can place at the murder, you're going to take all the blame. Again. Just like with the Jewish cemetery. That ain't fair, is it?"

Suddenly, the kid sat up, dropping his arms, piling up his spine like a soldier. "All right, I was there. I did it."

"Did *what?*" Vecchio asked.

"I shot him. I shot the Israeli guy."

Creegan studied the new pose, the hands flexed like they were reaching for a different purchase, the challenging tone that had been pulled out of storage someplace.

"Dwight, that man you say you shot was *not* an Israeli."

"His name was Sol and he had an accent. What else could he be?"

"Are you talking about the name he had stitched on his clothes? That was S-*A*-L, not S-*O*-L. And they were handed down from a guy that worked there before; they weren't his. His name was Turgot. Turgot Suleymanoglu. That's Turkish."

Dwight squinted, as if he was mentally reshuffling a swollen, sticky deck of cards.

"*What* was he?"

"A Turk."

"Like a towel-head, right? What have they done for us except sneak in and steal jobs?"

"He was here legally. Did you want the job he had? I didn't think so. And I fought alongside the Turks in Korea. They were tough, brave. Good soldiers."

"Well, that was in the old days. This guy was a migrant taking some American's job."

"Is that why he was killed?" Vecchio asked quietly. "This wasn't just a robbery that went bad?"

Dwight gave a quick head shake. "Nah. He was my target of the week."

Creegan didn't like that answer. If the eradication program was for real, having Apgard in custody might not stop it.

"Where's the weapon now, Dwight?" Creegan asked. "And where'd it come from?"

Dwight moved his tale into focus and said, "I chucked it in the harbor."

"Where in the harbor?"

"I don't remember. I was standing on one of the marina docks. By the gas pumps, maybe."

"The lieutenant also asked where you *got* the gun," Vecchio prompted.

Another hesitation. "I bought it off some guy in the city."

"And how did you get on to him?"

"I don't know. It was a long time ago."

"How long?"

Dwight shrugged.

"Why'd you chuck it? How were you going to hit your next target if your gun was in the harbor?"

"I can always get a gun."

His story didn't have much depth to it, but that didn't seem to bother him. The main thing was that he had laid claim to the killing.

It was Creegan's turn to prevaricate. Investigating crime was about the only situation in which he let truth take a back seat, matching lie for lie in line with some police wisdom his father had passed along to him: "To do a great right, do a little wrong."

"Dwight, try to remember how long it's been since you got the gun," Creegan said earnestly.

"Why?"

"Because it was used in another bad crime. How long's it been?"

"What crime?"

"How long? Think back and try to place it in time. What was going on in the world when you went into the Big Apple?"

"I don't know. It was late summer."

"Like August?"

"Yeah. Before the kids went back to school."

"You're real sure about that? *Real* sure."

"Positive. It was hot as hell."

"Ah, that's bad. What if I told you that that gun was used to kill a pregnant woman in Belmont? And not a Jewish or a foreign woman. She was a blond, all-American deli clerk. Why did *she* get shot?"

"I didn't shoot no pregnant woman."

"Yeah, but Dwight, it happened three weeks ago, early *October.* You had the gun then. So why a young, pregnant woman all the way in to Belmont? You want to see the pictures to refresh your memory?"

He rotated the file and opened it so that Dwight could see the Polaroids of the woman on the floor, the damaged face, the gravid stomach, the cross at her blood-stained throat. Carrie Hedrickson, killed in Belmont on the far edge of Peconic County five years ago by person(s) unknown. Even if her case had gone cold, it served a purpose in the here and now.

The persona Dwight was trying for seeped away as he worked out the implications of Creegan's lie. Some people would have asked for a lawyer at this point, but Dwight was at the tiller of a literal guilt trip, uncertain yet about the course he would follow.

"I didn't shoot a pregnant woman."

"Who did it then, Dwight?" asked Vecchio. "Did you loan the gun out to someone? You never knew what he used it for?"

Dwight did not know how to proceed. Creegan pitied the stunted mind and its vague, simplistic code, even though the deficiencies were to their advantage.

"That's what happened, isn't it, Dwight?" he prompted. "Like the detective said, you loaned it out and your friend used it for something you wouldn't have gone along with."

"It don't make sense," Dwight said. "Why would he go all the way to Belmont?"

"Who, Dwight?" Creegan asked. "Who are we talking about?"

Dwight shook his head.

"You don't even have a car. Your dad says you didn't borrow his last night either. So your buddy drove *his* car, the one you parked in the woods. You were not alone in this."

Vecchio said, "Dwight, in the little time we've spent together I can tell you're not like this other guy. You'll eventually have to tell us what went wrong at the gas station last night, but I don't see you doing this Belmont thing. It's too cold. What kind of person would kill a pregnant woman?"

Dwight was listening to something else inside his head.

"Dwight, listen to *us*," Creegan urged. "I can understand you not wanting to give up a friend. But what kind of friend would use your gun on such a bad thing and then not even tell you? Whoever he is, he's been holding out on you, leading you on. Setting you up. Hasn't that happened to you before?"

Dwight looked up at him and asked, "Is my dad still out there?"

"Yes, but you can't talk to him right now. We have to deal with this first."

"I don't want to talk to him. Can you tell him to go home?"

Creegan wondered if the kid would open up if he thought his father's dysfunctional aura was gone from here. He stood up and said, "I'll ask him to leave, Dwight, if that's what you want."

"Yeah, that's what I want. Does my mom know about this?"

Creegan looked toward Vecchio, who said, "We haven't been able to get hold of her yet. Would your father have called her?"

"*He* wouldn't say anything to her. They don't talk since she moved upstate. Can I call her?"

"When we finish here, Dwight."

The kid slumped back. Frank went outside and stood next to Stout. Fred had reloaded his cup, and the burnt smell annoyed even Frank's blurred receptors.

"I think he's getting ready," Frank said.

"His mutt of an old man is out there with Ivey."

"Have we checked *him* out?"

"Domestic violence. Drunk driving. That's it."

"Maybe we should try harder to get hold of the mother."

Stout pushed off like a rowboat. Inside, Vecchio was killing time until Creegan got back. He asked Dwight if he had any other family besides the split parents. There had been a little brother, but he had died of pneumonia. Sick little guy. And a girl cousin that he liked lived out in California. They had lost touch.

Frank went back in. "Your dad left already."

"Did he say anything?"

"The detective says he just got up and walked out."

Dwight disappeared a little deeper into his clothes. Was he feeling abandoned or relieved?

Creegan felt some real panic. "Jeez, Dwight, it wasn't your dad that went with you last night, was it?"

He felt Vecchio stir slightly. But Dwight was absolutely convincing when he shook his head no. "My old man won't even let me help him change spark plugs. He ain't got no patience with me."

"Well, he's gone now."

"Was this thing in Belmont maybe an accident?" Dwight asked.

"Look at the pictures again. Twice in the face. Once is maybe an accident, but not twice. He put two shots into Turgot too. It's a pattern."

Dwight took another sidelong look at the photos, his rickety faith collapsing further in on itself.

"It can't be."

"Is this guy the only one who treats you square?" Vecchio asked. "Is that why you're reluctant to tell us who he is?"

Dwight gave that some thought. "He doesn't mind having me along when he does things."

"What things?"

"Playin' pool. Bowling, once in a while."

"Any other things?"

"I've been along when he's gone into a few stores and bad-mouthed the help if they don't speak English good. We stole stuff on them. This thing that happened last night—it's something we kicked around for a while."

"Shooting someone instead of just bad-mouthing them?"

"Nah. I mean it was supposed to be just a robbery, a *real* robbery, not just shoplifting. We wanted to send a message to the ones stealing jobs."

"Sounds like your pal tried out the robbery angle on his own first. In Belmont."

"It wasn't my gun," Dwight said. "I lied about that."

Creegan said, "Our witness told us that you guys didn't hide your faces. If you didn't plan on killing the man, why would you let your faces hang out?"

Dwight leaned forward now, resting his chin on folded arms like a kid in school detention. "I didn't think he'd recognize me. I only been in there once or twice to fill lawn mowers."

"Hello, buddy!" Creegan said, imitating Turgot's voice and accent as best he could.

Dwight was startled. "Yeah. How'd you know he said that?"

"He said that to every guy that walked in. But he *may* have recognized you. At least your friend thought so, right? That's why he shot him. If the man could finger you, then you could finger your friend."

"Give us a name, Dwight," Vecchio said. "We know you didn't pull the trigger, but it's because he recognized you that this man was killed. Admit it."

Dwight stared at a point between the two men and said nothing. His face was desolate rather than defiant.

Vecchio's fingers tapped the crime photos, and Dwight's gaze was drawn back to them.

Creegan leaned forward with his fingers laced and waited until Dwight looked up at him. "Son, you're wasting good impulses on a bad person. This guy's not worth your loyalty after what he did to that young woman and to Turgot."

He waited a beat.

"If you keep quiet now, you'll be sending yourself away to a very dark and lonely hole that will go on and on forever. Never stops. Can't you feel it closing in on you now? You had so little to do with this. You hooked up with bad company, that's all. Basically all you did was grab a pencil and draw that little swastika, like when you went out that night with the kids in the graveyard, right?"

Creegan thought he sensed tiny connections closing.

"Who's the real bad guy, Dwight? He's still out there with that gun, and he's not about what you thought he was, is he? Dwight, save yourself."

Dwight's features seemed to enlarge, like a dilated pupil. He said a name. Vecchio got an address from him and looked at Creegan, who said, "It's yours, man."

Vecchio got up and left. Creegan watched the momentary luster fading from Dwight's face. He unlaced his fingers and extended a hand. "Thanks, Dwight. You did the right thing."

The kid looked at the hand.

He said, "You *talk* like a priest too."

Then he took the hand as if the act were something new to him. Creegan gave it a good, firm shake and let go. He grabbed Vecchio's pad and flipped it to a clean page. "Okay, let's get it all down and behind us. I'll stay with you through this."

"Can I call my mom after I'm done? I can call collect. She'll take a call from *me*."

"Sure. But before you do, we'll talk over the best way to break this to her. What about your dad?"

Dwight's only response was to pick up the pencil.

Later, when the grimy-looking paragraphs had all been set down, Creegan asked, "Dwight, do you want to see a real priest?"

"I ain't Catholic."

"What are you?"

"I'm nothing. I don't need a priest. I got you, right?"

On Sunday a steady rain held back the sunrise. Frank woke to the sound but did not try to go back to sleep. A ruthless, forgotten dream was waiting for him there.

While he got the coffee going, he thought about Dwight—and Curtis too, who had waited up for him with Ellen last night. The kid had had a good outing and did not let resentment get in the way of telling about it. Frank had done his best to relive the innings as if he'd been there. He would remember both boys at Mass today, along with Turgot—and Mike.

He used an umbrella when he went out to fetch the paper. The headline of the special edition said, "Marine and French Barracks Bombed in Beirut; Scores Killed."

Time charred to ash inside his head and heart. He was not sure how long it was before he was able to quiet his raging soul and hear the rain again.

He went in to wake his wife. As he stood over her, he glanced out the rear window and remembered the shy pride on Michael's face as the two of them had dragged the great tree limb into the shade.

ALBERT TUCHER

Bismarck Rules

FROM *Oregon Literary Review*

"HI," SAID MARY ALICE. "I'm Crystal."

The man in the doorway recognized the name. After more than ten years in the business, Mary Alice still welcomed the relief that followed. Once, early on, she had knocked on the wrong door. Getting away had taken some fast talking.

"I'm Steve. Come in."

His living room was down the hall and to the right. She liked it when he invited her to sit. Some men didn't. They stared at her and resented her for confronting them with their own needs.

She crossed her legs. As he enjoyed the view, she sized him up. He had the wiry build, weather-beaten features, and slightly graying hair of a man who could have been thirty or sixty.

So far he seemed okay.

"How can I help you?" she said.

"I want you to do something for me."

A lot of men started slowly. She waited for more.

"Nothing illegal," he said.

"Really?"

"Really."

"Okay. But it's still my time, and it's still two hundred dollars an hour for the first two, and a hundred after that. I've cleared my morning for you, so that's six hundred and counting."

"That's fine. Can you drive a stick shift?"

"I'm not sure what that means."

She hated to admit it. What kind of hooker knew less than the client?

"It means exactly what it sounds like," he said. "I'm talking about driving my car."

"Why do I need to drive your car?"

"Can you drive a stick? If you can't, we'll have to go in your car, and I don't think you want to do that."

He was right. She didn't like clients seeing her license plates. If they knew what to do with the information, they could penetrate her private life.

"I can drive a stick. I learned on a stick."

"Good. Then you can drive me to the doctor."

"Congratulations," she said. "You just came up with something I haven't done before."

He smiled.

"You could explain," she said. "If you wanted to, that is."

"I just turned fifty. Today I have to go for my first colonoscopy."

He seemed to think that explained everything. It didn't.

"They say I can't drive myself. I have to bring somebody to take me home. They won't even let me call a taxi."

She still didn't get it, and she could tell that her failure was starting to annoy him.

"I'm divorced. Five years now. I don't date. No wife, no girlfriend. My sister lives in Chicago, and she doesn't want anything to do with me, anyway. My parents are alive, and they're stuck with me. But that would be just too pathetic. Fifty years old, and my mommy and daddy have to drive me? Come on."

Mary Alice understood. This job was still hooking. He had no woman in his life, and he needed one.

"When I come out, I want to have a nice-looking woman waiting just for me. Of course, I didn't realize I was going to get this lucky. I love your kind of coloring."

He didn't know it, but he had scored with that comment. Mary Alice had grown up among Scandinavian blondes, and her dark hair and olive skin had always made her feel like an imposter.

He smiled so charmingly that she decided to do the whole job, even if he hadn't mentioned it.

"I'm not sure what the prep for that procedure is," she said. "Did they say anything about sex? I mean, are you feeling up to it?"

His surprise made her wonder, but she decided to let it go. She stood. He got up and led the way down the hall.

Steve kept his bedroom spare and tidy, and it made her feel inadequate. Mary Alice seldom made her own bed.

She went through the motions. They were good enough for most men, but not for her. Sex always reminded Mary Alice of a television left on in a neighbor's apartment. She couldn't enjoy the program, and she couldn't turn it off.

When Steve had finished, he rolled off her and lay on his back with his eyes closed. Mary Alice looked around. Something was missing from this room that the living room had also lacked.

No photos, she thought.

Steve opened his eyes.

"Photos are just another thing they can take away from you," he said.

"Not my business. Sorry. I was thinking out loud."

"Plus, I had to pose for my share of them. When they don't give you a choice, it's no fun."

She left that one alone.

"That felt vaguely familiar," said Steve. "Just now."

Mary Alice wondered whether she had been insulted.

"It's just about eleven years since the last time."

"Wait a minute. You're divorced for five. What happened to the rest?"

"I wasn't available."

It was starting to add up in a way that meant she would have to protect herself.

While he showered, she stood at the sink and freshened herself with a clean washcloth that he had laid out for her. As she watched him dry off, she thought about his way of standing as if he hoped to deflect attention.

In the car she depressed the clutch with her foot and turned the key in the ignition. The hand-foot coordination came back effortlessly. Nothing distracted her from thinking some more.

"Okay," she said. "You were in prison—for quite a while, is my impression."

"That was the eleven years."

"I don't care, except that going to prison is expensive. Lawyers, then you can't earn much while you're inside. I'll have to see some money."

She should have handled business up front. Something about him had thrown her off from the first moment.

Steve took an envelope from the left side pocket of his sport coat. He lifted the unsealed flap and let her glance at the bills inside. The top one was a hundred. She would check the rest at the first discreet opportunity.

"Thank you." She reached across her body and took the money with her left hand. "I'm sorry, but I have to protect myself. Collection agencies won't touch my problem accounts, if you know what I mean."

She tucked the envelope into the side pocket of her suit coat.

"Money's not a problem," he said. "Even after the civil suit. I have royalties from some patents."

"Civil suit. For what?"

"Let's not go into it."

Mary Alice wondered whether to turn the car around and go back. The bad feeling was getting worse, and she didn't know why. She had been with ex-convicts before. There must be something more.

Her indecision pulled the words out of him.

"Let's just say I was convicted of something. The State of New Jersey says I was guilty. I say I wasn't."

"I hear you," she said, for something to say.

"I'm not sure you do. People have a tendency to stop listening."

Mary Alice signaled right and steered to the curb. She stopped the car and sat staring straight ahead. Steve looked at her for a long moment and nodded.

"Keep the money. It spends."

He took a tiny cell phone from his other front pocket and began to punch in numbers.

"What are you doing?" she said.

"Canceling the appointment."

"I'm definitely keeping the money. But that means I'm going to earn it."

She checked her left mirror and pulled back into the traffic.

They left Lakeview, where Steve lived, and made their way into Witherspoon Township. The proctologist had his office in a small two-story professional building. She had passed it hundreds of times without noticing. The lot was half-empty, and she found a space right by the patients' entrance.

Inside, Steve led the way to the desk, where the receptionist greeted him.

"Mr. Golisard. We're running a little behind. You have someone with you?"

"My girlfriend."

"You understand you have to stay here the whole time?" said the receptionist to Mary Alice. "No shopping."

She smiled to soften the order. Mary Alice nodded. She joined Steve, who had already taken a seat on one of the long couches. Her shoulder touched his, which was just right for the relationship they supposedly had.

But something in the room felt wrong. She looked around the waiting room, until her eyes found a man on the other couch diagonally across the room. He was in his hard-used forties, and he wore a dark gray suit that was beautifully cut, but old. With both hands he gripped the handle of a battered briefcase that rested in his lap. He glared at Steve, who seemed not to notice. Mary Alice found it hard to ignore the man.

It was a relief when the receptionist called Steve into the consulting room. Mary Alice stood up with him. She kissed him and stroked his cheek.

"I'll be here."

When she took her seat again, she noticed that the man had transferred his glare to her.

"Stephen Golisard."

He made the name an accusation.

Mary Alice raised her eyebrows at him.

"I said, Stephen Golisard."

"I heard you."

"Your boyfriend. Do you know what he's really like? What kind of man he really is?"

Mary Alice broke eye contact and reached for the current *Time* in the magazine rack. She flipped some pages but found nothing new.

A few minutes later another couple came into the waiting room. They looked about fifty, but the woman could have been a defeated thirty-eight. They checked in with the receptionist and looked for seats

"Mr. Pilarczyk?" said the receptionist.

The new couple had just sat down. As the woman stood, she

turned in a full circle, as if she had no idea where to go. When she faced the window over the parking lot, the outdoor light made her seem defenseless. The woman froze for a moment before turning back to the waiting room.

Mr. Pilarczyk didn't move until he saw his wife get up.

Mary Alice realized that the man must be hard of hearing. She loved the moments that told her things about the people around her. Magazines couldn't compete.

The receptionist led the couple toward the consulting offices, which seemed to enrage the man with the briefcase. When she came back, he was ready for her.

"I don't appreciate being treated like this. I have an appointment. I'm prepared to pay for the doctor's time, although I don't see why I should. I'm offering to make him a lot of money."

"Doctor Roenn has told you he's not interested in investing in your idea. You made the appointment under false pretenses. You don't need a professional consultation, so you're not entitled to any of the doctor's time. Now excuse me, please."

For a moment the man looked as if he would hit the receptionist, who stopped herself in mid-flinch and glared back at him.

"I won't forget this," he said.

He turned sharply around and headed for the door, but as he passed the coffee table, he reached into the right side pocket of his suit coat and pulled out a handful of business cards. He dropped the pile of cards onto the table. When he saw Mary Alice watching him, he produced an effortful smile.

"I never let an opportunity go by. You might tell your boyfriend that."

He marched out of the office. The door banged shut behind him.

Mary Alice couldn't resist. She leaned forward and picked up one of the business cards. The man's name was Harold Mohn, and his card proclaimed him an inventor. She put the card in the right pocket of her suit coat.

There was no one else to entertain her. For a while Mary Alice stood at the window and counted cars in the parking lot. The receptionist had to call her twice.

"Mr. Golisard is ready to go."

In the examination room Steve had dressed, but he looked

woozy. With the nurse's help he stood up and crossed the room to Mary Alice. He put his arm around her shoulders, and his hand bore down heavily.

They left the office and made their way to the parking lot and the car. She helped him climb into the passenger seat and get settled. On the way home she decided to make conversation.

"There was a little excitement in the waiting room."

She told him about Harold Mohn.

"Oh, for Christ's sake," said Steve. "Mohn. He never gives up."

"You know him?"

"I know of him. We've never met. I'm not surprised I sat six feet away and didn't recognize him."

"You're not his favorite person."

"Losers like him always find somebody else to blame."

"How do you mean?"

"While I was in prison, he came out of nowhere and tried to take advantage of my . . . indisposition. Sued me for infringing some patents he holds. Total bullshit, but it happens all the time. Somebody takes a shot at you just to see what he can get."

"I had the impression he really believes you did something to him."

"Maybe he's convinced himself."

They waited silently at a red light. As Mary Alice started up on the green, Steve said, "I like you. I hope you believe me."

His voice had a different tone, one that she had heard before. It belonged to a client who had decided he was in love. Other women in her business exploited the situation or dumped the client, but Mary Alice had a weakness for men who fell for her, the more flamboyantly the better.

It was a problem. In her line of work she needed to stay uninvolved. She wished she knew how to fix the problem.

"Believe that you didn't do it?"

She heard her own voice soften to match his, and she scolded herself. That didn't mean she would stop what she was doing.

"That I'm not guilty."

The distinction seemed to matter to him, and she wondered why.

"The girl was a sexy little piece of work. She knew what she was doing. Nobody can say she didn't."

His pain medication must have destroyed his inhibitions. Mary Alice realized it later. But at that moment her insides lurched, and her throat clenched against the urge to vomit.

She welcomed the turmoil. It kept her too busy to look at him.

He didn't seem to notice the admission he had just made, or her silence. She kept driving. When they stopped in front of his house, Mary Alice wondered how she had remembered the route, and how many pedestrians she had hit. She turned the engine off and sat in the driver's seat, until she remembered that it wasn't her car. She would have to get out. Somehow she did. She didn't know how she had allowed him to touch her, but he was hanging on to her shoulder again as they approached his front door. He handed her his keys, and she opened the door. She gave the keys back to him and left him without a word. He called something after her, but she didn't answer. Some instinct made her turn left onto the sidewalk. After a while, maybe a few minutes, maybe hours, she found herself at her own car.

It was a bad idea to drive in her mental state, but she had no choice. If she waited until she was more in command, she might still be there the next day. She put the car in gear and lurched away from the curb without a glance in any direction.

Luck stayed with her all the way to her home, an apartment over the only pharmacy left in downtown Driscoll. She even found a parking space near her entrance at the side of the building. Normally she would have parked somewhere else for security, but on this day any distance would have felt like a death march.

She had started her day hours earlier than usual, and she hadn't tried to eat breakfast. In her refrigerator was a leftover portion of Chinese takeout that she had put aside to reward herself at lunchtime. Now she couldn't consider eating. Instead, Mary Alice went straight to the bathroom and knelt in front of the toilet. Her body had needs. Immediately she began to retch. Nothing came up but a few tablespoons of bile. That didn't stop her from heaving for several more minutes.

She had known she would vomit, and she knew what would come next. One at a time she moved her hands from the edges of the toilet bowl to the floor. She let herself sink until she lay curled up on her side on the bathroom tiles. As if it were happening now instead of twenty-five years earlier, she heard the hinges of her bedroom door squeaking. She was fifteen, and it had been going on for over a year, since her mother's death. Mary Alice heard Daddy's loud, wet breathing and felt his hands as they ran over her body, first on top of her nightgown, then underneath it. She smelled sweat, liquor, and cigarette smoke. His hand found her vagina. She always hated herself for lubricating, because it made her feel responsible for what came next.

She had read recently that women are hardwired to lubricate even under duress, but the knowledge had come too late.

Daddy came to her room many times, but this was the occasion she remembered. This was the night she decided to kill him when she got the chance.

Her mind took her to that frigid night a few weeks after she had turned eighteen. Her father lay unconscious where he had fallen, just short of the front steps. Mary Alice opened his coat and packed snow against his chest. When the snow melted, she packed more in. Each time it lasted longer, as he lost the battle against the prairie winter. She sat on the steps and watched. It seemed important to note his last breath, but at some point she realized that she had missed it.

When she had finished remembering, Mary Alice gathered herself up from the bathroom floor and studied herself in the mirror. Nothing in her reflection showed that this had been her worst day in years. That was good, because she had a lot to do. First she brushed her teeth and rinsed her mouth. Then she went to her bedroom and opened the closet door. In a shoebox on the shelf was a .32-caliber revolver and a box of cartridges. She popped the cylinder open and inserted six rounds.

Her father had taught her to shoot. He had never seemed to realize that a bullet could come looking for him.

She closed the cylinder and put the gun into her suit-coat pocket with Harold Mohn's card and her keys.

That reminded her. She pulled Steve's money out of her other pocket and stowed it in a dresser drawer.

Mary Alice walked down the stairs and out the side door of the building. She got into her car and drove back to Lakeview, where she parked in front of Steve Golisard's house. The midafternoon silence of the neighborhood made her believe that no one would see her.

Or maybe she didn't care if she was seen.

The gun was small but surprisingly heavy. It dragged her right hand downward as she approached the house. She reached out with her left hand, but she stopped it in midair, just short of the doorknob. After a moment she understood that she was reluctant to break in. She had come planning to kill the man in this house, but now she felt squeamish about damaging his property.

She would laugh about it another time.

But when she pulled the screen door open, she saw that someone had prepared the way for her. The inner door stood slightly open. Mary Alice pushed it farther.

Even as she looked, she pondered her indifference to what she saw. It was gruesome enough for anyone's taste, but it didn't bother her at all. Just far enough inside the house to avoid blocking the door, Steve lay dead on the floor. Blood told the story. Someone had shot him at least once in the chest and again through his open mouth, as he gasped or screamed or pleaded for his life. His face showed no damage, but a halo of blood had spread around him on the floor. Whoever turned him over would see a large exit wound in the back of his head.

That's that, Mary Alice thought.

With the gun still in her hand, she walked back to her car. She had to exchange the gun for her keys in her coat pocket. She drove carefully home and climbed the familiar stairs again. She sat on her aging sofa and waited.

The police would come. She had been arrested and finger-printed early in her career, and she remembered touching the fixtures in Steve's bathroom. Her experienced eye had told her that a good cleaning service came in regularly. Her prints and his would be the only ones there.

Unless she got lucky, and the killer had been careless.

She thought about her gun. Should she dump it somewhere, or should she let the police find it and work their magic to eliminate it as the murder weapon?

It's too complicated, she thought. Just get rid of it.

But the task would have to wait. The day had caught up to her and made her feel too heavy to move. The thought of getting up made her want to be sick again.

As if she had anything to vomit. At this rate she would never eat again.

At some point she realized that the room had become dark. It was time to do something. She rolled off the sofa and crawled to her bedroom. The last thing she did before climbing onto the bed was to strip off her suit coat and throw it toward the corner of the room. The gun in the pocket thudded on the carpeted floor.

When Mary Alice awoke, the bedside clock read five in the morning. She had the feeling that she had just missed something. The doorbell rang again. The infuriating sound pried her out of bed.

She looked down and saw that she still hadn't managed to change her clothes from the day before. If her morning breath bothered the cops, that was their problem.

Who else could it be but the police?

She trudged down the stairs and opened the door. Detective Eckert of the Lakeview police looked back at her. Eckert was very cute, but with her he was all cop and all business. He had another plainclothes cop with him, the kind of middle-aged man whose own wife can't remember what he looks like.

"This is Detective Rostow from Driscoll," said Eckert. "Can we talk to you?"

Mary Alice knew how to translate his words. He meant, "Let us in, or you're out of business." She turned and started to climb back up the stairs. That was all the invitation she felt like giving them. They followed.

She opened the apartment door and held it open for one of them to catch. They joined her in her small living room. She pointed to her sofa and waited for them to sit. She took the arm-chair, which was angled toward the two detectives.

"Stephen Golisard," said Eckert.

It was the same thing Harold Mohn had said, and it confused her for a moment.

"You know him?"

"Yes."

"When did you see him last?"

"Yesterday."

She saw no point in making them work for the information. The more effort they put into getting it, the more they would want to read into it.

"What time?"

"I got to his house before nine in the morning. I left him between twelve-thirty and one."

"And you stayed in the whole time?"

"I didn't say that. Let me ask you something."

She knew Eckert wouldn't be pleased, but she didn't care.

"Did you find an appointment book?"

Eckert didn't answer. He had a good poker face, but she still thought the answer was no.

"I drove him to the doctor's office. His proctologist."

Eckert blinked. It wasn't much of a reaction, but she enjoyed it.

"He's a friend of yours?"

"No, he's a client."

She had almost said, "Was."

This is fun, she thought. And dangerous.

She told him Steve's reasons for hiring her.

"So you were just the world's most expensive car service? No sex?"

"I figured he had bought a quickie."

"How did that go?"

"What is wrong with you today?"

"Your client has a history. A sexual history. Makes me wonder if he could perform."

Of course they knew about Steve. She shrugged.

"He managed. He seemed to like it. I'd hate to think neither of us did."

"What happened to the condoms?"

"One condom. I heard him flush."

Mary Alice wondered when she should lose patience and demand to know why the cops cared about Stephen Golisard. She decided that sooner was better.

"What's this about? You finally decided to shut me down?"

"No, you've got bigger problems than hooking. You say he was alive at twelve-thirty. Very soon after that he was dead. Shot. We have you at the scene. So far, we don't have anyone else."

He looked at her expectantly. She shrugged and looked back.

"So what was it?" he said. "Some kind of argument? Did he say something? Do something?"

This time she didn't bother to shrug.

"You don't like your work," he said.

"Not particularly."

"Or sex in general?"

"It doesn't do much for me."

"Ever wonder what you're missing?"

"Only about a million times."

"There's therapy for that."

"Where I come from, we don't do therapy. If something bothers us, we think about something else."

"Where's that?"

"Bismarck, North Dakota. Is that illegal?"

"Shooting him is. Which is why I'm thinking you might not want to play this by Bismarck rules. Your state of mind could make a big difference."

"And I'm thinking you're a really bad social worker."

"Okay. We don't know why you did it. Let's go on to the how. Would you consent to a search of this apartment?"

She didn't have to think. She was still a hooker without rights.

She looked defiantly at Detective Rostow, who was already holding out a form for her to sign. She accepted his pen and scrawled her name. Rostow took out his cell phone and made a brief call. Mary Alice and the two detectives sat without speaking or looking at each other, until the doorbell rang. Cops had a way of making the bell sound different. Rostow went down to answer it.

He came back with two uniformed officers, who joined in the search. It was the younger, cuter uniform who came out of the bedroom carrying her suit coat with the gun in the pocket. He seemed proud of himself. Eckert looked at the gun. He covered his disappointment well, but she saw it.

"Any other guns here?"

"That's it."

"I don't suppose you have a permit."

"No."

"We'll take this with us."

"You don't look very happy about it. I guess it's the wrong caliber?"

He said nothing, which was as good as saying yes.

"Now that we've got that out of the way," she said, "would you care to hear about somebody else who might have done it?"

Eckert gave her a sharp glance.

"Who would that be?"

She told him about Harold Mohn and about Mohn's card in her

pocket. Eckert held out his hand for the coat, which the young officer handed to him.

"And you didn't mention this before because?"

"Because you were taking things one step at a time. Step one being me. I know better than to tell cops something they don't want to hear."

He glared at her. When it didn't seem to make him feel any better, he dropped the suit coat on the sofa and turned to leave. The other cops went ahead of him. At the door he stopped and turned back to her.

"How does anybody get from Bismarck to Driscoll, New Jersey?"

"My ex was in the air force out there. I came back with him. It didn't work out."

"No kidding."

He stared at her for a while.

"We'll find that other gun. Count on it. And when we do, we won't owe you a thing."

He left the apartment, and his footsteps sounded on the stairs.

Mary Alice went around the apartment picking up what the cops had thrown around. She didn't need help making a mess of her home.

The day got worse. She had a regular lunch-hour client to see, one of the men she could do without. If the cops had to make her a suspect, couldn't they at least give her an excuse to miss this weekly appointment? The man was one of those who liked to be spanked and verbally abused.

When she got back from the date, Eckert and Rostow were waiting for her in their car. Again they followed her up the stairs.

"I just got off the phone," said Eckert when he and Rostow had seated themselves.

Mary Alice waited.

"I was talking to an old friend of yours."

"I don't have any old friends. I made a clean break when I came here."

"Somebody remembers you. John Stettinius. He said to tell you Johnny says hello."

"I doubt it."

"Good call. What he actually said was, is she in jail yet? When I asked him why he would think that, he told me about your father."

Mary Alice felt cold, which was strange on a warm day in May.

"He says it always bothered him that your father's death went down as an accident. He never believed it, but he couldn't prove anything. Your father had a broken leg, and his blood alcohol was high enough to stun a horse. He could have fallen and frozen to death on his own, but Detective Stettinius thinks he had help. From you."

She had to try twice to make her voice work.

"And why would he think that?"

"Timing, for one thing. A little earlier, and you'd have been a minor. You would have lost your brothers to foster care. As it was, they stayed with you. Then there were the rumors about your relationship with your father."

Relationship. It sounded as if her father had asked her out on a date, and she had said, "I'll have to ask my . . . oh, hey, no problem."

Mary Alice wanted to get her fingernails into Eckert's eyes. Instead she clenched her fists.

Eckert showed her his palms in a placating gesture.

"The way I see it, you couldn't possibly consent to something like that. I wouldn't call it your fault. And then when you found out about Stephen Golisard's history, well, I wouldn't expect you to swallow that. How did you find out about him?"

Mary Alice bit down until her back teeth threatened to break.

"What about Harold Mohn?" she asked, when she trusted herself to speak.

"Alibi. He went back to the doctor's office to make another scene. The cops were taking him out of there while Golisard was getting shot." Eckert grinned. "Tell you the truth, the uniforms said they didn't have much to do. The receptionist was handling her business just fine.

"The thing is, people remember you being very affectionate with Golisard in the office. To me that suggests you found out sometime later, maybe on the ride home. Or maybe even later than that."

Eckert's eyes focused on something. Mary Alice followed his gaze to her computer on the desk in the corner of the living room. He saw her looking, and annoyance at being caught crossed his face.

He had some kind of idea.

Eckert looked at Rostow. The two cops got up and left without another word to her.

Mary Alice knew what to do next. She picked up the phone and speed-dialed a number.

Her friend Diana listened without interrupting, as Mary Alice had known she would. Diana also didn't accuse Mary Alice of doing anything stupid. Diana knew from her own experience that trouble can come looking for a hooker.

"I think I know what's on his mind," Diana said. "But we can't use your computer. We don't want to leave a trail. Meet me at the library."

It was twilight when they met at the public library. Diana greeted the librarian and asked for one of the public-access computers.

"Step right up," said the librarian, a woman about Diana's age —early thirties. "Two machines, no waiting."

Diana called up Google and typed in "Megan's law registry." The first hit was the State of New Jersey's official list of released sex offenders. She clicked on "geographic search" and then Sussex County. There weren't many entries, and Steve's came up in moments. There was his mug shot, the date and particulars of his crime, and the make, model, and license plate of his car. The site stated ominously that offenders' home addresses might be added once the courts permitted.

Mary Alice thought she knew what had happened, and with the knowledge came a plan.

"What?" said Diana. Her smile said that she saw Mary Alice's mind working.

"Maybe later. It's probably better if you don't know."

"I'm here."

"I know," said Mary Alice.

When Diana had gone, Mary Alice made some notes from the website. Then she went low-tech and checked a name in the telephone book. She thanked the librarian and left. On the sidewalk she stopped and thought. It was time to stop using her cell phone for a while. The police might become interested in her calls. To her left were two pay phones, but they looked too exposed. She drove a mile down the road out of town, where she remembered another pay phone at the Shell station. The two young pump jockeys eyed her until she glared them into submission. She dropped coins into the phone and dialed.

Her client Gaylord answered. His nasal voice with its slightly wet consonants summoned a vivid picture of him to her mind—short and thin, with dark hair as manageable as a wire brush. He was a reporter who wrote for the *Newark Star-Ledger,* several small weeklies, and any magazine that bought serious stories on local corruption.

"Hi, sweetie, it's Crystal."

"Can't now."

He sounded surly. He usually did when he was in the middle of a story. When he had finished with his obsession of the moment, he became as friendly as a puppy, and he couldn't understand why other people hadn't forgotten his rudeness.

Mary Alice forgot things like that for a living.

"I need a favor," she said.

That got his attention. She had never asked him for anything except her money.

"What?"

"I'm guessing that you can find out more about sex offenders than they put in the Megan's law registry."

"That's big trouble," he said. "Contempt of court, maybe worse."

"But if anybody could, you could, am I right?"

"Maybe I could find some things out, but why do you want to know?"

"Sweetie, you're going to have to trust me on this. I really need to know. Nobody's going to get hurt. I can promise you that."

She hoped she was right.

"What do you need to know?"

"Addresses for the local ones."

"What's in it for me?"

"You're paid up for three months if you do this for me."

"A year. And it can only be one name. And there's one more thing."

"What's that?"

"What's your real name?"

"Why do you want to know that?"

"I just do," he said. "I want to know everything about you."

Mary Alice cursed silently. Here was one client she had managed to keep at a businesslike distance, and now he wanted to get closer.

"Come on," he said. "You know I could find out if I wanted to."

"That's coming pretty close to a threat. Not a smart move if you want to keep seeing me."

"I said I could, not that I would. I want to know your name, but I want it to come from you."

Mary Alice felt the resignation that came with making a mistake and knowing it. It struck her that she had a lot of experience with that feeling.

"Okay," she said. "One name, but it has to be the right one. It has to be one with a car. An older car."

He listened.

"And it's Mary Alice."

"They probably all have older cars. They can't get much in the way of jobs when they get out. I'll get back to you about it . . . Mary Alice."

"You know my pager."

She hoped the message was clear. He had her first name, but he wasn't getting her home phone number or anything else.

Mary Alice had driven home and was halfway up the stairs to her apartment when her pager beeped. She turned and went back down to the street. She walked for a good fifteen minutes, passing several pay phones before deciding on one that seemed remote enough.

"Hi, Gaylord, what have you got?"

"Peter Glebb." He spelled the name and gave her an address right in Driscoll.

Mary Alice rummaged in her bag for the notes she had made at the library. She read off the license plate to Gaylord, who verified it.

"It's a 1985 Chevy Caprice Classic."

That should work, she thought.

"He's got a busboy job at an Italian place in Morristown," said Gaylord, "but that should be the only time he's not home. He's still under supervision."

Mary Alice knew the restaurant. It served dinner only, which meant that Glebb should work from midafternoon until sometime after midnight. She decided to do what she needed to do at his home rather than his job.

She went home to wait. It was hard to do. She stared at her current romance novel for a while, and then at the television screen. She saw nothing. Twice she opened the refrigerator and verified that her Chinese takeout was still there. Maybe someday she would eat it.

Mostly, she sat in the dark.

At three in the morning she drove to the address Gaylord had given her. Peter Glebb seemed to have a basement apartment in a dilapidated two-story house. The location was perfect—on a side street for privacy, but close enough to Main Street for traffic noise. No lights showed in the apartment. She hoped that Glebb had gone to bed after a tiring night's work.

For a couple of years after killing her father, Mary Alice had looked for ways to punish herself. She had avoided drugs, because the state would have taken her brothers after all she had endured to keep the family together. Instead she drank, and took up with a succession of dangerous boyfriends. From one of them she had learned to steal cars.

She knew now that she had been lucky. The state would also have frowned on a conviction for auto theft, but the police had never caught her.

Mary Alice had no idea whether her skills applied to new cars, which was why she had asked Gaylord for an older model.

Her fingers remembered what to do with an old Chevy. In seconds she had opened the driver's door, and in a minute she had the engine running. She pulled away from the curb and looked both ways before turning left onto Main Street. Three blocks later she signaled a right turn up the hill.

The house was one of the Victorians on the north side of town. She passed the mailbox with the correct address on it, stopped, and backed into the driveway. It occurred to her that she had to get out and check something. Leaving the car running, she walked around and verified that the light over the rear license plate worked. She climbed the front steps, crossed the front porch, and rang the doorbell for a count of ten.

Only one person in the house would hear. The other occupant was deaf or close to it.

Back in the car, Mary Alice sat in the driver's seat and counted off three minutes on her luminescent watch. They seemed to take three hours.

She put the car in gear and drove slowly away. Somehow she knew she had been seen.

A block from the house she came to a stop sign. Mary Alice

braked and waited until she saw the headlights behind her. She led the other car to a small neighborhood playground.

In the parking area Mary Alice rolled her window down and shut the engine off. Trees shielded her from the few street lights. The darkness was so intense that she felt it on her face. Footsteps sounded softly to her left. She reached up and switched on the car's courtesy light.

"Hello, Mrs. Pilarczyk."

Mary Alice heard a sigh.

"Call me Mavis, I guess. I know you, but I can't quite come up with it."

"I'm not Peter Glebb."

"You don't say. Wait a minute. You were with that other one at the doctor's office. You're his girlfriend."

Mary Alice turned her head and looked. The woman's hand trembled even more than her voice. That was a problem, because the hand held a gun.

"I'm not his girlfriend. He had to hire me to pretend."

"So you're what, an escort?"

"Close enough."

"How did you know?"

It was time for the confrontation, but now Mary Alice tried to remember why she had worked so hard to make it happen. Who cared that Mavis had looked through the proctologist's window and seen Steve's car? Who cared that she had memorized the Megan's law registry and knew Steve's license plate, and Peter Glebb's? Who cared that Mavis had exploited the commotion around Harold Mohn to steal Steve's address from his medical file?

Mary Alice said nothing.

"Okay," said Mavis, "I killed Golisard. Why do you care?"

"I don't, really. But the cops think I killed him. And they'd have been right if you hadn't beaten me to it."

"Why did you want to kill him?"

"Probably for the same reason as you. Who was it, your father?"

"Don't you dare," said Mavis. Her hand started trembling again. "He was a good father."

"So was mine. To my brothers, anyway."

"Sorry," said Mavis in a calmer tone. "I have trouble with this."

She laughed.

"I know, 'No kidding.' It's weird, but this whole thing just came up recently."

She waited for some kind of encouragement, but Mary Alice didn't feel like giving it.

"I was on a jury. Not a child abuse case, but the creep on trial was making his daughter give him an alibi. I looked at him, and I looked at her, and I knew what was up with them. And I looked at that young girl, and I said, wait a minute. She's a kid, but I'm not. It's about time I took some responsibility."

Again she paused.

"Look at me. Would you say I spend a lot of time pushing people around? But you should have seen me. I wouldn't let up until we all voted guilty. They were afraid of me, the other jurors. It was fun. I could definitely get used to it."

Mavis closed one eye and sighted the gun at Mary Alice's forehead.

"Well, isn't this awkward? I don't have anything against you, far from it. But you're in my way. From now on, nobody gets in my way. Tell me, what would you do?"

Mary Alice looked at the gun inches from her face. She refocused on the other woman. The gun went strangely with Mavis's bathrobe and slippers.

"I would probably shoot me."

"Don't you care?"

"No," said Mary Alice, "not really."

That's interesting, she thought. How come I didn't know that until this moment?

"Good luck," she said. "I hope you get them all, before the cops figure it out. I have to doubt it, though. Things don't work out like that."

The scene would have held as much drama as commuters waiting for a train, except that commuters get dressed first, and they don't usually wait with guns. Mary Alice watched the muzzle and the finger on the trigger. It annoyed her, but she knew she was about to flinch. Her face didn't want to get shot, even if she didn't care.

Mavis dropped her gun hand to her side.

"I can't do it."

She seemed surprised.

"I guess you'd better run along. Tell the cops I'll be waiting."

"Okay."

"Okay? Is that the best you can do? I gave you what you wanted, didn't I?"

Mary Alice almost laughed. Who could give her what she wanted? What could that be?

But Mavis was waiting, and none of this was her fault.

"I guess."

KURT VONNEGUT

Ed Luby's Key Club

FROM *Look at the Birdie*

Part One

ED LUBY WORKED as a bodyguard for Al Capone once. And then he went into bootlegging on his own, made a lot of money at it. When the prohibition era ended, Ed Luby went back to his hometown, the old mill town of Ilium. He bought several businesses. One was a restaurant, which he called Ed Luby's Steak House. It was a very good restaurant. It had a brass knocker on its red front door.

At seven o'clock the other night, Harve and Claire Elliot banged on the door with the brass knocker—because the red door was locked. They had come from a city thirty miles away. It was their fourteenth wedding anniversary. They would be celebrating their anniversary at Luby's for the fourteenth time.

Harve and Claire Elliot had a lot of kids and a lot of love, and not much money. But once a year they really splurged. They got all dolled up, took twenty dollars out of the sugar bowl, drove over to Ed Luby's Steak House, and carried on like King Farouk and his latest girlfriend.

There were lights on in Luby's, and there was music inside. And there were plenty of cars in the parking lot—all a good deal newer than what Harve and Claire arrived in. Their car was an old station wagon whose wood was beginning to rot.

The restaurant was obviously in business, but the red front door wouldn't budge. Harve banged away some more with the knocker, and the door suddenly swung open. Ed Luby himself opened it. He

was a vicious old man, absolutely bald, short and heavy, built like a
.45-caliber slug.

He was furious. "What in hell you trying to do—drive the members nuts?" he said in a grackle voice.

"What?" said Harve.

Luby swore. He looked at the knocker. "That thing comes down
right now," he said. "All the dumb things—a knocker on the door."
He turned to the big thug who lurked behind him. "Take the
knocker down right now," he said.

"Yes, sir," said the thug. He went to look for a screwdriver.

"Mr. Luby?" said Harve, puzzled, polite. "What's going on?"

"What's going on?" said Luby. "I'm the one who oughta be asking what's going on." He still looked at the knocker rather than
at Harve and Claire. "What's the big idea?" he said. "Hallow-
een or something? Tonight's the night people put on funny costumes and go knock on private doors till the people inside go
nuts?"

The crack about funny costumes was obviously meant to hit
Claire Elliot squarely—and it did. Claire was vulnerable—not because she looked funny, but because she had made the dress she
wore, because her fur coat was borrowed. Claire looked marvelous,
as a matter of fact, looked marvelous to anyone with an eye for
beauty, beauty that had been touched by life. Claire was still slender, affectionate, tremendously optimistic. What time and work
and worry had done to her was to make her look, permanently, the
least bit tired.

Harve Elliot didn't react very fast to Luby's crack. The anniversary mood was still upon Harve. All anxieties, all expectations of
meanness were still suspended. Harve wasn't going to pay any attention to anything but pleasure. He simply wanted to get inside,
where the music and the food and the good drinks were.

"The door was stuck," said Harve. "I'm sorry, Mr. Luby. The door
was stuck."

"Wasn't stuck," said Luby. "Door was *locked*."

"You—you're closed?" said Harve gropingly.

"It's a private club now," said Luby. "Members all got a key. You
got a key?"

"No," said Harve. "How—how do we get one?"

"Fill out a application, pay a hundred dollars, wait and see what the membership committee says," said Luby. "Takes two weeks—sometimes a month."

"A hundred dollars!" said Harve.

"I don't think this is the kind of place you folks would be happy at," said Luby.

"We've been coming here for our anniversary for fourteen years," said Harve, and he felt himself turning red.

"Yeah—I know," said Luby. "I remember you real well."

"You do?" said Harve hopefully.

Luby turned really nasty now. "Yeah, big shot," he said to Harve, "you tipped me a quarter once. Me—Luby—I own the joint, and one time you slip me a big, fat quarter. Pal, I'll never forget you for that."

Luby made an impatient sweeping motion with his stubby hand. "You two mind stepping out of the way?" he said to Harve and Claire. "You're blocking the door. A couple of members are trying to get in."

Harve and Claire stepped back humbly.

The two members whose way they had been blocking now advanced on the door grandly. They were man and wife, middle-aged—porky, complacent, their faces as undistinguished as two cheap pies. The man wore new dinner clothes. The woman was a caterpillar in a pea green evening gown and dark, oily mink.

"Evening, Judge," said Luby. "Evening, Mrs. Wampler."

Judge Wampler held a golden key in his hand. "I don't get to use this?" he said.

"Happen to have the door open for some minor repairs," said Luby.

"I see," said the judge.

"Taking the knocker down," said Luby. "Folks come up here, won't believe it's a private club, drive the members nuts banging on the door."

The judge and his lady glanced at Harve and Claire with queasy scorn. "We aren't the first to arrive, are we?" said the judge.

"Police chief's been here an hour," said Luby. "Doc Waldron, Kate, Charley, the mayor—the whole gang's in there."

"Good," said the judge, and he and his lady went in.

The thug, Ed Luby's bodyguard, came back with a screwdriver. "These people still giving you a hard time, Ed?" he said. He didn't wait for an answer. He bellied up to Harve. "Go on—beat it, Junior," he said.

"Come on, Harve—let's get out of here," said Claire. She was close to tears.

"That's right—beat it," said Luby. "What you want is something like the Sunrise Diner. Get a good hamburger steak dinner there for a dollar and a half. All the coffee you can drink on the house. Leave a quarter under your plate. They'll think you're Diamond Jim Brady."

Harve and Claire Elliot got back into their old station wagon. Harve was so bitter and humiliated that he didn't dare to drive for a minute or two. He made claws of his shaking hands, wanted to choke Ed Luby and his bodyguard to death.

One of the subjects Harve covered in profane, broken sentences was the twenty-five-cent tip he had once given Luby. "Fourteen years ago—our first anniversary," said Harve. "That's when I handed that miserable b—— a quarter! And he never forgot!"

"He's got a right to make it a club, if he wants to," said Claire emptily.

Luby's bodyguard now had the knocker down. He and Luby went inside, slammed the big red door.

"Sure he does!" said Harve. "Certainly he's got a right! But the stinking little rat doesn't have a right to insult people the way he insulted us."

"He's sick," said Claire.

"All right!" said Harve, and he hammered on the dashboard with his folded hands. "All right—he's sick. Let's kill all the people who are sick the way Luby is."

"Look," said Claire.

"At what?" said Harve. "What could I see that would make me feel any better or any worse?"

"Just look at the wonderful kind of people who get to be members," said Claire.

Two very drunk people, a man and a woman, were getting out of a taxicab.

The man, in trying to pay the cab driver, dropped a lot of change and his gold key to the Key Club. He got down on his hands and knees to look for it.

The sluttish woman with him leaned against the cab, apparently couldn't stand unsupported.

The man stood up with the key. He was very proud of himself for having found it. "Key to the most exclusive club in Ilium," he told the cab driver.

Then he took out his billfold, meaning to pay his fare. And he discovered that the smallest bill he had was a twenty, which the driver couldn't change.

"You wait right here," said the drunk. "We'll go in and get some change."

He and the woman reeled up the walk to the door. He tried again and again to slip the key into the lock, but all he could hit was wood. "Open Sesame!" he'd say, and he'd laugh, and he'd miss again.

"Nice people they've got in this club," Claire said to Harve. "Aren't you sorry we're not members too?"

The drunk finally hit the keyhole, turned the lock. He and his girl literally fell into the Key Club.

Seconds later they came stumbling out again, bouncing off the bellies of Ed Luby and his thug.

"Out! Out!" Luby squawked in the night. "Where'd you get that key?" When the drunk didn't answer, Luby gathered the drunk's lapels and backed him up to the building. "Where'd you get that key?"

"Harry Varnum lent it to me," said the drunk.

"You tell Harry he ain't a member here anymore," said Luby. "Anybody lends his key to a punk lush like you—he ain't a member anymore."

He turned his attention to the drunk's companion. "Don't you ever come out here again," he said to her. "I wouldn't let you in if you was accompanied by the President of the United States. That's one reason I turned this place into a club—so I could keep pigs like you out, so I wouldn't have to serve good food to a ———" And he called her what she obviously was.

"There's worse things than that," she said.

"Name one," said Luby.

"I never killed anybody," she said. "That's more than you can say."

The accusation didn't bother Luby at all. "You want to talk to the chief of police about that?" he said. "You want to talk to the mayor? You want to talk to Judge Wampler about that? Murder's a very serious crime in this town." He moved very close to her, looked her up and down. "So's being a loudmouth, and so's being a ————" He called her what she was again.

"You make me sick," he said.

And then he slapped her with all his might. He hit her so hard that she spun and crumpled without making a sound.

The drunk backed away from her, from Luby, from Luby's thug. He did nothing to help her, only wanted to get away.

But Harve Elliot was out of his car and running at Luby before his wife could stop him.

Harve hit Luby once in the belly, a belly that was as hard as a cast-iron boiler.

That satisfaction was the last thing Harve remembered—until he came to in his car. The car was going fast. Claire was driving.

Harve's clinging, aching head was lolling on the shoulder of his wife of fourteen years.

Claire's cheeks were wet with recent tears. But she wasn't crying now. She was grim. She was purposeful.

She was driving fast through the stunted, mean, and filthy business district of Ilium. Streetlights were faint and far apart.

Tracks of a long-abandoned streetcar system caught at the wheels of the old station wagon again and again.

A clock in front of a jeweler's store had stopped. Neon signs, all small, all red, said BAR and BEER and EAT and TAXI.

"Where we going?" said Harve.

"Darling! How do you feel?" she said.

"Don't know," said Harve.

"You should see yourself," she said.

"What would I see?" he said.

"Blood all over your shirt. Your good suit ruined," she said. "I'm looking for the hospital."

Harve sat up, worked his shoulders and his neck gingerly. He explored the back of his head with his hand. "I'm that bad?" he said. "Hospital?"

"I don't know," she said.

"I—I don't feel too bad," he said.

"Maybe you don't need to go to the hospital," said Claire, "but she does."

"Who?" said Harve.

"The girl—the woman," said Claire. "In the back."

Paying a considerable price in pain, Harve turned to look into the back of the station wagon.

The back seat had been folded down, forming a truck bed. On that hard, jouncing bed, on a sandy blanket, lay the woman Ed Luby had hit. Her head was pillowed on a child's snowsuit. She was covered by a man's overcoat.

The drunk who had brought her to the Key Club was in back too. He was sitting tailor-fashion. The overcoat was his. He was a big clown turned gray and morbid. His slack gaze told Harve that he did not want to be spoken to.

"How did we get these two?" said Harve.

"Ed Luby and his friends made us a present of them," said Claire.

Her bravery was starting to fail her. It was almost time to cry again. "They threw you and the woman into the car," she said. "They said they'd beat me up too if I didn't drive away."

Claire was too upset to drive now. She pulled over to the curb and wept.

Harve, trying to comfort Claire, heard the back door of the station wagon open and shut. The big clown had gotten out.

He had taken his overcoat from the woman, was standing on the sidewalk, putting the coat on.

"Where you think you're going?" Harve said to him. "Stay back there and take care of that woman!"

"She doesn't need me, buddy," said the man. "She needs an undertaker. She's dead."

In the distance, its siren wailing, its roof lights flashing, a patrol car was coming.

"Here come your friends, the policemen," said the man. He turned up an alley, was gone.

The patrol car nosed in front of the old station wagon. Its revolving flasher made a hellish blue merry-go-round of the buildings and street.

Two policemen got out. Each had a pistol in one hand, a bright flashlight in the other.

"Hands up," said one. "Don't try anything."

Harve and Claire raised their hands.

"You the people who made all the trouble out at Luby's Key Club?" The man who asked was a sergeant.

"Trouble?" said Harve.

"You must be the guy who hit the girl," said the sergeant.

"Me?" said Harve.

"They got her in the back," said the other policeman. He opened the back door of the station wagon, looked at the woman, lifted her white hand, let it fall. "Dead," he said.

"We were taking her to the hospital," said Harve.

"That makes everything all right?" said the sergeant. "Slug her, then take her to the hospital, and that makes everything all right?"

"I didn't hit her," said Harve. "Why would I hit her?"

"She said something to your wife you didn't like," said the sergeant.

"Luby hit her," said Harve. "It was Luby."

"That's a good story, except for a couple of little details," said the sergeant.

"What details?" said Harve.

"Witnesses," said the sergeant. "Talk about witnesses, brother," he said, "the mayor, the chief of police, Judge Wampler and his wife — they *all* saw you do it."

Harve and Claire Elliot were taken to the squalid Ilium Police Headquarters.

They were fingerprinted, were given nothing with which to wipe the ink off their hands. This particular humiliation happened so fast, and was conducted with such firmness, that Harve and Claire reacted with amazement rather than indignation.

Everything was happening so fast, and in such unbelievable surroundings, that Harve and Claire had only one thing to cling to — a childlike faith that innocent persons never had anything to fear.

Claire was taken into an office for questioning. "What should I say?" she said to Harve as she was being led away.

"Tell them the truth!" said Harve. He turned to the sergeant who had brought him in, who was guarding him now. "Could I use the phone, please?" he said.

"To call a lawyer?" said the sergeant.

"I don't need a lawyer," said Harve. "I want to call the baby-sitter. I want to tell her we'll be home a little late."

The sergeant laughed. "A *little* late?" he said. He had a long scar that ran down one cheek, over his fat lips, and down his blocky chin. "A little late?" he said again. "Brother, you're gonna be about twenty years late getting home—twenty years if you're lucky."

"I didn't have a thing to do with the death of that woman," said Harve.

"Let's hear what the witnesses say, huh?" said the sergeant. "They'll be along in a little bit."

"If they saw what happened," said Harve, "I'll be out of here five minutes after they get here. If they've made a mistake, if they really think they saw me do it, you can still let my wife go."

"Let me give you a little lesson in law, buddy," said the sergeant. "Your wife's an accessory to the murder. She drove the getaway car. She's in this as deep as you are."

Harve was told that he could do all the telephoning he wanted—could do it after he had been questioned by the captain.

His turn to see the captain came an hour later. He asked the captain where Claire was. He was told that Claire had been locked up.

"That was necessary?" said Harve.

"Funny custom we got around here," said the captain. "We lock up anybody we think had something to do with a murder." He was a short, thickset, balding man. Harve found something vaguely familiar in his features.

"Your name's Harvey K. Elliot?" said the captain.

"That's right," said Harve.

"You claim no previous criminal record?" said the captain.

"Not even a parking ticket," said Harve.

"We can check on that," said the captain.

"Wish you would," said Harve.

"As I told your wife," said the captain, "you really pulled a bonehead mistake, trying to pin this thing on Ed Luby. You happened to pick about the most respected man in town."

"All due respect to Mr. Luby—" Harve began.

The captain interrupted him angrily, banged on his desk. "I heard enough of that from your wife!" he said. "I don't have to listen to any more of it from you!"

"What if I'm telling the truth?" said Harve.

"You think we haven't checked your story?" said the captain.

"What about the man who was with her out there?" said Harve. "He'll tell you what really happened. Have you tried to find him?"

The captain looked at Harve with malicious pity. "There wasn't any man," he said. "She went out there alone, went out in a taxicab."

"That's wrong!" said Harve. "Ask the cab driver. There was a man with her!"

The captain banged on his desk again. "Don't tell me I'm wrong," he said. "We talked to the cab driver. He swears she was alone. Not that we need any more witnesses," he said. "The driver swears he saw you hit her too."

The telephone on the captain's desk rang. The captain answered, his eyes still on Harve. "Captain Luby speaking," he said.

And then he said to the sergeant standing behind Harve, "Get this jerk out of here. He's making me sick. Lock him up downstairs."

The sergeant hustled Harve out of the office and down an iron staircase to the basement. There were cells down there.

Two naked lightbulbs in the corridor gave all the light there was. There were duckboards in the corridor, because the floor was wet.

"The captain's Ed Luby's brother?" Harve asked the sergeant.

"Any law against a policeman having a brother?" said the sergeant.

"Claire!" Harve yelled, wanting to know what cell in Hell his wife was in.

"They got her upstairs, buddy," said the sergeant.

"I want to see her!" said Harve. "I want to talk to her! I want to make sure she's all right!"

"Want a lot of things, don't you?" said the sergeant. He shoved Harve into a narrow cell, shut the door with a *clang*.

"I want my rights!" said Harve.

The sergeant laughed. "You got 'em, friend. You can do anything you want in there," he said, "just as long as you don't damage any government property."

The sergeant went back upstairs.

There didn't seem to be another soul in the basement. The only sounds that Harve could hear were footfalls overhead.

Harve gripped his barred door, tried to find some meaning in the footfalls.

There were the sounds of many big men walking together—one shift coming on, another going off, Harve supposed.

There was the clacking of a woman's sharp heels. The clacking was so quick and free and businesslike that the heels could hardly belong to Claire.

Somebody moved a heavy piece of furniture. Something fell. Somebody laughed. Several people suddenly arose and moved their chairs back at the same time.

And Harve knew what it was to be buried alive.

He yelled. "Hey, up there! Help!" he yelled.

A reply came from close by. Someone groaned drowsily in another cell.

"Who's that?" said Harve.

"Go to sleep," said the voice. It was rusty, sleepy, irritable.

"What kind of a town is this?" said Harve.

"What kind of a town is any town?" said the voice. "You got any big-shot friends?"

"No," said Harve.

"Then it's a bad town," said the voice. "Get some sleep."

"They've got my wife upstairs," said Harve. "I don't know what's going on. I've got to do something."

"Go ahead," said the voice. It chuckled ruefully.

"Do you know Ed Luby?" said Harve.

"You mean do I know who he is?" said the voice. "Who doesn't? You mean is he a friend of mine? If he was, you think I'd be locked up down here? I'd be out at Ed's club, eating a two-inch steak on the house, and the cop who brought me in would have had his brains beat out."

"Ed Luby's that important?" said Harve.

"Important?" said the voice. "Ed Luby? You never heard the story about the psychiatrist who went to Heaven?"

"What?" said Harve.

The voice told an old, old story—with a local variation. "This psychiatrist died and went to Heaven, see? And Saint Peter was tickled to death to see him. Seems God was having mental troubles, needed treatment bad. The psychiatrist asked Saint Peter what God's symptoms were. And Saint Peter whispered in his ear, 'God thinks He's Ed Luby.'"

The heels of the businesslike woman clacked across the floor above again. A telephone rang.

"Why should one man be so important?" said Harve.

"Ed Luby's all there is in Ilium," said the voice. "That answer your question? Ed came back here during the Depression. He had all the dough he'd made in bootlegging in Chicago. Everything in Ilium was closed down, for sale. Ed Luby bought."

"I see," said Harve, beginning to understand how scared he'd better be.

"Funny thing," said the voice, "people who get along with Ed, do what Ed says, say what Ed likes to hear—they have a pretty nice time in old Ilium. You take the chief of police now—salary's eight thousand a year. Been chief for five years now. He's managed his salary so well he's got a seventy-thousand-dollar house all paid for, three cars, a summer place on Cape Cod, and a thirty-foot cabin cruiser. Of course, he isn't doing near as good as Luby's brother."

"The captain?" said Harve.

"Of course, the captain earns everything he gets," said the voice. "He's the one who really runs the Police Department. He owns the Ilium Hotel now—and the cab company. Also Radio Station WKLL, the friendly voice of Ilium.

"Some other people doing pretty well in Ilium too," said the voice. "Old Judge Wampler and the mayor—"

"I got the idea," said Harve tautly.

"Doesn't take long," said the voice.

"Isn't there anybody against Luby?" said Harve.

"Dead," said the voice. "Let's get some sleep, eh?"

Ten minutes later, Harve was taken upstairs again. He wasn't hustled along this time, though he was in the care of the same sergeant who had locked him up. The sergeant was gentle now—even a little apologetic.

At the head of the iron stairs, they were met by Captain Luby, whose manners were changed for the better too. The captain encouraged Harve to think of him as a prankish boy with a heart of gold.

Captain Luby put his hand on Harve's arm, and he smiled, and he said, "We've been rough on you, Mr. Elliot, and we know it. I'm sorry, but you've got to understand that police have to get rough sometimes—especially in a murder investigation."

"That's fine," said Harve, "except you're getting rough with the wrong people."

Captain Luby shrugged philosophically. "Maybe—maybe not," he said. "That's for a court to decide."

"If it has to come to that," said Harve.

"I think you'd better talk to a lawyer as soon as possible," said the captain.

"I think so too," said Harve.

"There's one in the station house now, if you want to ask him," said the captain.

"Another one of Ed Luby's brothers?" said Harve.

Captain Luby looked surprised, and then he decided to laugh. He laughed very hard. "I don't blame you for saying that," he said. "I can imagine how things look to you."

"You can?" said Harve.

"You get in a jam in a strange town," said the captain, "and all of a sudden it looks to you like everybody's named Luby." He laughed again. "There's just me and my brother—just the two Lubys—that's all. This lawyer out front—not only isn't he any relative, he hates my guts and Ed's too. That make you feel any better?"

"Maybe," said Harve carefully.

"What's that supposed to mean?" said the captain. "You want him or not?"

"I'll let you know after I've talked to him," said Harve.

"Go tell Lemming we maybe got a client for him," said the captain to the sergeant.

"I want my wife here too," said Harve.

"Naturally," said the captain. "No argument there. She'll be right down."

The lawyer, whose name was Frank Lemming, was brought in to Harve long before Claire was. Lemming carried a battered black briefcase that seemed to have very little in it. He was a small, pear-shaped man.

Lemming's name was stamped on the side of his briefcase in big letters. He was shabby, puffy, short-winded. The only outward sign that he might have a little style, a little courage, was an outsize mustache.

When he opened his mouth, he let out a voice that was deep, majestic, unafraid. He demanded to know if Harve had been threatened or hurt in any way. He talked to Captain Luby and the sergeant as though they were the ones in trouble.

Harve began to feel a good deal better.

"Would you gentlemen kindly leave," said Lemming, calling the police *gentlemen* with grand irony. "I want to talk to my client alone."

The police left meekly.

"You're certainly a breath of fresh air," said Harve.

"That's the first time I've ever been called that," said Lemming.

"I was beginning to think I was in the middle of Nazi Germany," said Harve.

"You sound like a man who's never been arrested before," said Lemming.

"I never have been," said Harve.

"There's always got to be a first time," said Lemming pleasantly. "What's the charge?"

"They didn't tell you?" said Harve.

"They just told me they had somebody back here who wanted a lawyer," said Lemming. "I was here on another case." He sat down, put his limp briefcase against the leg of his chair. "So what's the charge?"

"They—they've been talking about murder," said Harve.

This news fazed Lemming only briefly. "These morons they call the Ilium Police Force," he said, "everything's murder to them. What did you do it with?"

"I didn't," said Harve.

"What did they *say* you did it with?" said Lemming.

"My fist," said Harve.

"You hit a man in a fight—and he died?" said Lemming.

"I didn't hit anybody!" said Harve.

"All right, all right, all right," said Lemming calmingly.

"Are you in with these guys too?" said Harve. "Are you part of the nightmare too?"

Lemming cocked his head. "Maybe you better explain that?" he said.

"Everybody in Ilium works for Ed Luby, I hear," said Harve. "I guess you do too."

"Me?" said Lemming. "Are you kidding? You heard how I talk to Luby's brother. I'd talk to Ed Luby the same way. They don't scare me."

"Maybe—" said Harve, watching Lemming closely, wanting with all his heart to trust him.

"I'm hired?" said Lemming.

"How much will it cost?" said Harve.

"Fifty dollars to start," said Lemming.

"You mean right now?" said Harve.

"The class of people I do business with," said Lemming, "I get paid right away, or I never get paid."

"All I've got with me is twenty," said Harve.

"That'll do nicely for the moment," said Lemming. He held out his hand.

As Lemming was putting the money into his billfold, a police-woman with clacking heels brought Claire Elliot in.

Claire was snow-white. She wouldn't speak until the policewoman was gone. When she did speak, her voice was ragged, barely under control.

Harve embraced her, encouraged her. "We've got a lawyer now," he said. "We'll be all right now. He knows what to do."

"I don't trust him. I don't trust *anybody* around here!" said Claire. She was wild-eyed. "Harve! I've got to talk to you alone!"

"I'll be right outside," said Lemming. "Call me when you want me." He left his briefcase where it was.

"Has anybody threatened you?" Claire said to Harve, when Lemming was gone.

"There's been some pretty rough talk," said Harve.

"Has anybody threatened to kill you?" she said.

"No," said Harve.

Claire whispered now. "Somebody's threatened to kill me, and you—" Here she broke down. "And the children," she whispered brokenly.

Harve exploded. "Who?" he said at the top of his lungs. "Who threatened that?" he replied.

Claire put her hand over his mouth, begged him to be quiet.

Harve took her hand away. "Who?" he said.

Claire didn't even whisper her answer. She just moved her lips. "The captain," her lips said. She clung to him. "Please," she whispered, "keep your voice down. We've got to be calm. We've got to think. We've got to make up a new story."

"About what?" said Harve.

"About what happened," she said. She shook her head. "We mustn't ever tell what really happened again."

"My God," said Harve, "is this America?"

"I don't know what it is," said Claire. "I just know we've got to make up a new story—or—or something terrible will happen."

"Something terrible already has happened," said Harve.

"Worse things can still happen," said Claire.

Harve thought hard, the heels of his hands in his eye sockets. "If they're trying that hard to scare us," he said, "then they must be plenty scared too. There must be plenty of harm we could do them."

"How?" said Claire.

"By sticking to the truth," said Harve. "That's pretty plain, isn't it? That's what they want to make us stop doing."

"I don't want to do anybody any harm," said Claire. "I just want to get out of here. I just want to go home."

"All right," said Harve. "We've got a lawyer now. That's a start."

Harve called to Lemming, who came in rubbing his hands. "Secret conference over?" he said cheerfully.

"Yes," said Harve.

"Well, secrets are all very fine in their place," said Lemming, "but I recommend strongly that you don't keep any from your lawyer."

"Harve—" said Claire warningly.

"He's right," said Harve. "Don't you understand—he's right."

"She's in favor of holding a little something back?" said Lemming.

"She's been threatened. That's the reason," said Harve.

"By whom?" said Lemming.

"Don't tell him," said Claire beseechingly.

"We'll save that for a little while," said Harve. "The thing is, Mr. Lemming, I didn't commit this murder they say I did. But my wife and I saw who really did it, and we've been threatened with all kinds of things, if we tell what we saw."

"Don't tell," said Claire. "Harve—don't."

"I give you my word of honor, Mrs. Elliot," said Lemming, "noth-

ing you or your husband tells me will go any farther." He was proud
of his word of honor, was a very appealing person when he gave it.
"Now tell me who really did this killing."

"Ed Luby," said Harve.

"I beg your pardon?" said Lemming blankly.

"Ed Luby," said Harve.

Lemming sat back, suddenly drained and old. "I see," he said.
His voice wasn't deep now. It was like wind in the treetops.

"He's a powerful man around here," said Harve, "I hear."

Lemming nodded. "You heard that right," he said.

Harve started to tell about how Luby had killed the girl. Lemming stopped him.

"What's—what's the matter?" said Harve.

Lemming gave him a wan smile. "That's a very good question,"
he said. "That's—that's a very *complicated* question."

"You work for him, after all?" said Harve.

"Maybe I do—after all," said Lemming.

"You see?" Claire said to Harve.

Lemming took out his billfold, handed the twenty dollars back
to Harve.

"You quit?" said Harve.

"Let's say," said Lemming sadly, "that any advice you get from
me from now on is free. I'm not the lawyer for this case—and any
advice I have to give doesn't have much to do with the law." He
spread his hands. "I'm a legal hack, friends. That must be obvious.
If what you say is true—"

"It *is* true!" said Harve.

"Then you need a lawyer who can fight a whole town," said Lemming, "because Ed Luby *is* this town. I've won a lot of cases in Ilium, but they were all cases Ed Luby didn't care about." He stood.
"If what you say is true, this isn't a case—it's a war."

"What am I going to do?" said Harve.

"My advice to you," said Lemming, "is to be as scared as your wife
is, Mr. Elliot."

Lemming nodded, and then he scuttled away.

Seconds later, the sergeant came in for Harve and Claire, marched
them through a door and into a room where a floodlight blinded
them. Whispers came from the darkness beyond.

"What's this?" said Harve, his arm around Claire.

"Don't speak unless you're spoken to," said the voice of Captain Luby.

"I want a lawyer," said Harve.

"You had one," said the captain. "What happened to Lemming?"

"He quit," said Harve.

Somebody snickered.

"That's funny?" said Harve bitterly.

"Shut up," said Captain Luby.

"This is funny?" Harve said to the whispering blackness. "A man and a woman up here who never broke a law in their whole lives— accused of killing a woman they tried to save—"

Captain Luby emerged from the blackness. He showed Harve what he had in his right hand. It was a slab of rubber about four inches wide, eight inches long, and half an inch thick.

"This is what I call Captain Luby's wise-guy-wiser-upper," he said. He put the piece of rubber against Harve's cheek caressingly. "You can't imagine how much pain one slap from this thing causes," he said. "I'm surprised all over again, every time I use it. Now stand apart, stand straight, keep your mouths shut, and face the witnesses."

Harve's determination to break jail was born when the clammy rubber touched his cheek.

By the time the captain had returned to the whispering darkness, Harve's determination had become an obsession. No other plan would do.

Out in the darkness, a man now said in a clear, proud voice that he had seen Harve hit the girl. He identified himself as the mayor of Ilium.

The mayor's wife was honored to back him up.

Harve did not protest. He was too busy sensing all he could of what lay beyond the light. Someone now came in from another room, showing Harve where a door was, showing him what lay beyond the door.

Beyond the door he glimpsed a foyer. Beyond the foyer he glimpsed the great outdoors.

Now Captain Luby was asking Judge Wampler if he had seen Harve hit the girl.

"Yes," that fat man said gravely. "And I saw his wife help him to make a getaway too."

Mrs. Wampler spoke up. "They're the ones, all right," she said. "It was one of the most terrible things I ever saw in my life. I don't think I'll ever forget it."

Harve tried to make out the first row of people, the first people he had to pass. He could make out only one person with any certainty. He could make out the policewoman with the clacking heels. She was taking notes now on all that was being said.

Harve decided to charge past her in thirty seconds.

He began to count the seconds away.

Part Two

Harve Elliot stood in front of a blinding light with his wife, Claire. He had never committed a crime in his life. He was now counting off the seconds before he would break jail, before he would run away from the charge of murder.

He was listening to a supposed witness to his crime, to the man who had actually committed the murder. Ed Luby, somewhere behind the light, told his tale. Luby's brother, a captain on the Ilium Police Force, asked helpful questions from time to time.

"Three months ago," said Ed Luby, "I turned my restaurant into a private club—to keep undesirable elements out." Luby, the expert on undesirable elements, had once been a gunman for Al Capone.

"I guess those two up there," he said, meaning Harve and Claire, "didn't hear about it—or maybe they figured it didn't apply to them. Anyway, they showed up tonight, and they got sore when they couldn't get in, and they hung around the front door, insulting the members."

"You ever see them before?" Captain Luby asked him.

"Back before the place was a private club," said Luby, "these two used to come in about once a year. The reason I remembered 'em from one year to the next was the man was always loaded. And he'd get drunker in my place—and he'd turn mean."

"Mean?" said the captain.

"He'd pick fights," said Luby, "not just with men either."

"So what happened tonight?" said the captain.

"These two were hanging around the door, making trouble for the members," said Luby, "and a dame came out in a taxi, all by

herself. I don't know what she figured on doing. Figured on picking up somebody on the way in, I guess. Anyway, she got stopped
too, so I had three people hanging around outside my door. And
they got in some kind of argument with each other."

All that interested Harve Elliot was the effect Luby's tale was
having on the mood in the room. Harve couldn't see Luby, but
he sensed that everyone was watching the man, was fascinated by
him.

Now, Harve decided, was the time to run.

"I don't want you to take my word for what happened next," said
Luby, "on account of I understand some people claim it was me
who hit the girl."

"We've got the statements of other witnesses," said the captain
sympathetically. "So you go ahead and give us your version, and we
can double-check it."

"Well," said Luby, "the dame who came out in the taxi called the
other dame—the dame up there—"

"Mrs. Elliot," said the captain.

"Yeah," said Luby. "She calls Mrs. Elliot something Mr. Elliot
don't like, and the next thing I knew, Mr. Elliot had hauled off
and—"

Harve Elliot plunged past the light and into the darkness. He
charged at the door and the freedom beyond.

Harve lay under an old sedan in a used-car lot. He was a block from
the Ilium Police Station. His ears roared and his chest quaked.
Centuries before he had broken jail. He had knocked people and
doors and furniture out of his way effortlessly, had scattered them
like leaves.

Guns had gone off, seemingly right by his head.

Now men were shouting in the night, and Harve lay under the
car.

One clear image came to Harve from his fantastic flight—and
only one. He remembered the face of the policewoman, the first
person between him and freedom. Harve had flung her into the
glare of the floodlight, had seen her livid, shocked face.

And that was the only face he'd seen.

The hunt for Harve—what Harve heard of it—sounded fool-
ish, slovenly, demoralized. When Harve got his wind and his wits

back, he felt marvelous. He wanted to laugh out loud and yell. He had won so far, and he would go on winning. He would get to the State Police. He would bring them back to Ilium to free Claire.

After that, Harve would hire the best lawyer he could find, clear himself, put Luby in prison, and sue the rotten city of Ilium for a blue million.

Harve peered out from under the car. His hunters were not coming toward him. They were moving away, blaming each other with childish querulousness for having let him escape.

Harve crawled out from under the car, crouched, listened. And then he began to walk carefully, always in shadows. He moved with the cunning of an infantry scout. The filth and feeble lights of the city, so recently his enemies, were his friends now.

And, moving with his back to sooty walls, ducking into doorways of decaying buildings, Harve realized that pure evil was his friend too. Eluding it, outwitting it, planning its destruction all gave his life inconceivably exciting meanings.

A newspaper scuttled by, tumbled in a night breeze, seemed on its raffish way out of Ilium too.

Far, far away a gun went off. Harve wondered what had been shot at—or shot.

Few cars moved in Ilium. And even rarer were people on foot. Two silent, shabby lovers passed within a few feet of Harve without seeing him.

A lurching drunk did see Harve, murmured some quizzical insult, lurched on.

Now a siren wailed—and then another, and yet another. Patrol cars were fanning out from the Ilium Police Station, idiotically advertising themselves with noise and lights.

One car set up a noisy, flashy roadblock not far from Harve. It blocked an underpass through the high, black rampart of a railroad bed. That much of what the police were doing was intelligent, because the car made a dead end of the route that Harve had been taking.

The railroad bed loomed like the Great Wall of China to Harve. Beyond it lay what he thought of as freedom. He had to think of freedom as being something close, as being just one short rush away. Actually, on the other side of the black rampart lay more of Ilium—more faint lights and broken streets. Hope, real hope, lay far, far beyond—lay miles beyond, lay on a superhighway, the fast, clean realm of the State Police.

But Harve now had to pretend that passing over or through the rampart was all that remained for him to do.

He crept to the railroad bed, moved along its cindery face, moved away from the underpass that the police had blocked.

He found himself approaching yet another underpass that was blocked by a car. He could hear talk. He recognized the voice of the talker. It was the voice of Captain Luby.

"Don't bother taking this guy alive," the captain said. "He's no good to himself or anybody else alive. Do the taxpayers a favor, and shoot to kill."

Somewhere a train whistle blew.

And then Harve saw a culvert that cut through the bed of the railroad. It seemed at first to be too close to Captain Luby. But then the captain swept the approaches with a powerful flashlight, showed Harve the trench that fed the culvert. It crossed a field littered with oil drums and trash.

When Captain Luby's light went off, Harve crawled out onto the field, reached the ditch, slithered in. In its shallow, slimy shelter, he moved toward the culvert.

The train that had whistled was approaching now. Its progress was grindingly, clankingly slow.

When the train was overhead, its noise at a maximum, Harve ducked into the culvert. Without thought of an ambush on the other side, he emerged, scrambled up the cinder slope.

He swung onboard the rusty rungs of an empty gondola in the moving train.

Eternities later, the slow-moving train had carried Harve Elliot out of Ilium. It was making its complaining way now through a seemingly endless wasteland—through woods and neglected fields.

Harve's eyes, stinging in the night wind, searched for light and motion ahead, for some outpost of the world that would help him rescue his wife.

The train rounded a curve. And Harve saw lights that, in the midst of the rural desolation, looked as lively as a carnival.

What made all that seeming life was a red flasher at a grade crossing, and the headlights of one car stopped by the flasher.

As the gondola rattled over the crossing, Harve dropped off and rolled.

He stood, went unsteadily to the stopped automobile. When he got past the headlights, he could see that the driver was a young woman.

He could see too how terrified she was.

"Listen! Wait! Please!" said Harve.

The woman jammed her car in gear, sent the car bucking past Harve and over the crossing as the end of the caboose went by.

Her rear wheels threw cinders in Harve's eyes.

When he had cleared his eyes, her taillights were twinkling off into the night, were gone.

The train was gone too.

And the noisy red flasher was dead.

Harve stood alone in a countryside as still and bleak as the arctic. Nowhere was there a light to mark a house.

The train blew its sad horn—far away now.

Harve put his hands to his cheeks. They were wet. They were grimed. And he looked around at the lifeless night, remembered the nightmare in Ilium. He kept his hands on his cheeks. Only his hands and his cheeks seemed real.

He began to walk.

No more cars came.

On he trudged, with no way of knowing where he was, where he was heading. Sometimes he imagined that he heard or saw signs of a busy highway in the distance—the faint singing of tires, the billowing of lights.

He was mistaken.

He came at last to a dark farmhouse. A radio murmured inside.

He knocked on the door.

Somebody stirred. The radio went off.

Harve knocked again. The glass pane in the door was loose, rattled when Harve knocked. Harve put his face to the pane. He saw the sullen red of a cigarette. It cast only enough light to illuminate the rim of the ashtray in which it rested.

Harve knocked again.

"Come in," said a man's voice. "Ain't locked."

Harve went in. "Hello?" he said.

No one turned on a light for him. Whoever had invited him in didn't show himself either. Harve turned this way and that. "I'd like to use your phone," he said to the dark.

"You stay faced right the way you are," said the voice, coming from behind Harve. "I got a double-barreled twelve-gauge shotgun aimed right at your middle, Mr. Elliot. You do anything out of the way at all, and I'll blow you right in two."

Harve raised his hands. "You know my name?" he said.

"That *is* your name?" said the voice.

"Yes," said Harve.

"Well, well," said the voice. It cackled. "Here I am, an old, old man. Wife gone, friends gone, children gone. Been thinking the past few days about using this here gun on myself. Just looky here what I would have missed! Just goes to prove—"

"Prove what?" said Harve.

"Nobody ever knows when he's gonna have a lucky day."

The ceiling fixture in the room went on. It was over Harve's head. Harve looked up at it. He didn't look behind himself, for fear of being blown in two. The ceiling fixture was meant to have three bulbs, had only one. Harve could tell that by the gray ghosts of the missing two.

The frosted shade was dotted with the shadows of the bodies of bugs.

"You can look behind, if you want," said the voice. "See for yourself whether I got a gun or not, Mr. Elliot."

Harve turned slowly to look at a very old man—a scrawny old man with obscenely white and even false teeth. The old man really did have a shotgun—a cavernous, rusty antique. The ornate, arched hammers of the gun were cocked.

The old man was scared. But he was pleased and excited too.

"Don't make any trouble, Mr. Elliot," he said, "and we'll get along just fine. You're looking at a man who went over the top eight times in the Great War, so you ain't looking at anybody who'd be too chickenhearted to shoot. Shooting a man ain't something I never done before."

"All right—no trouble," said Harve.

"Wouldn't be the first man I shot," said the old man. "Wouldn't be the tenth, far as that goes."

"I believe you," said Harve. "Can I ask you how you happen to know my name?"

"Radio," said the old man. He motioned to an armchair, a chair with burst upholstering, with sagging springs. "You better set there, Mr. Elliot."

Harve did as he was told. "There's news of me on the radio?" he said.

"I guess there is," said the old man. "I expect you're on television too. Don't have no television. No sense getting television at my age. Radio does me fine."

"What does the radio say about me?" said Harve.

"Killed a woman—broke jail," said the old man. "Worth a thousand dollars, dead or alive." He moved toward a telephone, keeping the gun aimed at Harve. "You're a lucky man, Mr. Elliot."

"Lucky?" said Harve.

"That's what I said," said the old man. "Whole county knows there's a crazy man loose. Radio's been telling 'em, 'Lock your doors and windows, turn out your lights, stay inside, don't let no strangers in.' Practically any house you would have walked up to, they would have shot first and asked questions afterwards. Just lucky you walked up to a house where there was somebody who don't scare easy." He took the telephone from its cradle.

"I never hurt anybody in my life," said Harve.

"That's what the radio said," said the old man. "Said you just went crazy tonight." He dialed for an operator, said to her, "Get me the Ilium Police Department."

"Wait!" said Harve.

"You want more time to figure how to kill me?" said the old man.

"The State Police—call the State Police!" said Harve.

The old man smiled foxily, shook his head. "They ain't the ones offering the big reward," he said.

The call went through. The Ilium Police were told where they could find Harve. The old man explained again and again where he lived. The Ilium Police would be coming out into unfamiliar territory. They had no jurisdiction there.

"He's all quiet now," said the old man. "I got him all calmed down."

And that was a fact.

Harve was feeling the relaxation of a very hard game's being over. The relaxation was a close relative of death.

"Funny thing to happen to an old man—right at the end of his days," said the old man. "Now I get a thousand dollars, picture in the paper—God knows what all—"

"You want to hear my story?" said Harve.

"Pass the time?" said the old man amiably. "All right with me. Just don't you budge from that chair."

So Harve Elliot told his tale. He told it pretty well, listened to the story himself. He astonished himself with the tale—and, with that astonishment, anger and terror began to seep into his being again.

"You've got to believe me!" said Harve. "You've got to let me call the State Police!"

The old man smiled indulgently. "Got to, you say?" he said.

"Don't you know what kind of a town Ilium is?" said Harve.

"Expect I do," said the old man. "I grew up there—and my father and grandfather too."

"Do you know what Ed Luby's done to the town?" said Harve.

"Oh, I hear a few things now and then," said the old man. "He gave a new wing for the hospital, I know. I know, on account of I was in that wing one time. Generous man, I'd say."

"You can say that, even after what I've told you?" said Harve.

"Mr. Elliot," said the old man, with very real sympathy, "I don't think you're in any condition to talk about who's good and who's bad. I know what I'm talking about when I say that, on account of I was crazy once myself."

"I'm not crazy," said Harve.

"That's what I said too," said the old man. "But they took me off to the crazy house just the same. I had a big story too—all about the things folks had done to me, all about things folks was ganging up to do to me." He shook his head. "I believed that story too. I mean, Mr. Elliot, I *believed* it."

"I tell you, I'm *not* crazy," said Harve.

"That's for a doctor to say, now, ain't it?" said the old man. "You know when they let me out of the crazy house, Mr. Elliot? You know when they let me out, said I could go home to my wife and family?"

"When?" said Harve. His muscles were tightening up. He knew he was going to have to rush past death again—to rush past death and into the night.

"They let me go home," said the old man, "when I could finally see for myself that nobody was really trying to do me in, when I could see for myself it was all in my head." He turned on the radio. "Let's have some music while we wait," he said. "Music always helps."

Asinine music about teenage love came from the radio. And then there was this news bulletin:

"Units of the Ilium Police are now believed to be closing in on Harvey Elliot, escaped maniac, who killed a woman outside of the fashionable Key Club in Ilium tonight. Householders are warned, however, to continue to be on the lookout for this man, to keep all doors and windows locked, and to report at once any prowlers. Elliot is extremely dangerous and resourceful. The chief of police has characterized Elliot as a 'mad dog,' and he warns persons not to attempt to reason with him. The management of this station has offered a thousand-dollar reward for Elliot, dead or alive.

"This is WKLL," said the announcer, "eight sixty on your dial, the friendly voice of Ilium, with news and music for your listening pleasure around the clock."

It was then that Harve rushed the old man.

Harve knocked the gun aside. Both barrels roared.

The tremendous blast ripped a hole in the side of the house.

The old man held the gun limply, stupid with shock. He made no protest when Harve relieved him of the gun, went out the back door with it.

Sirens sobbed, far down the road.

Harve ran into the woods in back of the house. But then he understood that in the woods he could only provide a short and entertaining hunt for Captain Luby and his boys. Something more surprising was called for.

So Harve circled back to the road, lay down in a ditch.

Three Ilium police cars came to showy stops before the old man's house. The front tire of one skidded to within a yard of Harve's hand.

Captain Luby led his brave men up to the house. The blue flashers of the cars again created revolving islands of nightmare.

One policeman stayed outside. He sat at the wheel of the car nearest to Harve. He was intent on the raiders and the house.

Harve got out of the ditch quietly. He leveled the empty shotgun at the back of the policeman's neck, said softly, politely, "Officer?"

The policeman turned his head, found himself staring down two rusty barrels the size of siege howitzers.

Harve recognized him. He was the sergeant who had arrested Harve and Claire, the one with the long scar that seamed his cheek and lips.

Harve got into the back of the car. "Let's go," he said evenly. "Pull away slowly, with your lights out. I'm insane—don't forget that. If we get caught, I'll kill you first. Let's see how quietly you can pull away—and then let's see how fast you can go after that."

The Ilium police car streaked down a superhighway now. No one was in pursuit. Cars pulled over to let it by.

It was on its way to the nearest barracks of the State Police.

The sergeant at the wheel was a tough, realistic man. He did exactly what Harve told him to do. At the same time, he let Harve know that he wasn't scared. He said what he pleased.

"What you think this is gonna get you, Elliot?" he said.

Harve had made himself comfortable in the back seat. "It's going to get a lot of people a lot of things," he said grimly.

"You figure the State Police will be softer on a murderer than we were?" said the sergeant.

"You know I'm not a murderer," said Harve.

"Not a jailbreaker or a kidnapper either, eh?" said the sergeant.

"We'll see," said Harve. "We'll see what I am, and what I'm not. We'll see what everybody is."

"You want my advice, Elliot?" said the sergeant.

"No," said Harve.

"If I were you, I'd get clear the hell out of the country," said the sergeant. "After all you've done, friend, you haven't got a chance."

Harve's head was beginning to bother him again. It ached in a pulsing way. The wound on the back of his head stung, as though it were open again, and waves of wooziness came and went.

Speaking out of that wooziness, Harve said to the sergeant, "How many months out of the year do you spend in Florida? Your wife got a nice fur coat and a sixty-thousand-dollar house?"

"You really *are* nuts," said the sergeant.

"You aren't getting your share?" said Harve.

"Share of what?" said the sergeant. "I do my job. I get my pay."

"In the rottenest city in the country," said Harve.

The sergeant laughed. "And you're gonna change all that— right?"

The cruiser slowed down, swung into a turnout, came to a stop before a brand-new State Police barracks of garish, yellow brick.

The car was surrounded instantly by troopers with drawn guns.

The sergeant turned and grinned at Harve. "Here's your idea of Heaven, buddy," he said. "Go on—get out. Have a talk with the angels."

Harve was hauled out of the car. Shackles were slammed on his wrists and ankles.

He was hoisted off his feet, was swept into the barracks, was set down hard on a cot in a cell.

The cell smelled of fresh paint.

Many people crowded around the cell door for a look at the desperado.

And then Harve passed out cold.

"No—he isn't faking," he heard someone say in a swirling mist. "He's had a pretty bad blow on the back of his head."

Harve opened his eyes. A very young man was standing over him.

"Hello," said the young man, when he saw that Harve's eyes were open.

"Who are you?" said Harve.

"Dr. Mitchell," said the young man. He was a narrow-shouldered, grave, bespectacled young man. He looked very insignificant in comparison with the two big men standing behind him. The two big men were Captain Luby and a uniformed sergeant of the State Police.

"How do you feel?" said Dr. Mitchell.

"Lousy," said Harve.

"I'm not surprised," said the doctor. He turned to Captain Luby.

"You can't take this man back to jail," he said. "He's got to go to Il-ium Hospital. He's got to have X-rays, got to be under observation for at least twenty-four hours."

Captain Luby gave a wry laugh. "Now the taxpayers of Ilium gotta give him a nice rest, after the night he put in."

Harve sat up. Nausea came and went. "My wife—how is my wife?"

"Half off her nut, after all the stuff you pulled," said Captain Luby. "How the hell you expect her to be?"

"You've still got her locked up?" said Harve.

"Nah," said Captain Luby. "Anybody who isn't happy in our jail, we let 'em go right away—let 'em walk right out. You know that. You're a big expert on that."

"I want my wife brought out here," said Harve. "That's why I came here—" Grogginess came over him. "To get my wife out of Ilium," he murmured.

"Why do you want to get your wife out of Ilium?" said Dr. Mitch-ell.

"Doc—" said the captain jocularly, "you go around asking jail-birds *how* come they want what they want, and you won't have no time left over for medicine."

Dr. Mitchell looked vaguely annoyed with the captain, put his question to Harve again.

"Doc," said Captain Luby, "what's that disease called—where somebody thinks everybody's against 'em?"

"Paranoia," said Dr. Mitchell tautly.

"We saw Ed Luby murder a woman," said Harve. "They blamed it on me. They said they'd kill us if we told." He lay back. Con-sciousness was fading fast. "For the love of God," he said thickly, "somebody help."

Consciousness was gone.

Harve Elliot was taken to Ilium Hospital in an ambulance. The sun was coming up. He was aware of the trip—aware of the sun too. He heard someone mention the sun's coming up.

He opened his eyes. Two men rode on a bench that paralleled his cot in the ambulance. The two swayed as the ambulance swayed.

Harve made no great effort to identify the two. When hope died, so too had curiosity. Harve, moreover, had been somehow drugged. He remembered the young doctor's having given him a shot—to ease his pain, the doctor said. It killed Harve's worries along with his pain, gave him what comfort there was in the illusion that nothing mattered.

His two fellow passengers now identified themselves by speaking to each other.

"You new in town, Doc?" said one. "Don't believe I've ever seen you around before." That was Captain Luby.

"I started practice three months ago," the doctor said. That was Dr. Mitchell.

"You ought to get to know my brother," said the captain. "He could help you get started. He gets a lot of people started."

"So I've heard," said the doctor.

"A little boost from Ed never hurt anybody," said the captain.

"I wouldn't think so," said the doctor.

"This guy sure pulled a boner when he tried to pin the murder on Ed," said the captain.

"I can see that," said the doctor.

"Practically everybody who's anybody in town is a witness for Ed and against this jerk," said the captain.

"Uh-huh," said the doctor.

"I'll fix you up with an introduction to Ed sometime," said the captain. "I think you two would hit it off just fine."

"I'm very flattered," said the doctor.

At the emergency door of Ilium Hospital, Harve Elliot was transferred from the ambulance to a rubber-wheeled cart.

There was a brief delay in the receiving room, for another case had arrived just ahead of Harve. The delay wasn't long, because the other case was dead on arrival. The other case, on a cart exactly like Harve's, was a man.

Harve knew him.

The dead man was the man who had brought his girl out to Ed Luby's Key Club so long ago, who had seen his girl killed by Ed Luby.

He was Harve's prize witness—dead.

"What happened to him?" Captain Luby asked a nurse.

"Nobody knows," she said. "They found him shot in the back of the neck—in the alley behind the bus station." She covered the dead man's face.

"Too bad," said Captain Luby. He turned to Harve. "You're luckier than him, anyway, Elliot," he said. "At least you're not dead."

Harve Elliot was wheeled all over Ilium Hospital—had his skull X-rayed, had an electroencephalogram taken, let doctors peer gravely into his eyes, his nose, his ears, his throat.

Captain Luby and Dr. Mitchell went with him wherever he was rolled. And Harve was bound to agree with Captain Luby when the captain said, "It's crazy, you know? We're up all night, looking for a clean shot at this guy. Now here we are, all day long, getting the same guy the best treatment money can buy. Crazy."

Harve's time sense was addled by the shot Dr. Mitchell had given him, but he did realize that the examinations and tests were going awfully slowly—and that more and more doctors were being called in.

Dr. Mitchell seemed to grow a lot tenser about his patient too.

Two more doctors arrived, looked briefly at Harve, then stepped aside with Dr. Mitchell for a whispered conference.

A janitor, mopping the corridor, paused in his wet and hopeless work to take a good look at Harve. "This him?" he said.

"That's him," said Captain Luby.

"Don't look very desperate, do he?" said the janitor.

"Kind of ran out of desperation," said the captain.

"Like a car run out of gas," said the janitor. He nodded. "He crazy?" he asked.

"He better be," said the captain.

"What you mean by that?" said the janitor.

"If he isn't," said the captain, "he's going to the electric chair."

"My, my," said the janitor. He shook his head. "Sure glad I ain't him." He resumed his mopping, sent a little tidal wave of gray water down the corridor.

There was loud talk at the far end of the corridor now. Harve turned his incurious eyes to see Ed Luby himself approaching. Luby was accompanied by his big bodyguard, and by his good friend, his fat friend, Judge Wampler.

Ed Luby, an elegant man, was first of all concerned about the spotlessness of his black and pointed shoes. "Watch where you mop," he told the janitor in a grackle voice. "These are fifty-dollar shoes."

He looked down at Harve. "My God," he said, "it's the one-man army himself." Luby asked his brother if Harve could talk and hear.

"They tell me he hears all right," said the captain. "He don't seem to talk at all."

Ed Luby smiled at Judge Wampler. "I'd say that was a pretty good way for a man to be, wouldn't you, Judge?" he said.

The conference of doctors ended on a note of grim agreement. They returned to Harve's side.

Captain Luby introduced young Dr. Mitchell to his brother, Ed. "The doc here's new to town, Ed," said the captain. "He's kind of taken Elliot here under his wing."

"I guess that's part of his oath. Right?" said Ed Luby.

"Beg your pardon?" said Dr. Mitchell.

"No matter what somebody is," said Ed, "no matter what terrible things they've done—a doctor's still got to do everything he can for him. Right?"

"Right," said Dr. Mitchell.

Luby knew the other two doctors, and they knew him. Luby and the doctors didn't like each other much. "You two guys are working on this Elliot too?" said Ed.

"That's right," said one.

"Would somebody please tell me what's the matter with this guy, that so many doctors have to come from far and wide to look at him?" said Captain Luby.

"It's a very complicated case," said Dr. Mitchell. "It's a very tricky, delicate case."

"What's that mean?" said Ed Luby.

"Well," said Dr. Mitchell, "we're all pretty well agreed now that we've got to operate on this man at once, or there's a good chance he'll die."

Harve was bathed, and his head was shaved.

And he was rolled through the double doors and put under the blinding light of the operating room.

The Luby brothers were kept outside. There were only doctors and nurses around Harve now—pairs of eyes, and masks and gowns.

Harve prayed. He thought of his wife and children. He awaited the mask of the anesthetist.

"Mr. Elliot?" said Dr. Mitchell. "You can hear me?"

"Yes," said Harve.

"How do you feel?" said Dr. Mitchell.

"In the Hands of God," said Harve.

"You're not a very sick man, Mr. Elliot," said Dr. Mitchell. "We're not going to operate. We brought you up here to protect you." The eyes around the table shifted uneasily. Dr. Mitchell explained the uneasiness. "We've taken quite a chance here, Mr. Elliot," he said. "We have no way of knowing whether you deserve protection or not. We'd like to hear your story again."

Harve looked into each of the pairs of circling eyes. He shook his head almost imperceptibly. "No story," he said.

"No story?" said Dr. Mitchell. "After all this trouble we've gone to?"

"Whatever Ed Luby and his brother say the story is—that's the story," said Harve. "You can tell Ed I finally got the message. Whatever he says goes. No more trouble from me."

"Mr. Elliot," said Dr. Mitchell, "there isn't a man or a woman here who wouldn't like to see Ed Luby and his gang in prison."

"I don't believe you," said Harve. "I don't believe anybody anymore." He shook his head again. "As far as that goes," he said, "I can't prove any of my story anyway. Ed Luby's got all the witnesses. The one witness I thought I might get—he's dead downstairs."

This news was a surprise to those around the table.

"You knew that man?" said Dr. Mitchell.

"Forget it," said Harve. "I'm not saying any more. I've said too much already."

"There is a way you could prove your story—to our satisfaction, anyway," said Dr. Mitchell. "With your permission, we'd like to give you a shot of sodium pentothal. Do you know what it is?"

"No," said Harve.

"It's a so-called truth serum, Mr. Elliot," said Dr. Mitchell. "It will temporarily paralyze the control you have over your conscious mind. You'll go to sleep for a few minutes, and then we'll wake you up, and you won't be able to lie."

"Even if I told you the truth, and you believed it, and you wanted to get rid of Ed Luby," said Harve, "what could a bunch of doctors do?"

"Not much, I admit," said Dr. Mitchell.

"But only four of us here are doctors," said Dr. Mitchell. "As I told Ed Luby, yours was a very complicated case—so we've called together a pretty complicated meeting to look into it." He pointed out masked and gowned men around the table. "This gentleman here is head of the County Bar Association. These two gentlemen here are detectives from the State Police. These two gentlemen are FBI agents. That is, of course," he said, "if your story's true—if you're willing to let us prove it's true."

Harve looked into the circling eyes again.

He held out his bare arm to receive the shot. "Let's go," he said.

Harve told his story and answered questions in the unpleasant, echoing trance induced by sodium pentothal.

The questions came to an end at last. The trance persisted.

"Let's start with Judge Wampler," he heard someone say.

He heard someone else telephoning, giving orders that the cab driver who had driven the murdered woman out to the Key Club was to be identified, picked up, and brought to the operating room of Ilium Hospital for questioning. "You heard me—the operating room," said the man on the telephone.

Harve didn't feel any particular elation about that. But then he heard some really good news. Another man took over the telephone, and he told somebody to get Harve's wife out of jail at once on a writ of habeas corpus. "And somebody else find out who's taking care of the kids," said the telephoner, "and, for God's sake, make sure the papers and the radio stations find out this guy isn't a maniac after all."

And then Harve heard another man come back to the operating room with the bullet from the dead man downstairs, the dead witness. "Here's one piece of evidence that isn't going to disappear," said the man. "Good specimen." He held the bullet up to the light. "Shouldn't have any trouble proving what gun it came from—if we had the gun."

"Ed Luby's too smart to do the shooting himself," said Dr. Mitchell, who was obviously starting to have a very fine time.

"His bodyguard isn't too smart," said somebody else. "In fact, he's just dumb enough. He's even dumb enough to have the gun still on him."

"We're looking for a thirty-eight," said the man with the bullet. "Are they all still downstairs?"

"Keeping a death watch," said Dr. Mitchell pleasantly.

And then word came that Judge Wampler was being brought up. Everyone tied on his surgical mask again, in order that the judge, when he entered, mystified and afraid, could see only eyes.

"What—what is this?" said Judge Wampler. "Why do you want me here?"

"We want your help in a very delicate operation," said Dr. Mitchell.

Wampler gave a smile that was queer and slack. "Sir?" he said.

"We understand that you and your wife were witnesses to a murder last night," said Dr. Mitchell.

"Yes," said Wampler. His translucent chins trembled.

"We think you and your wife aren't quite telling the truth," said Dr. Mitchell. "We think we can prove that."

"How *dare* you talk to me like that!" said Wampler indignantly.

"I dare," said Dr. Mitchell, "because Ed Luby and his brother are all through in this town. I dare," he said, "because police from outside have moved in. They're going to cut the rotten heart right out of this town. You're talking to federal agents and State Police at this very minute." Dr. Mitchell spoke over his shoulder. "Suppose you unmask, gentlemen, so the judge can see what sort of people he's talking to."

The faces of the law were unmasked. They were majestic in their contempt for the judge.

Wampler looked as though he were about to cry.

"Now tell us what you saw last night," said Dr. Mitchell.

Judge Wampler hesitated. Then he hung his head, and he whispered, "Nothing. I was inside. I didn't see anything."

"And your wife didn't see anything either?" said Dr. Mitchell.

"No," whispered Wampler.

"You didn't see Elliot hit the woman?" said Dr. Mitchell.

"No," said the judge.

"Why did you lie?" said Dr. Mitchell.

"I—I believed Ed Luby," said Wampler. "He—he told me what happened—and I—I believed him."

"You believe him now?" said Dr. Mitchell.

"I—I don't know," said Wampler wretchedly.

"You're through as a judge," said Dr. Mitchell. "You must know that."

Wampler nodded.

"You were through as a man a long time ago," said Dr. Mitchell. "All right," he said, "dress him up. Let him watch what happens next."

And Judge Wampler was forced to put on a mask and gown.

The puppet chief of police and the puppet mayor of Ilium were telephoned from the operating room, were told to come to the hospital at once, that there was something very important going on there. Judge Wampler, closely supervised, did the telephoning.

But, before they arrived, two state troopers brought in the cab driver who had driven the murdered woman out to the Key Club.

He was appalled when he was brought before the weird tribunal of seeming surgeons. He looked in horror at Harve, who was still stretched out on the table in his sodium pentothal trance.

Judge Wampler again had the honor of doing the talking. He was far more convincing than anyone else could have been in advising the driver that Ed Luby and his brother were through.

"Tell the truth," said Judge Wampler quaveringly.

So the driver told it. He had seen Ed Luby kill the girl.

"Issue this man his uniform," said Dr. Mitchell.

And the driver was given a mask and gown.

Next came the mayor and the chief of police.

After them came Ed Luby, Captain Luby, and Ed Luby's big bodyguard.

The three came through the double doors of the operating room shoulder to shoulder.

They were handcuffed and disarmed before they could say a word.

"What the hell's the idea?" Ed Luby roared.

"It's all over. That's all," said Dr. Mitchell. "We thought you ought to know."

"Elliot's dead?" said Luby.

"*You're* dead, Mr. Luby," said Dr. Mitchell.

Luby started to inflate himself, was instantly deflated by a tremendous *bang*. A man had just fired the bodyguard's thirty-eight into a bucket packed with cotton.

Luby watched stupidly as the man dug the bullet out of the cotton, took it over to a counter where two microscopes had been set up.

Luby's comment was somewhat substandard. "Now, just a minute—" he said.

"We've got nothing but time," said Dr. Mitchell. "Nobody's in a hurry to go anywhere—unless you or your brother or your bodyguard have appointments elsewhere."

"Who *are* you guys?" said Luby malevolently.

"We'll show you in a minute," said Dr. Mitchell. "First, though, I think you ought to know that we're all agreed—you're through."

"Yeah?" said Luby. "Let me tell you, I've got plenty of friends in this town."

"Time to unmask, gentlemen," said Dr. Mitchell.

All unmasked.

Ed Luby stared at his utter ruin.

The man at the microscopes broke the silence. "They match," he said. "The bullets match. They came from the same gun."

Harve broke through the glass walls of his trance momentarily. The tiles of the operating room echoed. Harve Elliot had laughed out loud.

Harve Elliot dozed off, was taken to a private room to sleep off the drug.

His wife, Claire, was waiting for him there.

Young Dr. Mitchell was with Harve when he was wheeled in. "He's perfectly all right, Mrs. Elliot," Harve heard Dr. Mitchell say. "He just needs rest—and so, I'd think, would you."

"I don't think I'll be able to sleep for a week," said Claire.

"I'll give you something, if you like," said Dr. Mitchell.

"Later, maybe," said Claire. "Not now."

"I'm sorry we shaved off all his hair," said Dr. Mitchell. "It seemed necessary at the time."

"Such a crazy night—such a crazy day," she said. "What did it all mean?"

"It meant a lot," said Dr. Mitchell, "thanks to some brave and honest men."

"Thanks to you," she said.

"I was thinking of your husband," he said. "As for myself, I never enjoyed anything more in my life. It taught me how men get to be free, and how they can stay free."

"How?" said Claire.

"By fighting for justice for strangers," said Dr. Mitchell.

Harve Elliot managed to get his eyes open. "Claire—" he said.

"Darling—" she said.

"I love you," said Harve.

"That's the absolute truth," said Dr. Mitchell, "in case you've ever wondered."

JOSEPH WALLACE

Custom Sets

FROM *The Prosecution Rests*

Martin County Courthouse, Shoals, Indiana. February

IT WAS LIKE A DANCE, Zhenya thought.

A strange, slow dance, full of rites and rituals she was just beginning to understand. Women and men in white shirts and dark suits, sitting behind long tables, reading from books, shuffling papers, popping up to talk, talk, talk to the grim-faced man sitting behind a desk up above the rest, and to the twelve silent, staring people trapped behind wooden railings on the side.

A performance where everyone else knew what would come next, as if the actors and the audience were all sharing a language, a vernacular that escaped only her.

A performance with a life at stake. Two lives.

Zhenya knew where she was, of course. She wasn't stupid. She'd traveled for two days, taking bus after bus, to a town, a state, a region she'd never even heard of before she found it on a map. To be here, in this big, pale stone building that looked like something built back home half a century ago to house a hundred families. She'd come all this way, to this uncomfortable wooden pew, just to watch the dance.

She'd watched a hundred similar performances on television before she'd come. There was a whole channel that showed nothing but them. But that was different—there were always words running across the screen, always people to explain what was going on, what all the endless talking meant.

But here she was on her own. Every once in a while, two of the men would step up to the big desk, to the judge. Then it would be his turn to drone on and on, sometimes speaking quietly, other times loudly enough for everyone to hear. She'd worked hard to learn English at school and since she'd been on her own, but his accent and the speed of his words made it hard for Zhenya to understand him.

So instead she just watched his face. It was round, pouchy, with flesh that sagged beneath the cheekbones and chin. But the judge's eyes were bright, and she could tell that he was following everything that was being said, even if she wasn't able to.

Good.

He had a strange nose. It started straight, but then bent sideways, as if it had been broken once and fixed badly. Perhaps he'd been a fighter. Or perhaps his father had hit him.

Zhenya reached up and touched the bump on the bridge of her own nose. She knew about broken noses. And about how hard you had to be hit for yours to break.

Most were strangers to her, of course, the people in this courtroom. All but one: the broad-shouldered man with the dark, wiry hair who sat at the table four rows in front of Zhenya, his back to her, facing the judge and the jury.

This man Zhenya knew too well, even though she'd never seen him before.

Yngblood. That's what he'd called himself. And now he must have felt the force of Zhenya's gaze, because he shifted in his chair, reached up to scratch his neck, and then finally twisted his head around to look at the small crowd in the pews. But before his eyes found her, his lawyer, a man in a suit that seemed too large for him, touched his arm and brought his attention back to the judge.

Zhenya's heart pounded.

Something must have happened, some decision made, because suddenly there were people moving around, a young woman carrying a big piece of cardboard to the front of the courtroom. The people in the jury box all leaned forward.

Speaking loudly, one of the lawyers lifted up a sheet of paper that covered the piece of cardboard, revealing the image, blown up to poster size, of a tall, slender girl with an oval face, luminous dark eyes, and black hair that fell thick to her shoulders.

The girl was wearing very short shorts and a bikini top. She was leaning forward and smiling at the camera.

She was, perhaps, thirteen.

People stirred and made noises. The judge barked at them. Yng-blood stared down at his lap, the back of his neck turning pink.

Now one of the lawyers was talking about the girl in the picture. Zhenya heard words like "graceful" and "childlike" and "innocent." All around the courtroom, people were nodding their heads.

Zhenya laughed, a sharp, sudden sound that made people stare at her. Biting her lip to keep the laughter inside, she shook her head in apology, then reached up and ran her hand through her short blond hair.

Childlike. Innocent.

He had no idea what he was talking about, this lawyer.

Arkhangelsk, Russia

In 1989, just a year before Zhenya was born, treasure hunters found a great trove on the banks of the Dvina River in Arkhangelsk. People said it had been buried nearly a thousand years earlier.

Most of the objects were silver coins. They had been brought from all over Europe, at a time when Arkhangelsk was a great port city. People traveled there to live, to seek their fortunes, or just to stop briefly on their passage through the great northern continent. Even the Vikings had come, once.

But now it was just a gray city, with faceless apartment blocks left over from the Communists, and garbage on the streets, and no place for a girl to escape to, unless she wanted to throw herself in the river.

Zhenya rarely even left her room. She was not permitted to, except to attend school, to study math and science and English. At school she was known as a quiet, pretty girl, with fair skin and long legs and big dark eyes and an expressionless face that never revealed anything about her soul.

Not that she believed in souls. All she believed in was surviving till the next day, and doing what her father and his brother, Mikhail, told her to do. She'd learned long ago that she had no choice but to listen and obey.

When they told her to stay away from strangers, to stay silent among acquaintances, she did. And so, at ages ten, twelve, Zhenya had no friends, no one she could trust, no one to talk to. She didn't know anybody.

But thousands of people around the world knew her.

United States District Court, Philadelphia. April

This was the one who'd called himself BMOC.

He was a high school teacher, it turned out, and girls' soccer and softball coach, though of course he'd lost those jobs months ago.

From what she could see from the back of the crowded courtroom, he didn't look much like an athlete. Soft and white, like the kind of bread you'd find on the grocery shelves here in America. If you pushed a finger into him, she thought, the dent you'd make would stay there.

Maybe he'd played sports as a child, in school, before he got so soft, and that was what made him an expert. Or maybe they couldn't pay much, the school, and he'd been the best they could get.

And maybe he'd taken the work so he could be close to the girls.

Zhenya had been sitting there all afternoon, waiting. Now it was time. One of the lawyers, a young man in a dark suit that reminded her of a knife blade, let his nasal, piercing voice get louder. Then, as happened every time, he pulled out the pictures. One, of Zhenya in a short sundress, lying back, bare legs spread, panties showing, was poster-sized, for all to see. But the others were smaller, private, for the eyes of the lawyers and the jury alone.

Protecting the audience from the shock. Still, the people around Zhenya shifted and murmured, a low, uncomfortable sound.

Innocents.

One by one, the members of the jury looked at the pictures, then raised their heads to stare at BMOC.

The girls' coach put his head in his hands and began to cry.

They beat her, of course, her father and Mikhail.

But they were careful about it. They'd punch her in the stomach, and then photograph her in lingerie that hid the marks. Or avoid showing her arms if they were bruised. But when they slipped, when they hit her in the face, they covered up the bruises with makeup. One kind when the marks were purple, another for when they had faded to yellow.

But they knew they couldn't go too far. And that, Zhenya knew, was the only thing that kept her alive.

Mikhail, he was the one who lost control. She could see it in his eyes, the way the whites would shine all around the black irises, the way his pupils would become as small as pinheads, the way his thick cheeks would flush and his mouth would hang open as he drew his fist back for the next blow.

He would have killed her, Mikhail, if her father hadn't been there to stop him. To pull him off, to shout at him and send him away to calm down.

Her father was more careful, because he understood that they'd have nothing if she died. That she was the reason they could buy a Lada, drink more expensive vodka, go out to restaurants while she hunted up a couple of eggs or a hunk of bread in the apartment.

But even so, her father never pretended that he felt anything else toward her, and he always let her know how easily he could withdraw his protection.

"You try to run off," he said to her, "and I will find you. I know everyone, and you know no one."

She said nothing.

"I will leave you alone with him. And then we will float your body down the river with the logs."

He brought his face close to hers. "Do you believe me?"

Of course she did. So she behaved herself, and waited.

And began to dream of an alternative future.

United States Courthouse, Fort Worth. May

These ones were mean. You could tell it by looking at them, even from a distance. They sent out waves of anger as they sat side by side in the echoing room, with their thick necks and red faces and stains under their arms. Looking at each other all the time, shaking their heads, as if they couldn't believe the way they were being treated.

Brothers, like enough to be twins.

Interceptor and ScrewU. They'd always seemed to be the first to comment when a new set of photos went up, and what they always said was coarse, lewd, cruel.

Zhenya noticed that no one came to the courtroom to support them. No wives, no parents, no friends sitting in the first row to offer words of comfort and encouraging looks. Just the two of them, with their smirks and their sweat, and an audience of curious strangers.

And Zhenya, of course, sitting in the back with her hands clasped together so tightly that her knuckles were white.

It had begun when she was ten.

Her father had come into her room carrying two big bags. One was full of new clothes. At first Zhenya had been thrilled — she couldn't remember the last time he'd bought her something — but as she dug eagerly through the bag, she could feel the smile freeze on her face.

"What are these?" she'd asked, pulling out something that looked like it was made from strings. "They are for me?"

"Put them on," he had said. "Those ones."

At first, she hadn't even been able to tell which end went where, but eventually she'd figured it out. While she dressed, he rummaged around in the second bag and came out with a camera.

Even then Zhenya hadn't been stupid. She'd understood.

In her new clothes, she'd looked down at her skinny body, then up at her father. At the camera's single eye.

"Who will see me?" she'd asked.

"Get on the bed" was all the answer he'd given her.

Pima County Justice Court, Tucson, Arizona. September

It was fall, but the sun was blazing in the sky, and the breeze that rattled the shaggy palm trees did little to cool the baking air. Zhenya and some of the others sought out scraps of shade and waited to be allowed to go back into the courtroom.

"Why are you here?"

Zhenya froze for a moment. She felt like she couldn't breathe. Her legs tensed, and without hesitation her eyes sought out the nearest corner, the closest spot where she could run, get lost in the crowd, disappear from view.

Then she regained control of herself, and turned to look at the woman who'd asked the question.

They were standing beneath the courthouse's green dome, which reminded Zhenya of the mosques back in Arkhangelsk. In-side, the judge, a woman with a face like a hawk's, had gotten an-gry over something, and everyone had been shooed outside so the lawyers could argue. Now they all stood here on the sun-baked plaza, sweating.

"Excuse me?" Zhenya asked.

The woman was old, at least fifty, with a too-tight tanned face and hair that had been bleached blond. But her expression was friendly. "I come to watch the show," she said. "It's something dif-ferent every week. Better than television or the movies."

Zhenya waited for a moment. Then, nodding, she said, "Yes, bet-ter than the movies."

The woman grinned and held out her hand. "I'm Bonnie, by the way. Bonnie Wright."

"Jane," Zhenya said, shaking the hand. It was hard and dry. "My name is Jane."

"Pleased to meet you, Jane. Where're you from?"

"New York."

Bonnie's eyes widened a little, but she didn't ask for any more details. "So, what do you think of this guy?" she said. "What's his name again?"

Zhenya nearly made a mistake. "Warlock," she almost said. "He calls himself Warlock." But then she realized that this hadn't been mentioned in the courtroom, that no one knew what he called himself when he wrote those horrible messages, when he described what he would do to her, and what she would look like by the time he was done. No one knew, except her.

"I'm not sure," she said finally. "I don't remember his real name."

That was a mistake too, which caused Bonnie to give her a curi-ous look. Even after all this time, it was hard for Zhenya to guess exactly what English words to use. You could get yourself in trouble so easily and barely be able to figure out why.

But it also protected her, this hesitation, this difficulty in putting sentences together. No one here, no one in America, was ever suspicious of her—they always gave her the benefit of the doubt. She could have used a vile word, and she had learned quite a few, and people would still have thought she didn't mean it.

"This man," she said. "Do you believe he is guilty?"

Bonnie shrugged and frowned. "I don't know," she said. "He *seems* like a nice guy. Not at all what I expected."

Someone called out from the front door of the courthouse, and they turned to go back inside. "And you," Bonnie asked. "What do you think?"

Zhenya just shook her head. She didn't yet have the words for what she thought.

They came to America when she was fourteen, Zhenya and her father and Mikhail. Leaving Arkhangelsk, leaving Russia, behind without a backward glance. Taking the train to Moscow, endless hours jammed between the two big, sweaty men in a crowded train car that smelled of old food and cigarettes, before boarding the enormous airplane for New York.

She could have escaped at any time, she knew that. Cried out, screamed, called attention to herself. In Pskov station, both her father and Mikhail fell asleep on the bench, and for ten minutes, perhaps more, Zhenya could have just walked away.

But she had nowhere to go. The streets of Russia were full of fourteen-year-olds who had run away. They did not have happy lives, or long ones. Zhenya was more afraid to leave than she was to stay.

Also, she was too busy revising her plan. She hadn't expected them to leave home so soon.

Thousands of men they had never met paid for the Aeroflot flight, at $24.95 U.S. a month, thirty euros, who knew how many yen or pounds. Men who waited each week to see Zhenya in teddies and short shorts and bikinis with the tops off, her hands covering her breasts.

Never quite showing them as much as they wanted, but always enough to leave them dreaming of more.

Unless they paid extra for custom sets. Then their dreams did come true.

*

"Why do they do this?" Bonnie Wright asked as they took their seats in the cool, dim courtroom.

"Look at those pictures, I mean," she went on, bringing her shoulders up. "Those men. How can they—think about children that way?"

Zhenya let her eyes blur. She knew. Of course she did. She knew exactly what it was that appealed to some men, a lot of men, when they looked at pictures of her. And not just her—because she had learned there were countless other girls out there, going through what she had.

"It's disgusting," Bonnie said.

No, Zhenya thought. *Much worse than that.*

They moved to Rego Park, Queens, a part of New York City that was already full of Russians. The stores had signs in Cyrillic, and the rhythm of the language she overheard on the street made it seem to Zhenya that they'd never left home. She knew her father had chosen this place because they would be completely invisible here. No one ever knocked on the door.

Two days after they arrived, he bought a new computer, a big new television set, and a new camera, much fancier than the one he'd had in Russia. Twice a week now, since she no longer went to school, he would photograph her dancing, holding stuffed animals, lying on her bed in a bathing suit, in lingerie. Wearing clothes sent by the men who were staring at her in their own homes, mere hours after her father took the pictures.

And the custom sets too got more frequent, more daring. Sometimes now, she had to stand there, in front of her father, naked. But it was all the same to him. From behind the camera, he looked at her with eyes as black and expressionless as a crow's.

At first the money poured in. Zhenya, allowed outside only rarely and under close supervision, spent the hours reading *Novoe Russkoe slovo* and sometimes copies of the American newspapers left behind by Mikhail.

And she watched the television, soon finding the channel that showed only court cases. After that, she watched it whenever she could, closely, even obsessively.

In this way she learned about America, and, saying words and sentences aloud in the empty apartment, practiced speaking English the way the Americans did.

She searched every inch of the four rooms when the men were out, discovering all the places her father had chosen to hide things he didn't want anyone to find. And for the first time, her heart pounding, sweat beading on her forehead, she went to his fancy new computer and saw herself the way others saw her.

In the weeks that followed, she went back many times and taught herself much more. How her father uploaded the photos of her. How he ran the site. How he could go anywhere he wanted online, and no one could ever see him.

And again, based on what she had learned in this new country, she dreamed of what she might do. Still, shaking with fear at the mere thought, she doubted that she would ever be brave enough to go ahead with it.

Until one day when Mikhail decided she was being too fresh with him and punched her in the stomach. As she lay there on the floor, he stood over her and looked down, and told her something she hadn't known.

"You're getting too old," he said. "Soon you will be worthless to us."

Zhenya was seventeen.

"But before that happens, we will make you someone else's problem," he said.

She could guess what *that* meant. So the next time they went out, her father and Mikhail, to drink vodka with all the other expatriate Russians, Zhenya finally, after seven years, began to act.

Warlock sat in a chair to the right of the judge's desk. He was tall, with curly blond hair and a well-trimmed beard. Blue eyes and a face that looked like it had done a lot of smiling. Long arms that rested on his knees in front of him, slender wrists and delicate hands emerging from the sleeves of a dark suit.

He showed none of the desperation that gripped Yngblood in Indiana or the girls' coach in Philadelphia, or any of the barely restrained rage of the brothers in Texas. Warlock looked like someone who had been brought here by mistake, who knew everything was just a misunderstanding, who expected to walk away and go back to his real life.

Explaining in a strong, convincing voice how mistakes had been made, how he had no idea, how in a million years he would never.

As Bonnie Wright had said, he looked and sounded like a nice man. An innocent man.

Zhenya knew the truth. But would the rest, the twelve silent ones in the jury box, see it too?

They talked about her.

All the time.

Her father had christened her the Divine Dvina, and the members of her forum called themselves her Dvotees. They acted like friends who shared a secret, who understood each other more deeply than anyone else in their lives understood them. For them, the forum was a refuge, a hiding place, *home.*

Dvina's Dvotees. Dozens of them talking there, some days, but five more than all the rest. The five who felt most strongly: Yngblood, BMOC, Interceptor, ScrewU, and, most of all, Warlock.

They talked about her eyes. Her smile. Her legs. Her breasts.

Her breasts, which, she discovered, had grown less appealing to them.

"Oh, the time is coming," BMOC lamented. "She's almost graduated to grannyhood already."

Grannyhood.

"Yeah, isn't it sad when they grow up?" asked Interceptor. "At least we'll always have the old sets, from when she was still cute."

"I hate fuckin' puberty," ScrewU said.

Zhenya looked down at her body. At the flaring bruises from Mikhail's most recent blow, the close-bitten fingernails, the fine hairs on her arms—which some Dvotees didn't like—the swell of her belly, her solid legs, her wide, high-arched feet.

When was the last time she'd studied herself so closely? She couldn't remember. Maybe never. Because it wasn't her body, it was theirs. And now they didn't seem to want it anymore.

"I'm letting my subscription lapse when it runs out," someone said.

"Me too," said someone else. "If I wanted to look at a teenager in a halter top, I'd just go down to the mall."

"Or the beach," BMOC said.

"Oh, shut the fuck up with all your whining."

That was Warlock.

"In a bad mood?" someone asked.

"He's always in a bad mood."

A pause. Then Warlock again: "I know some things you don't know."

"???" asked BMOC.

A longer pause. Then Warlock said, "Let's take this to chat."

Their screen names all disappeared from the forum screen. With a few quick strokes, Zhenya followed them into the private chat-room. Her father had set it up just as she would have: no one could see her there, but she could see them.

"So what's your secret?" BMOC asked.

"I'm going to meet her," Warlock said.

"WHAT?!"

"Spend as long with her as I want."

"Sure you are."

"Believe me or don't believe me, I don't give a fuck."

A long silence. Finally BMOC said, "How?"

"$$$$$."

And then Warlock went on to explain what he was going to do with Dvina once he had her. Do to her. The description took up half the computer screen, but Zhenya made it only through the first six lines before she lost control and found herself crouched over the bathroom toilet, emptying her insides into the still, stained water.

First the prosecutor stood and began to talk. She was beautiful, dark-skinned and black-haired, with high cheekbones and a mouth that turned down at the corners. Her voice was low, but somehow it still carried across the room.

"I have a question for you," she said to the jury. "Do you want this man out in the street, free, in the same room, on the same street, in the same *world*, as your daughters?"

Then it was Warlock's lawyer's turn. As short and lumpy as his client was tall and handsome, he jabbed the air with his right index finger as he talked. He told the audience and the jury about all the good works his client had done. And he talked about doubt. He said there was just too much doubt for the jury to convict. Proof was needed—and where was the proof?

"Don't let your emotions put an innocent man in jail," he said.

While Warlock stared down at the table in front of him, the picture of wounded innocence.

"Make the right choice," his lawyer said.

The audience seemed to be holding its breath. Watching from the back, Zhenya felt herself grow cold. They were going to believe him, those twelve people in the jury box. She could tell. They were going to believe all those pretty words, and Warlock was going to go free.

All around, Zhenya heard people exhaling. Beside her, Bonnie Wright turned her palms upward.

"I don't know what to think," she said.

"And after that," Warlock wrote, "I'll share her with you."

"Get real," Yngblood said.

"No, I'm serious—unless, of course, you think she's too old."

"I'd still do her," said Interceptor.

"When is all this happening?" asked BMOC.

"Very soon."

Zhenya sat looking at the words on the screen. *Very soon.*

"What if she doesn't want to?" BMOC asked.

"Oh, she will," said Yngblood. "She'll do whatever her father says."

Zhenya wondered if she'd waited too long.

Bending over the computer, she hit the "Reply" button, typed in, "Hi, guys!" and pressed "Send."

A moment later she saw her message pop up, under the screen name The Real Dvina.

Turmoil in the chatroom.

"Do you want me to tell you what I'm wearing right now?"

Torn jeans and a stained sweatshirt, her usual clothes when she wasn't being photographed. Her mouth had a sour taste, and she knew she still smelled of vomit.

"Fuck you," said ScrewU. "You're just some guy who hacked his way into here to dick with us. I'd like to put my fist through your face."

"Oh, it's me," The Real Dvina typed. "And I can prove it."

"How?"

"I have a new custom set, my best ever."

"Fuck you," said ScrewU again.

"Only people who ask nicely," The Real Dvina wrote, "will get it."

She logged off and went into her room to change. Then she went into her father's bedroom and retrieved his fancy new camera. She'd long since figured out how to work the timer, and now she took twenty-seven photographs of herself, doing things she had never done before.

Including some things she imagined Warlock would like.

When she went back to the computer, all five of the men had asked nicely.

In their fashion.

Guilty, said the jury in Shoals, Indiana.

And the one in Philadelphia.

And the one in Fort Worth.

The verdicts were no surprise, according to the audiences in each courtroom. "Cut-and-dried cases" was an odd phrase Zhenya heard more than once. "We don't have much tolerance in this country for child porn," one woman said.

But Zhenya already knew that. She'd learned it from the television.

In each case, the evidence was found right there on the men's computers. Sometimes the police, the FBI, had found pictures of more than just Zhenya. Worse pictures, with other girls in them.

Hearing his verdict, Yngblood sat as still as if he'd turned to stone. The coach, BMOC, collapsed, weeping, and had to be carried from the courtroom. Interceptor and ScrewU cursed the judge and jury, shouted and spat and ended up writhing on the floor, beefy policemen with red faces sitting on them, clicking on the handcuffs.

Zhenya was there for each of the decisions, just as she'd borne witness to nearly all the testimony. She took little pleasure, though, because always in the back of her mind was the one case that had not yet been decided. The most important one.

Warlock's trial was different from the rest. He had the best lawyers, the most money, and (it seemed to Zhenya) the most burning desire to stay free. His trial was delayed once, again, still another time. And then, when it finally started, his lawyers fought hard, brought in witnesses of their own, battled the prosecutors fiercely at every turn. By contrast, Warlock himself was always quiet, respectful, convincing.

When all the testimony was finished, when the lawyers had made their final speeches, the jury left the room and stayed out for a whole day, and another.

As the time passed, Zhenya became more and more certain that Warlock would go free. And then he would come after her, to punish her for destroying his life.

If that happened, if he managed to find her, Zhenya knew what she would have to do.

Her father slapped her across the face. Her feet left the ground, and for a moment she felt as if she were flying. But then gravity caught her again, and she fell to the floor. The wood was cool against her bruised cheek, and the taste of her blood was in her mouth.

They'd come home too soon, he and Mikhail.

"What have you done?" he asked her in Russian.

She didn't reply.

"You are not allowed to talk to those men."

She was silent.

"Get up," he said. But when she did, he knocked her down again, a blow to the stomach that made her think she would never breathe again.

"You think you can take our business? Make money for yourself, not us?"

She didn't reply.

"Get up."

She got onto her hands and knees, and this time it was Mikhail who stepped forward and kicked her, his heavy boot thudding against her ribs. Again she almost flew, but this time when she landed she rolled and twisted and got back to her feet faster than they expected. Making low, gasping sounds in her throat, she ran, but not for the front door. For her bedroom.

The two men followed. There was no lock on her door.

They found her lying on her bed, curled into a ball, hugging her pillow. "No," Mikhail said, laughing. "No time for sleep."

He reached down, grabbed her shoulder, and rolled her over. That was when she came up with the knife, the one she'd taken from the kitchen drawer weeks ago. Her arm swung around in a fast arc, and with open eyes she watched the four-inch blade enter Mikhail's throat just below his stubbly jaw.

There followed a moment of complete silence. Mikhail's eyes went wide as he stared at her. Then, choking and gasping, drowning, he fell backward onto the floor, leaving the knife clenched in her hand. His blood sprayed upward, a red fountain that drenched her and the bed alike.

Zhenya had been dreaming of this for years. She'd waited so long only because she needed to grow strong enough to carry it out. Never realizing that when the time came, her anger would give her all the strength she needed.

She came off the bed, and this time she flew, really flew. Landing on her father's back as he tried to run, hearing him cry out in terror, ripping upward with her right hand, feeling the blade slice through his flesh until it reached something harder, and then cutting through that too.

They went down together. Zhenya rolled clear and watched as he twisted and writhed and fought the air, watched until his crow eyes turned dull and he lay still.

Then she went and took a long, hot shower. When she was done, she inspected herself in the bathroom mirror. It wasn't as bad as she feared. Nothing seemed broken, and most of the blood hadn't been hers.

As she always had, she covered up her bruises with the makeup her father had bought for that purpose. Then she went to the secret drawer where, not believing in banks, he'd kept his money. *Her* money, really. A lot of it, enough to travel wherever she wanted to go in this big, empty country, if she so chose. And no one would ever find her. No one even knew she was here.

But she wasn't ready, not quite yet. Her father and Mikhail had come home before she had finished her preparations.

First she went back to the computer and sent her last custom set on its way.

Then she picked up the telephone and made a call to Washington, D.C. Whatever happened next—and she had hopes—she'd learn about it from the news media, which in this country never stopped talking.

Finally, as she had dreamed of for so long, she packed her clothes and left the apartment for the last time.

"We find the defendant guilty," the foreman of the jury said several times.

Warlock sat down hard on his chair at the defense table, looking as if he'd been hit in the head with a hammer. Beside him, his lawyer frowned and shrugged and started gathering his papers. The judge thanked the jury.

"Wow," said Bonnie Wright. "I just wasn't sure."

"Will he go to jail?" Zhenya asked.

Bonnie gave her a curious look. "Honey, weren't you listening? He's going away for two hundred years."

Zhenya gasped.

"It's the law here in Arizona," Bonnie said. "A mandatory sentence of twenty years per count for possession of child pornography, with no chance of parole. They found him guilty of ten counts. Do the math." She looked over at Warlock, who was slowly getting to his feet. "That man will die in jail."

As they watched, a pair of officers walked Warlock up the center aisle toward the door. His composure shattered at last, he seemed stunned, almost blind with shock and fear. As he passed, he suddenly lifted his head and looked directly at Zhenya. His gaze sharpened, and a muscle jumped in his cheek.

He knows me, Zhenya thought.

At the same moment Warlock started shouting. "It's her!" he said. "That's her—the one who set me up! The one who sent me those pictures. It's her—I swear—"

But for the first time Zhenya understood something others didn't. The officers merely glanced at each other and grinned. One of them wrenched Warlock's arm, so hard that his words changed into strange, guttural cries. Before he could get control of himself again, he was out the door, the sound of his garbled shouts still echoing in the quiet room.

Zhenya forced herself to look at Bonnie, afraid her new friend would see through her. Would she recognize in the face, in the body, of this short-haired, blond, well-dressed young woman the dull-eyed, half-naked girl of the photos?

But all Bonnie did was shake her head and laugh. "What was *that* about?"

Zhenya gave a cautious shrug.

"Well, good riddance to bad rubbish, I guess," Bonnie said.

Who knew what that meant? But it sounded like a final judgment she could live with.

*

She awoke disoriented and frightened. Then she remembered, and, stretching, leaned her forehead against the cool glass of the bus window.

The landscape outside was dry, sere. Where was she? Utah? Nevada?

It didn't matter, since she didn't yet know where she was heading. But one thing she did know: when she got there, when she chose to step off the bus, her life would begin at last.

MIKE WIECEK

The Shipbreaker

FROM *Ellery Queen's Mystery Magazine*

AT DAWN, the monsoon rains eased, and the long shantytown of Bhatiary grumbled to life. Low voices in the hostels, feet slopping through mud, occasional clanks from teapots on firebrick, all subdued in the damp, heavy air. Trucks groaned along the frontage road. Later the clanging and shouting and commerce would raise a constant roar along the beach, overcome only by the heaviest lashings of rain. But for now, a certain peace.

Mohit Kadir walked lightly, cheerfully. He smiled at the murky sunrise; glanced affectionately at poisonously bright chemicals in the runoff ditches. A day or two longer as a gang laborer, and then he was out, advancing to apprentice cutter—a promotion so difficult and so rare that strangers had come up and murmured their envious congratulations. Today, Mohit felt like he could haul a ton of steel single-handed and go back for more.

The foreman, Syed Abdul Farid, yawned at his door.

"*As-salaamu alaykum,* Mohit." He had gray hair and the solid build of a more-than-adequate diet. "You appear happy this morning."

"Yes, saheb." Mohit felt himself grinning. "A fine day."

They walked through the slum, collecting other members of the crew. Most lived together, six or seven men in scavenged huts. All came from the same town, Ghorarchar, in the far north of Bangladesh, a region of famine and desperate poverty. Mohit nodded greetings.

"*Kamon achhen?*"

"*Bhalo achhi.*"

The men wore similar lungis and cheap shirts, the thin garments uniformly tattered and stained, little more than rags. Their faces were gaunt, their arms thin to emaciation despite the appallingly heavy labor of their days. And they knew they were the lucky ones, the chosen. Ghorarchar offered nothing but slow starvation. Here on the long, trampled beach of Chittagong, they could earn sixty takas a day breaking ships, and be glad for it.

The ships! Five years since Mohit first saw them, colossal hulks of rust and steel, driven onto the strand and looming like mountains overhead. Half-dismembered, in the mist and rain of the monsoons, the dead ships seemed too massive, too huge to have ever been built by men. But now they were scrap, worth nothing but their metal, and other men were slowly taking them apart. For ten kilometers up and down the beach they sat one by the next, thirty at a time, slowly cut down with hand torches and carried away by barefoot gangs.

"How do you feel, Mohit?" Farid said as they crossed the frontage road, a brief pleasure of asphalt before their feet sank back into endless mud.

"Feel, *bhaiya*?" Mohit could be more familiar now, but Farid was still fifteen years older, and his boss.

"I'll be sorry to lose you, my best of workers."

"I will not lie." Mohit raised his eyes to the hull before them, leaning his head so far back, to see the top of the forepeak, that he stopped walking. "Once I'm up there, my only memories will be of my friends. I am happy to leave this behind."

"Cutting is dangerous work."

Mohit laughed. Five years he had worked like a Gulf-states slave; five years he had painstakingly put aside fifteen takas a day; five years he had deprived himself of the occasional glass of *tari*, or carrom wager, or bit of meat. He had saved 25,000 takas, a fortune by anyone's standards, all to buy his way into a cutter's crew. Tomorrow he would be free of the mud, slung high among the beams and steel, with a torch, a tolerable wage—and a better life.

"Pay close attention to Hasan." Farid was still in his role, father figure to the young men of Ghorarchar. "He has agreed to take you as his apprentice, and he will teach, but you must learn. Remember, you want to drop the plates onto the beach—not onto your head."

"Nor yours."

Mohit, orphaned at three years old, could not say he'd been a lucky child. But unlike so many other men in Bhatiary, he did not have to send money home to his family, for he had none. As a boy he had not a single toy; as a youth he survived by catching small fish from the rice paddies. Conditions that destroyed so many others had somehow granted him, instead, a determination to better himself. Today he was almost there. He had a plan: the cutter's job would let him save real money. Someday, by the will of God, he would have enough to buy a truck!—and then he would be a rich man, an independent operator ferrying scrap to the rolling mills. His cab would have the finest decorations, the best paint, the most brilliant chrome. Perhaps even . . . a house of his own. Such dreams were painful, and Mohit did not let himself imagine them often; but they drove him all the same.

Rain spattered lightly, *pock-pock* on the ship's hull, a vast, riveted wall before them. The vessel had been driven aground three weeks earlier, and the scavenging crews were just finishing the easy salvage—furniture and fittings and anything loose they could find inside.

"Cables," said Farid, and a sigh rustled through the men. Hauling the monstrously heavy steel plates, nearly a metric ton on fifteen shoulders, was hard enough. Dragging the metal hawsers up the beach, one man every four meters along the cables—which could be a kilometer long—was agony, as the sharp, pointy bits of galvanized wire shredded their skin.

"Soonest started, soonest done." Farid began to chivvy them into a line, beginning where the first cable descended from far above, so distant it disappeared threadlike into the mist.

But Mohit's mood could not be broken. He took his place cheerfully, glancing around while the others trudged into position.

Far down the ship's length he saw a trio of cutters examining the base of the stern. Squinting in the rain, Mohit thought he recognized Hasan, which made sense. Before dismantling could begin, the enormous fuel tanks had to be vented. They'd been almost empty when the ship grounded, naturally, and reclamation crews had pumped out the remainder for recycling, but sludge remained. If the fumes weren't released, someone's torch would ignite an explosion.

Of course, the vents had to be opened somehow, and even chisels could strike a spark. The experienced cutters knew how to do so safely, their years of knowledge allowing them to avoid nooks and joints where the gas accumulated. Hasan was the best, the most skilled, so Mohit was not surprised to see him leading the task. He felt a surge of pride—he would be working with Hasan, working with the finest cutter in all Chittagong.

"*Aste*," said Farid, calling from down the line, and Mohit bent to grasp the cable, ready to heave it up with the others. He shifted his feet in the mud, seeking stable purchase.

CRUNNK!

The blast sounded like the ship collapsing on itself, a hammer blow and a scream of metal. Voices cried out. Mohit spun around to see the dark hull buckle slightly, an enormous rent in the side. Torn steel gaped outward, a dark tangle littering the strand before it.

The cutters were gone, shredded in an instant. Mohit stared for a moment, before the shock hit him and he dropped to his knees and vomited into the mud.

Work halted. Men converged, uselessly, and stopped at the edge of the destruction, where gore spattered the twisted metal. Mohit, weak on his feet and wiping his mouth, stepped up. He saw a shoe atop a jagged piece of steel wreckage—he looked more closely and realized the foot was still inside, bone and skin sticking out. Then the rain sluiced it away.

Mohit had seen death before. Not so often as he'd imagined, but fatalities were inevitable in the breaking yards. Men fell from heights, were crushed beneath their loads, died instantly when towline cables snapped and whipped viciously across the beach, severing anything in their paths. The essential fragility of the human body was no surprise to him.

But this was Hasan—senior among the elite cutters, who had agreed to take Mohit on, and who, most importantly, had received his 25,000 takas.

And now . . . nausea rolled over Mohit again.

The deal was undocumented, of course. Bhatiary had no banks with stone pillars and armed guards, nor bureaucratic functionaries to seal and file the terms, in careful typewritten copies. Farid had arranged the negotiations, Mohit standing straight as he and Hasan talked. Hasan spoke quietly, soberly, then he smiled at Mohit and they bowed and called for a blessing from God, and no more was necessary. Farid had transferred the money later, discreetly.

Now Mohit had, quite possibly, nothing at all—no cutter's job, no position, no money. All gone, incinerated in the flash of one errant spark.

"Go," said Farid. "We will not work this morning. Recover yourself."

"But I—"

"We will stay and help." Farid nodded toward the road, where trucks had slowed and a desultory police flasher could be seen in the distance. "The master will be here soon, he'll handle it."

"Yes. All right."

Farid's shoulders slumped. "He'll need to find a new cutting team," he said softly. "I'm sorry, *bhai*."

Mohit said no more. He trudged up the beach, drenched in sheeting rain. Voices called to him, the curious and the idle wanting details to repeat, but he ignored them all.

Though it was still early, a few tea sellers were setting up at the roadway's edge, blackened pots under flimsy plastic awnings. For five years Mohit had passed them by, unwilling to spend a single taka that could be put toward his future instead. Now he slowed. What did it matter, now? What did anything matter? Abruptly he sat down, jerking his head at the vendor, and when the tea came he drank the cup off, hot and so sweet it stung his throat.

"*Dhonnobad,* saheb," said the tea seller. He was younger than Mohit, but one arm hung useless and twisted at his side, half his hand missing. He'd probably been a breaker, before. "The ship—the tanks exploded?"

"Yes."

"You were there?"

Mohit looked at him. "It is bad."

"I am sorry." The man accepted his cup back, and rinsed it in a pan of rainwater. "What will you do now?"

Ah, thought Mohit.

A truck roared past, horn blaring, water spraying off its massive load of black metal. The splash spattered the tea stall, causing the vendor to mutter and glare.

"Go back," Mohit said finally, answering the question for himself. "What else?"

But when he rose he turned away from the sea and the beach and the ships, and continued on into the shantytown. He had one more stop. One last possibility, before he abandoned the shining life he'd almost, almost achieved.

As a senior cutter, Hasan had been able to afford that most extraordinary of luxuries, his own house. It sat at the far edge of Bhatiary, where the encroaching sprawl of shacks was still tentative, and open fields began. The paddies were worked by the very old and the very young—men in their prime went off to the factories, or the beach, or the city. Glancing at the fields of water, where people in straw hats waded and tended the new plantings entirely by hand, Mohit thought he might be looking back a thousand years.

Or at Ghorarchar. A wave of despair flowed over him.

A group of schoolgirls went past, blue-and-white uniforms under plastic umbrellas, faces concealed by black veils. Mohit counted alleys and waded up the rushing torrent that had replaced a pathway to the street. Closer, he could hear a high, keening wail, even over the rainfall's din. The door to Hasan's house hung slack.

"*Maf korun,*" he called. "*Hasan bhabi?* Are you home?"

Hasan's widow sat in the room's single chair, leaning on the table, sobbing. The sparse furnishings were in disorder. A shelf was pulled loose from the wall, with clay cups on the hardpack dirt floor below; a pack of Star cigarettes lay torn open on the table; and several photographs on the wall hung crooked, in broken frames.

"Who are you?" A teenaged boy held the woman, one protective arm around her shoulders. Two older men stood assertively on either side, glaring.

Mohit explained, with as much deference as he was capable. "Perhaps Hasan saheb mentioned me . . ."

"Your sympathy is welcome," said one of the men brusquely. "One more tragedy granted us today."

"I'm sorry?"

"As if it was not enough that Hasan—" he broke off. "Some *gunda* heard what happened, and decided to take advantage. He broke in here, so soon he must have run over straight from Hasan's death."

His widow raised her face to Mohit, and he saw a dark, swollen bruise from one cheekbone to her nose.

"Keno?" she cried. "Why?"

"He did not—" Mohit stuttered. "What did he do?"

"He took," said the man bitterly, "everything Hasan had saved. His life and his livelihood, and all his money too."

"You!" The woman shouted at Mohit. "It was your fault!"

Shocked, Mohit said nothing, standing with his mouth open. The boy turned his mother away. The men looked at each other, uncomfortable, and the talker beckoned Mohit to the next room. It was the kitchen, cramped under a low ceiling, with walls of woven bamboo darkened by smoke and soot.

"The money, she means," the man said.

"I had just paid him," said Mohit. "To become his apprentice. It was—"

"I know. So much . . . the thief came for the money, of course. She thinks, perhaps you told too many people, and he heard of it."

"No." But Mohit had talked, among his friends, in the streets. How could he not, after such an accomplishment?

"It is unbearable," the man said. "The *gunda* burst in even before she had heard herself, only minutes before we arrived. But it was long enough for him to uncover Hasan's lockbox and flee." He hesitated. "She had to tell him."

"Yes."

"It is gone. All of it. Nothing remains."

Mohit thought he might fall, dizzy and weak. He forced himself straight. "Who was it?"

"She does not know, and no one else saw him. But he surely worked at the beach." The man eyed Mohit's scars and ragged clothing. "She says his left hand was missing four fingers, only the thumb remaining. He used rough language."

"Dukkhito," Mohit whispered. "I'm sorry."

"And I." The man's face sagged. "It is an awful day for us all."

An hour before dusk Mohit returned to the room he shared with another laborer. In the afternoon, with no money and nothing else to do, he'd gone back to the beach to haul cable. Life went on. A government inspector had come by, picking an annoyed path through the mud, to frown at the blast debris and threaten the master. Mohit had watched them talk, too far away to hear, as they left together, an assistant following five steps behind with the inspector's document case. The master seemed to be telling jokes; the inspector laughed. Money would be passed, the discreet transaction as natural as the rains bucketing down. Mohit had felt numb, glad he wasn't carrying steel plates, where a missed step could mean death rather than a little more cable burn.

At the hostel he squatted outside with his roommate, beneath an overhang of corrugated roofing. Sohel shared out the *khichari* he'd prepared. Usually they were so hungry that the dish was a feast, even when reduced by necessity to nothing but rice, dal, chili, and salt. Today Mohit let it go cold.

"An accident, yes, naturally, that is what they say." Sohel talked more than anyone and still finished his food first. "Was not Hasan the best cutter from here to Patenga? Had he not opened the tanks of twenty-five ships with never even a flare? How likely that he would slip, this once?"

Mohit looked up slowly. "Cutters are well paid not just for their skill. The torches are dangerous."

"And the weather — rain! Mohit, it was pouring down, no?"

"Yes," he said. "Yes, it was raining."

"So," said Sohel with satisfaction, always keen to find plots and conspiracy in any event. "How, then, could the spark ignite?"

Mohit glanced at the charcoal fire, now extinguished to conserve fuel, and raised an eyebrow.

"Yes, yes, surely, with a *match*." Sohel ran his fingers around his bowl, cleaning it, and nodded. "Are you even listening? I think you need to ask questions."

Mohit considered. "Why?"

"Not of me! Ask, who gained by Hasan's death?"

"No one." Mohit sank back. "But many lost."

"No." Sohel raised a finger. "Someone has Hasan's money." He paused. "Your money."

"My money," Mohit repeated. He felt again the accusing glare of Hasan's widow.

Darkness came with its accustomed quickness. The men rinsed their plates in streams of water coursing off the corrugated iron and entered their room, five square meters of packed dirt and a rough, splintery platform on which they slept. A murmur of other tenants came through the woven mats that served as interior partitions.

Standing, taking a few steps—the movement had stirred something inside Mohit. He looked at his bare pallet for a long moment, then turned back to the door.

"Where are you going?" Sohel sounded surprised.

"You are right." Mohit acknowledged Sohel's gratified expression, just visible in the murk. "The *dacoit* who robbed Hasan's house—perhaps he simply took advantage of the opportunity. Perhaps it was organized, somehow. Either way, he took what is mine."

"But . . . how will you find him?"

Mohit hesitated. Men drifted through Bhatiary by the tens of thousands, and missing fingers distinguished someone no more uniquely than missing teeth.

"I don't know," he said finally. A sense of resolution grew within him, at first faint and now increasing. "But I have nothing else to do."

Sohel reached out to hold his arm, a light, hesitant gesture. "You are—I am sorry to say this, but you are behaving oddly. I know, the shock, Hasan's death, your money, yes. Please." He paused. "Do not make this worse for yourself. I should not have suggested absurd theories."

Mohit grunted and pulled away. He felt Sohel watching him as he stepped back out into the rain.

It's my life, he felt like saying. It's not the money, it's my *life*.

When Mohit first arrived at Chittagong, he would sometimes spend a few takas gambling—a casual wager on a kabaddi match, or maybe a numbers bet, bought from the same fellow who sold Bangla Mad moonshine. He stopped after seeing another Ghorarchari, a few years older, lose his entire savings on a national cricket test. The man disappeared two days later, either just ahead of his Thuggee creditors or a few unfortunate steps behind. Conveniently, the fasting month of Ramadan had just begun, and Mohit foreswore all games as well as the usual food and drink. He was not often tempted after that.

But he knew where to go. In the jammed lanes of Bhatiary no one had privacy or secrets. Organized vice was run out of a shack alongside the "cinema," where members of the same gang screened

Bollywood DVDs on a television screen before rough-made wooden benches. Along with others too poor to pay the admission, Mohit occasionally loitered in the lane alongside, underneath a bedraggled string of colored lights illuminated when the generator was running. Sometimes a gap might appear in the blackout plastic tied to the walls. When the police were absent, pornographic videos slipped into the schedule, their indistinct soundtracks both fascinating and embarrassing to the eavesdroppers.

Tonight Mohit ignored the moviehouse and went straight to the entrance next door, which was overseen by a well-fed thug who nodded him to the door.

"I would see Chauhan saheb," Mohit said.

The man's gaze, which had wandered away, flicked back. "Would he know you, then?"

"No."

"Well." The man shrugged.

Yesterday Mohit would have retreated; yesterday he would never have come this far. Now, in the dark, his future demolished as thoroughly as one of the broken ships themselves, he found himself not just emboldened but reckless.

"It is about the men who died," he said.

The *gunda* frowned. "Dead men," he said. "So many of them, no?"

"The cutter, Hasan."

"Ah." After a long pause, the man stepped back and pushed open the door with one hand.

"At the carrom table," he said. "Don't interrupt the game."

Inside benzene lamps cast dull light on a scattering of tables and perhaps twenty men. Several sat along one wall, drinking *tari* from unlabeled, recycled bottles. Rain pattered on the metal roof, eased, came down hard again. A roistering group in the corner laughed loudly, arms around each other's shoulders. Mohit smelled sweat and oil and faint, bitter smoke.

A battery-powered lantern hung above the carrom table, spotlighting the meter-square surface and its black and white stones. As Mohit approached, one player flicked his striker, and a piece flew across the board to land cleanly in the pocket. His opponent grunted. Two more stones went in, and the men gathered around the table made noises of appreciation or dismay.

Chauhan would have been unmistakable even if Mohit were

straight off the bus from Ghorarchar. Short and broad, he stood at brooding ease, arms crossed, watchful. But it was the obvious respect of the others around him—distance, deference, careful glances—that made his status clear.

The match ended when one player ran five consecutive tiles, then pushed back from the table with a broad smile. The loser looked away and scratched under one arm.

Mohit stepped forward. "Chauhan saheb, *ektu somoy hobe?*"

"*Apni ke?*"

"I am Mohit Kadir, a gang laborer for Syed Abdul Farid. I have . . . an inquiry."

"*Ki?*"

Chauhan did not sound impatient or aloof, as Mohit had expected from someone whose name was always mentioned in low and wary tones. The carrom players were setting up another round, while spectators drifted away. Two men in polo shirts appeared at Mohit's side. He tried to ignore them.

"You have heard of the explosion today, and the death of three workers. I was there, and I later visited Hasan-*mia*'s house." Chauhan said nothing, and Mohit explained his arrangement with Hasan. "But a thief had already arrived, taking by violence all of Hasan's worth."

"We know." Chauhan nodded once.

"They said he was—that he had a bad arm, and missing fingers." Mohit swallowed. "I wonder . . . do you know who he might be?"

Chauhan's gaze narrowed, though his voice remained quiet. "Why would you ask me?"

"He might have come here, to spend his new riches." Mohit paused. "He might have done similar things before, and boasted of them. Perhaps rumors started. Perhaps you have heard something."

Hilarity rose from the party in the corner, and one man lurched off the bench to land on the dirt floor. His mates thought this even funnier, hauling him back up and reseating him. His shirt was now crusted with a swath of mud, which he didn't notice.

Chauhan looked at them for a moment, then back to Mohit.

"Do you know who that is?"

"I'm not sure . . . perhaps I have seen him on the beach."

"He will be taking Hasan's place tomorrow, as senior cutter on the ship. The sorrow of Hasan's family means great opportunity for him."

"But his hand—" Mohit stopped. "He is not crippled."

"No, of course not." Chauhan frowned.

"I'm sorry, saheb. I do not follow your meaning."

"Life is complicated, that's all. Actions and results may not be what one would expect." Chauhan sighed and took a glass from a shelf beside him. "We don't know the *dacoit*. He has probably fled, gone back to the country." He drank, replaced the glass, and regarded Mohit, who had not responded. "Your *ghush* is surely gone also. You will not recover your money."

"Five years," said Mohit softly. "Five years breaking my back for it."

Chauhan shrugged. "You are still young."

Another downpour rattled the roof. Two men came in, soaking wet, and a draft fluttered the lamps; the carrom players settled themselves and began again; Chauhan's attention moved on to other matters.

"Thank you, saheb." Mohit backed away.

"Go with God, *mashai*."

Although it was not late, the alleys were dark and empty, only a few people still out. Mohit stumbled through muck, feeling it splash up his legs. He pulled his lungi higher. Somewhere a generator chugged, probably for the grinding machines of a piecework reclamation shop, but the buildings and hovels all around were unlit. Candles were too dear; anyway, most of the inhabitants would be up before dawn for another day of toil.

In the dark, and distracted by his concerns, Mohit lost his way. He stopped, leaning against a wall of boards stripped from container pallets. He remembered his first nights in Bhatiary, arms too exhausted to lift, shoulders in raw agony, but thrilled simply to be among so many people. So many marvels to see. He never considered going back, though others did—perhaps because he had no family. He would make his way, or die.

The rattling sounds of trucks sharpened as the rainfall relented, and Mohit oriented himself to the main road. Once there, the passing headlamps illuminated his course, flickering across the shuttered stalls and tiny salvage yards along the verge.

Closer to his hostel, Mohit passed the concrete block housing elite employees from his breaking yard. He slowed. Farid's window was still lit, thin yellow light through the screen, and on sudden impulse Mohit went over and tapped at his door.

"Mohit, *ashen!* Come in!" Farid wore only a lungi, his torso bare in the sticky humidity. The cinder-block walls of his room were damp, and cooler night air entered sluggishly, if at all, through the small window's shutters. "You are out late."

"I am tired, but I cannot sleep."

"I understand. Hasan — it is difficult."

"Ji."

Farid gestured him to sit in the only chair, a stool before an ancient wooden desk that had once served in a sea officer's cabin. A decorated reed mat covered part of the cement floor. "I'm sorry, I cannot offer *cha*, the kettle is empty."

Mohit shook his head, it did not matter. Farid lowered himself onto his charpoy rope bed and they sat in silence for a time.

"You are, of course, welcome to continue in the carrying team," Farid said eventually. "Indeed, I would be grateful."

"Dhonnobad." Mohit nodded his thanks. He looked at the photographs on the wall — studio snapshots of Farid's daughter, posed against painted backgrounds of gardens and villas.

"She is well," Farid said, following his gaze. "In the madrassa already. I have trouble believing she has grown so fast."

"It is hard, being away from your family?"

"Of course." Farid lifted his shoulders, just a bit. "But how am I to support them, otherwise? School fees alone take nearly everything, forget food. It has been another difficult year. *Aii*, you know."

"Yes." Ghorarchar, like the rest of the northeast, had suffered even more than usual during the season known simply as Hunger.

"*Bhaiya*, I went to the *jua shala* just now."

Farid frowned. "You did not gamble, did you?"

"No. I spoke with Chauhan."

Farid coughed in surprise.

"Yes." Mohit described his earlier visit to Hasan's widow, and how he'd gone for help in seeking the housebreaker.

"But I fear he is escaped, with my money, and all of Hasan's."

"Insha Allah." Farid looked sad. "It is God's will."

Mohit started to brush off the mud streaking his legs, then remembered he was inside. He looked up at Farid. "*Bhaiya*, is it possible that the explosion was . . . arranged, somehow?"

"Arranged?"

"Not an accident. Set up. How else could Hasan, the most able of cutters, have made such a mistake?"

Farid considered. They heard a pair of men go by outside, fading voices complaining of the rain, their awful luck, the labor awaiting them in the morning.

"The *gunda* who robbed Hasan's family, I doubt he would have had the ability," Farid said. "It would be complex. To guess where Hasan would begin his vent, to place an incendiary of some sort—too much for a common thug."

"Perhaps not him." Mohit thought of the drunken cutter, celebrating his promotion.

"I don't know." Farid made an unsure gesture with one hand. "Possible, yes, by someone with much knowledge and luck. But to what end, I cannot see."

Mohit looked down again and said nothing.

"It was a terrible misfortune," Farid said. "For us all. You need not make it worse."

"Perhaps."

"Go home, Mohit. Sleep. Life goes on."

"Does it?"

Farid's lamp guttered, and Mohit noticed the tang of burnt kerosene.

"Do you remember when I recruited you?" Farid said. "In Ghorarchar, I needed just four men that spring, though thirty at least had already asked me, and more came every hour. You were young. Many others were stronger, or older, or, to be honest, more desperate. But I could see that you had the more important quality—you had courage. In five minutes I could see that."

Mohit shook his head, embarrassed.

"It was true," Farid continued. "Anyone can lift steel for a day or a week. Some endure long enough to become accustomed to the work, and fewer still can make a living of it. But the rare ones, they can look beyond, and plan for another life."

"Hmm."

Farid sighed. "You are still strong, Mohit. This is an enormous reversal, I can barely imagine how you must feel. But I know you will come through." He gestured—at the room, at the rain, at the shanties and mud and broken ships and tens of thousands of men of Chittagong. "You are better than this," he said.

After a while Mohit nodded and stood, feet and back aching, his shirt scraping painfully where the cable had wounded his shoulders.

"I wish you were right," he said.

Friday the rains stopped, the sun broke through for a few minutes, and Bhatiary took on a tenuous holiday feel, almost giddy. It was the week's day of rest. Most people wore their best clothes, shirts scrubbed clean and white, the breaking yards put out of mind for a few hours. Men stood in the open air, cheerful and dry, talking with friends. Some were the worse for alcohol, of course, and others squinted in the morning brightness, weary already. But most ambled along, glad to be out and free on a pleasant day.

Mohit, though not particularly religious, had gone to services that morning. He hadn't paid attention to the imam's long sermon, but the chants were nostalgic and comforting, and when he'd stretched out his arms and placed his head to the carpet—damp, yes, and suffused with the faint, inevitable reek of the beach—he'd felt more at peace than he could remember.

"*Khodahafez,*" said one of the mosque's acolytes as he left. "Thank you for coming this morning."

"It was a pleasure," said Mohit, and he meant it.

Outside he stood in the lane, glancing at the sky to see if the overcast might clear again. Perhaps. He lowered his gaze to the street and wondered, where now?

A crowd formed down the road, a cluster of onlookers suddenly achieving the critical number that drew more and more in, irresistibly. All right, thought Mohit, and followed the rest.

As he approached, he heard the flashover of rumor through the crowd: "A dead man—head smashed in, right here, can you believe it? Lying in the street, and no one saw him! Where are the authorities? Where is Chauhan?"

Mohit's mood collapsed. He hesitated, then pushed ahead, working his way to the front with muttered apologies.

The body was as described, a man face-down at the mouth of an alley—a narrow walkway, really, dark, between shuttered industrial shanties. A police officer had already appeared, tired and sweat-stained in his gray uniform, but a figure of uncontested authority nonetheless. He pushed back at the onlookers, snapping at two men so close they seemed about to roll the victim over for a better look.

Mohit stared. The dead man's arms were flung out, suggesting he'd been struck with great force from behind and fallen immediately. He'd come to rest on gravel spilling from a heap alongside one factory's wall, the back of his head a mass of gore and hair and bone. Blood pooled darkly on the damp stones.

His left arm ended in a stump, all four fingers missing. The thumb alone stuck out, pointed directly at Mohit like an accusation.

"We don't know who he was. How could we? Are we the police? Do we keep track of every single man in Chittagong? Solve every crime? Bah."

Chauhan stood outside the cinema, glaring. The sky had closed in again, and a slow drizzle showed no inclination to diminish.

"I'm only asking, saheb," said Mohit, glancing at the muscled cohort around him.

"People get hit on the head every day. Every night. This is a world of violence. Two *gadah* have a falling-out over some woman or a game of *tash,* and you come to me? Why is that?"

"*Dukkhito.* I'm sorry."

"*Thhik achhey.*" Chauhan abruptly calmed down. "Never mind, *mashai.*"

Twenty or thirty men had lined up under a long eave of corrugated roof, waiting for the cinema's next showing, and they were watching with open fascination. Chauhan swung his gaze past them, cowing several, then turned away.

"Come," he said. "We'll talk inside."

The *jua shala* was still and damp, a sour smell of *tari* hanging in the unmoving air. Some of the crew began to straighten up, brushing off tables and opening windows.

"I know as little as you, truly," Chauhan said.

"People think you are on top of everything." Mohit felt oddly disconnected from the situation, able to talk to the most danger-

ous man in Chittagong like he was the next laborer in the carrying
gang.

Chauhan barked a short, grunting laugh. "And that's a useful
reputation, to be sure."

"I'm sorry," said Mohit again.

"*Insha Allah.*"

Someone called from behind the hammered plank that served
as a bar, asking about inventory, and when was that lay-about bringing over more Bangla Mad, anyhow? Chauhan started to shout
back, then paused, returning to Mohit for a moment.

"I don't say that I know him." His voice was quiet. "I don't say
that I know anything about how he came to his end, or who did it,
or why. But I will tell you one thing."

Mohit watched him, waiting.

"He had no money when he died," said Chauhan. "And if one
were to follow back all the places he'd been recently, he was not
spending much. A little extra than usual, perhaps. No more."

"But Hasan—"

Chauhan held up one hand. "I say nothing of Hasan. I only tell
you what I know." Then he turned away, and Mohit knew he was
dismissed.

With nowhere to go, Mohit wandered around until he encountered Sohel, who was waiting in a long queue for the telephone
stall. The government offered cheaper service, but that was a half-
hour away in Chittagong proper. As for the post, even if both the
sender and recipient could read and write, it could take six months
for a letter to make its way across the country. Most of Bhatiary's
inhabitants kept in touch with their families at the stall, where an
entrepreneur kept a cell phone available twenty hours every day.
Friday, naturally, was the busiest time.

"It's been three weeks since I called," said Sohel. "And that time I
only reached a neighbor. He'll have passed on the news, of course,
but I miss talking to my family."

"They are well?"

"By God's will. We hope the next harvest will be better."

A boy walked down the queue, hawking fried groundnuts from
a folded palm leaf. Mohit shook his head at the solicitation, but
other men bought small handfuls, perhaps more from boredom
than hunger. The drizzle sputtered on.

"The dead man—you heard?"

Sohel nodded vigorously. "I went by, but the *poolish* had already taken him away. Typical of the police, so efficient only after the crime is over."

"He was the thief, the one who robbed Hasan's house." Mohit described what he'd learned.

"You spoke to Chauhan?" Sohel tilted his head and raised his eyebrows. "So directly? And he *answered* you?"

"He speaks straightforwardly," said Mohit.

"And why not?" Sohel decided. "He is too powerful to be concerned what you and I might think. He says what he knows, and then goes on with his business. Did you believe him?"

"Yes—about the money, I mean."

"*Hen.*"

"I don't understand, though."

"Perhaps Hasan's wife had taken it already . . . or the thief didn't find the real stash."

Mohit remembered the widow, sobbing in grief and anger, and the grim-faced relatives surrounding her. "No," he said. "I don't think so."

"A conundrum, then," said Sohel with the satisfaction of one who knows the world runs on secret plans and hidden motivations.

"Perhaps there is nothing to understand." Mohit stepped forward as the line advanced, gaining some shelter by the wall. "An accident, no more, and a crime of opportunity. Then the thief meets another blackguard. Just bad luck all around—as simple as that."

"No, no, no. Life is never simple. All events have reasons, or causes."

"Not always," said Mohit. "Not here."

When they reached the stall, Sohel retrieved several takas from a small cloth sack, holding the worn bills in his fist.

"Where are you calling?" the vendor asked. He sat bored under an awning of plastic, one wire running up to an aerial overhead and two others down to an automobile battery under the table. The current customer was still talking, rapidly now that he saw the vendor indicating his time was up, trying to say far more than the last few seconds could hold.

"Ghorarchar, in Rajshahi," said Sohel. He recited the number.

"Wait, wait," grumbled the vendor. "Here now—five minutes, ten takas."

"When he's done. What if the battery expires?"

The vendor shrugged. "Then you get your payment back. But why worry? I charged it fully this morning."

Neither man took it seriously, but they argued while the current caller finished up. Mohit watched. Finally the caller stood and left, Sohel sat down, and the vendor collected his fee.

"It will take a few moments to connect," he said, tucking the cash into his belt.

The money, thought Mohit.

A damp breeze ruffled the plastic sheet. The vendor glanced up as he finished dialing and put the phone to his ear.

Mohit put his hand on Sohel's shoulder. "I have to go."

"What?"

"Tell your wife—I don't know." And he left, almost running, as the wind increased and a smell of smoke and rain rolled over everything.

By the time he arrived at the row of concrete housing, the monsoons had burst again, a downpour slashing the muddy alleys and flimsy walls. A hundred meters away he came across another group of men, still out though most everyone had sought shelter. Mohit stopped long enough to exchange a few words, then ran on ahead.

He hammered the door with his fist and it swung open, unlatched. Farid, dozing on his charpoy, sat up in surprise.

"*Ki?* Mohit? What is happening?"

"*Aii,* saheb." He stood dripping rainwater onto the reed mat and panting. "Why? Why?"

Farid rubbed sleep from his eyes and pushed his hair back. "*Bhai?*"

"You never gave Hasan the money." Mohit thought he might cry. "That's why the thief was still here in Bhatiary—he didn't gain enough to leave, only enough to get himself killed."

"What are you saying?"

"Did you arrange that too?" Mohit stepped forward to stand above Farid, staring down at him. "Because he might tell?"

"No, no." Farid shook his head.

"You told me yourself—only someone with long experience and deep knowledge of the ships could have rigged the explosion. And who here has longer experience than yourself?"

"You don't know what you're saying!"

"Just tell me—" Mohit's voice broke. "I've known you my entire life, saheb. You are the hero of Ghorarchar, the only reason the village did not starve years ago. When you selected me to come to Chittagong, I was so proud, I could have floated off the ground. And now . . ."

A long pause. Farid's head dipped, and he mumbled something Mohit could not understand.

"What?" Mohit sank to one knee, to look Farid in the eyes.

"My daughter," Farid whispered. "I told you, the school fees— she would have had to leave." He hesitated. "She is not strong, like you. I would do anything for her."

Rain gusted in through the open doorway, spattering the floor and desk. Mohit looked at the pictures on the wall, and felt the tears finally run down his face.

"What now?" said Farid, slowly.

"It is too late." Mohit stood, stiff and aching. "I'm sorry, saheb. They figured it out, I guess, and they were already arriving. I came just before, but they'll be along now. They gave me only a few minutes."

"Who?" But Farid didn't need or want the answer.

"*Badai*," said Mohit, and he backed to the door. "Farewell, saheb."

As he stepped out, the rain fell even harder, hammering with painful force on his head and shoulders. The world was a blur, and he stumbled, to be caught and held up by a strong hand.

"Careful, *mashai*." Chauhan made sure Mohit was upright, then let go. They looked at each other for a moment. Finally Mohit nodded, once. Chauhan stepped past, up to Farid's door, followed by several of his men. None had any more attention for Mohit.

You are still young, Chauhan had said.

Mohit walked away, not looking back, into the darkening rain and his life, to start over.

RYAN ZIMMERMAN

Blood and Dirt

FROM *Thuglit*

MOSQUITOES PRICKED DOYLE'S SKIN. They whined in his ears. They tickled his eyelids. It had rained that afternoon, and Doyle should have known not to go into the woods after sunset, but he had to get out here, be by himself for a while. That's what he'd told Sheila. She always let him go when he said that.

The path that Doyle followed was hard to see in the day, almost impossible now in the dim moonlight that filtered through the trees. Even so, Doyle didn't have to pay the path much mind. He'd walked this way so often over the years that sometimes he expected to wake up some night and find that he'd sleepwalked his way to the patch of marijuana that grew at the end of the faint trail.

He walked through the pine flatwoods that radiated from the old family cabin that he and Sheila lived in, over a little clearing that his dad had called the prairie for as long as he could remember, and down into the swamp. He worried some about the cottonmouths that sometimes curled up around the cypress knees, and stomped his feet on this part of the path to warn them away. He kept to the high ground, avoided the black pools that could hide gators and snapping turtles that could take off a toe as easy as a pair of tin snips.

A rise of ground led to a hammock ringed by a thicket of vine and scrubby oak saplings. Once through the brush, the mature oaks spread out overhead, sheltering the marijuana plants underneath. Here, Doyle sat on a bare patch of ground, listened to the raucous frogsong that surrounded him, thought about what he had come here to do. Way back at the cabin, the dogs were barking, the sound traveling through the woods, over the prairie, and down into the swamp, muffled by distance, softened in the humidity, to where Doyle sat under the oaks. He resolved to take action, and whatever reaction that might come from it.

When he got back to the cabin, Doyle could see his brother Ray's pickup parked outside. That explained the dogs barking, he thought. He could see Sheila through the window talking to Ray's wife, Polly. Sheila looked like she was trying to be polite, but Doyle could see in her body language that she was tense. She held herself stiffly, back too straight to be relaxed, hands clutching a bottle of beer as opposed to gesturing freely as she sometimes did. Nevertheless, a smile played across her face. Always the hostess, Doyle thought.

He took the steps up to the front door and went inside. Ray was sitting on the couch, beer in hand, but it didn't look like it was his first of the night. "How's it goin', brother," he said. His eyes were red and he spoke slowly. Doyle had seen him like this many times over the years, and he knew that the sluggishness could be deceiving. Ray's temper lay coiled inside him like a moccasin that could strike out quickly and with little warning.

"Ray," Doyle said. "Looks like you done started without me."

"Don't be rude, little bro, say hi to Polly."

"Hi to Polly." Doyle nodded in her direction. Polly smiled in response. She was a meek woman, Doyle thought. Probably learned to lay low having to live with Ray over the years. Hell, in private she probably was limited to yessir and nosir. This must be a vacation for the woman. Polly was hard to talk to. Not much of a conversationalist. Doyle sometimes joked with Sheila that Polly was conversationally constipated. He got a big kick out of that, but Sheila never laughed. Instead, she would just frown and tell him to stop picking on poor women.

"Where's Ray Junior?" Doyle asked.

Polly looked to Ray before responding, gave him the chance to say if he wanted to. When he didn't, Polly said he was staying at her sister's.

Now Ray spoke. "Wanted to bring the little booger. Polly don't seem to think he's old enough yet. I say what the fuck? How old was we when Daddy took us on our first hog hunt? Six? Seven?"

"I think we was a bit older than that, Ray." Doyle walked to the fridge, pulled out a beer.

"I still say what the fuck. Don't want to raise a kid soft. Maybe that's what's wrong with you, Doyle." Ray grinned, more like a dog showing his teeth than anything else, waiting for Doyle to take the bait.

Sheila spoke up. "Come on, boys. I can vouch that Doyle's not soft. Least not till he's done."

"That woman of yours got quite a mouth on her," Ray said.

"Don't mind that." Doyle gave Sheila a knowing look. "It's just how she's raised."

In the night Doyle woke to the sound of barking dogs. "Shit." He put his feet on the floor and walked out to the living room. It was dark, but he could see that Ray wasn't on the couch where he had passed out a few hours before. He went to the extra bedroom. The door was cracked open so that he could see inside. Polly lay there on the bed alone, covered in mismatched sheets, facing the opposite wall. Doyle could hear her breathing. Slowly, she rolled toward him. Now he could see that she wore no nightclothes. The shadows of her ribs stood out in the pale light. Doyle saw her open her eyes, look right at him. She didn't say anything. He shut the door.

When Doyle went out front, he was only wearing his boxers. He could see Ray's silhouette over by the chain-link kennels where the dogs were so stirred up. Before going over to find out what the hell Ray was doing out here in the middle of the night, he pissed from the front steps onto the dirt in front of the cabin.

He skirted the wet spot on the ground and walked over to where Ray was. The pine duff felt damp and springy under his bare feet. He could hear Ray talking to the dogs, saying things in a low voice, but with urgency, almost like he were some kind of coach, trying to fire up his team but not wanting the other side to hear. He was calling them out by name — Dixie and Mylo, the Catahoulas; Otis, the bulldog; and Hammer, the pit bull. "Come on, Dixie, we're gonna find us a good ole hog. Hear that, Otis? Hear that, Mylo? Come on, Hammer, were gonna catch us a big motherfucker. A big motherfucker of a boar. Tusks four inches long."

Doyle stood there, and Ray went on like that for some time. Doyle didn't know what the hell Ray was trying to do. The dogs didn't need to get excited about going hunting. They needed their rest just like everybody else. In fact, he doubted that what Ray was saying was having any effect on the dogs whatsoever. They were just riled because they didn't like Ray. They'd hunt for him and all, but mostly just because they liked to hunt. Leave them alone in a room with Ray, and it would be interesting to see who came out the door.

Finally, Ray looked back at Doyle. "Little brother," he said.

"The hell you tryin' to do, Ray? If we had neighbors youda woke 'em."

"You sound like Ma. She didn't know shit either."

Ray could always use Ma to get under Doyle's skin. He didn't know whether it was purposeful or not, but Ray was full of sharp little jabs and fond of picking at sores where Ma was concerned. Doyle had only known his mother to be loving, but she left when he was six. Ray was ten. He couldn't argue. Ray had known her better. Thankfully, Ray steered away from the subject.

"That's the beauty of livin' out here, Doyle. Raise holy hell and it ain't nobody that gives two shits. I sure wouldn't mind it, Doyle. Not one bit. But, hey. You was always the good boy. What the hell was Daddy supposed to do? It ain't like he was goin' to leave the place to me where I was."

This was the same conversation they'd had over and over again. The one about Daddy drinking himself to death while Ray was locked up for cutting a guy's neck with a broken bottle. Doyle knew already how it would play out, but he always tried to avoid it anyway.

"Come off it, Ray. You know it ain't like that. Daddy was just tryin' to do right by both of us. You got that money he saved up all that time."

"Yeah, but money gets spent, little brother. Now look. I'm livin' in some fuckin' trailer park. Polly don't respect that. I can see it. She's thinkin', Ray, why don't we live in some nice house like a fuckin' respectable family? You think that don't hurt? She knows it hurts. That's why she don't never say nothing when I get too mad sometimes. You ain't got them problems, little brother. Land and houses don't get spent. They just get history in 'em. That's what's respectable. History." Ray looked hard at Doyle. His eyes appeared clear now. Sober.

"Don't be getting all deep on me this late at night, Ray. You know I can't argue with you. You always was the smart one."

"Don't you forget it, little brother." Ray slapped Doyle on the back of the neck. Squeezed a little too hard and gave him a shake. "Don't you forget it."

Next morning Doyle lay awake in bed, just listening. The house was quiet. Birds were singing outside. He could pick out the song of a mockingbird that he knew was sitting in that old longleaf pine right out back. He heard the whistle of a red-shouldered hawk not far away. He felt Sheila roll over next to him and closed his eyes, hoping to buy a few extra minutes of silence.

"I know you're awake, so don't even pretend you can't hear me." Sheila leaned up on one elbow, smiled down at Doyle.

He opened one eye. "Now you're just talkin' to spite me. I'll bet you ain't even got nothing to say."

"You should know me better than that, mister."

"Okay. What is it?"

"It's Ray. I think he's getting worse."

"I didn't know he was ever any better."

"You know what I mean, Doyle. Polly barely talks. It's like she's scared to death of him. And I heard the dogs last night too. What was all that about?"

"What can I do? Ray's family, whether we like him or not. He's the only family I got left." Doyle rubbed the sleep from his eyes, stretched and yawned. He meant that he was getting tired of the subject.

"All I'm saying is maybe you should talk to him, Doyle." Sheila put his hand on her breast, clutched it there like she was trying to send him a message.

"Don't worry. I'll get us sorted out." Doyle moved as if to get up out of bed, but Sheila squeezed his hand tighter to her chest. Maybe he'd just lay there another minute.

When Doyle made it out to the kitchen, Polly was sitting there at the table, knees to her chest, perching on a chair like a bird. Doyle noted that she had her clothes on. "Polly," he said.

"Mornin', Doyle." When Polly talked, it always sounded like someone had turned her volume down. "Made some coffee. Hope you don't mind."

"Hell, Polly. Mi casa es su casa." When Polly didn't respond, Doyle said, "Means my stuff is your stuff. Do as you like round here, don't have to ask nobody's permission."

Polly frowned at this. "You're a good man, Doyle." She furrowed her brow, as if it were painful to say this.

"No, just family is all. Don't go overestimatin'. I'm not likely to live up to your thoughts of me." Doyle poured himself a cup of coffee, took a sip. "You always did like it strong. This is likely to get a person movin' in the morning. I'm fixin' to whip up some breakfast. What'll you have?"

"I'm fine. Thanks."

"Nonsense. How's eggs and sausage for you? Put some meat on those bones." Doyle rummaged through the cabinets, fishing out a big skillet. Polly made no more objections, so he got some extra eggs from the fridge. "You should always fry up the meat first, sausage, bacon, whatnot. That's the way Ma always did it. That way the eggs'll soak up the grease when you cook 'em afterwards. Soak up the flavor too." He glanced over his shoulder at Polly, saw her looking at him. "Hell. Look at me, just ramblin'. You know all this stuff. Just tell me to shut up."

Ray emerged from the extra bedroom, crossed over to where Polly sat, put a hand on her shoulder without affection. "What are y'all two talkin' about?" He looked to Doyle for the answer. "Sounds mighty friendly out here, like y'all was havin' some real fine discussion." He chuckled a little, looked down at Polly.

"You know me, Ray. Always blatherin' on about something or other. Your little Polly there's quiet as a churchmouse, but real friendly. Won't even tell me to shut up when she knows I oughta." Doyle put some sausage links on a plate, set the plate on the table. "Eat up, guys. Don't wait for me."

Polly got up, took a plate off the counter for Ray, got a fork and knife from the drawer, a napkin. She set his place at the table, loaded his plate with sausage links, and returned to her seat. Doyle looked at Ray. "Like you're king of the castle or somethin'."

"That's how I raised her."

After breakfast Doyle went out to the kennels to get the dogs set for the hunt. He felt optimistic about the results. He had seen pigs, and the signs of pigs, all over his property. Seemed you just couldn't get rid of them if you tried. He let the four dogs out of the kennels one by one, buckling thick leather collars on Dixie and

Mylo, his bay dogs, and strapping Otis and Hammer into cut vests.
They were the catch dogs, the ones that did the gritty work of running in and seizing the wild boar by the ear and holding him until
the situation could be reconciled in some way. Most of the time
that meant the hog would be tied, taped up, brought back to a pen
where its meat could sweeten up a while before slaughter. Sometimes the hog would be shot where the dogs trapped it. Doyle liked
to make sure that part went quickly. Ray sometimes had other
ideas.

"Hey, Doyle. Got a surprise for you," Ray called, coming out the
front door of the cabin. He walked to his truck, reached into the
bed, and pulled out two six-foot-long spears. Each had a wooden
shaft fitted with an eighteen-inch steel spearhead.

Doyle tried not to wince. "What you got there, Ray?" He knew
full well what the spears were for. He just thought he'd see what
Ray had to say for himself.

"What's it look like? Boar spears, man. We're gonna do it the
old-time way. None of this blastin' away with guns, scarin' every
man and beast within hearin' distance. This is the way real men
used to do it." Ray was grinning. He held a spear in each hand,
shafts rested in the dirt at his feet, points toward the sky. His eyes
ran up and down first one, then the other. He tossed one out toward Doyle, as casually as if it were a broomstick.

Doyle reached out to grab the spear, but his positioning was awkward. The end of the shaft caught on the ground and the point accelerated downward, glancing off Hammer's cut vest. "Damn, Ray."
The dog scampered a few feet away. Stood glaring at Ray.

"Aw, he'll be fine. Had his vest on. No big fuckin' deal. Pick up
the damn spear and let's get this show on the road."

"Fuckin' spears, Ray?"

"It's only for your sake it's not just knives."

Not too far from Doyle's front steps, he turned Dixie and Mylo
loose. They went off, zigzagging their way into the woods, and
Doyle and Ray followed, each one with a catch dog on a leash. Ray
had Otis, the big bulldog, and Doyle had Hammer. Neither dog
liked Ray too much, but Doyle figured Hammer probably liked
him a little less after being hit with the spear.

Doyle didn't mind hog hunting. Hell, he had even supposed

that he enjoyed it. What he really enjoyed, though, was just being out tramping around in the woods with his dogs. The meat for the table was nice. When he looked at Ray, he saw a whole different story. In the woods, Ray's face constricted into what Doyle thought of as a pine knot. His brows furrowed between his eyes, his mouth held tightly, lips seeming to disappear. With Ray, it was all about the kill.

Crossing the prairie, a big king snake slid through the grass in front of Doyle, each scale reflecting a bead of sunlight. Hammer whined, wanting to lunge at it, but Doyle held him back. He paused to watch the serpent go on its way. As he watched, Ray came up beside him with Otis. Out of the corner of his eye, he saw Ray take his spear by the shaft and swing it like a hatchet, the head whistling down upon the king snake, chopping it neatly in half on the ground. Doyle stood and stared at where the snake writhed in two pieces, dark and gleaming against the yellow grass. He couldn't help but think it had the look of a creature surprised that its normal mode of locomotion had failed it.

Ray laughed a big belly laugh. He bent over, put his hands on his knees. Acting like he'd never seen anything so funny. Doyle just looked at him. Too mad to say anything, he marched off in the direction of the dogs past the snake, now slowing in its contortions as it bled into the dirt.

"Come on, Doyle," Ray called from somewhere behind him. "You gotta admit that was goddamned funny."

Doyle let Hammer drag him into the swamp, happy to get clear of Ray for a while. He could catch up when he caught up. Be just as fine if I didn't see that fucker for the rest of the day, he thought.

Just then, the bay dogs let loose, their barks resounding through the cypress forest. Hammer pulled harder, knowing what was to come, and Doyle had to jog behind, gripping the dog's leash in one hand, his spear in the other. He imagined what he looked like running around the woods with a spear. A damned lunatic, that's what.

Hammer took him on the straightest line to where the other dogs were making all the racket. Doyle busted through palmettos, waded creeks, not thinking much now about gators or turtles, only wanting to catch up to the chase. Finally, he caught sight of some movement through the trees. The two leopard dogs were circling a big boar. The hog was turning, trying to keep both dogs in front of him, grunting and looking for a chance to slash at the dogs with his tusks.

Hammer tugged at the lead, and Doyle had to drop his spear and hold on with both hands. He considered letting Hammer go in by himself, but it would probably be safer to wait until Ray showed up with Otis.

He stood there watching the dogs and the boar, Mylo and Dixie dancing just beyond the reach of the tusks, occasionally darting in to nip at the hog's hindquarters. The boar's eyes seemed so small in that massive head, and yet they burned with a primal hatred. Doyle had been charged before, and he had always heard horror stories of hunters getting treed for hours by an angry pig, or worse, slashed up and left to bleed in the woods. His daddy had always told him that there wasn't nothing meaner than a big old boar, all them male juices running through his body for so many years made him gristly and ornery to the point he couldn't see straight.

Mylo danced a little too close just then, and the hog spun around and slashed wildly, catching the dog on the hindquarters and opening up a gash. The dog yelped a little and blood leaked down his leg. "Dammit, Ray," Doyle said. He looked behind him to see if he could find his brother somewhere.

The sound of the boar's high-pitched squeal, like a woman's scream, brought his attention back to the fray. As if by magic, the hog suddenly had a big white dog hanging from his ear as he thrashed and turned. Otis. What the fuck? Ray must have come in from a different direction. What the hell was he doing just letting Otis go in there alone? Doyle unclipped Hammer's leash and the dog flew in to latch onto the boar's other ear.

He looked around for Ray and found him standing stiffly by the trunk of a huge cypress tree. Ray wasn't watching the dogs, though. He was staring right at Doyle. "What the fuck, Ray?" he called.

Ray didn't answer back. Instead, he walked forward to where the dogs now had the boar's head pinned to the ground, waiting until he got within a few feet before taking his eyes off Doyle. He shifted his gaze to the boar, the dogs still moiling around, Mylo still too wound up to take notice of the cut on his hip, blood drying and matting in his fur, and lifted his spear. Brought it down with force behind the pig's shoulder, into its rib cage. The squeals increased in volume. Ray pulled the spear out. Stuck the boar again. Again. Again.

The two bay dogs, now smelling the blood, grew even more riled, danced even closer, yearning to lick the boar's wounds, roll in the blood on the ground. Mylo, in his excitement, bumped the back of Ray's knee, causing it to buckle. In a flash, Ray turned and kicked the dog hard up under its belly, lifting it off the ground. Mylo landed with a thump, tried to drag himself away, but Ray was quicker. He stabbed the dog in the back of its neck and it went limp.

"Goddamn you, Ray." Doyle walked up and looked down at his fallen dog. There was nothing he could do to help Mylo. The dog just lay there, twitching. "Why'd you have to go and do something like that?"

Ray stared back at him and Doyle thought he saw something of the boar's eyes in his own brother's face. "What's a matter, little brother? Sad you lost your pup?"

"That don't answer my question, Ray." Doyle felt his breath fast and shallow in his chest.

"I think we both know what's upset me so. I seen what you did, Doyle." Ray hefted the spear in his hand, took a step toward Doyle.

Doyle sidestepped, keeping the dead boar between him and his brother. "What are you talkin' about, Ray? You must be outta your head. I ain't done nothing to upset you."

"Course not, Doyle. You was always the good boy. Wouldn't do nothing to upset no one. Not even his ex-con scum of a big brother."

"That's right, Ray. Come on. We'll get these dogs back to the house, come back with the four-wheeler, pick up the hog. We'll all be eatin' barbecue this evenin'." Doyle wished he hadn't dropped the spear back there dealing with Hammer.

Ray continued as if he hadn't heard anything Doyle had said. "No, you would never even think of lookin' at your poor brother's wife." He continued stalking Doyle around the boar, his face seeming calm, but his eyes on fire.

"Ray, come on. I ain't sniffin' around your wife, if that's what you're getting at. That was an accident. I was only lookin' for you. The dogs was barkin', I didn't know what was goin' on." Doyle tripped over Otis, the dog still worrying the boar's ears at his feet.

He sprawled on the ground, caught himself, scrambled to get back to his feet and slipped again in the dirt, now slick with blood. In that instant, Ray was over him.

"I saw what you did to our little garden."

Doyle stared back at him.

"Every one of them plants knocked down and trampled on. Might not mean much to you, brother. Means a hell of a lot to me. I got a kid to worry about. I need the money that stuff brings in. You got everything you need. You didn't want to be involved, coulda said so. I coulda left you out of it. I guess you're in it now, though." Ray spit on the ground next to Doyle's hand.

"Fuck you, Ray. That stuff is on my land. I don't want to end up spendin' time in prison over a few extra bucks." Doyle could feel a bead of sweat running down his forehead. Felt the sting of it as it got into his eye, but tried not to blink.

"That's right. Your land. I done forgot." Ray reached out one hand as if to help his brother up, but still clutched the spear tightly in the other. "Come on, Doyle. We're family."

Doyle didn't take Ray's hand. Instead, he pushed himself up off the ground. Ray standing there the whole time with his hand out like a statue, wanting to make sure the gesture didn't go unnoticed. Doyle was conscious of the dogs whining behind Ray, sniffing at the dead boar, his dead dog. "I guess it's true what they say, then. You can't pick your family."

Ray lunged at him with the spear. Doyle jumped back, but was too slow. He couldn't believe that this was happening. At least not to him. The spear point sunk an inch into his belly. He felt the blood running into the waistband of his pants. When Ray tried again, he grabbed at the spear, got it just behind the point, and didn't let go.

Ray pushed forward, grunting, his eyes narrowed, and Doyle fell back to the ground. He gasped for breath, but it wouldn't come. The shaft of Ray's spear slipped a little in his sweaty hands, the point inching closer to his face.

Ray started screaming. He let go of the spear. Doyle rolled away and looked up to see Hammer gripping Ray by the hamstring, shaking his whole body back and forth, but making no sound. All the sound was coming from Ray, who was swinging his fists back at the dog, but only hitting the Kevlar cut vest, doing no damage.

Doyle found Ray's spear still in his hand. He got to his knees, and then up to his feet, breathless from the fall and lightheaded with adrenaline. He looked at Ray's eyes. They were still furious, burning pinpricks set into his skull. He looked at Hammer, the dog still gripping and shaking, Ray's blood on his muzzle. Dixie and Otis were barking, but keeping their distance.

Doyle stepped forward with the spear and drove it deep into Ray's rib cage. He let go of the shaft, left the spear sticking out of his brother. Ray stopped struggling with Hammer. He fell back, landing on the dog still hanging on his leg. Hammer let go and grabbed him by the shoulder, holding Ray as if he were a pig, pinning him down. Doyle sat next to his brother. Tugged on the dog's collar to get him to let go. Ray's chest fluttered up and down with his breath. Blood gurgled in the back of his throat. His eyes were wide open, staring up into the cypress trees and the sky above. "Damn it, Ray," Doyle said. He stroked his big brother's hair for a long time after he died, after the dogs had filled their bellies on the carcass of the boar and wandered off to nap, after the sun had traveled its course long enough to drag shadows across Ray's face, and watched as the dirt swallowed the last of the bad blood under the cypresses.

Contributors' Notes
Other Distinguished Mystery Stories of 2009

Contributors' Notes

Gary Alexander has written nine novels, including *Disappeared*, which will be in print this year. He's also written more than 150 short stories, most for mystery magazines. Back in the good old days (five to ten years ago) when newspapers were buying freelance travel, he sold articles to six major dailies, including the *Chicago Tribune* and the *Dallas Morning News*. He lives in Kent, Washington, with his wife Shari and teaches creative writing at the Kent Senior Activities Center. Please visit him at www.garyralexander.com.

▪ We visited Campeche City, Mexico, in 1997. It was a wonderful city full of colonial history, nice people, and thanks to lousy beaches, very few gringo tourists. I sold a travel piece on Campeche City to the *New Orleans Times-Picayune*, which was a lot of fun as well as a tax write-off for the trip. It's gratifying to finally get this terrific place into a mystery yarn.

R. A. Allen has published fiction in the *Barcelona Review* (64), *SinisterCity*, *PANK*, *Sniplits*, *Calliope*, and other publications, and poetry in *Boston Literary Magazine*, *The Recusant* (U.K.), *Word Riot*, *Pear Noir!*, and elsewhere. Nominated by *LITnIMAGE* for Dzanc Books' Best of the Web 2010, he lives in Memphis. For more information, visit www.nyqpoets.net/poet/raallen.

▪ This story explores the relationship between two career criminals who have been friends since their impoverished childhoods in an area of the United States known more as a leisure destination for its spectacular beaches. As they enter their thirties, they are faced with choices made unique by their status as ex-convicts. One of them wants to go straight, the other wishes to become a more efficient criminal. While fleeing a violent confrontation in a stolen car, they accidentally stumble into a horrific incident being perpetrated on one of those spectacular beaches. I tried to write a story about the same things that fascinate me on a day-to-day basis: human relationships, human motivations, and the role the unexpected plays in rearranging our lives.

Award-winning author **Doug Allyn** has been published in English, German, French, and Japanese, and more than two dozen of his tales have been optioned for development as feature films and television. The author of eight novels and more than a hundred short stories, his first story won the Robert L. Fish Award for Best First from Mystery Writers of America, and subsequent critical response has been equally enthusiastic. He has won the coveted Edgar Allan Poe Award (plus six nominations), three Derringer Awards for novellas, and the Ellery Queen Readers' Award an unprecedented nine times, including this year.

Mr. Allyn studied creative writing and criminal psychology at the University of Michigan while moonlighting as a guitarist in the rock group Devil's Triangle and reviewing books for the *Flint Journal*. Career highlights are sipping champagne with Mickey Spillane and waltzing with Mary Higgins Clark.

- "An Early Christmas" touches on two of my favorite themes: the beauty of the lake country, and the social turmoil seething just beneath the surface.

Mary Stewart Atwell lives in Springfield, Missouri. Her short fiction has appeared in *Best New American Voices 2004*, *Epoch*, and *Alaska Quarterly Review*, and she recently completed her first novel.

- Having "Maynard" included in this anthology feels appropriate, since the story and its protagonist are still in many ways a mystery to me. I woke up one morning with the image in my head of a baby floated down the river on a cheap plastic raft, and though I don't usually use dreams as source material, I decided to see where it led. Originally that image began the story, but as I went on, I found that the narrator's voice had taken over. I was going through a period of worrying that all my first-person narrators sounded a little bit too much like me, so I was thrilled to find myself hearing this new voice—naive, bold, and capable of saying almost anything.

The reason that I was able to let the story take its own course, guided by the strangeness of that confident voice, is that I wrote it on a deadline. At the time, I was part of an unofficial writing workshop with some friends from the University of Virginia. It had been several years since I'd been part of an official writing community, so I was, and am, hugely grateful for the discipline and camaraderie that the group provided. I'd like to thank those friends here, excellent writers and critics all: Will Boast, Erin Brown, Drew Johnson, and Emma Rathbone. Thanks also to Ronald Spatz for publishing the story in *Alaska Quarterly Review.*

Matt Bell is the author of the fiction collection *How They Were Found,* published in October 2010 by Keyhole Press. He is also the editor of the literary magazine *The Collagist* and can be found online at www.mdbell.com.

▪ In "Dredge," I wanted to write a failed detective story, one in which the person acting as the detective could not carry out the duties of his assumed position: Punter is incapable of solving the "crime" he sets out to solve, mostly due to his mental and social limitations. He tries to act as he believes a detective should act, but because he fails to completely process what he experiences, he isn't able to draw the appropriate connections between the few clues he manages to uncover. Partly, this is because he has been isolated for so long. He has no family, no friends, and everyone else in his life—his counselors, his coworkers—have all been removed from his life by the time the story begins. What happened to the drowned girl in this story is something that Punter can only understand if he understands the people around him, and since that's impossible, the story becomes about what he chooses to do in the absence of that understanding. I've always thought about what happens at the very end of "Dredge" as a positive thing for Punter, as dark as it seemingly is. For me, it's a hopeful ending, even though an outside observer would think that much about his life is now going to be worse than it was before (and even though he's inflicted misery upon others to get there). When looking at the story purely from Punter's perspective, his getting to release his awful history has got to be a triumph, no matter what it eventually costs him. That kind of "hard win" interests me a lot—what if the best we can hope for from our efforts is still a bad outcome? We still have to try, right?

Jay Brandon is the author of fifteen novels, from *Deadbolt* (1985), which won *Booklist*'s Editor's Choice Award, to *Milagro Lane* (2009). Five of his novels feature district attorney Chris Sinclair and child psychiatrist Anne Greenwald, the most recent being *Running with the Dead* ("a brilliant entry in a series that just keeps getting better"— *Kirkus*). His novel *Fade the Heat* was nominated for an Edgar Award and has been published in more than a dozen foreign countries. Jay holds a master's degree in writing from Johns Hopkins and is a practicing lawyer in San Antonio.

▪ My only nonfiction book is a history of practicing law in San Antonio. While doing research for that book, I came across this incident from 1842, when a Mexican general and his troops marched into San Antonio (Texas was not at war with Mexico at the time), went straight to the courthouse, and captured nearly every lawyer in town. What a time it must have been when an enemy thought he could strike a crippling blow by taking away the lawyers. The lawyers were all eventually released, but some were gone for nearly two years. I was fascinated both by the idea of a city without lawyers and by what their captivity must have done to those prisoners. Other than that historical event, the story is entirely fiction.

I want to mention two other things: "A Jury of His Peers" is written in a slightly archaic style to fit the time period. And yes, this attack on our own soil that San Antonians remembered for the rest of their lives did happen on September 11. You couldn't make that up. Real life is shameless.

Phyllis Cohen was a resident of Manhattan. After retiring from a thirty-five-year career in the New York City school system, she undertook a mini second career as a freelance writer, writing nonfiction at first, mostly science reporting; when that petered out, she moved on to fiction. About her fiction, she said: "My short stories are of many genres—crime, science fiction, relationships—but there is a common element throughout of character and human interest." Phyllis Cohen died on January 26, 2009. (*Note:* This brief bio and the note that follows were written by the author's widower, Herbert Cohen.)

▪ When Phyllis first heard of the call for stories for the Mystery Writers of America anthology, she pulled "Designer Justice" out of the trunk and swore this would be her last attempt to get a story published before absolutely quitting. She'd sold only one story, some twenty years earlier, to *Buffalo Spree*. Whenever she submitted stories, they were returned with the usual rejection wallpaper. Many times she'd get an editor's letter praising her style but requesting that she remove some pointed political opinion or rewrite a section. Ripping the letter up, she'd sneer, "I don't do surgery on my babies!"

"Designer Justice" presented a different problem, however: it was more than 1,500 words over the MWA anthology word allowance. It took over a month to bring the story down to size. She called the editing her "literary liposuction." When she was finally finished, she lifted the story out of the printer tray and thrust it at me: "Read the crap!" Then she stared out the window trying to look nonchalant, but once or twice I caught a furtively anxious glance. Ten minutes later I looked up at her. "Kiddo! This stuff you think is crap is ten times better than the original." She didn't believe me until she received the acceptance letter.

In May 2008, Phyllis was diagnosed with terminal cancer. The first words out of her mouth were, "Shit, I knew I'd never see that damn story in print!" Unfortunately, she never did. I received the preproduction copy on January 27, the day after Phyllis died.

John Dufresne is the author of two story collections, two books on writing fiction, and four novels, most recently, *Requiem, Mass.* His story "The Timing of Unfelt Smiles" appeared in *The Best American Mystery Stories 2007.* He teaches creative writing at Florida International University in Miami.

▪ My job was to write a story set in South Boston. I grew up in an Irish neighborhood, attended Irish Catholic schools for twelve years, and was an altar boy in an Irish parish church much like St. Cormac's in the story. I wanted to be a priest. I wanted to write about sin and evil in the context of a sacred place. The epidemic of priestly abuse of children seemed like a natural place to begin. When I started the story, I didn't know if the sin was abuse or if the sin was false accusation. Or both. I remembered the McMartin preschool abuse trials and was aware of false memory syndrome. So I began writing the story during the first week of the fall semester. I wrote five or six pages that week and stopped when I got to a point in Father Mulcahy's dream where Jesus won't stop tickling him. I wasn't expecting that to happen. I brought the pages to school and read them to my undergrad class. I told the students I'd appreciate any feedback, any thoughts. They began to e-mail questions and suggestions. Every couple of weeks I'd read some more. When I found myself unexpectedly in Mrs. Walsh's head in the opening act, I knew I could now go into anyone's head that I wanted. Maybe even Jesus's. When a representative from the cardinal's office stopped by the rectory, I knew there would be plenty of sin —and crime—to go around. I promised the students that I'd finish the story by the end of the semester. I e-mailed them copies with their grades.

Lyndsay Faye spent years working in musical theater (she is a soprano and a proud member of the Actors' Equity Association) before her meatpacking district day job was razed by bulldozers and she seized the opportunity to finish her first novel: *Dust and Shadow: An Account of the Ripper Killings by Dr. John H. Watson.* Her latest short story appears in the 2009 holiday issue of *The Strand* magazine. She is an avid lover of food culture, Sherlockiana, and historical fiction and lives in Manhattan with her husband (Gabriel) and cat (Grendel). Visit www.lyndsayfaye.com for more information.

▪ When I was asked to contribute a story for the anthology *Sherlock Holmes in America,* I was thrilled to say yes, and to volunteer to use my Bay Area birthplace as a setting. I was equally as confused regarding how to get both Holmes and Watson all the way across America from London. That's a long trip, and I didn't care to lose Watson's narrative voice by recounting Holmes's days in America alone. And then I recalled that during an unfinished play called *Angels of Darkness,* Conan Doyle made mention of a young Dr. Watson practicing medicine in San Francisco. That solved half my problem. The challenge of writing a case narrated by Watson that Holmes is able to solve from his armchair *à la* Poe's Dupin was very daunting; no investigation could happen, of course, and none of the dangers were immediate. But Conan Doyle himself used the format of Holmes retelling an old case by the fireside at Baker Street in two tales, which bolstered my confidence, and I simply added two new twists: Watson is doing the storytelling on this occasion, and the case is solved in real time instead of being a relic of Holmes's college days.

Gar Anthony Haywood is the Shamus and Anthony Award–winning author of eleven crime novels, including six in the Aaron Gunner series, two in the Joe and Dottie Loudermilk series, and three stand-alone thrillers. Haywood's first Gunner mystery, *Fear of the Dark,* won the Private Eye Writers of America's Shamus Award for Best First Novel of 1989, and his first Aaron Gunner short story, "And Pray Nobody Sees You," won both the PEWA's Shamus Award and the World Mystery Convention's Anthony Award for Best Short Story of 1995. Haywood has written for both the *New York Times* and the *Los Angeles Times,* has penned such television dramas as *New York Undercover* and *The District,* and twice has coauthored a "Movie of the Week" for ABC Television. His latest novel is the urban crime drama *Cemetery Road.*

• I am a monster fan of the Showtime-era Los Angeles Lakers, and Earvin "Magic" Johnson remains my favorite player of all time. A superstar first in sports and now in business, I don't think there's a sinister bone in Magic's body, but he grew up in East Lansing, Michigan, so it's probably safe to say there's more edge to the man than his disarming smile would otherwise indicate.

This story came out of my curiosity about just how much "edge" there might be. As so dramatically illustrated by the Tiger Woods scandal, at the time of this writing, we never really know the people we elevate to celebrity status. What we see of them is only what they choose to expose to the light. The men and women who reside beneath the skin—the real people behind the public facades they project—are a complete unknown. And, I would venture to guess, some of them are killers you wouldn't want to cross.

Jon Land is the author of twenty-eight books, seventeen of which have been national best-sellers. *RT Reviews* magazine honored him in 2009 with a special achievement award for being a "Pioneer in Genre Fiction." *The Seven Sins* was named one of the Top Five Thrillers of 2008 by *Library Journal* and was optioned for film by Moritz Borman (*Terminator: Salvation*). Jon's latest series, commencing with *Strong Enough to Die* in 2009 and followed by *Strong Justice* in 2010, features female Texas Ranger Caitlin Strong. *Strong Enough to Die* has been optioned as a film property by Hand

Picked Films, with Carl Franklin (*Devil in a Blue Dress, Out of Time, One False Move*) attached to direct and Jon writing the screenplay himself.

Jon graduated from Brown University in 1979 Phi Beta Kappa and Magna cum Laude. He serves as vice president of marketing for the International Thriller Writers (ITW) and lives in Providence, Rhode Island.

▪ "Killing Time" offered me an opportunity to write a story that harks back to the days of hardboiled noir. I'd always wanted to write from the viewpoint of a dark hero, and the fish-out-of-water concept of a professional killer hiding out in the guise of a middle school teacher grabbed hold of me from the start. The real fun of the story for me was watching Fallon come to embrace his role and the moral dilemma he faces when the school is taken hostage by terrorists. I got the idea from the real-life tragedy a few years ago in Chechnya. But that's the great thing about writing fiction: you can reinvent reality with any ending you want.

Dennis Lehane is the author of eight novels, including *The Given Day; Mystic River; Gone, Baby, Gone;* and *Shutter Island.* He is currently writing a screen adaptation of "Animal Rescue" for 20th Century Fox. He lives with his wife and daughter in Boston and west central Florida.

▪ "Animal Rescue" originated, like a lot of my work, from a central obsession with loneliness. Every day we interact with people who go home to empty apartments and numbing isolation from which there is no reasonable expectation of escape. On any number of levels, this is heartbreaking, and I wanted to write about it. I started with Bob, and that led me to Nadia and even Cousin Marv—three people lost in their aloneness. And then along comes this dog . . .

Lynda Leidiger's short stories have appeared in magazines ranging from *Playboy* to *Prairie Schooner.* She is a recipient of an NEA grant and was the first woman to win the International Imitation Hemingway Award. She lives in Iowa.

▪ I wrote "Tell Me" after my sister-in-law became a victim of a random shooting by two teenage boys in rural Wisconsin. The true story took a twist far more amazing and powerful than anything I could have invented. Although the shooting left her legally blind and permanently disabled, she not only has forgiven the boys—now men—but visits them in prison. Her new career is traveling to schools and correctional facilities around the country, talking in her soft, halting voice about the consequences of violence. She changes lives. Knowing her is a gift. I'd like to dedicate this story to Jackie Millar.

During a twenty-five-year career as a criminal defense attorney, **Phillip Margolin** appeared before the U.S. Supreme Court and represented approximately thirty people charged with homicide, including a dozen who faced the death penalty. All fourteen of his novels have appeared on the *New York Times* best-seller list. *Heartstone,* his first novel, was nominated for an Edgar. *Executive Privilege* won the Spotted Owl Award for the Best Mystery in the Pacific Northwest. *The Last Innocent Man* and *Gone, But Not Forgotten* have been made into movies.

• Never throw away anything you write. You never know when it might come in handy. About a year ago, I was going through some very old files in a metal filing cabinet in my laundry room, when I came across a folder with scraps of short stories I had started and never finished. To give you an idea how old these stories were, the one that eventually became *The House on Pine Terrace* was written on a typewriter. I had forgotten about the story in the intervening years. The scrap I read was only a few pages long, but it sounded interesting. I took it down to my office and spent a few days expanding it into a whole story, and now it's in this anthology. As soon as I finish writing this note, I'm going back to that ancient file. Who knows?

Chris Muessig and his wife Susanne left an emptied nest on Long Island several years ago to resettle in Cary, North Carolina. During the day he performs editorial work at North Carolina State University, and in the odd hours he writes to fill the vacuum created by the diaspora of their three children. "Bias" was his first published piece of fiction, chosen by Janet Hutchings for Ellery Queen's Department of First Stories. Such blatant encouragement, after many decades of polite but firm rejection, has led to the sale of two more tales, including another of Creegan's encounters with the spirit of the '80s.

• "Bias" gestated for at least twenty years. It originated in the confluence of a number of nagging contemplations: a series of senseless and unsolved killings of Long Island gas station attendants, the loosening of anarchy upon the world, and the use of violence as a means of expression reaching everywhere. Of course, these conditions are not unique to the early 1980s. As Frank muses, every generation seems to have its Barbary shore.

Albert Tucher is the creator of prostitute Diana Andrews, who makes a cameo appearance in *Bismarck Rules.* Thirty short stories about her have been published in *Lynx Eye, Thuglit, Out of the Gutter, Beat to a Pulp,* and other print and online magazines and anthologies. He has also written a series of unpublished novels about his character.

• The idea for "Bismarck Rules" came to me in 2003, when I went for my first colonoscopy. I discovered that my proctologist would not let me transport myself to and from my appointment. I had a friend who was available to drive me, but it occurred to me that some patients would not. Men hire prostitutes to do many things that are only distantly related to sex. Why not have a client pay my character Diana Andrews to pose as his girlfriend and take on the driving chore?

Two things happened. What I thought would be a comedy quickly turned very dark, and I realized that Diana Andrews has a biography that is incompatible with the plot developments in the story. I came up with a sidekick for Diana, another prostitute named Mary Alice Mercier, aka Crystal. She has since figured in my novels and several other short stories.

Kurt Vonnegut was one of the most influential writers of the twentieth century. Known for his unique blend of satire, black comedy, and science fiction, he was the author of works such as *Slaughterhouse-Five, Cat's Cradle,* and *Breakfast of Champions.* His first short story, "Report on the Barnhouse Effect," was published in *Collier's* on February 11, 1950. *Player Piano,* his first novel, was published a year later. His writing career spanned fourteen novels and numerous collections of essays and short stories. The asteroid 25399 Vonnegut was named in his honor. Kurt Vonnegut died in Manhattan on April 11, 2007.

Joseph Wallace's stories have appeared in *Baltimore Noir, Hard Boiled Brooklyn, Bronx Noir, Ellery Queen's Mystery Magazine,* and the Mystery Writers of America anthology *The Prosecution Rests,* where "Custom Sets" first appeared. His debut novel, *Diamond Ruby* (expanded from a story in *EQMM*), was published in May 2010. Set in 1920s New York City, it details the perilous life and times of a teenage girl with the unusual ability to throw a baseball as fast as any (male) pitcher alive.

▪ A few years ago I wrote a thriller that attracted some interest, though no buyers. It had as a secondary character Zhenya, a Russian girl who travels to the United States under appalling circumstances. I've since come to believe that if I had placed her at the center of the story, I would have ended up with a far better novel. Having learned my lesson, I decided to make Zhenya the protagonist of "Custom Sets." In several of my other stories and my novel *Diamond Ruby,* I've also chosen to write about teenage girls, whose strength, toughness, and resilience tend to be underestimated by villains and readers alike. I love writing the moments when the truth becomes known to all.

Mike Wiecek is the author of *Exit Strategy,* which was short-listed for a Thriller Award by the International Thriller Writers. His short stories have received wide recognition, including a Shamus Award. In his younger days Mike spent several years in Japan and traveled widely in Asia. He now lives outside Boston with his wife and two children. For more information, visit: www.mwiecek.com.

▪ I've never been to Chittagong, but several years ago I saw an essay on the shipbreakers. One photo stood out: a long line of men ascending the beach, the cable on their shoulders stretching back and disappearing into mist. Their faces, worn by effort and pain, made a striking contrast to the colossus of rusted steel they were dismembering. And I thought, *Story.*

Though poverty grinds down those who suffer it, even the shantytowns have a certain dignity. People have dreams, make plans, and take pride in their achievements, however modest they might seem. There is always a future. Though it may be hard to believe, the Bangladesh shipbreaking yards have grown too expensive. The trade is now shifting to even cheaper, crueler, less safe countries: Sri Lanka, Myanmar, Vietnam. The stern logic of globalization dictates, but I hope we remember Mohit and his companions, who do the hard work.

Ryan Zimmerman attended the University of Florida, where he majored in wildlife ecology until he realized how much math he'd need to take. He ended up graduating three times from the University of South Florida (where he took no math classes), most recently with an MFA in fiction writing. Ryan lives in Tampa with his wife, his daughter, and his dog.

▪ I believe that the original inspiration for this story came when I happened across a hunting show on TV in which a couple of guys were hunting hogs with nothing but dogs and knives. I have to say, I was a bit repulsed, but also fascinated. I have nothing against hunters, but when I tried to imagine the type of guy who would enjoy stabbing an animal to death, I came up with Ray, the domineering backwoods sociopath of "Blood and Dirt." I gave him a nice kid brother, put the two in the steamy pressure cooker of a Florida summer, and this is the story that resulted.

Other Distinguished Mystery Stories of 2009

HAYCOCK, BRIAN
  Alaska. *Amarillo Bay,* vol. 11, no. 4
HURWITZ, GREGG
  Back and Forth. *Uncage Me,* ed. Jen Jordan (Bleak House)

IRVIN, JANET E.
  After the Dreamtime. *Alfred Hitchcock's Mystery Magazine,* January/February

KELLEY, Z.
  Anything Helps. *Two of the Deadliest,* ed. Elizabeth George (HarperCollins)

MALEENY, TIM
  Prisoner of Love. *Uncage Me,* ed. Jen Jordan (Bleak House)
MANFREDO, LOU
  Central Islin, U.S.A. *Ellery Queen's Mystery Magazine,* August
MAYER, BETH
  The Way to Mercy. *The Sun,* July
McCRACKEN, ELIZABETH
  The Lost and Found Department of Greater Boston. *Zoetrope All-Story,* Winter

NELSON, SHANE
  That One Small Thing. *Ellery Queen's Mystery Magazine,* February

ROESCH, MATTOX
  The Maluksuk. *The Sun,* September

SELWOOD, JONATHAN
  The Wrong House. *Seattle Noir,* ed. Curt Colbert (Akashic)
SMITH, R. T.
  Maggard. *Grist,* no. 2
STROBY, WALLACE
  Heart. *Inside Jersey,* August
SWINGLE, MORLEY
  Hard Blows. *The Prosecution Rests,* ed. Linda Fairstein (Little, Brown)

TAYLOR, ART
  A Voice from the Past. *Ellery Queen's Mystery Magazine,* August

WARREN, JAMES LINCOLN
  Shanghaied. *Alfred Hitchcock's Mystery Magazine,* January/February
WINSLOW, DON
  Wipeout on Van Buren. *Phoenix Noir,* ed. Patrick Milliken (Akashic)
WOLVEN, SCOTT
  Jockamo. *Thuglit,* November/December

ZELTSERMAN, DAVE
  Julius Katz. *Ellery Queen's Mystery Magazine,* September/October